"DON'T GO, KENT," SHE WHISPERED.

Torment tightened his features. "For God's sake, Juliet! Why must you make this so damned easy . . . and yet so damned hard?" He spun toward her, the lean strength of his body pressing her to the sofa.

His first kiss plunged her into rough splendor. The shock of his tongue against her lips ignited a scandalous fire inside her.

Her palms embraced the hard heat of his chest as she slid them upward over his shirt. Her heart thumped madly, the blood beating in her ears. She felt submerged in a sea of sensation, drowning in a floodtide of feelings.

"So proper," he murmured, his breath warm on her lips, "and so very tempting."

DREAMSPINNER

BARBARA DAWSON SMITH

AVON BOOKS NEW YORK

DREAMSPINNER is an original publication of Avon Books. This work has never before appeared in book form. This work is a novel. Any similarity to actual persons or events is purely coincidental.

AVON BOOKS
A division of
The Hearst Corporation
105 Madison Avenue
New York, New York 10016

Copyright © 1990 by Barbara Dawson Smith
Inside cover author photograph by Ralph Smith
Published by arrangement with the author
Library of Congress Catalog Card Number: 89-91536
ISBN: 0-380-75921-7

First Avon Books Printing: May 1990

AVON TRADEMARK REG. U.S. PAT. OFF. AND IN OTHER COUNTRIES, MARCA REGISTRADA, HECHO EN U.S.A.

Printed in the U.S.A.

RA 10 9 8 7 6 5 4 3 2 1

To the West Houston Chapter
of Romance Writers of America

I am deeply indebted to Robert Nunes for the Hindustani translations; to Carla Luan for sharing her expertise on gems; and especially to Susan Wiggs, Arnette Lamb, Alice Borchardt, and Joyce Bell for their unfailing support and astute criticism.

Prologue

Castle Radcliffe, August 11, 1885

A distant scream drifted through the copse.

Kent Deverell, Duke of Radcliffe, reined in the prancing gray gelding. Cocking his dark head, he sorted through the chitter of a thrush, the tinkle of a sheep's bell, the whisper of the wind through the oaks. The heavy sweetness of honeysuckle wafted through the evening air. Nothing stirred in the dense shadows of the woods; the scene looked as it had a thousand times before. Yet the hairs at the back of his neck prickled.

He subdued the sensation. He must have heard one of the pair of peacocks that roamed the south garden. It wouldn't be the first time someone had mistaken their shriek for a human cry of distress.

He lightly slapped the reins and the horse resumed its walk down the murky path. Beyond the stand of oaks rose the ancient turrets of Castle Radcliffe, starkly outlined against the purple sky of dusk. A breeze swirled up from the river and tugged at his loose-sleeved shirt. After a long day helping his men with the reaping, Kent welcomed the coolness. Weariness weighted his bones, yet it was a good feeling. The crop promised to be bountiful; he prayed the fruits of his labor would be enough to pay off the creditors. Enough to take Emily on that belated honeymoon trip to Italy.

Regret wrenched his heart. God forgive him for speaking so angrily to her that afternoon. All she'd been trying to do was preserve harmony in the house-

1

hold; he shouldn't have come down so hard on her for receiving a visit from that miserable snake. . . .

Kent swallowed the bile of hatred and resolved to apologize to his wife. For Emily's sake, he'd make the effort to forget their bitter quarrel. He'd leash his pride and keep the peace. Tender affection welled inside him. She'd brought only goodness into his life, kindness and caring and quiet joy. Soon she would present him with the greatest gift of all, a baby, his heir—

The cry came again, sharper, higher-pitched. And this time he knew it wasn't a peacock.

Emily?

Impossible. Yet that had been a woman's scream.

Fear forced the breath from his lungs. His bootheels sank into the horse's flanks. As the gelding leaped to the command, Kent hunched over the silken mane. Alarm hammered at his skull. The baby? It was too early. Four months too early. And why would Emily's scream carry all the way out here?

The vast expanse of lawn sloped upward to the castle perched on a rocky knoll overlooking the Avon River. Nestled within the crumbling fortress walls, the chimneys of the manor house puffed smoke into the darkening lavender sky.

A movement on the battlements caught the anxious sweep of his eyes. From the parapet abutting the north tower something hung pale against the age-streaked stone. He strained to see. Linens a servant had put out to air? No one ventured up there anymore, especially not at so late an hour.

His gaze fixed on the parapet, he urged the horse onward, over the grass. Through the gloom, he discerned two slim arms clinging to an embrasure. And golden hair tumbling down a slender back.

Disbelief paralyzed him. "Emily," he said in a guttural whisper.

Another bloodcurdling scream rent the air.

Terror swamped him like a nightmare. He kicked the horse to a faster speed. The wind swayed her hair. Her arms shifted as if she were scrabbling, struggling to climb to safety. An impossible task for a woman so frail, so weighted by the burden of pregnancy.

"I'm coming," he shouted. "For God's sake, hang on!"

She fell. Her skirts billowed; her cloak flapped. Her thin, petrified cry penetrated the pounding of hooves.

Horror dried his throat. Time eroded into eternity. He sucked in a searing gulp of air. Then she vanished into a tangle of bushes on the rocky slope beside the water.

No . . . no . . . no.

Nearing the curtain wall, he jerked on the reins. Even before the gelding cantered to a halt, Kent leapt from the saddle and ran.

Dear God, let him be wrong. Let it be an illusion . . . a trick of the evening light.

Scrambling over the rocks, he forced a path through the prickly undergrowth of brambles and nettles. A branch tore his shirtsleeve; a thorn embedded in his palm. Heedless, he plunged onward, gasping out her name.

"Emily! Where are you?"

Only the harsh sob of his breathing answered. The scrape of his footfalls mingled with the lapping of the river.

No one could survive such a fall. No one.

Please, let her live . . . please . . . please.

He nearly stumbled over her. She lay in the shadows, one arm at her side, the other lying across the gentle mound of her belly. She might have been sleeping.

He dropped to his knees. An inky splash of color marred the pale oval of her face. He cupped her cheeks and felt the sticky heat of blood at her temples. "Emily!"

No answer. No movement. Tears of panic blurred his vision. Christ, she couldn't be dead. Not his beloved wife.

He ran shaking hands down the length of her. She felt warm, soft, limp. He felt cold, numb, devastated.

Oh, God, this couldn't be happening. She was too

sweet, too dear . . . the single shining goodness lighting his life. Without her, he would be lost to the depths of darkness.

He took hold of her shoulders; they felt like the delicate bones of a wren. "Darling, please, please, answer me!"

She stirred. Her eyelids fluttered. Through the gathering dusk, she stared blankly up at him.

Hope blazed like a miracle in his chest. "You're safe, darling," he muttered. "Safe! We'll get you inside, fetch the doctor—"

Her spine arched and her hands lifted. She gripped the loose linen of his shirt with a strength that startled him. Her lips moved as if she were frantic to tell him something.

He heard only the breath rattling in her throat. Blood trickled darkly from a corner of her mouth.

Alarm invaded him anew. "Lie still! Don't try to talk. You'll be all right. You have to be. . . ."

Her head rolled from side to side; she murmured something he couldn't distinguish. Desperate to soothe her, he stroked her brow. Precious moments were ticking away. He didn't dare try to lift her for fear of causing further injury.

"Emily, I must seek help—"

He gently pulled at her wrists, but her fingers tightened on his shirt. As if exerting every last seed of energy, she clung to him. Her lips moved again. She coughed, and the gurgling sound chilled his soul.

Her grip slackened and her eyes glazed. On a final wisp of breath, she choked out one distinct word: "Dreamspinner!"

Chapter 1

London, June 1888

Was he staring at her or at the house?

Clutching the bucket, Juliet Carleton peered past the wrought-iron fence that bordered the front garden of Carleton House, near Belgrave Square. Across a cobbled street teeming with elegant broughams and hansom cabs, a landau was parked. A faded gold crest adorned the black door of the carriage. In deference to the balmy afternoon, the top had been folded down, and a coachman perched like a brooding oak on the driver's seat. But it was the man sitting inside the landau who interested her.

Lounging in the rear seat, an arm stretched along the side of the vehicle, he gazed straight toward her. A huge plane tree overhung the curb and cast him in shadow. Yet she could discern keen dark eyes and the slash of proud cheekbones. Clad in a white stock and fine coat, a top hat crowning hair as black as a raven's wing, he might have been any one of scores of gentlemen out enjoying the exceptional weather. Except that this stranger watched with an intensity that verged on insolence.

Was it only her fancy that cloaked him in an air of mystery?

Yes, Juliet told herself firmly. He must be waiting for someone. He merely passed the time by studying the architecture of her father's magnificent mansion.

She tipped the wooden bucket and poured the last of the pungent manure water over the soil. Sunshine heated her shoulders as she inhaled the fertile scent of

newly turned earth. With a jaundiced eye, she surveyed the ornamental row of bushes bearing an array
of crimson and yellow blooms. Roses were pretty, but
dull. Someday she'd have her own house and grow a
garden of more unusual flowers, red campion and
white water soldier and purple speedwell . . . so many
names she'd only encountered in textbooks. And she'd
have a vegetable garden to cultivate more useful plants.

Her gaze strayed to the stranger. She oughtn't stare
back, yet his very presumption stirred a reckless alertness within her, a fluttery sensation like rose petals
tossed by a gust of wind. Did he believe her to be a
servant girl assigned to assist in the garden? With the
apron thrown over her navy silk dress, she might give
such an impression.

Setting down the bucket with a sharp click, she
squared her shoulders. Let him think what he pleased.

A draft horse trudged by, pulling a dray piled high
with beer kegs. At least it blocked that annoying
stranger from her view. Spying the curled leaves of a
dock weed half-hidden beneath a rosebush, she
stepped off the path, the heels of her kid leather shoes
sinking into the soft, wet loam. Hitching up her hem,
she angled sideways to evade the thorns.

"Juliet Diana Carleton! Whatever are you doing?"

The scandalized murmur was almost lost to the rattle
of carriage wheels and the clopping of hooves. She
turned to see her mother gliding down the flagged
path; the immense gray stone mansion formed a stately
backdrop for her elegance. A gown of mauve striped
silk hugged a figure as slender as a debutante's, and a
wide-brimmed straw hat guarded her lily complexion
and perfectly groomed fair hair.

Juliet crouched to tug at the weed; it gave a sickly
sucking noise and snapped in half. "Good afternoon,
Mama. I'm preparing the garden for tonight's party."

"You're making a spectacle." Dorothea Carleton
spoke in an undertone to avoid attracting the attention
of the fashionable folk promenading the street. "Now
come out of there before someone of consequence sees
you mucking about like a common laborer."

He saw. Juliet resolutely kept her gaze from wandering to the landau. "In a moment, Mama."

Without troubling to fetch her trowel, she plunged her fingers into the damp soil and loosened the long taproot.

Dorothea shook her head in despair, setting her bonnet ribbons to bobbing. "We do have gardeners, darling. One would think two years at a finishing school would have taught you—" She paused, her nose poised upward. "Gracious, what *is* that abominable odor?"

"Manure," Juliet said, blithely aware of the ripe smell that mingled with her mother's subtle fragrance of Parma violets. "The rose bushes must be fertilized if they're to bloom well."

Distaste turned down the corners of her mother's fine mouth. "A lady should be content with cutting and arranging flowers."

"A botanist must get her hands dirty."

Dorothea released a long-suffering sigh. "You're not to speak such nonsense." Her voice a sharp whisper, she handed Juliet a handkerchief. "Here, do wipe your hands before the neighbors see you looking as filthy as a . . . a crossing sweeper."

Stepping back onto the pathway, Juliet tossed down the weed and held on to her patience. Arguing served no purpose; she must simply persevere and hope that one day her parents would relent.

"Oh, darling, I do detest scolding, but you should be resting. Don't you realize the importance of this evening? Lord Breeton has accepted the invitation to your come-out ball. If you mind your manners, you may someday become a marchioness."

Juliet grimaced. "And spend the rest of my life listening to his lordship's braying laugh? No, thank you."

"He's a fine man with an impeccable lineage."

Wiping the grime from her fingers, she glanced idly toward the black bulk of the landau in the shade. Her heart gave a leap; the dark stranger sat watching with that peculiar bold interest. "What about love?" she asked idly.

"Admiration and respect are far more important. You must find a man who can offer you a fitting place in society and a title to pass on to your children."

She studied her mother's aristocratic features. "You married beneath your station. Grandfather was a baronet, and Papa hasn't a title."

Her back a graceful bow, Dorothea pretended to inspect a yellow hybrid tea rose. "Your father's status will be rectified when the queen honors the work he's done on behalf of charity."

"And all the money he's contributed."

"Juliet! Don't be crass."

Shame stirred inside her. Though her mother's view was narrow, she did mean well. "I'm sorry, Mama. But even you must admit that Lord Breeton's true interest is the size of my marriage portion."

"It's indelicate to speak of such matters." Dorothea wagged a gloved finger at her daughter. "And you do know how to behave, if only you'll set your mind to the task. You managed superbly at the Queen's Drawing Room."

Juliet recalled the interminable wait in the antechamber at Buckingham Palace and the long walk up the white marble staircase to the State Apartments. One of a stream of debutantes dressed in elaborate court gowns and tiaras, she had executed a deep curtsy, then kissed Victoria's age-mottled hand. That brief action had officially propelled her into the ranks of adulthood.

She giggled. "You ought to have seen Maud. She nearly tripped on her train when we had to walk out backwards."

Dorothea affectionately tucked a strand of russet hair behind Juliet's ear. "Maud may be the Earl of Higgleston's daughter, but *you* possess a natural noble grace. Soon you'll have a title to match."

As her mother rambled on, Juliet let her gaze drift to the stranger. Was he observing her or the house? Beneath the stiff brim of his top hat, his eyes watched with uncanny directness. Despite the warmth of the sun, a chill tickled her skin.

"You're gawking like a shopgirl," Dorothea chided. Affecting a genteel interest in a gold tea rose, she swept her gaze along the street and gasped. Straightening, she lifted a hand to her mouth. "Oh, dear. Oh, dear, dear me."

Surprised to see her mother so flustered, Juliet frowned. "What is it, Mama?"

"It's *him*. Oh, dear heavens. What shall I do?"

"It's who?"

Dorothea whirled, presenting her back to the road and wringing her gloved hands. "The man in that landau over there," she murmured. "It's Kent Deverell, the Duke of Radcliffe."

Deverell. The name grabbed Juliet by the throat. Memory came flashing back, of a time when she was nine years old and a playmate had taunted that the powerful Deverells hated the lowly Carletons. Hurt, she'd run to Papa for reassurance; instead he'd exploded with anger and slapped her cheek, the only time he'd ever displayed physical violence toward her.

She looked sharply at the man inside the carriage. A devil, Papa had said. But this lean, dark stranger bore no horns or forked tail. Beyond his air of aggressive interest, he appeared no more dangerous than an ordinary gentleman.

"He's Papa's rival," she mused. "You warned me a long time ago never to speak the Deverell name in front of Papa."

"Yes. Oh, dear me," Dorothea fretted to the rosebushes. "Whatever can he be doing across from our home?"

"Perhaps he has a business meeting with Papa."

"Never! If Mr. Carleton spies the duke here, he'll be furious. It'll ruin our ball."

Surely her mother exaggerated. Yet why not find out for herself? "I'll go speak to him. I'll ask him to leave."

"Darling, I don't think that's wise—"

Even as Juliet took a step toward the gate, he leaned forward and spoke to the driver. The coachman flicked the reins and the carriage started briskly down the crowded street. As the vehicle disappeared into the throng, the duke never once looked back.

Disappointment wove an uncertain ribbon around her senses. "You can rest easy, Mama. He's gone."

Dorothea cast a cautious glance from beneath her bonnet brim. "Oh, praise heavens! I was afraid he might be planning to upset your father."

"He must have stopped to admire our new home, that's all."

"Yes, you're right. Mr. Carleton says he's the jealous sort, always coveting our wealth. Run along inside now, darling. I'm simply beset with duties today. . . . I must check with Potter on the extra champagne he ordered. And make certain the parlor maid cleaned that bit of woodwork she missed in the music room."

Mrs. Carleton started toward the portico with its huge fluted columns. Already forgotten, Juliet felt uncomfortably like another chore that had been ticked off her mother's list.

As she went to collect her bucket, she found her gaze straying down the street where Kent Deverell's carriage had vanished.

Three hours later, considerably cheered by a leisurely bath and luxurious primping, Juliet floated down the grand staircase. The white tulle of her gown rustled as she adjusted the rosettes of satin ribbon that framed her bare shoulders. A spray of creamy gardenias adorned the coil of russet hair. As she caught a glimpse of her elegant form in one of the beveled mirrors that flanked the front door, a sudden intense longing swept over her.

Perhaps something magical would happen tonight. She imagined herself gliding into the arms of a handsome gentleman, a man who would applaud her intelligence and appreciate her wit, a man who would share her passion for plants.

The anonymous face resolved into the saturnine features of Kent Deverell. Reaching the base of the stairs, she paused. Nonsense. She was as likely to see a costermonger tonight as the Duke of Radcliffe.

Near the front door, a liveried footman stood at rigid attention, awaiting the arrival of the first guests. A battalion of maids had cleaned the house until every inch of the floor gleamed and every bit of brass sparkled. The vivid scent of roses and carnations drifted from a scattering of cloisonné vases.

Her heels scuffed softly across the marble floor as she moved toward the drawing room with its emerald silk paneled walls. Before she could enter, the butler emerged. "Ah, Miss Carleton. Mr. Carleton asked to see you in the library."

"Thank you, Potter."

As she started down the long, echoing corridor, uneasiness pricked her spirits. Now what had she done wrong? Surely Mama wouldn't have reported such a minor transgression as weed pulling.

Portraits of people in old-fashioned garb stared down from the walls; this sprawling house had come equipped with noble ancestors, Juliet decided with a smile. The success of her father's myriad business interests had enabled her parents to move here last year while she had been away at boarding school. Unlike the smaller town house of her youth, this place felt cold in spirit, more a museum than a home.

The library doors stood ajar; she pushed open one carved panel. Twisted loops of gold cord fastened the crimson velvet curtains. Scattering the room were mementos of her father's trips to India: brass pots from Benares, an elephant's foot stool, a collection of exotic figurines from his import business. The air bore the scent of leather book bindings and the rich tobacco of her father's cigars.

Emmett Carleton stood by a window, his head tilted toward the dusk light filtering through the Nottingham lace panel. He cut a handsome figure in a black evening suit and white cravat. With his robust frame and his mane of thick gray-streaked hair, he reminded Juliet of a lion, king of his domain.

Lost in thought, he stared down at something cradled in his palm. With the other hand he smoothed his sweeping mustache. The unexpected sadness on his leonine face touched her heart and awakened her curiosity.

Keeping impulsively silent, she tiptoed nearer and saw that he held a filigreed gold locket. Tucked into either side was a tiny photograph; both images appeared to be of women, though Juliet could not discern their features. Then her petticoats rustled and Emmett pivoted toward her.

In the same swift motion, he snapped the locket shut and tucked it into a pocket of his waistcoat. She had the oddest impression that he looked guilty before his face settled into a familiar jovial expression.

"Ah, Princess," he said, his green eyes crinkling. "I didn't expect you so soon."

"Whose locket is that, Papa?"

His smile seemed a trifle forced. "It belongs to a business associate. He left it by mistake in my office and I thought to return it to him tonight."

"He's one of our guests? Who?"

"No one important. Now, allow me to say, you look radiant tonight."

The matter of the locket was closed, Juliet knew by the firmness of his voice. And when Emmett Carleton made a decision, no amount of persistence could turn him onto another course.

She reluctantly stifled her questions and twirled, her snowy skirts swaying. "Do I pass muster, then?"

"The noble swells will be smitten," he declared, fists planted at his waist. "No doubt your mother and I shall soon be entertaining an endless stream of titled suitors."

She laughed. "Poor Papa. If the prospect disturbs you, perhaps we should cancel the ball and avoid the headache of launching me into society." Sobering, she added, "I could always study botany at Trinity College—"

"No daughter of mine is going to turn herself into a bluestocking. I prefer blue-blooded grandsons to carry on the family tradition."

The reference to their long-standing debate stung.

With a cool stare, she said, "And what of what *I* want?"

His bushy gray brows lowered. But he merely said, "No arguments, Princess . . . not tonight." Reaching into a pocket of his frock coat, he withdrew a strand of pearls. "Your mother asked me to present you with this. Your grandmother—the Lady Beckburgh—wore these pearls on the occasion of her debut." Stepping behind her, he fastened the cool silver clasp at her nape.

Her annoyance sank beneath a rush of warm emotion. The sentimental gift meant more than a maharaja's treasure trove. She brushed her fingertips over the glossy pearls. "Oh, Papa, I never expected—"

Bursting with affection, she swung around to embrace him, pressing her cheek to the fine fabric of his lapel. His scent of cigars enveloped her, bringing back fond memories of childhood, when her favorite time of day had been the brief moments each evening in which she visited her parents to bid them good night.

For an instant, he held her tight; then he drew stiffly back. Clearing his throat, Emmett Carleton adjusted his impeccable cravat. "A simple 'thank you' will suffice. One never knows when a servant might walk in."

Vaguely disappointed, she nodded. Couldn't he for once forget the rigid rules of propriety? "Of course, Papa."

"Shall we proceed to the foyer? I can't wait to show you off, Princess . . . the jewel in my crown of achievements."

Her vision of the future failed to match that of her parents, Juliet reflected uneasily. She suddenly recalled Kent Deverell, but decided against mentioning his strange appearance. No need to ignite the short fuse of her father's temper, especially not now, and spoil his pleasure in the ball.

As she took his arm, she felt a fluttery mix of excitement and disquiet. Half of her looked forward to the magic of the evening. The other half felt like a choice plum being placed on display at the greengrocer's.

* * *

"Who has your first waltz?" Lady Maud Peabody squinted at the dance programme Juliet held in her white-gloved hands. "Egad, the inimitable Lord Bree-ton. Or shall I say, Lord *Brayton*?"

Juliet grinned, then glanced around the crowded ballroom to see if anyone had overheard the impudent pun. No one paid attention to the two debutantes, who stood in a nook half-hidden by the feathery foliage of an aspidistra. The gas jets cast a blaze of smoky golden light over the assembly of ladies and gentlemen. Glit-tering like a fairyland, the ballroom had huge, gilt-framed mirrors and an arched ceiling from which hung several crystal chandeliers. The buzz of voices mingled with the tuning of instruments from the musicians' al-cove.

"My father encouraged his lordship to sign my card for two waltzes and a polka," Juliet whispered, grim-acing. "I'm afraid my parents regard him as a potential son-in-law."

"You could do worse." Her fair features as dainty as a snowdrop, Maud fluttered a silk fan and confided, "*My* parents are favoring that beastly Roger Billings-gate. Imagine . . . I saw him spit into a vase of carna-tions when he thought no one was watching."

Juliet laughed. "What did you do?"

"Affected not to notice, of course." A gleam entered Maud's nearsighted blue eyes. "On the other hand, he does have pots of money. Perhaps the right woman might tame the savage beast."

Amused, Juliet shook her head. "I wouldn't count on it. If you're wrong, you'll be staring at him over the breakfast table for the rest of your life."

"Oh, fiddle," Maud said with a dismissive wave of her fan. "I can scarcely see past my nose, anyway. Besides, we're not schoolgirls anymore; I can manage any man—" Her words broke off as she squinted at the crowd. "Don't look now, but I think that's Breeton heading this way. Searching for you, no doubt."

Juliet kept her gaze longingly trained on the French doors leading to the formal gardens. "I'm tempted to hide on the terrace until the first dance is over."

"He'd only come after you. You're too rich an heiress to let slip through his greedy fingers. Now, *smile.*"

She assumed a civil expression just as Lord Breeton ambled out of the throng. The pompous dandy wore a stiff boiled collar and a shiny formal coat sporting a red rosebud on the lapel. Muttonchop whiskers and a thatch of curly brown hair framed his pallid face. His features were regular, except for the fact that nature had failed to provide him with a chin.

"Your ladyship," he said, bowing first to Maud, then to Juliet. "Miss Carleton, I was beginning to despair of ever finding you. Rather like chasing down a fox at a hunt."

The comparison irritated her. Dipping into the obligatory curtsy, she said sweetly, "Perhaps your lordship ought to have brought his pack of hounds."

He looked momentarily puzzled; then he let loose a braying laugh. "Hounds at a ball, you say—hee-haw—now, that would create quite the stir, wouldn't it?"

Maud lifted the fan to her face and uttered a choked cough. Juliet wanted to sink into the polished parquet floor, but thankfully, his loud guffaw attracted little attention.

"Are you all right?" she asked Maud in mock solicitousness. "A pity if you fell ill and had to leave the festivities."

"I'll be fine." Her eyes twinkled above the zealous wagging of her fan. "It's this stuffy air. Settles in the throat, you know."

"I say," interjected Lord Breeton, "the musicians are striking the first notes. Do pardon us, your ladyship."

Taking firm hold of Juliet's arm, he whisked her toward the dance floor. The lively whirl of a waltz restored her sparkling gaiety; for all his faults, Lord Breeton was a superb dancer. So what if he could only converse on the horse and the hunt?

Afterward, he delivered her to her mother's side, where a morose young nobleman awaited his turn to partner Juliet. Another hopeful, she decided, as he droned on about the disrepair of his country estate, and then belatedly added a gushing testimony to the heritage of the house and his own ancient lineage.

Never lacking for escorts, she danced away the hours. Between sets, she stood surrounded by a bevy of admirers as she drank champagne. The effervescent wine sped straight to her head. She couldn't deny a giddy delight in being the center of attention. Flattered by the number of gentlemen who requested an introduction, she had to remind herself the attention stemmed from her extravagant dowry as her father's sole heir.

Then she saw him.

She was laughing at a long-winded tale told by Viscount Hazlitt, of a soda siphon battle with the Prince of Wales, when an odd prickly sensation pulled her gaze to the musicians' alcove.

A man stood there, one broad shoulder propped negligently against a pillar. His hand rested in the pocket of his formal coat, drawing back the black fabric and emphasizing the superb fitness of his body. A light breeze wafted through the opened French doors and ruffled his black hair. Clean-shaven, his features were handsome in an aggressive sort of way, with striking cheekbones and a proud set to his jaw.

Kent Deverell.

Her heart tripped over a beat. Beneath black brows, eyes dark as pitch studied her with frank absorption. His scrutiny unnerved her. Unlike the refined admiration she'd received from other gentlemen, this man radiated a dynamic intensity, a disturbing aloofness. With a twist of chagrin, Juliet realized she couldn't tell what he thought of her.

Why had he come here?

Obeying reckless impulse, she raised her chin and shot him a haughty glare. His mouth quirked into the hint of a smile, half-mocking, half-mysterious. Unaccountably the breath squeezed from her lungs. He seemed disinclined to come forward and make her acquaintance, so why did she feel the overwhelming urge to defy convention and introduce herself to her father's business rival?

"What a handsome devil," whispered Maud. "Who *is* he?"

Juliet tore her gaze from the duke to see her friend squinting over the fan. Lord Hazlitt and the others had wandered off, leaving them alone with Lord Breeton. Before Juliet could gather the shreds of her composure, the marquis spoke.

"Radcliffe," he said, his lip curling in cultured distaste. "I say, what do you suppose he's doing here?"

"Radcliffe?" piped Maud, her eyes owlishly wide. "Do you mean the *Duke* of Radcliffe?"

Breeton nodded. "Kent Deverell, none other. He and I attended Harrow together."

Juliet frowned, puzzling over his presence. Her mother hadn't issued an invitation to the duke. Unless she'd been wrong this afternoon . . . unless Papa had invited Kent Deverell without informing Mama. Was it possible the feud had been settled?

Burning with curiosity, she swung sharply toward him again. But the place by the pillar stood empty; the duke had vanished.

"I say," Breeton went on, "this must be the first time Radcliffe's come out in society since the scandal."

Maud perked up; her fan dipped to reveal an avid expression. "What scandal?"

Breeton rubbed his receding chin. "I'm no backstairs gossip . . . but I heard Deverell's wife took her own life three years ago. Leapt from the parapet of Castle Radcliffe."

Shock and pity struck Juliet speechless.

Maud gasped. "Egad!"

"A sad tale, indeed," Breeton mused. "Especially since the duchess was . . . er . . . *enceinte.*"

"Oh, the poor man!" Maud exclaimed. "To lose both his wife and his heir. But are you certain this is true?"

"Of course, my lady," Breeton said, puffing out his thin chest. "My valet has a cousin in service near Radcliffe's estate. Said the local vicar tried to refuse to bury Emily Deverell in consecrated grounds. Radcliffe went half-mad and claimed the death was an accident. Actually threatened the vicar with bodily harm until he relented."

"Perhaps it *was* a tragic accident," Juliet said.

Lord Breeton held himself pompously erect. "You are doubtless unaware of the late duchess's background. She was born on the wrong side of the blanket, poor thing. Talk has it, she was prone to melancholia."

"How typical of an ill-bred commoner," she murmured dryly.

"Yes . . . er . . . no." Breeton flushed beet-red to his ears. "I say, Miss Carleton, I meant no offense—"

"Then don't repeat rumors," she snapped, glancing from his disconcerted expression to Maud's guilty countenance. "Pray excuse me."

Pivoting, she swept into the swarm of guests. Almost immediately she regretted her outburst. Breeton merely acted his usual priggish self; Maud obeyed her compulsion for gossip.

So why, Juliet wondered, had she leaped to the duke's defense?

The image of his darkly handsome face invaded her mind. He'd lost his wife and unborn child to calamitous circumstance; no wonder he gave the impression of brooding emotions hidden within those midnight eyes.

Sympathy softened her heart. What if his wife really *had* committed suicide? What could make a woman so unhappy that she sought death as her sole escape? Juliet shivered, baffled and curious. Unless Kent Deverell *was* a devil in disguise . . .

Concentrating on her thoughts, she nearly bumped into her mother at the doors to the ballroom.

"Oh, darling, there you are." Stunning in Nile-green faille, Dorothea Carleton spread the pearl sticks of her fan and looked to the couple beside her. "Have you welcomed Lord and Lady Higgleston?"

Juliet greeted Maud's parents warmly, though she scarcely knew them, for they took scant interest in their only daughter, a child of their middle age. Like a pair of matched cobs, both were stout, gray-haired, and stoop-shouldered. Lady Higgleston spent part of each year as lady-in-waiting to the queen and the other part pursuing philanthropic causes, while Lord Higgleston hibernated at his club.

Her ladyship snatched Juliet's hand and squeezed it with evangelical fervor. "Dorothea has been telling me about the banquet Mr. Carleton is sponsoring next month for the orphans of the Rosemary Lane Hospice. Such generosity is to be commended! Don't you agree, Arthur?"

Lord Higgleston cupped a hand to his ear. "Eh? Whatever you say, m'dear. Whatever you say."

"We all have a duty to succor the less fortunate," said Mrs. Carleton.

Lady Higgleston gave a vigorous nod, setting the ostrich feather in her coiffure to bouncing. "Indeed so. I shall make certain the queen hears of your benevolence when she returns from Balmoral. Her Majesty is a champion of the downtrodden, you know. Did you hear what she did for Lady Frith?"

Bemused, Juliet shook her head and extracted her hand. "No."

"Her ladyship's father was a commoner who made his fortune in the sausage trade. He disapproved of her eloping with that penniless Earl of Frith and tried to cut her off, but the queen interceded and made him pay the dowry. Isn't that so, Arthur?"

"Eh?" He blinked. "Yes, m'dear. Whatever you say."

"Pray excuse us," said Lady Higgleston. "I see Reverend Wilder by the punch bowl. I must question him on his interpretation of last Sunday's scripture." Tugging at her husband's sleeve, she hauled him through the crowd.

"What a marvelous night this has been." Blue eyes sparkling, Dorothea Carleton bent nearer in a waft of violet perfume. "When the queen hears the news, your father could win his knighthood."

"I'm glad," Juliet said sincerely.

"And you've hardly had a moment alone. The dance has been quite the success, don't you think?"

She bit her lip. She ought to report Kent Deverell's illicit presence, but a strange reluctance held her back. He wasn't disturbing anyone, she reasoned, so why trouble her mother?

Abruptly Mrs. Carleton frowned. Drawing herself up straight, she gazed across the ballroom. At the same moment, the din of conversation lowered and whispers swept the gathering like wind through a woodland.

Curious, Juliet turned to follow the line of her mother's attention. And caught her breath.

Moving with the smooth self-possession of a man accustomed to command, Kent Deverell strode directly toward them.

Chapter 2

She wasn't quite what he'd expected.

As he cut a path through the murmuring crowd, Kent subjected Juliet Carleton to a dispassionate appraisal. Tall and willowy. Huge green eyes. Hair the rich red-brown hue of cinnamon. In her delicate features she favored her mother; fine cheekbones and pure ivory skin lent her an air of fragility. She wore a white gown that skimmed her slender curves and left her shoulders and bosom all but bare. The steadiness of her gaze stirred a reluctant admiration in him. She held herself as erect and proud as a goddess, a goddess with the contours of a flesh-and-blood woman. Yet somehow she looked heartbreakingly young.

His throat ached suddenly. She must be the same tender age Emily had been at the time of his marriage to her. Almost the same age Emily had been at her death.

The dull pain of loss welled from deep within him. Then resentment choked Kent, resentment that Juliet Carleton could inspire a comparison to Emily. The two women looked vastly different, and doubtless the disparity was more pronounced in temperament. His wife had been all gentleness and virtue; a woman raised in the shadow of Emmett Carleton could only be corrupt.

What the hell *had* he expected, anyway? A snake-haired Medusa? A sloe-eyed temptress? A female replica of Emmett Carleton?

Like frost over a barren field, resolve chilled Kent's soul. He must focus on his purpose and disregard sentiment; he must concentrate on capturing her trust.

He must avenge Emily's death.

21

As he drew closer, he noted a faint blush on Juliet Carleton's cheeks; she must be wondering why he'd stopped outside her house today, why he'd come here tonight. Grim anticipation gripped him, for the chase was about to begin.

Relaxing his mouth into a well-bred smile, he turned to her mother. Dorothea Carleton retained her girlish figure, though her fair features bore a tracery of wrinkles around the eyes and mouth. They had met years ago, at a charity reception to which the hostess had inadvertently invited both him and the Carletons. To Kent's dark satisfaction, Emmett had seethed all evening.

"Mrs. Carleton," he said. "How pleasant to see you again."

Dorothea hesitated. One elegant gloved hand lifted to touch the brilliant diamond pendant at her throat, a pendant that must be worth far more than he spent annually on seed and labor. Kent reflected cynically on her dilemma: should she order him to leave and risk a scene, or yield to his superior rank?

She curtsied. "Your Grace," she said, her voice composed. "This is most unexpected."

"I hope my presence won't cause you any inconvenience."

She gazed at him uncertainly. "Is it wise for you to stay? If Mr. Carleton should come out of the drawing room . . ."

"But I'm here to hold out the olive branch, nothing more. It's time we put old enmities aside, don't you agree?"

"I . . . yes, of course, but—"

"Then you won't mind introducing me to your daughter."

With inbred civility, Dorothea said, "Your Grace, I should like you to meet Miss Juliet Carleton. Juliet, His Grace, the Duke of Radcliffe . . . Kent Deverell."

Juliet dipped a curtsy that was a shade shy of complete homage. "I'm honored," she murmured.

Despite her words, she didn't look deferential in the least. Her eyes were green rimmed with gold, and annoyingly similar to Emmett's piercing gaze, except for her long lashes. Kent gritted his teeth against the rising bile of hatred as the opening notes of a waltz wafted through the ballroom.

"Then perhaps," he said, taking firm hold of her arm, "you won't mind granting me the honor of a dance. Do excuse us, Mrs. Carleton."

Looking alarmed, Dorothea murmured, "But Your Grace—"

Juliet missed the rest of her mother's protest as the duke propelled her toward the multitude of couples gathering on the dance floor. She tilted her head to look at him; he stood taller than her other dance partners. His features, both rugged and noble, held an undeniable force of character. A curious exhilaration beat in her blood. With a faint shock, she realized that from the moment she'd seen him in the landau, she'd wanted to meet him. Yet she could forget neither his identity nor his audacity.

"You might have asked me instead of ordering me."

Sliding an arm around her waist, he clasped her hand in his. "Would you have agreed?"

"Of course not. Lord Breeton signed my card for this waltz."

"Breeton," he scoffed. "He'd only bore you with his exploits at the hunt."

She swallowed an unexpected bubble of laughter. "He's a superb dancer."

"So am I," Kent Deverell said with unashamed conceit. "And since you've already danced with that popinjay—and every other man here—it's my turn now."

As he guided her around in perfect time to the Viennese waltz, Juliet felt as graceful as a lily petal scudding over a crystal pond. Through her thin glove, his hand felt strong and callused, unlike Breeton's baby-soft palm. When she spied, on the fringe of the crowd, his lordship's sulky face, she could summon no remorse. Her gaiety faltered only when she noticed a number of guests staring and murmuring.

Because a Carleton was dancing with a Deverell? Or

because of the scandal surrounding the death of the duke's wife?

The impulse to defend him seized her; absurd, because he looked more than capable of defending himself. Yet she lifted her chin in studied nonchalance and softened her lips into a smile. Let people talk. She would enjoy her dance with the handsome duke.

"When a woman smiles like that," he said, "it generally means she's up to something."

"Or that she simply enjoys a fine waltz."

"I'm glad you find dancing with me such a pleasure."

His nearness, his bold stare, unsettled Juliet. She lowered her gaze to the white, bell-like blossom adorning his lapel. "Where did you get that foxglove bloom? You weren't wearing it when you came in."

"I noticed you prefer a man who sports flowers."

"Lord Breeton again?"

"None other." His voice lowered to a husky undertone. "And I do so want to win your favor."

A slow heat suffused her. "Why?"

"Are you angling for compliments, Miss Carleton?"

Her cheeks grew hotter. How easily he could fluster her. "Foxglove is an odd choice. The flower of a poisonous plant."

"Rosebuds are too tame. You strike me as the sort who prefers something wilder, more exotic."

"Perhaps," she said breathlessly. "But you never answered my question. We haven't any foxglove in our garden."

"On the contrary. I'll show you."

In a smooth motion, he spun her through the throng of dancers and out an opened doorway. The terrace lay in moon-dappled shadow, the formal gardens lit by strings of festive lanterns that bobbed against the starry sky. Couples strolled the concentric pathways. After the stifling closeness of the ballroom, the balmy night air caressed her skin and aroused a reckless anticipation inside Juliet. The breeze carried the vivid odors of blooming roses and fresh-turned loam, along with a heady hint of the duke's masculine scent.

He released her hand, but kept his arm curved around her waist as he escorted her down the marble steps. "Far more agreeable out here, isn't it? Not only do the Carletons sponsor the finest ball of the season, they manage to order perfect weather as well."

The trace of derision rang a discordant note into the music drifting from the ballroom. Stepping away, she turned, searching the lean angles of his face through the velvety shadows.

"Why did you wait outside the house this afternoon?"

"Because I heard Emmett Carleton had a pretty daughter. And for once, the gossipmongers told the truth."

The silken words warmed her. "You must have had more reason than that," she persisted.

"As I told your mother, I want to end the hostility."

"But why now? Why tonight?"

His tall form limned by moonlight, Kent Deverell stood silent, drawing an oak leaf through his long fingers. "This is my first chance," he said quietly. "You see, I've been in mourning, so I've not visited London in quite some time."

Her heart ached with compassion. Impulse urged her to lay a hand on his sleeve. "I'm so sorry, Your Grace. I heard what happened to your wife and child—" Unsure if he'd resent her presumption, she drew back. "Excuse me, I'm being forward."

"Please, don't apologize for a gesture of friendship," he said, dropping the leaf to fold her hands in his. "I want you to be frank with me."

"Then tell me, why does Papa hate you so?"

"He hates me because he hated my father, Miss Carleton. As my father has been dead for four years, I see no reason to extend the feud to the second generation." He lowered his voice to a husky murmur. "Let's not spoil the evening with ancient hostilities."

The warm squeeze of his fingers echoed his sincerity. "My father may not agree with you," she warned. "He's not one to easily forget a slight. He'll be furious if he finds you here."

The duke shrugged. "I'll be glad to talk to him . . . later."

Misgiving shivered inside her; then longing blotted out the sensation. She wanted to close her mind to the dispute, to open the night to magical possibilities. . . .

Grasping her arm, he steered her away from the gardens and toward the southern side of the mansion. Pools of light spilled from the windows, leaving great shadowed areas that wrapped the footpath in intimacy. Expectation fluttered inside her belly. "Where are we going?" she asked.

"To find that foxglove. Remember?"

Enthralled, Juliet let him lead her into the gloom as the sprightly tune of a lancers set drifted from the house. She stole a glance at his strong profile as he peered ahead into the darkness. No other couples had strayed so far. She risked her reputation by going off alone with him, yet she would not turn back, not even to please her father. It was time she began making her own decisions.

"Here we are," he said, halting midway along the wall.

There, nestled against the gray Portland stone of the house and half-hidden by a row of clipped boxwood, three foxglove spikes reached toward the yellow light from the drawing room. Each scraggly stalk bore a line of large, tubular white blooms.

"They're lovely!" Heedless of her skirts, she sank to her knees and stripped off a glove to run her fingertips over one velvety flower. "What an odd place for wildflowers to spring up."

"The wind probably blew some seeds from another garden."

"Probably." Curious, she tilted her face toward his towering figure. "How did you know they were here?"

His smile gleamed through the shadows. "You forget, I wouldn't have been let in through the front door. I was forced to find an alternate entrance."

"You came through one of the garden gates?"

"No, straight over the fence there."

Following his pointing finger, Juliet glanced at the

wrought-iron enclosure bordering the property. Flattered and amused, she imagined His Grace, the Duke of Radcliffe, clad in formal attire, skulking through the darkness and leaping the wall.

"You're quite the athlete," she teased.

He hunkered down beside her. "I had considerable incentive. Once I saw you this afternoon, I knew I'd do anything to meet such a beautiful woman."

His husky words caught her off guard. "I thought you were staring at the house."

"You truly think I'd prefer cold gray stone to you? You're too modest, Miss Carleton."

Aware of his nearness, she felt an unseemly urge to reach out and trace his sculpted cheek as she might caress a perfect orchid. Flustered, she looked down at the foxglove. "*Digitalis purpurea,*" she said in a breathy rush. "They're usually purple blooms. I wonder if the white variety flourishes better in the city."

"How do you know the Latin name?"

At his sharp tone, Juliet flushed. Would he, too, disdain her unladylike interest? Lifting her chin, she met his eyes and said, "I devote a great deal of time to studying plants, Your Grace."

With that disquieting alertness, he stared back. Then his gaze dipped over the billows of tulle surrounding her crouched form, and lingered an instant on her breasts. "A lady botanist?"

"Yes. I can't claim a university education, but I've learned on my own through reading books and working in the garden and greenhouses."

"You're better off without a degree. Experience has taught me far more than all the agriculture lectures I heard at Trinity."

She sat back on her heels. "Agriculture?"

He inclined his head. "Put plainly, I'm a farmer. Even a duke must sometimes earn his living."

Her gaze fell to his strong and callused hands. Absently she drew the long kid glove between her fingers. Odd, that her father would consider a farmer his rival. She burned to pursue the puzzle, but a reluctance to shatter the spell held her back.

"What was Trinity like?" she asked.

"A lot of highbrows more involved in sculling than studying." Scooping up a handful of soil, he let it filter through his fingers. "This is how you'll learn best, Miss Carleton, just as you've been doing. With a plot of ground and a sack of seeds."

Thrilled that they shared an interest, she said, "It's amazing how beautiful flowers can spring from something so mundane as dirt. Sometimes I feel like an artist plying a brush, helping nature create a lovelier palette. Have you ever felt that way?"

"Farming isn't quite so aesthetic."

His indulgent smile made her feel suddenly shy. "You probably think I'm being fanciful." A poignant memory tugged at her, and copying Kent, she reached down to sift the cool earth through her fingers. "Whenever I made up a whimsical story as a child, my father used to call me his little Dreamspinner."

His hand convulsed around a handful of dirt, his knuckles going white. *"What did you say?"*

The ragged quality of his voice yanked her gaze to his face. His jaw was rigid; his lips thinned. Confused and wary, Juliet studied him. The mere mention of Papa angered the duke. . . .

"Dreamspinner," she repeated. "It's just a silly name from my youth. Papa hasn't called me that in a long time."

"How long?"

"Oh, three or four years at least." Cocking her head, she peered closely at him. "I thought you wanted to end the rivalry. You look ready to go to war, not make peace."

His fingers slowly unclenched, dropping the soil. He brushed off his hands. "I'm sorry. My mind strayed to another matter."

Despite the formal apology, shadows lingered in his eyes, shadows that suddenly alarmed her. Kent Deverell could be charming and open, yet she sensed a well of secrecy within him, a secrecy that both fascinated and frightened her. She really knew so little about him.

"I should like to get up," she said.

"Of course."

Rising with negligent ease, he extended a hand. When his fingers closed around her gloveless ones, the shock of his warm, roughened skin struck the breath from her lungs. Her legs felt about to buckle. He kept their hands inexorably joined, and the black bitterness in his eyes made her shiver.

Pulling free, she took a step toward the lighted gardens. "I'd better return to the ballroom or people will talk."

Something flickered in his eyes. "Come now, you don't appear the sort to let a little gossip bother you."

Juliet busied herself with tugging the long glove up her arm and over her elbow. "Of course not," she said firmly. "But a lady can be ruined by the slightest infraction, Your Grace."

She started down the path; he fell into step beside her. "And you, of course, don't wish to be ruined. Else Breeton might beg off marrying you."

Annoyed, she shook her tulle skirt free of the clinging dirt. "I've no plans to wed his lordship, not that it's any of your concern."

"Pardon, I was merely speculating that your father would want his only daughter to wed a titled man."

"He'll allow me to make my own choice."

"Will he?" Kent gave a short laugh. "I wonder."

That satirical note returned to his voice, making Juliet feel as uncertain as a foxglove battered by a storm. "If you truly wish to forget the past," she said, tilting her head at him, "then why do I have the feeling you still despise Papa?"

Only the barest faltering of his gait betrayed any emotion. His expression remained congenial, polite as any gentleman escorting a lady on her walk. "I didn't mean to give that impression," he said. "Please try to understand, I learned to dislike Carletons at my father's knee. It's hard to shake a belief so deeply ingrained, but I'd like to try."

She bit her lip. "How do I know you're sincere?"

"You'll have to trust me."

Candor etched that austerely handsome face, a candor that softened her heart. Perhaps it was naive, but something about him inspired faith. She gave Kent a tentative smile, then watched with pleasure as his stern mouth eased into an answering grin.

As they rounded the corner of the house, her skirts swished to the lilt of another waltz. Through the bright-lit windows of the ballroom, she glimpsed the dancers, the ladies' gowns forming a jeweled bouquet that contrasted with the formal black attire of the men. Couples still wandered the garden, their figures silhouetted by strings of lanterns.

Why did she feel surprised that everything around her appeared so normal? she wondered whimsically. Had she expected a hue and cry to be raised over her brief disappearance?

As they reached the terrace steps, Kent caught her wrist. "Let's not go in, Juliet. Not yet."

He spoke her name like music, and those devilish eyes radiated an invitation that beckoned to her. Despite the barrier of her glove, the caress of his thumb against her inner wrist sparked shivers over her skin. Somehow the night seemed charged with magic, and a scandalous longing flamed inside her, a longing that quickened her blood. She wanted to press her cheek to his silk shirt, to feel his arms holding her close, to smooth away the harsh lines etching his face. . . .

A movement near the house caught her attention. Emmett Carleton had emerged from an opened French door at the far end of the terrace. As he paused to peer toward the gardens, dismay drove the joy from her. As much as she wanted he and Kent to settle their differences, she felt a half-guilty desire to avoid a confrontation.

"There's Papa now," she said.

Even as she spoke, Emmett started straight toward them, and his vigorous stride bespoke displeasure.

Kent tightened his fingers around her wrist. "Meet me tomorrow at the Embankment," he murmured. "Eleven o'clock by Cleopatra's Needle. Can you manage that?"

Torn between prudence and passion, she shook her head. "I don't know. . . ."

"Promise me, please. I must see you again, Juliet. I want the chance to know you better."

His eyes glowed dark and fathomless as the midnight sky. A drowning sensation swept over her, and she yearned to succumb to the whirlpool, to give herself in to his keeping, to let him spin her away wherever he willed. . . .

"Yes," she heard herself whispering. "Yes, I'll be there."

The approach of footsteps shattered the spell as Emmett descended the marble steps. Fury tightened his leonine features, a fury thinly concealed beneath a rigid mask of civility. His fingers clenched and unclenched at his sides, as if he contemplated violence and held himself back through force of willpower.

"Take your bloody hand off my daughter," he bit out in a brutal undertone.

Kent aimed a lordly look at her father; then he let his arm drop to his side. "Hello, Emmett."

"You aren't welcome here. Get out."

Though her father spoke quietly, rage radiated from him. Juliet hastened to his side. "It's all right, Papa. The duke means no wrong. He came here tonight to make peace with you."

"Yes," Kent agreed, "I thought it was long past time you and I wiped the slate clean."

The men exchanged a hard stare. Then Emmett said, "The only thing I want to wipe clean is the floor with your face."

The vicious statement shocked her. "Father!"

"Stay out of this, Princess," he said, without taking his eyes from the duke. "This scoundrel isn't fit to kiss your feet."

Kent wore a slight smile. "I heard a rumor that you're angling for a knighthood. Shall we engage in fisticuffs in the ballroom? Or would that ruin your chance at impressing the queen?"

Emmett's lips tautened beneath the handlebar mus-

tache. He swung toward Juliet. "Go wait by the door.
I'll have a word alone with this villain."

She had no choice but to obey. Kid slippers dragging, she walked away, casting a worried glance over
her shoulder at the two men.

The moment she was beyond earshot, Emmett said,
"I'll accept your presence here under one condition. If
you've come to sell me Dreamspinner."

Kent gave a brusque laugh. "You'd like that,
wouldn't you?"

"It should belong to me. If William hadn't stolen
it—"

"My father stole nothing. I'd have thought you'd
have given up on Dreamspinner. Since it brought about
Emily's death . . . or have you so conveniently forgotten that fact?"

Sweat beaded Emmett's upper lip. Fists tight, he
took a step closer. "Why, you devil—"

"You murderer."

The quiet words were almost lost to the lovely music
from the ballroom. The blood drained from Emmett's
face, leaving it chalk-white. His chest swelled with the
effort to draw in air.

"I'll give you one chance to get out," he snarled.
"Then I'll summon a pair of footmen to toss you into
the gutter like the rubbish you are."

The duke clenched his jaw. For a long, fierce moment he stared before lifting his hand in a sardonic
salute. "As you wish, then. Far be it from me to provide the evening's entertainment."

Pivoting, he retraced his steps down the footpath.

From her stance by the door, Juliet watched in despair as his tall form vanished into the shadows. She
forgot her father's presence until he appeared at her
side. Burning to know why that short exchange had
driven all color from his cheeks, she asked, "What did
the duke say to you?"

"Nothing of consequence." His fingers bit into her
arm. "Now come along."

"Where are we going?"

"Inside. The gossips have had long enough to speculate. Let's hope it's not too late to undo the damage that devil has wrought."

"But Papa, the duke was the soul of kindness—"

"We'll speak of him later," Emmett cut in, his eyes frosty. "And your behavior as well, young lady. Now, by God, look as though nothing's happened."

His blunt words stung, but she couldn't reply, for he was half hauling her into the ballroom. After the cool night air of the garden, the heat smothered her. At his side she worked her way through the press of people, stopping occasionally to speak to a guest. Now, more than ever, her father brought to mind a lion who prowled his domain and dared anyone to challenge his authority. With mingled awe and dismay, she realized the extent of his power. Though a few lords and ladies looked speculative, no one openly questioned her scandalous disappearance with the Duke of Radcliffe.

While she smiled and chatted, her mind remained fixed on the encounter between Kent Deverell and her father. Had so many important people not been present, Papa would have instigated a fist brawl. The thought staggered Juliet. She had always suspected he had an aggressive side, but the proof of such poisonous hatred left her sickened.

Once they'd made the rounds, Emmett delivered her to his wife's side. "Dorothea, I'd like to return to my business discussions. Can you manage here?"

Mrs. Carleton nervously touched her diamond pendant. "Yes, Mr. Carleton, of course."

"I trust you'll do better at chaperoning this time."

He swung to Juliet, and the stern warning on his face transmitted clear: she was to behave like the perfect lady. Chin held high, she met his angry gaze.

The moment he strode away, Dorothea murmured fretfully, "Oh, dear, he's so very furious. How could you have done this to me?"

Regret assaulted Juliet; she'd never meant to cause her mother any trouble. As several suitors assembled to request their dances, she forced herself to flirt and converse. Maud ventured by, bubbling with questions about the duke and whispering commentary on the guests. But not even her cheery chatter held much interest for Juliet.

The sparkle had gone out of the evening . . . gone with a man who had midnight eyes.

"What the devil induced you to go waltzing off with that scoundrel?"

Her father clicked the library doors shut. His glare pinned Juliet as she sank into a gold brocade chair, her legs aching from hours of dancing, her cheeks cramped from smiling. The instant the last of the guests had departed, he'd marched her straight into his private den.

"You raised me to be gracious to all guests," she countered, peeling of her gloves and laying them aside. "He acted the perfect gentleman."

"Gentleman, pah." Emmett prowled the Persian carpet. "Give him half a chance and he'd have tossed up your skirts and had his way with you."

"Father!" Hot color seared her cheeks; fighting a scandalous warmth, she gripped the chair arms. "We only went for a walk in the garden, no different from scores of other couples."

Emmett splashed brandy into a glass and took a swallow. The gesture gave testimony to the degree of his displeasure; he never drank alcohol or smoked cigars in her presence.

"Pardon my indelicacy," he said gruffly, "but it's best you realize the sort of man Deverell really is. Despite that smooth appearance, he isn't to be trusted."

She leaned forward. "He came here to offer peace, an end to this hostility."

"He came here to mock me," Emmett snapped. "Deverell knows how important it is to me to secure a proper marriage for you. He knows and he tried to ruin your reputation."

"He didn't ruin anything." To herself, she added, *And he did have the opportunity.*

"Because I caught him in time."

Studying his ruthless expression, she shook her head. "Surely you can separate a professional rivalry from a personal one. I don't see why you despise the Deverells so much."

"It's a business matter, Princess. A lady might find it difficult to comprehend."

Vexed by his supercilious attitude, she struggled to keep her voice level. "Tell me anyway, Papa."

He hesitated, then set his glass down with an abrupt click. "Perhaps it *is* better you know." His eyes took on a distant look. "Some twenty years ago, I owned a vast tea garden in the Assam region of India. I sold the plantation to Kent's father, William. When the tea market crashed just days later, William said I'd deliberately misled him . . . and cheated him by charging an inflated price."

"Cheated!" Indignant, Juliet sat up straight. "Surely you couldn't have predicted what would happen."

"That's what I said, too. But he'd suffered a huge loss and had to blame someone, rather than face his own faulty judgment." Emmett picked up a small ivory elephant and studied it. "Not long afterward, he embroiled himself in a scandal. You see, the Indian government was shipping all their opium to China under a trade agreement. William got caught bringing a pilfered supply into England along with a tea shipment. The incident might have died, except that an anti-opium group got wind of it and decided to make William their scapegoat." Putting down the figurine, Emmett gave a snort of disgust. "They blasted him as the high-and-mighty duke who'd stooped to drug peddling. William had the audacity to blame it all on me."

"How could he do that?"

"He claimed I'd planted the opium to invent a scandal. And when his business enterprises went into a downslide, he said I'd used my influence to induce the banking community to refuse him loans. He was just a gambler who never learned how to hedge his bets." Emmett waved a hand around the room. "Everything I have, Princess, I earned. I wasn't born with a fancy title and a castle. William Deverell never knew the value of hard work."

"That's no reason for you to hate his son."

"Isn't it, now." Stroking his handlebar mustache, he went on scornfully, "Kent inherited the tendency to make poor investments. He squandered the last of the Deverell fortune developing some newfangled threshing machine that never worked."

"What he does with his money is his own concern."

"Perhaps. But mark my words, he's cut from the same cloth as his father."

"You're not being reasonable—"

"You don't know the whole story." Yanking back a panel of Nottingham lace, Emmett peered into the black night. In a flat voice, he added, "Kent Deverell drove his own wife to suicide."

Despite her knowledge, shock shook her. "That's hearsay."

"Hearsay usually has a grain of truth. He neglected his wife in favor of his farming."

Unable to contain her agitation, Juliet rose on weary legs and paced the library. "I thought you disliked gossip. Won't you even give him a chance to exonerate himself?"

He swung around, his gaze keen. "Why should it matter to you? I trust you aren't entertaining any notion of letting that devil court you."

Recalling her promise to meet Kent, she hid a throb of guilty longing by pretending to examine an engraved brass vase. "Of course not."

"Good. Because by God, he'd better not lay a hand on my daughter again."

"I doubt he'll return here, Papa. I just wish . . ."

His heavy footsteps came closer. "Wish what, Princess?"

Juliet raised troubled eyes to his face; those robust features, so dear to her heart, now seemed harsh and obstinate. "I wish I could wipe away the past. Why must your feud be mine as well? It's not fair to make your hatred a family tradition."

As the mantel clock chimed four times, Emmett patted her shoulder. "You let me worry about the Deverells, Princess. They're not worth bothering your pretty head over. Now, you'd best get some sleep.

Come the afternoon, we'll doubtless be under siege by gentlemen callers.'' Looking considerably cheered by the prospect, he motioned her to the door.

On leaden feet she mounted the grand staircase. She'd been dismissed, dumped back into the category of vacant-headed debutante. Rebellion flared, fueled by resentment. Why did everyone assume she *wanted* gentlemen callers, that she looked forward to a life empty of all but inane conversation about the latest fashion or a dull tidbit of gossip?

In the confines of her elegant bedroom, she barely noticed as a sleepy maid helped her undress and settle into bed, then extinguished the gas sconces. Alone, Juliet stared up at the darkened canopy and imagined how furious her father would be if she dared disobey him.

She tossed onto her stomach and restlessly rubbed her cheek against the smooth feather pillow. Something ached inside her, a frustrated yearning for adventure, a feeling akin to reaching out for a perfect foxglove only to have the wind snatch it from her grasp. An image burned into her mind and fired her with unbearable longing: Kent Deverell with his devilish eyes.

Should she go meet him or shouldn't she?

Chapter 3

She'd kept her promise.

As Juliet Carleton followed the path through the Embankment gardens, elation and guilt battered Kent in a storm of emotion. With studied nonchalance he stood with one elbow propped on the pedestal of the bronze sphinx. He spared only a glance for her girlish companion; then his eyes fixed on Juliet. Slim and graceful in a high-throated gown of lemon-yellow silk, she shone like a ray of sunshine, brightening the overcast day and piercing the darkness of his heart.

Spying him, she waved and walked faster. Her fresh young face and lush, lithe body awakened an absurd longing in him. Desire, pure and simple, he assured himself. She aroused nothing more than physical passion in him, a passion that would play an integral role in executing his plot. Any capacity in him for affection had died forever nearly three years earlier, on the rocky slope below Castle Radcliffe.

So why did shame sour his soul? He'd half expected Juliet Carleton to change her mind; he'd prayed she would foil his plan. It was as if he wanted her to stop him from committing this cold-blooded act. Yet here she came, her eyes the gold-edged green of a forest and her smile as soft as a dream.

Dreamspinner. The name scourged his mind and fortified his resolve. Today he would make no more mistakes; today he would permit no more slips of temper to spark her suspicions. But God! Who could have blamed him for forgetting himself when she'd uttered that cursed name? Who could condemn him for feeling bitter fury that Emmett Carleton had had the temerity to dub his daughter Dreamspinner?

Forcing an amiable smile, Kent repressed the events that had driven him to this reckless stratagem. Juliet Carleton was his best weapon, his only weapon. Principle had no place in his scheme. Honor would bring no victory in this fight, not when he battled a man as ruthless as Emmett Carleton.

With gentlemanly courtesy, he straightened as the two women stopped before him.

"Good morning, Your Grace," Juliet said, and sank into the obligatory curtsy, one hand balanced on her folded yellow parasol.

The sight of a Carleton paying homage to a Deverell should have pleased him; instead, he felt vaguely irritated. "Please," he said, keeping his voice congenial, "there's no need for such formality between friends."

"I'd like you to meet the Lady Maud Peabody," she said. "Maud, His Grace, the Duke of Radcliffe."

Kent dragged his gaze from her pretty smile and over to her companion. Clad in a gauzy pink gown, Lady Maud reminded him of an elegant iced confection.

"I'm honored." His ladyship dipped a curtsy, but she was squinting at him so avidly, she almost tripped on her voluminous skirts.

He reached out to steady her arm. Her myopic regard told him she'd heard the scandalous rumors and hoped to find out more. He had no intention of having her tag along as chaperone.

"Peabody," he said. "Would your father be Lord Arthur Peabody?"

"Yes, Your Grace. Are you acquainted with him?"

"We're both longtime members of Brooks's Club. Although I've been away from London for some years, I'm sure he'd be more than happy to vouch for my character."

She nodded with a shade too much vigor. "Oh, yes. Yes, I'm sure he would."

"Then perhaps you won't mind leaving Miss Carleton and me—"

"Gracious, will you look at that!" One hand supporting her ostrich-plumed hat, Lady Maud tilted her head back and gazed up the colossal length of the obelisk, the tip shrouded in fog. "Egad, it's tall, isn't it? Do you suppose it really belonged to Cleopatra?"

"The Pharoah Thothmes the Third," Juliet read from the plaque on the granite pedestal.

Lady Maud bent closer, her nose nearly brushing the bronze tablet as she peered at the inscription. "Fashioned in five hundred B.C.," she gushed. "Or is that fifteen hundred? Ah, well, no matter, it's all so terribly ancient. Imagine, Cleopatra's Needle once baked beneath the hot sun of Egypt. Isn't that fascinating, Your Grace?"

Kent repressed a grin at her transparent attempt to distract him. "Quite. However, I'd far prefer to take a stroll with Miss Carleton than suffer a history lesson."

"In a moment," Lady Maud said. "I haven't yet examined either of the sphinxes—"

"Then please feel free to remain here." He offered his arm to Juliet, whose eyes danced with laughter. An answering humor quirked the corners of his mouth. "Shall we, Miss Carleton?"

She tucked her hand in the crook of his arm. "As you wish, Your Grace."

Lady Maud sucked in a dramatically deep breath of pungent river air. "Ah, it's such an invigorating morning. I do believe I shall take my constitutional with you."

"I'd like a *private* chat with Miss Carleton. Might we escort you back to your carriage?"

Even her ladyship couldn't ignore such a blatant directive; she looked as woebegone as a child denied a sweet. "Oh, fiddle. No need to bother yourselves. Digby's waiting right over there." She made a vague gesture toward the roadway beyond the gardens. "But is this quite proper, Your Grace?"

"I give you my solemn vow not to ravish Miss Carleton on the Embankment." He regarded the tip of Juliet's parasol. "Besides, she's undoubtedly quite capable of defending her own virtue."

Maud uttered a sound halfway between a gasp and a giggle. "How boldly you speak! Surely Juliet would prefer me to stay." A hopeful light gleamed in her eyes.

Smiling, Juliet shook her head. "I shan't be long, I promise."

Feet dragging, Maud walked off, casting an occasional disappointed glance over her shoulder.

"She's quite the determined character," Kent said as they started down the broad walkway that hugged the curving north bank of the Thames. "Is she always so difficult to dislodge?"

"Only when she thinks she's missing out on the excitement."

"Do *you* find me exciting, Miss Carleton?"

The quiet question shook Juliet. Despite the barrier of his gray morning coat and her gloves, she could detect the powerful muscles of his arm beneath her fingers, and the sensation made her blood surge with unnerving heat. She could gaze for an eternity into the jet-black mystery of his eyes, listen for eons to the husky cadence of his voice, inhale forever the heady spice of his scent.

"Yes, I do," she admitted.

He stared. "May I presume, then, you're not afraid of me?"

An ironic smile touched her lips. "The only thing I'm afraid of is what my father will do should he learn I've come to meet you."

"He didn't raise a hand to you last night, did he?" Kent stopped and gripped her arms; as if searching for bruises, his gaze raked her face. "How can I make peace with a man who mistreats you?"

The protective menace he radiated both gratified and dismayed Juliet. "He's never mistreated me," she hastened to say. "He's no monster, despite what your father might have told you. Papa forbade me to see you, that's all."

"Yet you're here."

Replete with dark satisfaction, his eyes glittered down at her. His hands rubbed gently over her thin sleeves. She stood paralyzed by the warmth flowing through her, sluggish as honey, pooling deep inside her belly. Even as he let her go, the phantom feel of his touch lingered on her skin.

Somehow with Maud along, this meeting had seemed less like an act of disobedience, less like a clandestine tryst. Juliet suddenly worried that the duke might misread her unladylike eagerness to see him again.

"Papa harbors a great dislike for you," she said. "But I prefer to form my own opinions."

"Where did you tell him you went today?"

"I didn't. . . . I told Mama that Maud and I were going to the glover's shop."

"I've no wish to cause trouble between you and your parents. Yet I can't bear to think I might never see you again." Again he touched her, his fingertips brushing her cheek in a feathery caress. "You're like a hothouse rose, sealed off from me."

His low-pitched words burned into her heart. To cover her confusion, she walked to the border of the path, where a sapling stood, its trunk encircled by a wrought-iron fence in figured arabesques. "Sometimes I feel like this elm," she murmured, reaching up to finger a leaf. "Allowed to thrive, yet confined to a pretty cage."

"Except today," he said, close beside her. "Today no one is fencing you in."

Was it only her wild fancies that imbued his voice with a suggestive undertone? Uncertain, she studied the sun-bronzed angles of his face; he seemed so much older and more experienced. Did Kent Deverell understand the reckless needs churning inside her, the ache for adventure that drew her to him?

"A lady isn't supposed to have independent ideas," she said. "What do you think of a woman pursuing an interest in botany?"

"I think it's no sin to be young and full of ideas. Do you see that statue over there?" He pointed to a sculpture of Prince Albert, standing in romantic elegance on a gray granite pedestal beyond the row of elms. "It was done by Elizabeth Ware, the Countess of Hawkesford. She's managed to succeed in both pursuing her dream and being a lady, all at the same time."

Intrigued, Juliet stepped closer, leaning on her parasol as she examined the fine detailing on the bronze statue. A tiny swan imprint was stamped into the base. "I read about her latest gallery showing, though I don't believe she socializes much. She was raised in America, wasn't she?"

Kent nodded, bending to pluck a blade of grass. "I've a passing acquaintance with Nicholas Ware, enough to know he encourages his wife's desire to pursue art."

"I wish I could convince my parents that a woman can do more with her life than make a brilliant match."

"Perhaps," he said, idly feathering the grass blade along her jaw, "my Lady Botanist should try to find a man as tolerant as Lord Hawkesford."

The caress made her shiver, made her blurt out the thought that had hugged her heart since she'd drifted into a fretful sleep the night before: "*You* could court me."

His fingers tensed; then methodically he began to shred the stalk of grass. "I believe I already am."

A wild flurry of longing drove her breath away. "Then you'll call on me?"

"You're forgetting your father. After last night, I doubt Emmett Carleton will ever invite me to enter his house."

"You mustn't give up so easily. Give me time to work on him, and he'll come around, you'll see."

"Will he?" Sounding cynical, he took her arm and guided her along the footpath curving toward the black iron expanse of the Charing Cross railway bridge. "I've no taste for dodging fist brawls."

Her fingers tightened around the parasol handle "I'll speak to him again, try to make him see the senselessness of the feud—"

"No!" The word sliced through the misty air. Turning her to face him, Kent went on in a husky tone, "You'd only enrage him. He might send you away, and I couldn't bear to lose you. Not now, Juliet, when I've only just found you."

His callused fingertips grazed the soft skin below her ear in a way that left her giddy and breathless. A few passersby glanced curiously, and she tried to summon outrage that he should take such liberties, as if she were a parlor maid accustomed to open caresses. But she could find only exhilaration within herself and a shocking desire to feel his body pressed to hers.

"I don't want to lose you, either," she whispered.

"Then let's not chance telling your father. We mustn't allow the shadow of family rivalry to taint our precious time together."

In her heart she knew he was right; she couldn't be certain how Papa would react if she spoke in support of a Deverell. A thrill pulsated through her veins, the thrill of obeying her own instincts and learning all the secrets of this intriguing man.

"All right," she said. "I'll keep quiet—at least for now."

The vow seemed to satisfy Kent. He shifted the conversation to the plantings of shrubs and flowers in the Embankment gardens, then to speculation on the people they passed.

"That one's definitely a schoolmaster," said Juliet, as a man scurried by, pince-nez glasses perched on his beak nose.

"Then why isn't he in the classroom? I say he's a detective from Scotland Yard." Kent cocked a dark eyebrow. "In disguise."

She laughed. "It's just as likely he's a musician going to rehearsal at the Savoy Theatre. His shoulders are stooped from bending over the piano."

"He's heading in the wrong direction, then. The Savoy's behind us." His expression sobered. "Excuse me a moment."

Letting go of her arm, Kent veered toward a street sweeper. The white-bearded man wore a turban and tattered robe as he wielded a broom, slowly and steadily cleaning the pathway beside the granite wall overlooking the river. Kent said something in a foreign tongue and pressed a coin into the sweeper's palm. The man's wizened brown face lit up. Chattering gratefully, he bowed.

The duke's humane gesture struck Juliet with a mixture of admiration and chagrin. She'd walked right past the laborer without even noticing him.

The moment Kent returned, she said, "That was kind of you. What did you say to him?"

"Just a greeting in his native tongue."

"What language is that?"

"Hindustani."

"Where did you learn to speak it? In India?"

"Yes. I visited there as a boy."

Juliet recalled what her father had said about the ruin of the Deverell business interests. "Have you ever been back?"

"No, never."

As Kent gazed toward the fog-veiled spires of Westminster, his face looked somber, his features drawn tight into an expression that verged on sadness. She had the impression his thoughts had drifted to somewhere far beyond this chilly gray morning, and she ached to share his musings and ease his troubles.

"Do you spend most of your time at Castle Radcliffe?"

As if he'd forgotten her presence, he stared at her. "Yes. I farm my lands there."

"Do you live alone?"

"My cousin and his wife make their home with me." In a distracted voice, he added, "The Embankment will be growing crowded soon, Miss Carleton. We mustn't risk word getting back to your father, so I'll return you to your carriage now."

His sudden formality left Juliet hurt and disappointed. She sensed that any effort to probe into his confidential affairs would prove futile. If he wanted to court her, why did he shut her out the moment she asked questions about his life? Perhaps she was too impatient. Perhaps he only worried that this was too public a place for private conversations.

He held her arm as they walked through the gardens and toward the roadway. Was the brush of his leg against her skirt by accident or design? Her heart trembled, fragile as a new-blooming violet. Kent Deverell was a riddle; she wanted to probe the depths of a man who had loved and lost, a proud man who had suffered such tragic misfortune. . . .

"I presume that's your carriage?"

His note of dry humor made Juliet look down the street to see Maud, her head topped by the lavishly feathered bonnet, peeking out the brougham window in unashamed interest. Self-consciously Maud whipped off her gold-rimmed spectacles, then screwed up her features and strained to see.

Juliet bit back a smile. "She'll beg me to recount every word you and I exchanged. Not, of course, that I intend to indulge her."

"She won't tell your father, will she?"

"Not if I ask her to keep silent. Maud adores a good secret."

"Then perhaps we should give her something more substantial to withhold."

Before she could guess his meaning, Kent caught her hand and pulled her in front of him. He bent closer and brushed his lips over hers. Headier than sandal-wood, his scent enveloped her; softer than an orchid petal, his mouth caressed hers. When he straightened, she felt shaken, her blood brimming with that exciting turmoil of danger and desire. No gentleman would kiss a lady on a public street, yet she wanted him to do so again, to take her into his arms and hold her close, to nurture the tender bond growing between them.

He stood motionless, watching her, and for an un-guarded moment she read the same fierce yearning in him, a yearning that enchanted her. "Have you ever been to Highgate Wood?" he asked.

Unable to trust her voice, she shook her head.

"Tomorrow, can you get away most of the day?"

This time she managed to whisper, "Yes."

His fingers squeezed hers. Through clenched teeth, he said roughly, "My God, Juliet. You shouldn't be so bloody agreeable."

The torment in his voice bewildered her. "I don't understand, Kent. Don't you *want* me to meet you?"

"You hardly know me. You shouldn't trust a man so readily."

Gentle feeling washed away her confusion; his pro-test stemmed from concern for her reputation. Brushing her thumb over the broad back of his hand, she murmured, "I know that a man who shows kindness to a street sweeper couldn't possibly harm me."

His jaw tightened and she thought he meant to deny his considerate nature. But he merely drew a deep breath. "Tomorrow, then," he said in a subdued tone. "Meet me here at ten o'clock."

Pivoting, the duke strode away, past the carriage where Maud gawked openmouthed. Juliet watched him, her spirits soaring dizzily, until his broad-shouldered form disappeared into the throng of laborers and tradesmen.

"You've made plans to go *where?*" Her fine brow drawn into a frown, Dorothea Carleton laid down her pen on the gilt-edged writing desk and gazed up at her daughter.

That displeased look made Juliet quake with guilt. What if her mother saw through the lie? Glancing out the window of the morning room at the dull gray sky, she thought longingly of Kent and gathered her courage.

"I promised Maud I'd go with her to Wimbledon tomorrow," she repeated, forcing her eyes back to her mother. "Her grandmother is having another of her spells, and you know how demanding the dowager Lady Higgleston can be. Maud is afraid to go alone."

"Lady Maud Peabody has never been afraid of anything."

At the suspicious tone, Juliet swallowed. "What I meant was, Maud is hoping to use my presence as an excuse to return on the late train. If she goes alone, her grandmother will coerce her into staying for weeks, and then she'd miss half the Season."

Dorothea pursed her lips. "Your father will be none too pleased about this. Lord Breeton left his card while you were gone. I was about to compose an invitation to tea tomorrow."

"Couldn't we invite his lordship the day after? After all, you wouldn't want him to think we're overeager."

Mrs. Carleton tilted her head in resignation. "You

have a point, darling. All right, then, you may go. But next time," she added, shaking a slim finger, "do consult me before making your plans. Mr. Carleton has charged me with the task of seeing you married well."

"Yes, Mama. Thank you so much."

Awash with giddy relief, she bent and kissed her mother's cheek. Only at Dorothea's startled expression did Juliet recall she wasn't supposed to act excited at the prospect of spending the day in the company of a querulous old lady. Lowering her lashes, she veiled her glorious anticipation of freedom and hugged her excitement inside her heart.

The outing with Kent stirred her romantic dreams and fired her botanist's blood. Highgate Wood skirted the northern edge of the city, and sheltered a vast variety of wildflowers: honeysuckle, wood violet, yellow archangel, sorrel. Few people frequented the park on this quiet Friday; a man walked a terrier, two boys stalked a fox, an elderly couple shared a pair of opera glasses to study the birds. Even though she could glimpse the red brick houses of the village, Juliet felt as if her spirit had been set free from the restrictions of an uneventful life. The warm summer day held the thrill of a treasure hunt, a search for rare species of plants, many of which she recognized only from her textbooks.

Kent acted the consummate gentleman and the benevolent host. When she dirtied her hands, he smiled indulgently and offered her his linen handkerchief. He'd brought a picnic luncheon, which they shared beneath the spreading branches of an ancient oak. As they ate a simple meal of cheese and bread, the air sang with the mellow cooing of wood pigeons and the staccato notes of a nuthatch. Afterward, he stayed close by her side, calling her attention first to a patch of stitchwort, then to a clump of wild garlic.

Too content to worry about her sapphire silk skirt, she knelt to examine a jagged-toothed leaf. "*Leucanthemum vulgare*."

He chuckled. "A fancy name for the common oxeye daisy."

She smiled back. "But still an uncommonly pretty flower."

His relaxed mood made him all the more endearing. He crouched beside her, so close she detected the heat radiating from his body. Today no tension marred the handsome angles of his face. Even his eyes shone lighter, a mellow walnut-brown beneath the slash of charcoal brows. The musky odor of humus blended with his faintly earthy scent. How happy he made her, Juliet thought in sudden melting warmth.

Impulsively she said, "Do you remember the first plant you grew from seed? Watching those tiny leaves push out of the soil and unfurl must be like seeing your child for the first time."

A shadow passed over his face. Only belatedly did she recall that his unborn baby had died, that Kent had been denied that unique joy. With a blush of dismay, she stammered, "I'm sorry, I didn't mean to remind you . . ."

His strong hand closed around hers. "Don't apologize for opening yourself to me, Juliet. You're right . . . there *is* a certain magic to life. A magic I've let myself forget."

"Because you're afraid of being hurt again," she ventured.

His eyes devoured her, and she feared she'd touched a nerve. He looked down, studying the clasp of their hands, her skin a delicate ivory against his tanned fingers. "Yes," he admitted quietly. "I suppose I am."

"What was she like . . . your wife?"

"Why don't you tell me first what you've heard about Emily?"

"I know only that she fell from the parapet of the castle."

"Who told you so?"

His grip tightened and she wondered at the interest burning in his eyes. "Lord Breeton, when he saw you at the ball."

"Breeton," Kent said in disgust, releasing her hand. "When that popinjay's not talking about hounds, he's spreading more gossip than a flap-jawed servant."

Determined not to be distracted, Juliet moistened her dry lips. "Your wife . . . was she at all like me?"

He cast her an oblique look before glancing down to toy with a daisy. "Actually not. Emily lacked your frankness, your zest for life. She was shy and frail, the kindest person I've ever known."

He made her sound like a paragon of womanly virtue, the sort of woman Juliet could never tolerate being. Then why did she feel so suddenly wretched? "You must have loved her very much."

"Why do you say that?"

"You married her, despite the circumstances of her birth."

"Are you referring to Emily's bastardy?"

His tone of chilly detachment sparked heat in her cheeks. She fought to hold her gaze steady. "Yes. I . . . I wondered if people ever shunned her."

"I never brought her into London society. She preferred a quiet country life." He stood, a towering figure limned by the filtered rays of sunlight. "It's getting late. Shall we go?"

The finality of the gesture closed the discussion. Somehow, without her noticing, the afternoon shadows had lengthened. Regretfully she accepted his hand as he helped her into the cabriolet. He sat down beside her, and the gray gelding started toward the city. Kent stared straight ahead, brooding and silent. Despite the pleasant breeze and the mesmeric sway of the carriage, Juliet felt troubled, longing for a return of their easy companionship.

"Why did you come to London?" At his sharp glance, she added hastily, "I don't mean to pry. It's just that I've never asked you before. . . . I presume you've business here.'

He returned his gaze to the road. "I needed to see a banker."

"Did it have to do with the threshing machine you're developing?"

He cast her another biting look. "Where did you hear about that?"

She bit her lip. "Somewhere. I don't recall."

"From Emmett, no doubt."

His frosty tone made her happiness wilt like the nosegay of wildflowers in her lap. Resentment suddenly stiffened her spine. "I wonder why you bother with me, then," she snapped. "I'm a Carleton, too."

His hand descended over hers on the leather cushion. "Forgive me, Juliet. I had a lot of unhappy memories weighing on my mind. Can you spare me a little patience, please?"

The contrition in his voice drew her gaze to his face, where concern gentled those sternly handsome angles. Her frustration eased, yet she couldn't let go of her anger, not just yet.

"I only want to make sure you've really set aside the feud."

"I have. It just takes some getting used to, that's all."

Could she trust his word? She stole another glance and found him watching her. She could drown in the dark sea of his eyes. When he looked at her like that, she wanted to surrender herself into his keeping, to let him do with her whatever he willed.

"All right," she whispered, turning her hand so that her palm nestled within his. "I just wish . . . ."

"Wish what?"

How could she express the newborn needs and hopes and dreams trembling inside her heart? "I wish that everything could stay as perfect as it was earlier."

"I know."

A shared sensitivity shone on his face, and for one breathless moment she thought he meant to kiss her. Then he swung his pensive gaze back to the smartly trotting horse.

"Unfortunately," he said in a voice so low she had to strain to hear, "life is rarely perfect."

"Perfect . . . absolutely perfect," Dorothea Carleton proclaimed. "Turn around now and let me see the back."

Juliet dutifully twirled before the cheval mirror in her

bedroom. The jade-hued gown sported a sash of black watered silk that cinched her tiny waist, and the low, square bodice of shirred gauze dramatized the fullness of her breasts. A modest cluster of green ribbons adorned one side of her chignon, and russet curls fringed her face. If only she were dressing to meet Kent . . .

Rebellion stirred in her. "I wonder if Lord Breeton will judge me to be as superior as the horseflesh in his stable."

"Oh, darling," Dorothea chided, "don't be contrary. Someday you'll realize the value of this extraordinary opportunity. Come now, we must hurry if we're to be downstairs when he and his mother arrive."

Some thirty minutes later, Juliet selected a slice of saffron cake from a silver tray offered by a footman. Absently she listened to her father and Lord Breeton debate the merits of various horses entered in the upcoming Ascot races. Across from her, seated in matching chairs of emerald damask, Mrs. Carleton and Lady Breeton sipped tea and compared milliners.

Her enormous bosom swathed in gray silk, the marchioness leaned forward, looking like a well-fed pouter pigeon. "You must take care," she cooed, "to check your account very closely. Why, just last week, I was charged for an ostrich plume when the bonnet I'd ordered only had a cock's feather."

She shook her head disapprovingly and her fleshy neck jiggled. Juliet gulped back a grin. Curious, how Lady Breeton possessed such an abundance of chins, while her son had been deprived of even one.

As Dorothea uttered a polite reply, Juliet's mind strayed to the previous day's outing with Kent. *Life is rarely perfect.* Over and over she'd mulled his somber words, and each time they left her with an aching sympathy, with the need to soothe his suffering and rekindle the light of joy inside him. He'd seemed so at ease tramping through the woods, and younger somehow, as if the cares of a lonely life had lifted from his shoulders.

Until they'd spoken of Emily.

Perhaps the right woman could make him forget the morbid past and seek a happy future. Her heart

warmed at the memory of the smiles they'd shared over
each remarkable wildflower. If she closed her eyes, she
could recall the rousing earthy essence of his scent. . . .

"I say, Miss Carleton, you look positively blissful.
Did you enjoy Wimbledon?"

Jerking her gaze toward Lord Breeton's pallid face,
Juliet drew a blank. "Wimbledon?"

"That *is* where you went yesterday, isn't it?"

Everyone stared at her. Cheeks burning, she recalled
the lie. "I . . . yes, of course. Lady Maud Peabody and
I went there to visit her grandmother."

"How is the dowager Lady Higgleston faring?" demanded the marchioness.

"Quite well, though her arthritis has been acting
up." Juliet took a sip of tea to ease her dry throat.
"Might I say, my lady, that's a stunning brooch you're
wearing. It's a lovely match for the blue of your eyes."

Preening, Lady Breeton patted the dainty sapphire
pin, half swallowed by her huge breasts. "Why, how
kind of you to say so. It was a gift from my dear departed Quentin." The chair groaned under her weight
as she swiveled toward the men. "Such a well-
mannered girl you have, Emmett."

"Yes, she is, isn't she?"

At her father's proud expression, Juliet felt herself
sinking deeper into a swamp of guilt. Her ploy might
have diverted the discussion, but it had also won her
praise when she didn't wish to encourage Breeton's
suit. Looking from beneath her lashes, she studied his
lordship and tried to imagine being his wife. Those
spindly arms would hold her close, those muttonchop
whiskers would brush her cheek as he kissed her—

A shudder seized her insides. No, she could not endure that, not even to please her parents. Emmett
Carleton recounted an amusing tale about a mixup in
negotiating the purchase of their house from the lord
chancellor. He looked so bent on impressing the Bree-
tons with his wealth that Juliet felt the stir of nausea.

What would he do if he knew the only man who
fascinated her was the Duke of Radcliffe?

Chapter 4

S he fascinated him.

Kent Deverell sat at the desk in his study and stared at the silver fountain pen he rotated in his hands. Before him lay a half-finished sketch for the mechanical thresher, but improving upon the invention failed to hold his attention. These past two weeks he'd lost the ability to concentrate.

Except on Juliet.

Dropping the pen, he picked up a wilted stalk of tansy, the yellow flowers gone brown and brittle. He smiled, remembering how she'd playfully tucked the stem into his buttonhole on an outing to Hampstead Heath. He'd always considered tansy a weed, but she made him see beauty in the most mundane of plants.

The moment he'd planned for so long now approached with inexorable speed. At this very instant, unaware of his intent to seduce her, Juliet Carleton was on her way here. His loins burned with the anticipation of possessing her body.

Instead of seeing her wed to a man of noble title, Emmett Carleton would endure whispers and gossip. He'd be hard-pressed to find an aristocrat desperate enough to marry a fallen woman, even the heiress to a fortune.

And how would Juliet survive being shunned?

For the hundredth time, he conjured up her sparkling eyes and artless smile, the fine-boned face that reflected her vibrant interest in life. She made him feel young again . . . sent him back to a time when he'd still believed that dreams could come true.

Dreamspinner.

Abruptly he crushed the stalk of tansy; its strong aroma wafted through the air. Sentiment had no place in his plan. He should be grateful for her naïveté; it made her so damned easy to manipulate. Yet his throat constricted with an absurd tenderness, a tenderness he hadn't felt toward any woman since Emily.

Emily. The bitter blow of memory struck the softness from him. His mind burned with the image of her gentle face. She'd been too fragile to fight the wickedness of a world that wouldn't accept the circumstances of her birth, too kind to comprehend the evil of men who would treat her as something less than perfect.

He had no such compunction. Like a blast of winter wind, resolve froze his soul. Lowering his hands to the desk, he gripped the edge so hard, his blunt-tipped nails scored the green leather surface.

His grip slowly eased. Methodically he brushed the tansy remains into the rubbish bin. No matter what the cost, he must vindicate his wife's death.

Emmett Carleton must pay for driving her to suicide.

"Are you certain this is wise?" Maud asked.

Clutching the door strap as the brougham rounded a corner, Juliet smiled at her friend. "After all your madcap escapades, I never thought I'd see the day when *you'd* be lecturing *me.*"

"But to go to the duke's town house, unchaperoned . . ."

Juliet knew the risk. To meet a man in a public place bent the rules of convention; to visit him alone broke every dictate drummed into her by her mother. She could be ruined; Papa had warned her that Kent meant to do just that. . . .

"I trust him," she said firmly. "Someday, when you meet the right man, you'll understand how I feel."

An unholy glint entered Maud's eyes. "Do you suppose he'll try to do *that* to you?"

"That?"

"You know. Lure you into his bedroom so he can do all sorts of unspeakable things to your person."

Heat washed through Juliet. At boarding school, she

and Maud had spent hours speculating about the secret act between men and women. "Don't be absurd. Kent has acted the perfect gentleman."

Then why had he asked her to his home? He'd mentioned a surprise, but what could it be? She hugged the breathless hope that his feelings for her had deepened, that today he meant to declare himself.

Over the past fortnight, they'd shared glorious stolen hours: an afternoon wandering the stalls at a horticultural exhibit, a morning studying the flora of Hampstead Heath, even an entire day roaming the greenhouses in the Royal Botanic Gardens at Kew. Her mother had arched an eyebrow at the sudden obsession with shopping that Juliet and Maud had developed, but thankfully Dorothea was preoccupied with planning a schedule of dinner parties and soirees designed to lure Lord Breeton into the family fold.

Through the broad front window of the carriage, Juliet saw the opulent shops of Regent Street. Hands trembling with excitement, she pulled out the vanity drawer hidden in the maroon satin panel before her, then checked her appearance in the small mirror and adjusted the pearl-tipped pin securing her straw hat. Was the bodice of the apricot gown cut too low for afternoon wear?

She bit her lip. "Oh, dear. Perhaps I ought to have worn the lavender silk after all."

Maud drew out her gold-rimmed spectacles and peered closely. "Egad. You'd have looked as if you were in half mourning."

"Then maybe the new Du Barry rose gown?"

"Stop fretting. His Grace, the most noble Duke of Radcliffe, will be utterly entranced by your immortal beauty."

They looked at each other and giggled, and the moment of anxiety lifted. Exhilaration kindled inside Juliet, an exhilaration that stoked the blaze of longing in her heart. Ever since she'd met Kent, the world glowed vibrant and rich . . . a richness of the senses. Colors seemed more vivid, tastes sharper, scents keener. The clatter of carriage wheels sang like a symphony; even this cool gray day felt brisk and brilliant.

"There's the dressmaker's," Maud said, squinting at the traffic.

She tugged on the velvet bell pull to signal the coachman, and the brougham rumbled to a stop. A liveried footman helped the two women down in front of a confectioner's shop. The scent of fresh-baked pastries wafted through the air. A bright-hued array of shoppers strolled the sidewalks and peered into the store windows.

Maud seized Juliet's gloved hands. "I wish *I* were off to such an adventure with a man."

Affection flooded Juliet. "Your time will come. Then I'll have a chance to help *you.*"

Turning, she walked swiftly down the street. The throng of elegant shoppers thinned as she neared Picadilly, yet she kept her face lowered on the chance that an acquaintance might spot her.

Suddenly, from the corner of her eye, she spied the approach of a familiar plump pigeon form. Lady Breeton! The woman minced down the street, her maid a step behind. Juliet ducked into a milliner's shop and affected an interest in a display of fans. Curbing her nervousness, she let the proprietress show her one of violet silk gauze.

She forced herself to tarry for ten minutes. When she stepped cautiously from the shop, Lady Breeton was nowhere to be seen. The close call alarmed Juliet. Discreetly lifting a hand, she hailed a passing hansom, and gave the address to the rear-seated driver. Her stomach still aflutter, she settled herself in the small interior of the cab.

The breeze flowing through the open front cooled her heated cheeks; her heart thudded in rhythm with the swift clop-clopping of the horse's hooves and the jangle of harness. At last . . . at last the interminable hours of waiting were nearly over.

Like a light-starved plant reaching for sunshine, her need for Kent grew with each meeting. She loved the low melody of his voice, the absorption on his face as he drove his carriage, the brush of his callused fingers as he handed her a flower. Not since that day at the

Embankment had he kissed her. She ached to relive the tender touch of his lips. . . .

The hansom jolted to a halt before the stately town homes of Grosvenor Square. She handed the fare through the trapdoor in the roof, then mindful of her skirts, she stepped down.

As the cab rattled away, Juliet stood still, caught by the sudden snare of conscience. How horrified her mother would be if she knew her daughter was about to visit a man unchaperoned! And how furious her father would be if he knew that man was Kent Deverell.

To calm her galloping heart, she took as deep a breath as her tight-laced corset would allow. She was an adult now, capable of directing her own life. Capable of judging the merits of a man.

Taking a swift glance around, she hastened up the steps and rapped with the brass knocker. A minute dragged past.

Then the knob rattled and the door opened. A man stood there, but he resembled no butler or footman she'd ever seen. A flat gray turban topped his head, and a pale muslin robe swathed his lean body. For one astounded instant, Juliet blinked, sure he was the ancient street sweeper. But this man looked younger, his skin dusky, his shoulders straighter.

Recovering herself, she held out her calling card. "I've an appointment to see the duke."

The servant studied the small, engraved square. A corner of his thin lip lifted slightly; then he bowed and waved her inside.

"His Grace is in the study," he said, a musically foreign note to his voice. "If you would care to wait, I'll inform him of your arrival, Miss *Carleton*."

The faint inflection on her name radiated disapproval. He pointed a dark finger to a doorway, then glided silently away, leaving her standing in the entrance hall.

Taken aback by his rudeness, Juliet walked through the doorway and discovered a small drawing room. The furnishings were warm and charming, yet the peacock-blue sofa was faded, the dhurri carpet frayed at the edges. A tiger-skin rug lay before the hearth. As in her father's library, brass and ivory artifacts scattered the room. Odd, that despite the differences between the two families, both their homes held that one distinct similarity.

The muted noises of traffic emphasized the eerie silence within the house. The sensation of solitude puzzled her a moment; then she realized why. She was accustomed to servants bustling about, unobtrusive yet ever present. Kent's town home seemed empty and forlorn, like a neglected winter garden.

Parting the yellowed lace at a window, she peered outside. Carriages and drays rattled along the street; a nursemaid wheeled a pram; a pair of elderly ladies strolled past. So ordinary a scene. Yet she felt as if she were trembling on the brink of a great adventure.

The heavy fall of footsteps emanated from the hall. She swung to the doorway as Kent walked into the room. His handsome face wore a welcoming smile that made her heart leap with gladness. Today he'd left off his formal coat; in a plain white shirt and dark trousers he looked alert and vital.

"Juliet," he said, taking both her hands. "You're like sunshine in this musty old place."

Bending, he planted a kiss on her cheek, and even that chaste gesture nearly made her knees wilt. She loved the feel of his fingers around hers, his large, solid hands holding her tenderly.

"I'm delighted to be here." Laughing, she shook her head. "I'm sorry, that sounds like a platitude . . . and it seems so inadequate to express how I feel right now."

His dark lashes lowered a bit, making his eyes appear blacker. "And how *do* you feel?"

"Happy," she whispered. "Happy to be with you, no matter where we are."

For a moment his face remained soft; then a muscle in his jaw tightened and he released her hands. "Come along," he said, pivoting. "I promised you a surprise, and I won't have you accusing me of reneging."

As they headed down the shadowed hall, Juliet sensed that she'd stirred deep feelings in Kent. Excitement shivered through her. Surely he'd reveal those feelings today.

"Did you have any difficulty getting here?" he asked

"No . . . and no one saw me."

"I wish you'd have let me come for you."

"It's better this way," she said firmly. "We agreed not to risk someone seeing me getting into your carriage."

He nodded, then led her through a doorway. Juliet found herself in a study lined with glass-fronted bookcases. A camelback sofa sat on a Turkish carpet, both in jeweled shades of burgundy. Like the drawing room, the air held a trace of staleness, though a pair of long windows stood open, the floral drapes undulating in the summer breeze.

Intending to put down her gloves, she walked to a mahogany desk, where a pungent odor made her sniff. She tilted her head at Kent. "Tansy?"

He glanced away. "The flower you gave me last week got accidentally crushed. I had to throw it away."

"Then I'll be sure to give you another," she teased. On the desk, a silver pen lay carelessly across a drawing. "Is this your work?"

"Yes."

"May I look?"

He smiled. "If you like."

Picking up the paper, she studied a cutaway view of a curious boxy machine. Neatly labeled were several conveyor belts, fans, and wheels. "What is it?"

"The mechanical thresher. It runs on petrol."

"Petrol?"

"A fuel used by the horseless carriage."

"I've never seen one of those, but I heard my father speak of them." Fascinated, Juliet stared at the drawing. "Does it really work?"

He laughed at her questioning look. "I hope it will someday. Right now it's only an experiment."

Admiring the precise beauty of the sketch, she felt a flash of resentment that her father could disparage Kent for having the vision to dream, to create. "Have you invented anything else?"

"A few odd things here and there. But enough about me. This is what I wanted to show you."

He walked to the fireplace, where a pair of brass peacock andirons guarded the empty hearth. Atop the marble mantelpiece stood a row of unframed watercolors. The brilliant hues of exotic flowers lured her as forsythia beckons a honeybee.

"Oh, Kent, look!"

Indulgent pleasure lit his eyes. "Do you like them?"

"They're lovely," she said, picking up a picture of a phalaenopsis orchid, the golden flowers marked with chestnut brown. "Where did you get them?"

"The other day I came across my father's drawing case, tucked in a cupboard. He sketched as a hobby."

"So that's where you inherited your artistic talent."

A corner of his mouth quirked. "Alas, mine extends solely to dull technical drawing."

She surveyed the other designs. "Plumbago, bougainvillea, hibiscus . . . These plants are all native to India, aren't they?"

Kent nodded. "I'm afraid they're the only flora I could find among the sketches. For the most part, my father drew people and places, odd things he saw on his travels."

"May I see the other pictures?"

Surprise gleamed in his eyes. "Are you really interested?"

"Yes."

He motioned her to the sofa, where a flat leather satchel lay against a rosewood table. Sitting beside her, so close their knees nearly touched, he began to flip through the stack of vellum sheets. The majority of the scenes were of India, where, Kent explained, the Deverell family had long had an interest. Captivated, Juliet studied the contrast of images: a trio of filthy children in a poverty-stricken village, a proud native perched atop an ornately saddled elephant, a beautiful blond Englishwoman reclining on a bullock-hide boat as it drifted down the Ganges.

"Is she your mother?" Juliet asked.

Kent slanted a look at her. "No. Her name is Chantal Hutton. She is, or rather was, a friend of my father's."

She wondered at his strange expression; then he

pulled out the next sketch and her heart went liquid. The smooth pen strokes depicted a boy, his chin tucked shyly, sitting astride a pony. The youthful angles of his face held a promise of strength.

"Ah, now, that's you."

"You're right. I was eight years old there."

"And the servant beside you," she said, noting the turbaned Indian standing at stiff attention, "he looks like the man who answered the door today."

"Yes. Back then, Ravi acted as my father's *chaprassi*, or messenger. He was my father's most trusted servant."

"He didn't seem to care much for a Carleton visiting you."

"Don't pay him any mind." Kent kept his gaze fixed on the sketch he held. "Odd, how that day brings back memories. The sun was beating down, and I can still smell the suffocating heat that weighted the air. I felt ready to faint, but when my father said sit still, I sat."

"He was strict?"

"Yes, but it was more than that. My mother had died the previous year, and I wanted to please him, to make him smile, to lift him out of his melancholy."

The sympathetic portrayal of William Deverell intrigued Juliet. Was Papa biased? "Tell me about him, please."

A shadow passed over Kent's face. "What do you want to know?"

His sudden cool manner irritated her, but she kept on, determined to learn more about the man her father hated. "What sort of person was he? I had the impression he was a relentless businessman, yet these sketches are the work of a sensitive man."

"In part, he was a dreamer." He tucked the drawing back into the case, then propped his elbows on his knees and looked down at his clasped hands. "Yet he also held an unshakable conviction about class differences. He believed that a man born to the dukedom, a man with the noble blood of the Deverells, was superior to other men and destined to rule."

"You must not feel superior if you're a farmer."

He smiled. "Father never understood why I'd want to work in a field, like a common laborer."

"What did he want you to do with your life?"

"He thought I ought to follow in the footsteps of generations of Deverells." He shot her an enigmatic stare. "To uphold the family honor and join him in the fight against your father."

On impulse, she shaped her hand around his clenched fingers, her arm resting along his. "I'm glad you didn't, Kent. I'm glad you saw the sense in forgetting the feud."

A spark flickered in his dark eyes; then he looked down at their joined hands. Did he share her awe at seeing her lily-pale skin against his sun-browned flesh, at feeling her softness against his strength?

"Some called my father an arrogant fool," he said, his gaze still lowered, "but I admired him for living what he believed. He tried to fulfill his ideals, to excel at everything he did, no matter what the consequences."

Then why had William Deverell stolen opium? A selfish desire to maintain the treasured closeness of this moment kept Juliet from voicing the question.

"He certainly excelled in art. What are you going to do with all these drawings?"

"Take them to Castle Radcliffe when I leave tomorrow."

Shock and dismay ripped through her contentment. Pulling her hand back, she studied his aloof expression. "You're leaving?"

"I must. I've neglected my duties at home for far too long already." His narrowed gaze flitted to her lips. "Besides, my business here is nearly concluded."

His dispassion chilled her, yet she detected a flame of feeling beneath that frosty exterior, a flame that melted the bleak storm of pain in her heart. Did he, too, feel shattered at the prospect of parting? Was he afraid to nurture the tender bud of affection growing between them, afraid to open himself to the risk of loving another woman?

Placing her hands on his forearm, she studied the

harshly handsome angles of his face, a face she suddenly saw as dearer to her than any other. "Don't go, Kent," she whispered. "I can't bear to part from you."

A muscle in his jaw clenched and she sensed violence raging inside him. From outside drifted the hollow cheep of a sparrow and the distant rattle of carriage wheels. She held her breath and prayed that whatever unknown powers in him fought to resist her, his feelings for her would prove strong enough to triumph.

Torment tightened his features. "For God's sake, Juliet! Why must you make this so damned easy . . . and yet so damned hard?"

Before she could puzzle through his brusque words, he spun toward her, the lean strength of his body pressing her to the sofa. Where his first fleeting kiss had been gentle, this one plunged her into rough splendor. The shock of his tongue against her lips ignited a scandalous fire inside her, a blaze of passion that compelled her to open her mouth. His tongue delved inside, then retreated in a wildly exciting rhythm.

Her palms embraced the hard heat of his chest as she slid them upward over his shirt, her unsteady fingers discovering first the taut cords of his neck, then the coarse silk of his hair. His mouth carried the heady taste of man, tinged with an arousing trace of musk. Her heart thumped madly, the blood beating in her ears. She felt submerged in a sea of sensation, drowning in a floodtide of feelings.

"So proper," he murmured, his breath warm on her lips, "and so very tempting." Removing her hat, he tossed it aside, then plucked out the tortoiseshell pins that secured her upswept hair. The heavy mass cascaded down her back, and the admiration darkening his eyes made her toes curl with pleasure.

"You're beautiful, Juliet . . . so temptingly beautiful."

As he feathered kisses along her temple and cheek, one of his hands cradled the nape of her neck; the other trekked downward, following the shape of her shoulder. Whether by accident or design, the base of his palm brushed the curve of her breast, and despite the barrier of her corset, the contact stunned her. Heat clenched her belly, and a startling liquid tightness throbbed between her legs. She didn't understand how or why he aroused such a tumult inside her, but she longed for more.

Kissing his smooth-shaven cheek, she felt the words rise from deep within herself: "I love you, Kent. I love you so much."

His hand froze on her arm. For an instant his heart beat a frantic tattoo against her breast. Then he jerked away.

She opened her eyes to see him sitting back against the sofa, his chest rising and falling. His gaze glittered with black fury.

"You don't know what you're saying," he snapped.

His abrupt mood shift bewildered her. "Yes, I do. I know my own mind, my own feelings—"

"Do you? You've known me for barely a fortnight, and already you claim to love me?" He laughed, a harsh sound that held no humor. "You can't begin to comprehend what I'm really like, Juliet. You're caught up in girlish dreams."

Passion ebbed, leaving her drenched in cold reality. *Was* she responding with indecent haste? Imagining a need in him because she herself was lonely? She swallowed the lump in her throat. "I may not know everything about you, Kent, but I do love you."

"Enough to risk your own reputation? Enough to go upstairs with me right now, to my bedroom?"

Staring at his icy countenance, Juliet bit her lip. She recalled her vague perceptions of the private act of love, something permitted to married couples, but forbidden to her.

Something no gentleman would ask of a lady he respected.

Yet the bone-deep bitterness she sensed in him and the need within herself reached past her pain and her scruples. If she truly did love him, she must trust him as well.

"Yes."

Chapter 5

The single, soft word hit him like a blow to his midsection.

Kent couldn't move, couldn't breathe. He could only stare at Juliet. Her eyes warm and certain, her lips reddened and vulnerable, she met his gaze with unflinching pride. Her hair formed a glorious cinnamon waterfall around her shoulders. She looked like a goddess sculpted in alabaster, the image of heartbreaking beauty and untrammeled innocence.

Desire surged in him, a desire so acute, his limbs trembled. He had seen that expression in only one other woman's eyes, that utter adoration, that shining devotion, that absolute trust.

Emily. Oh, God, Emily.

His throat closed, suffocating him.

He shot to his feet. Striding to a window, he braced one palm against the frame and sucked in a searing breath. *I love you.* He'd never thought to hear those words again from any woman. Never.

Especially not from Juliet Carleton.

Tilting back his head, he struggled to regain an emotional equilibrium. The breeze fluttered the curtains and fanned his overheated body. God! What the hell was wrong with him? He should be gloating over her compliance. Like a ripe plum, she had fallen straight into his hands. So why couldn't he follow through with the perfect finale to his plan?

Because she would bear the punishment for her father's crimes and the pain of Kent's revenge.

Shame weighted his soul. What had grief done to him? He'd been so caught up in hatred that he'd failed to consider her future. He wanted Emmett to suffer, not Juliet. With the bitter taste of defeat in his mouth, Kent acknowledged the truth. He couldn't dishonor her and turn her into a social pariah, not even to avenge himself on Emmett Carleton.

"Kent?"

At the uncertain quaver of her voice, he swung his head around. Juliet stood behind him, the curling strands of her hair drawing his eyes to her bosom, where the apricot silk bodice clung to her breasts. Her fingers were laced in front of her, graceful fingers that had glided over his chest and threaded into his hair. The memory of her passionate response made his groin ache anew.

"Perhaps I shouldn't have spoken so boldly a moment ago." She hesitated. "Please understand, I'm not retracting my words. I just don't want a quarrel to spoil our last day together."

The tilt of her chin displayed courage, a courage he couldn't help but admire. *Emily would never have had the fortitude to face you so squarely. Or to acknowledge her passion so openly.*

The comparison pricked him into stiff formality. "For pity's sake, if anyone's erred here, it was me. I spoke out of turn. I treated you like less than the lady you are."

"Is that really why you walked away, Kent? Because you made a mistake?" Her hands clenched convulsively. "Or because you can't accept my feelings?"

He focused his gaze on a crimson cabbage rose embellishing the drapery. "You're too young to know your own mind."

"And that's too pat an answer." She stepped in front of him, forcing him to look at her. "You've not considered me too young these past weeks. You enjoyed my company. Why else would you have courted me?"

How the bloody hell could he answer *that?* "Juliet, I never wanted to hurt you—"

"Unless this all has to do with my father."

She looked stunned at the thought. His chest tightened. He couldn't bear for her to guess his diabolical plan; he couldn't bear for her to hate him. "He has nothing to do with us."

"I wonder." Angry suspicion shadowed her eyes. "You've befriended me, yet you've not made any attempt to settle your differences with Papa."

"You saw what happened the one time I did. He's never going to change."

"Because you'll never give him the chance. Perhaps Papa was right. Perhaps you only want to ruin my reputation."

His mouth went dry; he could only stare at her.

She gave him a measuring look, a look that made him feel hollow and vile, as if he'd fallen far short of her expectations. "I see. Thank you for at least being gentleman enough to tell me you're leaving tomorrow."

She walked away, her carriage stiff as she bent to collect the hairpins scattered over the sofa. Her bitter dignity sliced into his heart. In numb silence he watched her coil the long strands of hair atop her head, then don the jaunty straw bonnet. As she walked to the desk to collect her gloves, the sight of her slim back and exquisite profile twisted his belly with a confusing mix of tenderness and desire and panic. If she walked out now, he'd never see her again. God! How could he let her go?

Yet what right had he to keep her?

An idea seized his mind, a solution so stunning and so perfect, he wondered why he'd not considered it before. He could give Juliet at least part of what she wanted. He could sate the hunger gnawing at his loins. And he could still punish Emmett Carleton by stealing what he valued most.

Without looking his way, she headed to the door.

"Don't go."

She turned, her face pale but composed. "There's nothing more to say, Kent."

"That's not true." His palms broke out in a cold sweat. He couldn't let himself think she'd be happier with a man who would shower her with love. He couldn't give himself time to consider that he might be making the worst mistake of his life. He forced out the words he'd never meant to speak to any woman again.

"Will you marry me?"

The quiet question penetrated the mire of misery enveloping Juliet. Shaking with disbelief, she stared at his rugged features, at the tanned skin and black hair that formed so dazzling a contrast to the white of his shirt. He couldn't be serious. He couldn't be. Yet the very thought of becoming his wife made her heart slam against her ribs.

Quelling the riot of hope, she shook her head. "How can you ask me that? You yourself said we hardly know one another."

"We know enough." Striding to her, he tenderly took her cheeks into his palms. "When I saw you about to walk out of my life, Juliet, I suddenly knew the truth. I can't let you go."

Candor gentled his face. Her hands clenched the soft kid gloves as she struggled to sort through the doubts and dreams clashing inside her. "What about my father? What if he forbids the marriage?"

"We won't tell him. We'll elope."

"I can't simply run off—"

"It's the best way. When it's too late to obtain an annulment, Emmett will be forced to accept the inevitable."

The grim certainty in his voice told her that Kent saw his way as the only sensible solution. Was he right?

"But how can we keep our plans a secret? The instant the banns are announced, someone will congratulate my parents."

"Not if we marry by special license. I may not be wealthy, but I wield a duke's influence."

His cool self-possession disturbed her. He'd spoken no words of love, no promise to cherish her. Did he want her for money? She tried to banish the thought, but it seared like a hot coal in her stomach.

"My father is sure to cut me off without a penny."

"He can burn his millions for all I care. I want *you*, Juliet, not the Carleton fortune."

This time his eyes blazed with feeling and his hands

held her tightly. She felt dizzy and reckless, caught in a whirlpool of happiness. "Oh, Kent, I want to believe you. Truly, I do."

"If it will ease your mind, I'll have my solicitor draw up papers renouncing any claim of mine to your father's money." His lips brushed hers in a petal-soft caress. "Think about it, Juliet. By this time tomorrow, we can be man and wife."

His palms slid down her back, his fingers splaying over her hips, pressing her to him, stroking a torrid longing that melted all reason. She drew a shallow breath. How could he ask her to think when their bodies were fitted so tightly together, when his earthy scent enfolded her, when his musky-sweet taste lingered in her mouth?

"Come home with me as my duchess, Juliet. Share my life and my bed. Bear my children. I need you. We'll never be apart again."

Like leaves before an autumn wind, her doubts scattered. He was asking her to banish the darkness from his soul. He was asking her to make him forget the tragedy of his past. He was asking her to reawaken his ability to love.

"Yes, I'll marry you."

His arms relaxed. He gently cupped her jaw, and in his hand she detected a faint tremor of emotion that made her spirits soar.

"I'll make you happy, Juliet," he vowed, as if trying to convince himself. "I'll grant you all the freedom your parents denied you . . . the freedom to pursue your interest in botany. You can spend your days restoring the neglected greenhouses at Radcliffe. I'll never cage you like that sapling."

"As long as we're together, I'll be happy."

She brushed her lips across his work-roughened palm; his sharp intake of breath thrilled her. "I'll set your spirit free," he whispered. "I'll unlock all the sensuality hidden inside you."

"I want that, Kent. I want everything you can give me."

He tilted her chin and his mouth caught hers again.

Wanting to bind herself to him, she wreathed her arms around his neck and pressed her breasts to his chest. He kissed her lips, her cheeks, her eyes, and his thumbs rubbed her temples, the combination of caresses drawing a deep and magical response from her body.

When at last his mouth ceased its sorcery, he continued to hold her, his hand drifting over her back, as if he could not bear to let her go. She nestled her cheek in the hard hollow of his collarbone and let herself float. Like wingbeats of joy, her pulse joined with his. She wanted to bask forever in the heat of his body, the strength of his arms.

Too soon, he drew back. "I must go. There's still time today for me to see the bishop about the license."

"Shall I accompany you?"

Kent shook his head. "I've no wish to subject you to any embarrassment."

"I'm not ashamed of my love for you."

"You don't understand." He hesitated. "I'll have to say that we've consummated our relationship."

Perplexed, she cocked her head to the side. "We've *finished* our relationship? But isn't it just the opposite—?"

Those dark eyes gleamed; a slight smile softened his mouth. "You *have* been sheltered, haven't you, my Lady Botanist?" Tucking a wisp of hair behind her ear, he added, "I'll have to tell him that I've compromised you, taken you to my bed."

Understanding flamed in her cheeks. Such a declaration would brand her a fallen woman. People would speculate about the abrupt marriage; her parents would endure stares and malicious gossip.

"Is there no other reason you could give?"

"Trust me. It's the only way to ensure that our marriage takes place immediately." He paused, and although his hands still rested on her shoulders, she had the curious impression of his withdrawal. "You see, the bishop will grant a special license only if he believes you may be carrying my child."

He walked away to tug on the bell cord. Juliet wondered what had triggered his sudden aloofness. Was it the mention of a child? He must still mourn the unborn baby who'd died with his beloved wife.

Wife. The thought sent shivers down her spine. She slowly bent to retrieve the gloves, which she'd dropped during the kiss. Kent stood by the sofa, his broad back half-turned as he gathered his father's drawings and tucked them into the satchel. The sight of his lean body brought a rush of reckless rapture. Once they were married, she would bear him a baby, an heir. He'd be so proud and happy. . . .

"Yes, sahib?" Ravi stood in the doorway. His brown eyes impassive, the servant flicked a glance at her.

"Tell Hatchett to bring the landau around. Immediately."

"As you wish, Your Grace." Bowing, the servant left, as silently as he'd arrived.

"Will you wait while I fetch my coat?" Kent asked her. "This once, I insist on escorting you home—or at least as close as we can risk. The future Duchess of Radcliffe shan't be going about London in hired hansoms."

She stood still, staring as he strode out of the library. Her heart beat fast under the force of a stunning thought. She would be a duchess. . . . Her parents wanted her to wed a titled man, and she could scarcely do better than a duke. Once they understood that Kent intended not dishonor but marriage, wouldn't her father set aside his animosity?

Excited resolve built within her. The moment Papa came home today, she'd gently break the news. He'd be angry at first, but Mama would help ease him into acceptance. Given time, he would concede to Juliet's determination and realize how important his blessing was to her. At last he'd regard her as an adult. . . .

She took a deep breath. Better that Kent shouldn't know her plan; like her father, he'd order her to leave such matters to the men. But she would prove to him that Papa could love as fiercely as he could hate. Like Romeo and Juliet, she would bring together the two feuding families.

Some thirty minutes later, she sat beside Kent in a closed landau that smelled of ancient leather, the wheels creaking as the carriage jolted over the cobbled street. The contemplative look in his eyes revealed little of his private thoughts. The absentminded drumming of his fingers on the seat exhibited the only sign of nerves. But even his preoccupation couldn't dim the sunshine inside her. She could sit for hours and study the strong angles of his profile, the black hair that curled slightly behind his ears, the raven slash of his eyebrows, the noble set of his jaw. She envisioned them married, passing a quiet evening in the drawing room, children gamboling at their feet while Kent held her close and told her about his day. . . .

He turned abruptly to her. "We'll have to get our start during the night. Can you manage to be in front of your house at two tomorrow morning?"

His words dashed her into dismay. "So soon? I thought we'd wait a few days—"

"I cannot wait to make you mine, Juliet." He gathered her hands in his. "Unless you've doubts about becoming my wife."

He bent his head, and his warm lips caressed the back of her hand. His mouth lingered a moment; then he looked up, his face mere inches from hers. His eyes gleamed with a dark fire that nourished the flame of longing inside her. She could no more resist him than she could stop the wild beating of her heart.

"No, Kent. I've no doubts."

His hands tightened before releasing her. "It's settled, then. We'll leave tonight."

Her soul sang with excitement. She wanted to run away with Kent, to experience the heady thrill of escaping propriety, to let him initiate her into all the mysteries of womanhood.

Still, she yearned to banish the need to steal away in the middle of the night. She had no wish to damage her parents' dearly bought position in society. A long engagement period followed by an elaborate wedding would fulfill her mother's dreams and swell her father's pride.

Regretfully Juliet tucked away her craving for adventure. Once she settled things with Papa, she'd send Kent a message that at last the feud was over. He'd come and make amends with her father. Perhaps Papa would even finance Kent's inventions. . . .

Around the corner from Belgrave Square, the landau halted and Kent helped her down. He caressed her cheek and murmured good-bye; she hoped tonight she'd be able to tell him all this secrecy was unnecessary. The black door with its faded gold ducal crest clicked shut. She stood on the curbstone and watched as the carriage drove off into the congestion of traffic.

Juliet started toward her house. Feeling blissful, she grinned at a liveried footman who hurried down the walkway. Feeling generous, she pressed a silver half crown into the grimy palm of a flypaper vendor. Feeling mischievous, she waggled her fingers at a housemaid who polished a brass door knocker.

Occupying an entire corner of the square, Carleton House stood with fluted gray columns supporting a portico that towered to the third floor. The palazzolike mansion seemed warm and inviting today. As she climbed the marble steps, the approach of a carriage drew her attention.

Her father's brougham rounded the circular drive and stopped near the entryway. Before the footman could reach the handle, the door burst open and Emmett Carleton stepped out.

Her heart danced over a beat. The chance to speak to him had come sooner than expected. She could scarcely contain the eagerness and anxiety roiling inside her.

Like a lion closing in on its prey, he surged up the stairs. His mind must have been on unpleasant matters; his lips were thinned beneath the handlebar mustache.

Juliet took a deep breath. "You're home early, Papa."

"And a damned good thing, too."

The curse shocked her as much as the fury beneath his taut mask of civility. Seizing her arm, he jerked her toward the door. Potter held open the mahogany panel and stared straight ahead.

She half stumbled as her father hauled her into the house. "Papa? What's wrong?"

His glance scorched her. "Don't play the innocent with me."

A second shock wave struck. She felt the blood drain from her cheeks. *Dear heaven, he must have found out about Kent.*

Emmett marched her up the grand staircase. Her arm throbbed as he drew her down the hall and into her bedroom. He released her abruptly. She caught at the doorjamb to steady herself.

Her maid, Charlotte, stood before the dressing table. She froze in the act of pouring perfume into a cut-glass bottle. The rich scent of oil of jasmine wafted through the air.

"Out," Emmett growled.

Charlotte hastily corked the vial. Her wide-eyed gaze darted from father to daughter; then she bobbed a curtsy and scurried out, shutting the door.

Fists clenched, he swung toward Juliet. His chest rose and fell with terrible fury. "You faithless liar. How long have you been sneaking off to see Deverell?"

She struggled to control her disgust and hurt that he'd treat her so crudely. As soon as he knew the truth, he'd calm down. "Papa, things aren't what they seem—"

"Don't deny that you got out of his carriage. I was close enough to see that much."

"I wasn't denying—"

"I saw the way that damned blackguard touched you. The way a man would caress his mistress. Now answer me: how long has this abomination been going on?"

His thundering voice alarmed her, but she refused to flinch. "I've met him a few times, but you must understand—"

"That conniving devil! I should have guessed he wouldn't stop at invading my home." He slammed his palm onto the dressing table so hard, the bottles and jars clinked. "By God, he won't get away with stealing you, too!"

"Too?" Cocking her head, she sensed that something simmered below the surface of his anger, something beyond her perception. "What do you mean?"

Emmett turned away, his expression hidden. "A Deverell can't be trusted," he growled. "That's all you need remember. He means to smear your reputation so that no decent man will want you."

Juliet stepped in front of him. "Where do you get such horrible ideas? Kent would never dishonor me."

He glowered. "Hah! He's ruined more lives than you can know."

Her lips softened into a reassuring smile. "But he's asked me to marry him. And I agreed, Papa. I agreed because I love him. I've never wanted anything more than I want him."

Emmett stood perfectly still. "You betraying bitch."

With a snarl of fury, he lunged at her. His palm struck her cheek. Reeling from the blow, she staggered backward until her spine met the carved bedpost. Pain shot up her back.

Shaking with disbelief, Juliet stared at her father. The echo of the slap hung in the quiet air. She cupped her red-hot cheek. Without the support of the bedpost, she would have wilted like an ice-stung bloom.

His harsh expression dissolved into horrified regret, and he took a step toward her. "Princess, forgive me," he said in a hoarse voice. "I shouldn't have lost my temper."

Bewildered, she shook her head slowly. "Didn't you hear what I said? Kent wants me for his *wife*."

A muscle ticked in his jaw. "He'll never have you. Never."

Bitter disillusionment soured her soul, and she swallowed a choking upsurge of tears. "Then you aren't apologizing for what's really important. You can't bear for me to love Kent because that would mean you've been wrong all these years."

"I know him better than you think, Princess. I just don't want him to hurt you."

"You've already hurt me." She touched her stinging cheek. "I didn't realize how much until a moment ago."

"Put that bastard out of your mind, do you understand me?" Her father shook a finger. "He's no better than a dirt farmer—"

"Mr. Carleton! What's going on here?"

Her mother stood with her hand on the doorknob, her figure trim and ladylike in a gown of gentian-blue silk.

"I've not invited you into this discussion, Dorothea."

She hesitated, her gaze moving from him to Juliet. Then Dorothea took a determined step forward. "I'm aware of that, Mr. Carleton. But Potter informed me that you'd dragged Juliet up the stairs in a most extraordinary fashion. Now I see you've struck her, and I wish to know why."

"She's been lying to both of us. For the past fortnight, she's been sneaking off to meet Kent Deverell."

Dorothea gasped and turned to her daughter. "Is this true?"

Juliet held her head high. "Yes. But you needn't worry about scandal. Kent and I wish to be married."

"Married! Dear me . . ." Eyes alight, Dorothea looked at Emmett. "Darling, imagine! Our daughter, the Duchess of Radcliffe!"

"She'll be the Marchioness of Breeton. That's prestigious enough for me."

"But Mr. Carleton, your grandson could be a duke—"

He cut her off with a downward slash of his hand. "I said that's enough. I'll not hear another word on the matter."

The enthusiasm left her delicate features, and she lowered her gaze. "Yes, of course."

Their argument left Juliet sickened, for neither of her parents considered her happiness. "You might ask me what *I* wish."

"I know what's best for you, Princess." Emmett stalked toward the door, then pivoted, his expression stony. "Go near that devil again and by God, you're no longer my daughter."

Though his words cleaved her heart, she lifted her chin. "You're not treating me like your daughter, but a share of stock to be traded at your command. I'm old enough to make my own decisions."

"You're acting like a child. I'll leave you alone to think about your unseemly conduct."

Seizing his wife's hand and snatching the brass key from the inside lock, he slammed the door shut behind them. Before Juliet realized his intent, the key rattled in the lock. The heavy tread of footsteps marched away.

She rushed to the door and shook the knob. A sob lodged in her throat and tears blurred her eyes. She sank to her knees and pressed her cheek to the door. The cool wood soothed her cheek, but the rent in her heart burned with the heat of her father's callous words. Kent had been right all along; Papa hadn't even been willing to listen. He didn't trust her to make wise choices. He'd never offer his blessing on the marriage. And she couldn't depend on her mother for help; no matter what her private feelings, Dorothea Carleton would bow to her husband's wishes.

Go near that devil again and by God, you'll no longer be my daughter.

Her mind a maze of grief, Juliet buried her face in her hands and wept. The burst of raw emotion gradually subsided, leaving her as desolate as a storm-lashed garden. If she went through with the elopement, she would lose her parents forever. Yet could things ever be the same again? To make them happy, she'd have to forfeit the man she loved and shackle herself to that shallow, fox-hunting Breeton.

She had the sudden, unbearable need to feel Kent's arms around her, to lay her head on the firm warmth of his chest, to hear the reassuring beat of his heart.

Tonight she would pledge her life to him.

The decision cleared her mind. Rising, she looked around the bedroom. French gilt furniture, an ornately plastered ceiling, a silk-hung four-poster bed with a pale blue counterpane. *A pretty cage.* The expensive de-

cor reflected her mother's style and her father's appetite for luxury. Only the vase of dried wildflowers and
the botany books on the nightstand marked the room
as her own.

Going to an opened window, she peered down. The
stone ledge above the terrace looked alarmingly narrow, and extended to an enormous oak at the corner
of the house. She *had* to escape. Could she manage to
inch her way to those thick branches?

For Kent, she would try anything.

In her dressing room, she selected the largest hatbox
and tossed aside its lavishly ribboned contents. Buoyed
by nervous energy, she packed the makeshift portman-
teau and hid it under the bed. Then she waited. Hours
passed in measured ticks of the ormolu mantelpiece
clock. At eight, Charlotte brought a dinner tray. From
her sidelong looks, Juliet knew the maid burned to discover why the master had imprisoned his daughter. To
avoid suspicion, she accepted Charlotte's aid in donning a nightdress. The servant murmured a good-night
and locked the door behind her.

Too overwrought to sleep, Juliet forced herself to sit
in a chair by the window. With a pang of regret, she
gazed over the darkened gardens in which she'd spent
many contented hours. There would be other gardens
at Radcliffe, a place of her own. What was his castle
like? And Kent's cousin?

The sky was cloudy, the night chilly with rising mist.
Gaslight shone in the windows of neighboring houses
and in the mews, where the stable lads and coachman
resided. The ever-present odor of smoke pervaded the
air. From downstairs came the occasional rise of a voice,
though the words were indistinct.

Her mind replayed the awful confrontation with her
father. *He won't get away with stealing you, too.* What
could the Deverells have done to turn her father into
such a beast? Swallowing hard, she buried the memory
beneath thoughts of Kent . . . the beauty of his smiles,
the taste of his mouth, the gentleness of his touch.

One by one the lights vanished and the voices
ceased. The clock chimed once. The house creaked and

settled. Certain that everyone slept, she exchanged her nightdress for a simple gown of forest-green silk. The task seemed to take forever as her fingers fumbled with corset hooks and frock buttons.

Then she sat down at her desk and composed a note to her parents. Her emotions numb, she left the folded letter and poked her head out the window again. The ledge lay hidden in gloom. A shudder ran through her. She might lose her footing, tumble to the flagstoned terrace.

Just as Emily Deverell had fallen to her death.

Yet what other choice did she have?

A startling idea sent Juliet rushing to the door. Crouching, she peered through the keyhole. The key blocked the opening.

From her desk she fetched a sheet of stationery and slid it under the door. Using a hairpin, she gently dislodged the key. A ping sounded as the metal struck the floor of the hall. Dropping to her knees, she peered beneath the door and saw the key lying just past the paper. "Drat!"

Now what? She ran into her dressing room and yanked open a drawer. Fingers trembling, she pushed aside fans and combs, hatpins and handkerchiefs. At last she found a buttonhook.

Hurrying back, she thrust the long hook under the door. It took four tries before her shaking hand maneuvered the key onto the paper. She slowly drew it inside. Elated, she snatched up the cold brass in her fist. Then her exultation drained. No doubt, Charlotte would be held to blame for forgetting the key.

Yet Juliet couldn't turn back now.

The clock chimed twice as she swiftly donned her best braided jacket. Catching the hatbox handle in her hand, she unlocked the door and crept out. A low-lit gas sconce at the far end of the hall shed enough light for her to see. She relocked the door and left the key, so that nothing would appear amiss.

Silence hung heavy as she tiptoed along the dark hall and past her parents' suite of rooms. She headed down the grand, curving staircase, her shoes tapping on the marble risers, the ungainly hatbox bumping her thigh.

Turning the latch, she opened the front door. Across the square, in a deep-shadowed area between the street lamps, she saw the misty outline of a familiar landau. Pivoting, she took one last look around the lofty foyer. Regret choked her throat, regret that her parents could not accept the man she loved.

Then she stepped into the chilly night and closed the door on her childhood.

Chapter 6

Kent forced himself to stand rigidly before the altar steps.

Seeking a distraction to calm the churning in his stomach, he glanced around the small church. This remote sanctum in the rolling hills of Hampshire suited his requirements superbly. Sunshine flowed through the stained glass and cast jeweled light over the rows of empty pews. The congregation consisted of Ravi and Hatchett, who sat together at the rear. On one side of Kent stood the gangly vicar; on the other, a rabbit-toothed young curate gawked with ill-concealed awe.

Everyone waited for the ceremony to begin.

Panic swept Kent in a sickening wave. The urge to run out of the church swamped him. He could yet stop himself from committing this ignominious act. He could turn back, cancel the wedding, and restore Juliet to the life she deserved. Fleeing would be not the act of a coward, but of a hero.

Go. Now. If you have any humanity left in the void of your soul, you'll give her back.

His foot moved. A hand touched his arm. Numbly he looked at the ink-stained fingers on his gray sleeve. His eyes followed the arm to the surpliced clergyman.

"I don't blame you for your impatience, Your Grace," whispered Wesley Elphinstone. "Here's your bride now. And she's well worth waiting for, if I may say so."

Kent jerked his gaze down the aisle. Juliet stood framed by the open doors of the church, the late afternoon sunlight gilding her slender figure. A wreath of orange blossoms crowned her upswept hair, and a crepe de chine gown in a shade of aged gold warmed her skin. In her arms she cradled a spray of lavender marsh orchids. The blooms drew his eyes to her breasts, where the prim bodice and pearl necklace accented her womanly fullness. Tonight he'd possess the right to undress her; tonight he'd run his hands over her ripe curves; tonight he'd make long, sweet love to her.

His groin tightened with unholy heat. Christ. Now he was lusting in a church. To what depths had he sunk?

Go, his mind urged again. *Go, before it's too late.*

Yet his feet remained rooted to the stone floor; his eyes remained fastened on the beautiful girl.

The organ wheezed, yanking his gaze to the choir loft, where he could see Mrs. Elphinstone's pudgy back bent over the keyboard. The feathers on her enormous green hat bobbed as she lurched into Wagner's *Lohengrin March*.

Juliet started down the aisle. The sadness and exhaustion of the girl who'd run to him so early this morning no longer shaded her face. Now her eyes were steady with resolution, her features serene with love.

A love he'd taken by trickery. A love he couldn't return.

Self-loathing twisted like a knife inside him. He was about to achieve the ultimate revenge; he was about to gain legal control of Emmett Carleton's daughter.

Yet he felt lower than a worm slinking beneath the fields of Castle Radcliffe.

In desperation, he dipped into the black well of memory. Emily. Think about Emily. Think about Dreamspinner.

But the images were fleeting, insubstantial compared to the vibrant picture of Juliet walking toward him.

Skirts swishing, she glided to his side. As she met his gaze, uncertainty flashed in her eyes; then her mouth curved into a tender smile. She slipped her hand into his, and his mind went blank to all but the inviting fullness of her lower lip. He wanted to kiss her, right here and now, to submerge himself in the magic of her youthful charm and let reality fall away.

Elphinstone cleared his throat. "Er . . . as there's no one to give the bride away, shall we begin?"

Oh, God. Kent's palms turned to ice. Rather than trust his voice, he gave the clergyman a curt nod.

Elphinstone commenced reading the service, his black prayer book held at arm's length.

Only a few words of the prefatory address pierced the roaring in Kent's ears: ". . . answer before God at the day of doom . . ." A wave of dizziness almost made him sway. All that kept him upright was the feel of her small hand enclosed in his. ". . . if you know any lawful hindrance why you may not be wedded together at this time, say it now."

Elphinstone paused and looked up, his bushy gray brows raised. Kent bit back a rude command: *Good Christ, why don't you just get on with it?*

"Ahem." Hastily lowering his eyes, the vicar droned out the wedding contract. Like stones, each word sank into Kent.

". . . from this day forward, for better for worse, for richer for poorer, in sickness and in health, to love and to cherish, till death do us part."

"I will," Juliet said, her voice soft but firm.

Turning to the duke, Elphinstone began to intone the vow a second time.

An awful agitation stirred inside Kent. He could offer Juliet neither love nor riches. What right had he to cheat her of a happy future? In despair he looked down at her, and the faint bruise along her cheekbone caught his eye. Fury surged inside him, a fury that swept the guilt away. God, how he'd wanted to kill Emmett Carleton for striking her!

Perhaps he should have told her the whole sordid story.

Then she wouldn't have married him.

Oh, Christ. At least he was doing her a favor by saving her from that brute. He would keep his pledge to protect her.

Time folded back; years dropped away. Once again, a Deverell would give asylum to a Carleton. . . .

"Your Grace?"

He jerked his head toward the vicar. Kent swallowed the knot in his throat. "I will."

His steadfast tone brought a trembling joy to Juliet. When she'd walked down the aisle to join him, his aloof demeanor had dismayed her. Now, through a haze of happiness, she watched him place his heavy gold signet on her finger. She held her fist tight to keep the ring from sliding off as he bent to give her a brief, stirring kiss.

Elphinstone murmured the closing prayers and blessings; then the organ began thumping out a recessional march. With one arm holding the stalk of orchids and the other looped with her husband's, she entered the vestry to sign the register. Footsteps clumped down the choir stairs, and Mrs. Elphinstone's stout figure appeared in the doorway. She clasped a handkerchief to the bosom of her green and garnet striped gown.

"Oh, my, wasn't that romantic?" She dabbed her eyes with the handkerchief, then noisily blew her nose. "Never have I seen a more radiant bride, Your Grace. You two make a handsome couple indeed."

"We appreciate your hospitality," Kent said. "It was kind of you, Vicar, to marry us on such short notice."

Elphinstone's gaunt chest swelled with self-importance. "Say no more. It is my holy duty to perform God's tasks."

"Yet perhaps you won't refuse a modest donation in exchange for a few days silence on this matter." Kent pressed a gold coin into the parson's palm.

Elphinstone's eyes gleamed bright as the sovereign. "Thank you, Your Grace. The less fortunate in our district will benefit from your generosity."

His wife looked crestfallen and curious. "A few days, Your Grace? Won't you tell us the cause for such secrecy?"

Kent's expression went frigid. "My reasons are my own. If you'll excuse us now." Hand at the base of

Juliet's spine, he steered her toward the arched doorway.

"Oh, but Your Grace!" Mrs. Elphinstone burst out. "Surely you're not leaving so soon? The Vicar and I would be honored to have you share our tea."

Standing witness to the wedding of a duke must be the pinnacle of Mrs. Elphinstone's dull life, Juliet thought in wry sympathy. Impulsively she lay a hand on Kent's arm. "We can spare a few moments, can't we?"

His mouth tightened, and she thought by his frosty glare that he would refuse. Then he turned away and said, "My wife and I would be delighted to join you."

The delay displeased him, Juliet reflected, as the foursome trooped out of the church and toward the stone vicarage. Or was he angry with *her*? Did he expect her to be as subservient as her own mother? The magnitude of the step she'd taken struck with dizzying force. She had bound her life to the tall and sternly handsome man who walked beside her, a man who could be both bitter and tender, cold and kind.

As they passed beneath a trellis crowned with pink cabbage roses, trepidation weighed upon her as heavily as the ring upon her finger. A thought had been hovering at the back of her mind since the quarrel with her father, a thought she had refused to ponder during the long, numbing carriage ride. How well did she really know Kent?

In the vicarage parlor, she took her seat beside him on an ancient sofa. The watercress sandwiches tasted dry as sand in her mouth and the sticky black gingerbread settled like a lump in her stomach. Kent took command of the conversation; he deftly flattered Mrs. Elphinstone and politely solicited the vicar's pompous opinions. With startling clarity, Juliet saw another facet of this complex man who was now her husband.

Afterward they found Hatchett waiting outside with the landau, the top folded down to the balmy summer evening. Ravi stood beside the carriage, and his swarthy face wore no expression as he handed Juliet inside. Yet she sensed contempt in his eyes, a contempt that added to her unease. He resented her . . . because she had Carleton blood. Would the others at the castle resent her, too?

The servant took his place beside the burly coachman, and the carriage started down the narrow country road.

Late sunlight gleamed through a stand of elms and settled on the hedgerows and fields. Alongside the ditch grew yellow marsh marigolds and an occasional patch of purple orchids, like the stalk in her lap. Her wedding bouquet. Running a fingertip over the velvety lip of one bloom, she tried to recapture the reckless hope that had borne her through the marriage ceremony.

Yet the man beside her seemed a stranger now. She felt awkward and tongue-tied, naive and nervous. Could she truly cure his cynicism and win his love?

His hand settled over hers, the calluses firm against her soft skin. His keen dark eyes studied her. "Second thoughts?" he asked, his low-pitched words almost lost to the rattle of wheels.

She lowered her gaze to their joined hands. "All my life I trusted my father, but he turned on me the moment I ceased doing as he commanded."

Almost imperceptibly, his fingers tightened. "And now you're wondering if you can trust me."

"Yes."

He said nothing for a moment; the shrill cry of a peewit mingled with the rhythmic clopping of hooves.

"Juliet, look at me."

An underlying roughness made his words more an entreaty than an order. Lifting her chin, she found her skin prickling from the intensity of his gaze.

"I'll never raise a hand to you," he said, his voice soft but steadfast. "You have my word on that."

"I know."

He watched her closely. "Then why do you still doubt me?"

How could she tell him that her misgivings stemmed not from the threat of abuse but from the absence of affection? She touched the pearls encircling her throat.

Go near that devil and by God, you're no longer my daughter.

She swallowed hard. "I'm wondering about something odd that my father said to me last night. Something about you not stealing me, too. What did her mean?"

His eyes widened, then narrowed. He released her hands and sat back. "Doubtless Emmett referred to his belief that my father cheated him out of a piece of property."

She tilted her head. "But I thought it was the other way around. I thought *your* father believed Papa had cheated *him.*"

"There were many arguments between them. Let's not let their feud spoil our honeymoon."

Juliet couldn't forget her father's furious face. "But what will Papa do? He's surely gotten my letter by now."

Kent shrugged. "You're my lawful wife. You needn't worry about your father."

"And if he comes after us?"

"He'll expect us to travel by train to Radcliffe. The last thing he'll suspect is that we took a carriage to Hampshire."

"What if he's waiting at the castle?"

"Then we'll invite him in and have a feast." Tenderly he brushed her hand again. "Don't torment yourself, Juliet. Let's enjoy the few days it'll take us to reach home."

Home. That single word boosted her spirits because, consciously or not, he'd drawn her into the circle of his family.

"Let's set aside the future and the past," he went on, his voice lowering to a husky whisper. "Nothing should mar your memory of our wedding. I'll do my best to make everything perfect for you tonight. You can trust me in that."

His thumb drew slow circles over her wrist, and the warmth of his grip flowed into her. Kent had married her because he, too, felt this burning ache for physical closeness. Impulsively she leaned toward him and said,

"My father deceived me into thinking he was a decent, fair-minded person. What I love about you, Kent, is that you've been so honest with me."

Something dark leaped into his eyes, that frustrating veil hiding his thoughts. The breeze blew a lock of black hair against his forehead. He nodded and turned to gaze at the scenery.

Beset by disappointment and determination, Juliet fingered her pearls. Tonight, she thought. Tonight he wouldn't shut her out.

They stopped for the night at an ancient posting inn. The second-story room had a steep-pitched roof and a gabled window open to the night breezes. The tassels on the drawn-back draperies stirred with each puff of air. Candlelight glowed over the whitewashed walls and cast shadows in the corners.

Standing before a minuscule washstand, Juliet dipped her hands into a chipped china bowl and rinsed the travel dust from her face, then shined the heavy gold wedding band. Kent had gone downstairs, ostensibly to order dinner, more likely to give her a few moments privacy. His considerate nature warmed her heart and made her shiver with anticipation. Would he be as patient with her inexperience tonight? *Trust me. . . .*

Restlessly she walked to the bed, the floorboards creaking. The pink and white striped hatbox looked incongruous against the claret-colored counterpane. She focused her attention on the meager task of unpacking her few toilet articles, a favorite botany text, the crumpled green gown she'd worn this morning. The wrinkles dismayed her. She tried to shake out the silk folds, then gave up and draped the garment over a chair.

A sharp rapping made her pulse jump. Kent. She hastened to the door. When she saw only the innkeeper's plain-faced wife, Juliet felt her smile droop.

The woman dipped a curtsy, made awkward by the tray balanced in her hands and the admiration reflected in her eyes. "I brung supper, Your Grace."

For an instant, the title startled Juliet; then she moved aside. "Come in, please."

As the woman lay cutlery and dishes on a small table by the hearth, Juliet wandered to the window seat and gazed outside. The dense foliage of a walnut tree obscured the quarter moon. Through an occasional break in the woods, she could see the silver gleam of the Itchen River. The stamp of a horse's hoof came from the nearby stables, then the lonely hoot of a barn owl. Directly below, the ground glowed with lamplight that spilled from the kitchen. A faint burst of laughter drifted from the public taproom at the front of the inn.

Was that where Kent had gone?

Then she saw him, a solitary figure in the gloom beneath the trees. He walked slowly from the direction of the river, and as he passed through a patch of moonlight, she saw that his hands were in his trouser pockets, his shoulders hunched slightly beneath his white shirt. For some unfathomable reason, she recalled the drawing of him as a little boy sitting astride a pony and anxious to please his father.

"Might I 'elp you undress?"

The hesitant voice intruded upon the memory. Turning, she saw the innkeeper's wife standing before the hearth, her chapped hands worrying her white apron.

"Don't mean t' seem bold, Your Grace," the woman added hastily. "I just saw you didn't 'ave no lady's maid."

And neither luggage nor nightdress. Embarrassed, Juliet shook her head. "I can manage, thank you."

"Then I'll iron your gown. I'll do a fine job, I will. Often's the time I've cleaned and pressed silk." The woman picked up the rumpled green frock.

"Thank you."

"Anythin' else, you just call." She bobbed a curtsy and left.

The instant the door clicked shut, Juliet peered outside again. Shadows stirred and swayed beneath the trees, but she could no longer see Kent's tall form. A gust of wind raised goose bumps over her skin. Rubbing her arms, she stole a glance at the bed.

I'll do my best to make everything perfect for you.

The thought of the night ahead brought a confusing flurry of emotions. She tried to put a name to those feelings: longing and curiosity and an odd pulsing excitement deep in her belly. Savory scents emanated from the covered dishes on the table, but she felt no stirring of appetite, only a dim, undefinable ache. Would his kisses tonight let her into his heart? What happened between a man and a woman? She wished there were someone to ask, someone familiar to whom she dared pose her questions. The one time she'd asked her mother, Dorothea had blushed and turned away.

Restively Juliet wandered to the nightstand and picked up the stalk of orchids. Like her courage, they were drooping. To revive the flowers, she went to the table and poked the stem into a glass of water.

The door opened. Heart thumping, she turned to see Kent, his broad shoulders filling the entryway. The wind had tousled his hair, yet the disorder made him more rakishly handsome. His jet-black eyes met hers; then he shut the door and walked toward her.

Holding out a spray of small, brilliant blue flowers, he said, "I found these. Thought you might like them."

His manner seemed curiously hesitant. As she took the stem, her fingers brushed his; the contact flustered her. "Water forget-me-not. *Myosotis* . . ." She searched her memory for the specific name; then she turned toward the nightstand and her botany text.

"*Scorpioides*," he supplied, before she could open the book. "You're slipping, my Lady Botanist. Perhaps I shall have to devise a quiz for you."

His teasing invited a similar response. "Tonight?"

The gleam of humor in his eyes darkened. "No," he murmured. "Tonight we'll have too much else to occupy us."

His gaze dipped to her breasts, and her legs suddenly seemed on the verge of wilting. Her fingers tightened around the fragile stalk of forget-me-nots. Just a look from him made her flush. . . .

He glanced at the neatly laid table, then went to the

washstand, where the slope of the roof forced him to bend his head. "Forgive me. I've kept you waiting."

"No, you haven't. The innkeeper's wife only just brought the meal." Juliet watched as he poured a fresh bowl of water and began to soap his hands. His precise movements held her in strange fascination, and the quiet splashing of water filled the silence. She sensed that he'd withdrawn from her, and the notion puzzled and frustrated her. Venturing closer, she studied his powerful profile, the imperious forehead and sculpted mouth, the black hair that curled slightly behind his ears.

"I saw you out walking. Did you go as far as the river?"

"Not quite. It was dark, and the ground got a bit marshy."

"Tomorrow morning, will you show me where you found the forget-me-nots?"

"If you like."

His distracted tone hardly encouraged conversation. Unsure of his mood, she twirled the stalk of flowers as nervousness jittered inside her. *How well do you really know him?* While he dried his hands on a linen towel, he looked at her and she endeavored to smile, but her face felt stiff.

A subtle gentling touched his expression. "Shall we eat?"

She nodded and sank into a chair. While he lifted the cover off a soup tureen, she occupied herself with adding the forget-me-nots to the tumbler holding the orchids.

He ladled the watercress soup into their bowls. She picked up her pewter spoon, but the tightness in her throat kept her from taking a mouthful. The atmosphere seemed suddenly, overwhelmingly intimate. The candelabrum on the wooden mantelpiece isolated the table in a soft cocoon of light. She had never before dined alone with a man, not even with her father. Footmen had always hovered in the background, waiting to whisk away an empty plate or to offer a tempting dish.

The candleglow illuminated Kent's inscrutable features. Her husband. How strange that seemed. Had he shared such a wedding night meal with his beloved Emily? Uncertainty swamped Juliet, along with a keen awareness of her own inexperience.

He cocked his head to the side. "If the soup isn't to your liking, I can ring for something else."

His concern loosened the ball of tension inside her. She managed a spoonful; the chilled blend of potatoes, cream, and watercress slipped down her throat easier than she'd expected. "No, it's fine."

"It's Mrs. Fitter's specialty."

"Who?"

"The innkeeper's wife."

"Oh . . . yes."

Chagrined that she'd been too embroiled in her own thoughts to ask the woman's name, Juliet took another spoonful of soup, then a sip of white wine. The act of eating began to melt the tension from her limbs. As she finished her soup, Kent lifted the covers from the other dishes. Heady aromas wafted through the air as he placed a portion of poached trout on her plate, then a slice of roast chicken in a sticky cherry sauce, and a hunk of crusty bread. As she watched him work, a sense of mischief sprouted inside her.

"Why are you smiling?" he asked.

"Because this is a luxury I never learned about in finishing school . . . to be served by a duke."

He grinned. "I wouldn't do this for just anyone, only for my duchess."

His gaze flicked to her lips. Her humor dissolved into that odd throbbing heat inside her belly. Flustered, she picked up her fork and toyed with the meal. For long moments the only sounds were the whisper of the draperies and the clink of the cutlery.

"Tell me about your childhood," he said.

The unexpected question drew her eyes to his. "What do you want to know?"

"Anything. Everything. When did you become interested in botany?"

His look of interest encouraged her. "The summer I

turned eight," she said, "my parents went to the Continent. Whenever I wasn't in the schoolroom, I'd play in the garden with my dolls. One day I wanted a bouquet for a mock wedding, and the gardener cut a few miniature roses for me." Pensively she stirred her fork in the remains of her fish. "Bennett was a kind old man. I spent a lot of time with him asking questions while I watched him work. Gradually I started to help him out."

He leaned back, studying her over the rim of his wineglass. "Did our wedding live up to your girlhood fantasies?"

The slight quirk of his black eyebrows gave Juliet the sudden, stunning impression that he, too, felt vulnerable, anxious to please. A wave of love lapped at her apprehension. "Yes," she said firmly, "I couldn't have dreamed of a lovelier wedding."

"You don't regret giving up a big society celebration?"

"All I need is the man I love." On impulse, she leaned forward. "It's hard to believe that a fortnight ago we didn't even know each other."

His fingers tensed around his glass, though his eyes were downcast, studying the play of candlelight through the pale gold wine. "Yet we knew of each other."

"I didn't. I mean, I'd heard of the Deverells, but not you in particular." She paused, intensely curious. "What did you know about me?"

"Just what I told you the night we met . . . that I'd heard Emmett Carleton had a beautiful daughter. I wanted to see for myself."

His sudden bold stare made her shiver. "Yet you already had," she said in a breathy whisper. "The afternoon of the ball, your carriage was across from my house."

"What I saw then intrigued me all the more."

Again his gaze swept downward, to her bosom. In an abrupt impatient gesture, he whisked the linen napkin from the last dish, this one piled with plump strawberries in cream.

"Would you care for some?" he asked.

The beauty of the fruit enticed her. "Yes, please."

Kent regarded the disarray of cutlery and china. "No clean dishes. Will you share with me?"

He picked up a ripe berry, but made no move to push the bowl into the center of the table; instead he reclined in his chair, the fruit a vivid red against his tanned fingers.

"Come here, Juliet."

Uncertain, she met his stare. A faint breeze fluttered the candles and sent shadows dancing across his features. She pushed back her chair, the scrape of the legs jarring the silence. Slowly she walked to him. No sooner did she reach for the strawberry than he caught her by the waist and pulled her onto his lap.

Her shoulder met the solid wall of his chest. His masculine scent made her pulse surge; his face loomed so close, she could see the dark stubble shadowing his cheek. The room grew hot, though a cool wind glided through the opened window.

One arm looped around her waist, he leaned forward to dip the strawberry in cream, then raised it to her lips. Too shy to look at him, she took a bite. The blend of rich cream and sweet berry melted on her tongue, and the juice trickled down, cool against her chin. She reached for a napkin, but his low growl of protest stopped her.

"Allow me."

His hands cupped her cheeks as he bent to touch his lips to her chin, and the lick of his tongue sent a flutter of longing through her. The heat of his body warmed the sleek linen of his shirt. Her head felt light, as if she'd drunk too much wine, yet her belly felt weighted, heavy with fever.

"More?" he murmured.

Unable to speak, she nodded. He selected another strawberry, but this time he took a bite first before offering the rest to her. His fingers brushed her lips as he helped her eat the morsel, and the fleeting caress prickled over her skin. Closing her eyes, Juliet fancied she could taste his unique male flavor along with the fruit.

She curled against him, her cheek settling into the crook of his neck. He uttered a sound deep in his chest, a sound that sent a shiver tickling down her spine.

"So you liked that, did you?"

She only half registered the satisfaction in his tone; then he tipped up her chin. "Yes," she breathed in the moment before his mouth found hers. His tongue slipped inside and lingered, savoring the richness of strawberries and cream and wine. His hard thighs pressed into her bottom; an intense awareness of him swept her. Against her breasts she detected the heavy thumping of his heart and the butterfly beat of her own blood. He smelled clean and faintly musky, as stirring an aroma as the outdoors.

"Touch me," he whispered against her lips.

Hesitantly she sought the strong column of his neck, then the powerful muscles of his shoulders. His hands slid to her nape and freed the button there from its mooring. He continued to kiss her as his fingers moved steadily downward, until the back of her gown lay open to the waist. Somehow he must have untied her petticoat tapes as well, for his hand slid down her corset to cup her hip, where only thin lawn underdrawers shielded her nakedness.

A scandalous pleasure burned between her thighs. The alien sensation brought a stirring of alarm that overwhelmed the languor in her limbs. Never had she imagined him touching her with such blazing intimacy.

Pulling back against his arm, she gulped in air. "What are you doing?"

With a quizzical frown, he regarded her; then a speculative glint entered his eyes. "You really don't know, do you?"

A flush crept up her throat. "Know what?"

"What happens in the marriage bed. Didn't your mother ever tell you—?"

At her waist his hand remained still, though his warmth penetrated her underdrawers and nourished the strange disturbance inside her. She pulled in another shaky breath. "I thought . . . it must be rather like pollinating a flower . . . isn't it?"

He rolled back his head and laughed, the sound emerging from deep within his chest. Stung by embarrassment, Juliet tried to get up, but his hands tightened, pinning her in his lap. She sat stiffly upright, conscious of his devastating nearness and aware of his superior knowledge.

"I'm so glad you find me amusing," she snapped.

The mirth slid from his face, though a certain softness lingered around his eyes. His palm cupped her cheek as if it were a rare orchid. "On the contrary, darling, I find you adorable."

The endearment dissolved the starch from her spine, though wariness remained. "I'm surprised a man of your experience could desire a woman so naive."

His eyes blazed with black fire. "I do, Juliet. I intend to show you just how much." Reaching to the water glass, he plucked out the orchid stem and studied it. His finger probed the mouth of one delicate flower, and for some obscure reason, heat suffused her. With a subtlety that made her quake, he feathered the velvet petals along her jaw. "Unlike flowers," he murmured, "people have been blessed with the ability to reap great pleasure from the act of procreation."

He lay the orchid stalk on the table, then his hand resumed that leisurely, alluring caress over her hip. She was aware of the inviting heat of his body, the hard circle of his arm, the sensual promise of his mouth. Hot and vibrant, yearning for him bloomed inside her.

"What do we do next?" she asked breathlessly.

"First we take our time about undressing. We have all night."

Slowly Kent pulled the pins from her hair, letting the heavy mass cascade down her back. Tangling his hand in her tresses, he held her still and caught her lips, his tongue gaining entry to the warmth of her mouth. The magic of his kiss spun her away into an exquisite realm of pleasure. Hypnotized by the need to bind herself to him, she wriggled closer, a growing restlessness making her shift in his lap, her hips twisting against his.

His growl of appreciation vibrated against her lips. With rough tenderness, his thumb probed the corner of her mouth. "Nectar," he murmured. "That's where you're akin to a flower . . . you offer me sweet nectar."

For long, lovely moments he sipped at her mouth; then he dropped small, stinging kisses over her face. He peeled the gown off her shoulders and down her arms, the crepe de chine slithering to her waist like a bud shedding its golden sheath. Cool air struck her skin; she had scarcely time to draw a breath before he pressed his lips to the wild pulsebeat in her throat.

Instinctively her hands lifted to shield her breasts. He drew her fingers away. "Don't cover yourself," he said. "You're too beautiful."

His mouth moved downward, caressing the soft swells above the lace-edged corset. The feel of his tongue against her flesh stoked the fire inside her; she tilted her head back and twined her fingers in his hair. His palm embraced her breast, and his heat burned through the stiff undergarment.

Seeing his dark head bowed over her bosom stirred a flurry of feelings inside her, feelings she could no longer repress, feelings that transcended the fear that he felt no more than physical desire for her. "I love you, Kent. I love you so."

The quiet words flowed past his passion and into his heart. Kent found himself forsaking the scented warmth of her breasts and lifting his gaze to hers. The adoration in her green eyes hurled him into a vortex of turbulent emotion.

He couldn't speak; he couldn't move. She regarded him with such trust, such tenderness, that his throat choked with guilt. Could he ever say those words back to her? The temptation to give her what she wanted almost overpowered him.

He swallowed hard. He couldn't lie to her. At least not about love.

What if she saw through his deception? Suddenly he could bear her rapt gaze no longer. He stood, his arms steadying her as her feet met the floor. She looked winsome yet sultry, her clothing in disarray, her cinnamon hair tumbling around her bare shoulders.

Bewilderment shadowed her face. "Kent?"

"Shh." His finger came down over her lips, the supple flesh still moist from his kisses. "Just a moment."

Releasing her, he stepped to the mantel and blew out the candles; darkness swirled through the room. In the faint moonlight, Juliet stood as silent as a silver shadow.

Yet she lured him like the brightest beacon.

With unerring ease, his hands found her slender waist. The gown and petticoats had fallen away, and her undergarments shone pale as her ivory skin. He pulled her to him, matching his hardness to her softness. His woman. His wife.

Clenching his teeth, he willed away a tide of tenderness. He tried and failed to summon satisfaction that he'd bested Emmett Carleton at last. No longer did Kent know which motive pulsed stronger inside him: revenge or passion.

She's only a woman, he told himself. In the darkness he could pretend she was not the daughter of his enemy but an anonymous female. Shadows would hide her wide-eyed innocence and his own self-loathing. He could forget the past and the future; he could sink into her warmth and lose himself, shed the suffocating blanket of shame and regret.

"Turn around," he muttered, even as his hands rotated her.

With unsteady fingers he plucked at her corset laces, but the complicated pattern baffled him. Christ, he should have had the foresight to unlace her in the light. A flash of memory blinded him. . . . He'd never undressed Emily like this . . . she had always waited timidly in bed with the covers drawn to her chin. . . .

Juliet's breathy laugh floated over her shoulder. "It might be simpler if I undid the front hooks," she said.

Through the shadows he saw the dark blur of her head; through the silence he heard the brush of her fingers on the fastenings. Feeling foolish and remorseful, he said stiffly, "You should have a lady's maid. It wasn't fair of me to ask you to leave with so little."

"So little? Kent, I have more than I'd ever dreamed of."

Though darkness veiled her expression, the fervor of her words made his chest ache with self-disgust. "Juliet, I wish—"

He stopped, unsure of himself. What *did* he wish? To shower her with the riches she'd relinquished for him? To be at liberty to promise her a lifetime of happiness? To rinse away his guilt and begin their marriage with truths instead of lies?

Like a kitten seeking affection, she rubbed her cheek against his shoulder. "I don't need wealth," she whispered. "We agreed that money didn't matter so long as we have each other."

The feel of her submissive body fueled the flame of his passion. Physical love, at least, he could offer her. "I want you," he muttered. "God help me, I want you so much."

Stepping behind her, he drew off the corset, leaving her clad in chemise and underdrawers. He put his hands beneath the froth of lace, splaying his fingers over the warmth of her abdomen and giving her a moment to accustom herself to the intimacy of his touch. Recalling her earlier alarm, he prayed that desire accounted for the swift rise and fall of her chest.

"Afraid?" he murmured.

"No . . . I want everything you can give me."

He was swamped by a need so fierce, he shook from it. In that moment he no longer knew or cared who he desired more, his wife or Emmett Carleton's daughter. Slowly he slid his palms upward until he cradled her bare breasts. He passed his thumbs over her nipples; both were pebble-taut. Her sharp intake of breath pierced the darkness. Angling her head, she cuddled her cheek on his chest and arched her spine, the action thrusting her breasts more fully into his hands.

Her ardent response shot fire through him. He wanted to toss her down, rip open his trousers, and plunge inside her. The fantasy enveloped him so thoroughly that he pulled her to the bed before reality penetrated. She was a virgin; he mustn't frighten her by unleashing the raw power of his lust.

Forcing a deep breath to clear his mind, he gently drew the chemise over her head. Moonlight filtered over the curves of her body, the full breasts, the narrow waist, the womanly hips. Under his scrutiny, Juliet held herself proudly, the earlier shyness gone. Before he could even reach for her, she pressed herself to him, tilting into the back-to-chest position he'd abandoned.

"Hold me, Kent . . . hold me as you did a moment ago."

He could no more resist her request than he could stop the blood from blistering his loins. His hands massaged her breasts again, but only for a moment. Lured by secrets beyond her realm of knowledge, he glided his palms downward, over her drawers, to trace the open seam between her legs. She flinched and gasped, her hands catching at his arms.

"Kent, what are you—?"

"Shush, darling . . . trust me . . . trust me."

Her muscles relaxed. Half turning her in his arms, he tipped up her chin and subjected her to a deep and drowning kiss. His fingers found her center, already hot and slick, and her sigh gusted against his mouth, her hips moving against his hand. Her passion startled and delighted him. He'd meant only to caress her a little, to help prepare her for his entry, yet her unrestrained response made him greedy for more.

"Kent, I've never felt so strange . . . so full of need. . . ."

"Give in to your feelings," he whispered. "Give yourself to me, darling."

Suppressing his own urgency, he stroked her in a slow, seductive rhythm. She twisted her face to his chest and moaned his name, her fingers clutching restively at his shirt. He sensed her need swelling in tempo with the savage pounding of his own blood. Somehow he found his back against the bedpost, his

arms supporting her weight, his fingers coaxing her
until she cried out, her body convulsing against his.

Her fulfillment infused him with primal exultation.
Holding her tight, he gritted his teeth and strove for
control. *Wait*, he commanded himself. *Wait a moment
for her to recover. By God, you owe her that much and more.*

Her breathing gradually eased. "Kent . . . that was
. . . I never imagined anything could be so glorious."

Gazing down at the pale oval shadow of her face, he
grinned, seized by the impulse to strut. "We're not
through yet."

"No?"

He rolled his hips against hers, the movement stinging him with a pleasure that verged on pain. "I've yet
to plant my seed, Lady Botanist."

"How—?"

"Don't ask so many questions," he chided gently,
reaching around to untie her drawers. "Some things
don't translate well into words."

He peeled away the wisp of cloth, then sat her on
the bed and knelt to remove her shoes and stockings.
The feel of her silken skin threatened his grip on himself. Keenly aware of her watching him, he shed his
own clothing and then pressed her down onto the mattress. He adjusted her lush body against his so that she
could not fail to feel the hard heat of his arousal.

A shiver passed through her; his belly clenched and
he lifted a hand to touch her cheek. "We'll go slow,
until you're ready."

She sighed, her hair a dark halo against the white
linen pillow. "I'm ready now," she said, and guided
his hand to the soft, sweet curve of her breasts.

Emily had never been so uninhibited. The memory fled
his mind as swiftly as it had entered. "Juliet . . . this
could hurt you the first time. I'll try to be gentle."

"You will be. I trust you."

Her certainty curled around his heart. She made him
feel like a youth again, unfettered by twisted secrets.
Bending his head, he kissed her long and slow, his
hands caressing her. He turned his mouth to her
breasts and suckled her until she arched her spine and

sighed his name. Instead of causing him to forget her identity, the darkness seemed to enhance his awareness.

No other woman tasted like Juliet; no other woman possessed her ripe curves. Each breath seduced him with her scent; each murmur of delight tempted his self-control. He stroked her moistness, and her thighs opened in instinctive invitation. Determined to hear her moan again with the ultimate pleasure, he held back his raging impulses until he sensed her readiness.

No longer able to contain himself, he pressed into her, breaching the barrier of her maidenhead. She cried out, clutching at his shoulders, and he paused, torn between remorse over hurting her and elation at her perfect satin sheath.

Limbs trembling, loins aching, he nuzzled her hair. "Darling Juliet . . . I didn't mean to be rough. . . . You're so small and I'm so—"

"Perfect . . . you feel perfect."

Her breath came hot and uneven against his throat. She moved her hips and he teetered on the brink of exploding. Sucking in a deep breath to temper his hot blood, he commenced the measured, unbearably magical rhythm. Her legs gripped him in a honeyed vise. Only when she uttered his name in a sobbing cry, her body racked by tremors, did he succumb to the lure of his own release, and reality fell away beneath a wild pulsebeat of ecstasy.

For a time he lay saturated in sweat and peace. Her body curved into his, her cheek nestled against his neck. Tenderness flowed through him, a tenderness that both stunned and scared him, a tenderness so powerful he wanted to weep. In consummating their marriage, he'd found an uncommon closeness, a rare rapport.

He'd found only extraordinary satisfaction, he corrected himself, because Juliet was such a responsive woman.

Yet he wanted to hold her like this forever, cloaked in dark anonymity, hearing her heart beat in rhythm with his, inhaling the jasmine aroma of her skin. And if their lovemaking bore fruit? The thought stunned him. Perhaps someday he would feel their baby kick within her womb—

As his child had moved inside Emily.

The vow of vengeance sucked all the joy from him. His muscles tensed with the need to escape the quicksand of memory. He started to lift himself from the bed. At the same instant Juliet stirred. Her soft arms encircled him, her gentle hands trapping him in a bond stronger than steel.

"*Now* I see what you meant," she said in sleepy surprise. "That wasn't in the least like pollinating a flower."

The declaration caught him unawares. Humor invaded his panic. He couldn't stop the chuckle that swelled deep within himself and somehow that awful pressure eased.

She swatted his chest. "Don't you laugh at me again."

He rubbed his cheek against her hair. "It's all right to laugh in bed. Don't take this too seriously."

"Mmmm," she murmured in contentment. "I like this side of you, Kent. Not so serious and bitter. I love you."

She pressed a kiss to his neck. His throat went taut, but she didn't seem to notice. She yawned and stretched, and he found himself turning onto his side, fitting her back to his chest and weaving his fingers through the silken spill of her hair.

What I love most about you is that you've been honest with me.

He tried to shake the disquieting feeling that he'd cheated her. He'd given her a title and the freedom to follow her own inclinations. Many marriages survived on less.

What would happen when she found out the truth?

He ought to tell her himself, but he couldn't force out the words that would lay bare his deceit. Yet once they reached Radcliffe, someone, sometime, was bound to let slip a telling fact. And when that happened . . .

He drew a heavy breath. Christ, she'd despise him. She'd run straight back to Emmett Carleton.

Opposing emotions raged inside Kent. His arms tightened around her. He didn't know if he wanted her to stay because of this powerful physical passion, or because he couldn't bear to surrender her back into his enemy's hands.

A baby would bind her to him forever. Suddenly the notion possessed a perfect, pleasing appeal. He wanted a second chance at becoming a father. He wanted a daughter with Juliet's brilliant smile or a son who'd tag along with him in the fields.

He shaped his fingers to the fertile curve of her hip. If she were ever to leave him, the courts would award him custody of his heir. The child would act as a magnet, luring her back to Radcliffe and her husband.

She snuggled against him, her breathing soft and even in slumber. The action was so trusting that a wave of self-loathing inundated him. He had no right to plot the direction of her life without offering her love. Yet he could not let her go.

A tide of exhaustion swept away his guilt. He pressed his chin to her fragrant hair and closed his eyes. Tomorrow was soon enough for regrets.

Tomorrow . . .

Chapter 7

She awoke to a lonely bed.

Lifting onto an elbow, the counterpane falling from her bare breasts, Juliet blinked groggily around the room. Sunshine poured through the window to bathe the simple furnishings with the golden radiance of midmorning. Only a depression in the adjoining pillow gave testimony that Kent had slept beside her.

Where had he gone?

Missing him already, she stretched, her limbs awash with luxurious laziness. The dishes had been cleared from the table, the clothing folded neatly on the chair. The forget-me-nots and orchids in the water glass reminded her of their intimate meal.

The innkeeper's wife must have crept inside to tidy the place.

Juliet blushed. No sound had penetrated her exhausted slumber . . . no clink of china, no creak of the floorboards, no click of the closing door. For the first time she had slept without a nightdress . . . for the first time she'd learned the wanton joy a woman experienced in the arms of the man she loved.

Swinging her naked legs over the side of the bed, she drew the counterpane around herself. Last night she hadn't been so modest. Last night she had burned with the fever of physical need. The memory brought an echo of that exquisite ache deep within her. Now she understood why an unchaperoned girl was forbidden to visit a man. Once seduced, she'd never again be content to live without that special intimacy.

A grin shaped her lips. She liked being married . . . yes, she did. Her steps quick and eager, she walked to the window and peered through the opening in the curtains. Sunlight washed the yard with the hazy hues of summer and glinted off the slate roof of an outbuilding. A pair of wrens flew busily in and out of the rustling leaves of the walnut tree. Tending their nest, Juliet thought, just as she and Kent would build a life together.

The fanciful comparison deepened her smile. Yet, silly or not, she looked forward to sharing every part of herself with him.

Abruptly Ravi and Hatchett walked out the doors of the stone stable. Ravi spoke to the coachman, who shrugged, scratching his salt-and-pepper hair. With a suddenness that startled her, the Indian tilted his turbaned head and looked up at her window. Even at a distance the malevolence in those dark eyes pierced her. Though the draperies concealed her, Juliet found herself shrinking back, her happiness shriveling.

She lifted her chin. His prejudice against the Carletons shouldn't disturb her. After all, she was a Deverell now, the Duchess of Radcliffe.

The thought infused her with trembly excitement, roused the urge to find her duke. Swiftly she drew on her undergarments, then the freshly ironed green gown, which hung from a hook near the door. After pinning up her hair, she hastened out the door.

Flashes of memory held her enthralled as she headed down the narrow staircase. Kent kissing her, Kent caressing her, Kent murmuring tender encouragement until that radiant pleasure had burst inside her. *Trust me. . . .*

She had, and he'd made her his woman. Even the odors of sour ale and lamp smoke smelled wonderful as she passed through the deserted taproom and went into the cool morning. She paused to inhale the exhilarating sweetness of the air, to relish the warmth of the sun. Alongside the country road, a blackbird tugged at a clump of chickweed, shaking loose the seeds and eating them.

Her shoes kicked up the hem of her skirt as she wandered toward the side yard. A fat bumblebee zoomed past, aiming straight at a patch of silverweed, the flowers bright yellow against the pale leaves. Rounding the corner of the inn, she saw the landau now parked outside the stable. His brawny back to her, Hatchett stood polishing one of the brass lamps.

At the opposite end of the yard, beneath the dappled shade of an oak, Ravi sat on a wrought-iron bench, the breeze stirring his gray robe. His spine was straight, his attention focused on the small book in his hands.

A reluctance to confront his malice kept Juliet rooted to the spot. Like a botanist guarding a new hybrid, she held fast to her happiness. Then she buried her reluctance. She must make a place for herself in Kent's life; she must nurture an amiable relation with his most trusted servant.

Head held high, she marched toward the Indian. He looked up, his muddy brown eyes studying her, but he made no move to rise.

She ignored the slight. "Good morning, Ravi."

He inclined his head, but said nothing.

"Would you know where my husband went?"

"Fishing."

She blinked at the river. "Fishing?"

"It is an amusement of his." He paused, one dark eyebrow cocked. "His Grace did not tell you of his passion for the sport?"

His disdain conveyed the message that she knew little of her husband's habits. Despite her determination to remain unruffled, Juliet felt embarrassment sting her cheeks.

"Which direction did he go?" she asked.

"He wishes to be left alone."

"I'm sure he wouldn't include me in such an order."

Ravi shrugged. "I tell you only his words, that no one must disturb him. No one."

The firm ground of her contentment quaked beneath a shock of doubt. What if Kent truly *didn't* want to see her? What if last night had meant no more to him than the gratification of physical desire, the securing of her as his wife? What if he'd found her too bold in comparison to his shy Emily?

Thrusting the book into a pocket of his robe, Ravi stood, his turbaned head towering over her. "Perhaps while you await the master's return, I might fetch you some breakfast?"

Triumph gleamed in his murky eyes. A sudden fury swept her, a fury that he dared to sow mistrust in her heart. "No, thank you," she snapped. "I intend to find my husband."

She started toward a copse of wych elms beyond the yard, but the bite of fingers on her arm brought her to an unceremonious halt. Stunned by Ravi's insolence, she jerked her eyes to his face and summoned all the hauteur she had seen her mother direct at a recalcitrant servant.

"Kindly remove your hand."

He made no move to comply. "You mean to go, after what I have told you?"

"Yes. I'll not tolerate your interference between my husband and me." Despite a thickening in her throat, Juliet kept her voice steady.

Eyes narrowed, he regarded her; she matched him stare for stare. A grasshopper hummed into the heavy silence and a breeze struck her hot cheeks. His grip slackened and Juliet stepped away.

"Memsahib."

The soft foreign word stopped her; she swung back to meet that inscrutable gaze. He pointed a dusky finger to the left, where sunlight glinted off the river.

"Walk that way," he said. "You will find His Grace on the bridge, where the river turns."

Wary, she tilted her head. "Why are you telling me now?"

He bowed, this time with the homage of a servant for his mistress. "Because perhaps the daughter is forthright . . . as forthright as the father is devious."

Stunned speechless, she watched as Ravi walked toward the stables, the robe swishing around his lean form. Her skin bristled. If he meant to compliment her, he'd chosen a backhanded manner. How dare he de-

nounce Papa as wicked when William Deverell had
dealt in stolen opium.

She caught herself. After the callous way Papa had
tried to deny her the man she loved, she shouldn't leap
to his defense. He had treated her like a choice piece
of property, rather than a cherished daughter. She
didn't trust Ravi's judgment, yet how well did she really know her father, the businessman?

Swallowing her uncertainty, she struck out toward
the elms. Now, more than ever, she needed to talk to
Kent. She needed to reassure herself that the closeness
of last night still existed, that their bond had been no
insubstantial dream. *Dreamspinner.* The pet name her
father had once called her slipped into her mind. But
no longer did she spin girlish fancies; now she ached
with a woman's longing, a woman's need for love and
companionship.

As she emerged from the trees, the dusty heat of the
morning enveloped her. She veered to the left, where
a water meadow stretched toward the river. The
mauve-pink grass heads blended with brick-red sorrel
blooms and purple thistle. Against the cloudless sky,
a hawk sailed, wings spread.

Lifting a hand to shade her eyes, Juliet peered ahead,
but a stand of chestnut trees hid the bend in the river.
She kept walking until she reached the bank, where
she picked a sprig of water mint and idly chewed it,
the taste sharp and refreshing. The beauty of the undergrowth called to her, the pink and white blossoms
of bramble, the red-brown buds of a figwort, the feathery white flowers of meadowsweet. Yet she pressed
onward, her steps quick, the need in her heart out-
weighing scientific curiosity.

Rounding the curve in the river, she came upon the
bridge that spanned the flowing water. Kent stood in
the middle of the small structure, his broad back to
her, his elbows planted on the stone arch as he plied
a fishing rod. The breeze fingered his black hair and
rippled the white shirt against his powerful shoulders.

A storm of longing drenched her. How well she recalled the feel of those naked muscles beneath her fin-

gertips. As her husband straightened to recast the fishing line, he caught sight of her. He turned to watch her approach, but with the sun dazzling her eyes, Juliet couldn't discern his expression. Driven by doubts and dreams, she walked toward him until her feet met the stone pavings of the bridge.

"Good morning, Kent." Before her courage withered, she added in a rush, "Ravi said you wanted to be left alone. I wondered if that order included me."

A swallow swooped past in a flurry of small brown wings. Beneath the bridge, water gurgled over the rocky bed.

Propping his fishing rod against the rail, Kent closed the few feet between them and extended a hand. "Of course not," he said, his tone smooth. "Ravi should have known that."

But she had caught his hesitation; it weighed her with indecision. Why did she so often sense he withheld a part of himself? Hadn't last night altered him in the same magical way she felt altered?

As he drew her up the gentle slope of the bridge, his palm, rough and warm, held hers. Sharp and sweet rose the memory of him caressing her, his fingers gliding with the sureness of expertise, coaxing a response until her body bloomed with pleasure. She longed for him to draw her into his arms, but to her disappointment, he loosened her hand and crouched to open a hamper.

"Would you care for some refreshment?" he asked, glancing up. "I'm afraid the tea is cold, but the oast cakes are fresh."

"Oast cakes?"

"A Hampshire specialty. Try one."

He handed her a flat, currant-studded biscuit, then poured her a mug of tea from a pottery jar. He seemed bent on keeping the mood impersonal, a situation that perplexed Juliet.

"Ravi called me memsahib," she said. "What does that mean?"

" 'The master's woman.' " His gaze penetrated

hers. "In India, it's a title of respect. He's accepted you as my wife."

"I wonder. Whenever he looks at me, I get the impression he's not seeing me . . . he's seeing a Carleton."

"Put him out of your mind," Kent said, an offhand edge to his voice. "You're a Deverell now."

As if to close the topic, he picked up his fishing rod and cast the fly in a smooth arc upon the water. Juliet sipped the tea to ease the dryness in her throat; she couldn't shake the uneasy feeling that she intruded upon his privacy.

Yet she had no intention of leaving.

Leaning on the stone ledge, she nibbled at the crusty oast cake and watched as the current carried the iridescent green hook-fly on a slow drift. A movement near the bank caught her eye. A fin flashed silver as a fish rose in the clear sunlit river and sucked in a live fly buzzing along the surface.

"There's one," she said.

"I see him." Kent reeled in his empty line. "That trout has been eluding me half the morning."

As he recast, she studied his profile, the planes of his face strong in the sunshine. The striking cheekbones and firm jaw looked so familiar, yet so foreign. She yearned to know every facet of his life, to explore his mind as she had explored his body. Could two people bare their souls as completely as they bared their bodies?

She crumbled the remains of the oast cake. "Are there trout streams close to the castle?"

"Radcliffe is on the Avon."

"Is that where you usually fish?"

"Yes."

He kept his gaze on the river. Despite his reticence, she kept on. "How long have you been out here this morning?"

"Hours. I'm a farmer . . . I always get up before sunrise."

"You should have awakened me. I'd have come with you."

He looked at her. "I couldn't bear to disturb you when you were sleeping so peacefully."

His smile bore a trace of the tenderness that had enthralled her last night, the tenderness that nourished her heart. Did he truly care for her beneath that mask of reserve?

Her fingers tensed around the mug of tea. "Do you fish much?"

"Not as often as I'd like. Gives me a chance to be alone with my thoughts."

"I can understand the need to be alone. Except . . ."

"Except?"

She took a deep breath of country air. "Why this morning after the closeness we shared last night?"

A neutral expression came over his face and he turned back to the river. "No particular reason. It's peaceful, that's all."

Dear God, was he already having misgivings about their impulsive marriage? She had to know. "Kent, why did you marry me?"

His dark eyes widened slightly; then he cocked his head in a watchful pose. "What do you mean?"

"You said you needed me, that you wanted me—"

"I do. Now more than ever."

His answer was too swift, too sterile, and he fixed his gaze on the river. Feeling as aimless as the hook-fly, Juliet cast about for the right words.

"Last night," she said slowly, "I felt closer to you than I ever have to any other person. You seemed to feel that closeness, too . . . you called me 'darling.'" Her voice went husky at the memory. "Yet today I have the impression you're unwilling to share all of yourself with me."

He shot her a glance, quick and unsmiling. "Because I came fishing? I assumed you needed your rest."

"Is that the only reason?"

"Marriage shouldn't deny us separate interests, individual pursuits. It isn't all moonlight and orchids."

"Marriage isn't all physical love, either. What if . . ." She paused, sickened by a fear she had never imagined in her girlish dreams. "What if someday your passion for me dies? What will be left for us then?"

His gaze jerked from the fishing rod to her. "I'll never stop wanting you, Juliet. You can be certain of that."

An unbearable longing beat in her throat. "But will you ever love me?" she whispered.

His eyes held hers as water burbled over the rocks and a squirrel chattered. Abruptly his free arm shot out to settle her snugly against the hard length of his body.

"Juliet . . . Juliet." He spoke over her head, his voice low and grating. "I don't know if I can ever love you the way you want me to. I thought you understood that when you agreed to marry me."

The heaviness to his voice burrowed into her heart. Dear God, how could she have forgotten that he'd once suffered the loss of an adored wife? She would simply have to work harder at healing his wounded heart.

Drawing back slightly, she touched his cheek. "I'm glad you've been so candid. I'd rather have that than a thousand false pledges of love."

His face tensed beneath her fingers and his gaze slid away to stare moodily at the river. "Maybe our life together won't always be easy, but I'll do my best to make you happy."

"You have," she said softly. "Believe me, you have."

"You'll have the freedom to pursue your botany," he went on, as if trying to convince himself. "We'll build a life together . . . you'll bear our children."

Joy warmed her as she imagined cradling their baby, a son with black hair and midnight eyes. His heir. "Yes," she breathed. "I want children so much."

His lips touched her brow. "Don't ever leave me, Juliet."

The harsh entreaty mystified her . . . until she realized he must be thinking of Emily again. She rubbed her cheek against his smooth linen shirt and cherished the hard-knit muscles beneath. "I'll be with you forever."

Taking her chin, he tilted her face to the bright heat

of the sun. His thumb caressed her lower lip; the rasp of his callused skin brought her skin to life. "You smell of mint," he murmured.

Then his mouth met hers and all rational thought melted under the heavy stroke of his tongue and the bruising urgency of his kiss. Her heart seemed to pound deeper and deeper within her body. Eager and willing, she arched her back and lifted onto her tiptoes—

Kent pulled abruptly away. "Good God!"

He seized the fishing rod with both hands. Swaying, Juliet steadied herself on the stone rail and peered down at the river. A loud splashing at the end of the line told her the trout was hooked. The fish shook its head from side to side and dove into the weeds.

"What's it doing?" she asked.

"Trying to dislodge the fly." He shot her a dazzling grin. "You must be good luck."

He focused his attention on reeling in the fish. Sunlight illuminated the absorption on his face. Exasperated yet entranced, Juliet contented herself with watching the play of muscles in his arms and chest until at last the brown trout lay wriggling and gasping soundlessly on the stones of the bridge.

With all the pride of a true angler, Kent crouched down and regarded his catch. "Ah, now there's a beauty."

"Poor thing," Juliet couldn't help saying.

He grinned up at her. "I seem to recall you ate trout for supper last night, Duchess, without the slightest qualm."

"I didn't have to watch it flopping about first."

"Well." Reaching inside the mouth, Kent extracted the hook. "We'll fix that, then."

Picking up the slippery fish, he flung it over the rail. A loud splash sounded as the trout landed in the river. With an insulted flick of its tail, the fish ascended to the surface of the water.

"Kent!" Aghast and amused, Juliet stared at him. "Why did you do that? You spent all morning chasing that thing."

"The thrill is over. Besides, I've no wish to offend my wife's tender sensibilities."

He winked, and the sensual slant of his mouth echoed the pleasure of the night before. Heat bathed her with the scandalous longing to lie naked beneath him, with the rough, warm stones of the bridge against her back and his lean, hard body stroking her hips and breasts.

She took a step toward him. "Make love to me, Kent."

He went still, his lashes half lowering. "I will . . . tonight."

"We're alone now. Couldn't we do it here . . . in the sunshine?"

"That's out of the question. We're hardly peasants to be rutting in the open countryside."

His brusque words hurt, yet when his gaze dipped to her bosom, the heavy heat of desire spurred her to recklessness. Not giving herself a chance to think, she gripped his forearm. "Please, darling, I'm your wife. Show me the joy we shared last night."

His muscles went rigid beneath her hand. "I'm sorry," he said stiffly. "You ask the impossible."

He turned away and began to collect his fishing gear. As sharp as the hook that he tossed into the hamper, pain pierced Juliet. Her passion drained away, leaving a hollow ache.

Slumping against the rail, she watched him; his brisk actions and inflexible features radiated disapproval. Did her impetuous outburst fail to meet his image of the demure wife?

Suddenly she could no longer bear the awkward silence. "Kent, surely you don't condemn me for admitting a perfectly natural desire."

Frowning, he straightened, hand on his hips. "I'm not condemning you for anything."

His cool manner crushed her; she let her gaze follow a martin swooping along the bank. "Yes, you are," she said. "Men don't care for boldness in a wife. I should have learned that from my own parents' behavior."

The liquid music of the river played into the silence. "Juliet, look at me."

The gentle exasperation in his tone lured her eyes to his face. To her utter amazement, a smile flirted at the corners of his mouth. Coming closer, he lifted a hand to her neck and his thumb passed over the pulsebeat in her throat.

"I thought scientists gathered all the facts before arriving at a conclusion," he said, his voice a husky murmur. "Don't try to second-guess what I like in a woman. Be yourself."

His gaze moved to her lips, her breasts, then back to her mouth. Passion burned in his eyes, a passion that made her heart clamor against her ribs. Her spirits lightened like the breeze that stirred his thick black hair.

"Then why did you refuse me?"

"Because I'll not chance any other man seeing what's for my eyes alone."

His possessive words made her toes curl with pleasure. Releasing her, he bent to pick up the hamper and fishing rod, then extended a hand. "Come, Duchess, I've yet to show you those forget-me-nots."

Touched that he'd recalled his promise of the previous evening, she slid her hand into his. They wandered along the bank, where sunlight filtered through the rustling leaves of chestnut and poplar and elm. Near a marshy bed of reeds stood the clump of forget-me-nots, the flowers playing host to several bumblebees. Kent picked a spray of the tiny blue stars and tucked it behind her ear. Charmed, she entwined her arm with his as they walked toward the rolling meadow. Wild roses abounded in the hedgerows and the call of a cuckoo enriched the summer air.

Her contentment held even as they spied the whitewashed walls and thatched roof of the inn. After a leisurely luncheon they started off in the landau. That day set the pattern for the ones ahead. Kent seemed determined to cater to her every whim. When she spied an early-blooming bush of purple loosestrife, he stopped the carriage and fetched her a stalk. When she happened to mention her thirst, he brought forth a basket of refreshments. When she asked him questions about Radcliffe, he obliged with a humorous commentary on the fine art of farming.

He told her little about his cousin and heir, beyond that Gordon was a scholar of philosophy who spent his days in the library, while his wife, Augusta, tended the district poor. For the first time, Juliet learned he had a sister, Rose. "We've never been very close," he said, "because she's nine years younger than me."

"Is she married?"

He shook his head. "I'd like to see Rose settled well, but she claims to have little interest in suitors. Since she's only eighteen, I haven't pressed the issue."

Juliet looked forward to having someone close to her own age at the castle. She interrogated Kent until he begged for mercy.

"I'll say no more," he teased. "You're to form your own opinions of my family."

The nights stretched into sultry hours of passion. She knew by the way he rarely lingered over supper that he was as impatient as she to shed the bonds of civility, to let loose the wild longings they held in check all day. Spending each night at a different inn, they made love with the darkness heightening their senses. She learned the texture of every part of his body; where he was hard, she was soft, and where he was rough, she was smooth. He explored her as well, bringing her to life in ways she had never before imagined, coaxing her with his mouth and hands until she whimpered and writhed in erotic abandon. She cherished the aftermath when they lay together in sated serenity, when she could fancy that their hearts and bodies and souls were joined as one.

Each morning she awoke to an empty bed. Farmer's hours, Juliet reminded herself to counteract a nagging sense of loss. Then would come the memory that he'd never returned her whispered words of love. And next she would tell herself to cease expecting too much too soon, to disregard the aloofness that sometimes shadowed his eyes.

Still, the days and nights seemed suspended in time, idle yet exciting, each moment a jewel to be treasured. Juliet wanted the interlude to last forever. Yet she also yearned to fit into the routine of his life, to see the castle his ancestors had built, to meet the other people who mattered to him.

Three days later, she awoke to a dismal morning with a gray sky that threatened rain. Happy despite the weather, she dressed quickly and joined Kent in the small dining room for breakfast; then they went for a stroll along High Street. The town of Chipping Campden typified the other Cotswold villages they'd passed through, with cramped buildings of honey-colored limestone, tall gables, and steep, tiled roofs. In the roadway, a swaybacked cob pulled a cart piled high with cabbages. The sidewalk teemed with life: housewives burdened with parcels, a boy racing after a dog, a workman trundling a wheelbarrow filled with nails.

From the wares displayed in front of a greengrocer's, Kent purchased a small sack of peaches. He plucked one out and handed it to Juliet. As they walked off, she caught the scrutiny of the shopkeeper and slanted an impish look at her husband.

"Everyone's staring at you," she whispered. "They probably find it hard to believe such a handsome lord would deign to mingle with the common folk."

He smiled as she took an unladylike bite of peach. "More likely they're wondering at the identity of my lovely companion. Dressed in gold, you're a ray of sunshine on this gloomy day."

Pleased that he could be so complimentary about her limited wardrobe, she teased back, "An odd description, considering my brown hair."

Slowing his steps, he cocked his head at her. "It's more red than brown . . . cinnamon, actually. That day you came to meet me at the Embankment, I remember having the same thought, that you reminded me of sunshine."

"Truly?"

He nodded. "You looked radiant and warm, pure as light."

His rare fanciful portrayal enchanted her. "I shouldn't be surprised," she murmured. "I was already half in love with you."

His eyes turned opaque. With a nod, he shifted his gaze to the street ahead. Sighing, she used a handkerchief to wipe the peach juice off her fingers. Would she ever mention love without her husband withdrawing?

The wrought-iron sign over a dressmaker's shop caught her attention. Inside the bow window, amid a rainbow array of fabric and notions, lay a small oblong patch of blue.

"Look, Kent," she said, pointing. "Maud would adore having that case to hold her eyeglasses. May we go inside and see it, please?"

He frowned at the item; then his eyes softened. "As you wish."

A bell tinkled overhead as they entered, and a matron in a white shirtwaist and gray skirt bustled out of the back. Upon seeing them, she paused, and a shrewd look came over her fleshy face, as if she were calculating the cost of their clothing and contemplating how much they might spend.

"Good morning. Might I show you some fabrics? I carry only the softest silks, the richest brocades." Her thimbled finger indicated the bolts of material behind the counter.

"Her Grace wishes to see the blue case in the window," Kent said.

The seamstress's eyes perked up at the title. "Oh, yes. Yes, indeed, Your Grace." She scurried to the window. "There you are, Your Grace," she said, handing the item to Juliet. "A fine piece you've selected. Did the beadwork myself."

As Juliet studied the pretty pattern of white bugle beads, the woman said, "You must be attending the Breedloves' weekend party."

"No."

Kent's haughty reply would have frozen a more sensitive woman; Juliet hid her amusement as the shopkeeper continued, "You're visiting Lord Wrocktonbury, then?"

"No."

"Ah well, even if you're only passing through, I do have a select number of ready-made gowns. I've just finished one for Lady Wrocktonbury's approval. . . . Perhaps I might show it to Her Grace instead."

Without awaiting a reply, she scurried into the back room and returned a moment later, her arms laden with a cloud of apple-green faille and cream satin. She shook out the dress, and Juliet caught her breath. Gold embroidery adorned the low-cut bodice, and loops of green ribbon embellished the sleeves and skirt. She fingered the sleek fabric and imagined herself the image of ladylike elegance as she descended from the landau to meet Kent's relations.

"It's exquisite," she said wistfully.

The shopkeeper's eyes gleamed with the anticipation of a sale. "Lady Wrocktonbury is rather wider in the waist, but given an hour or two, I can have the seams taken in to suit Your Grace."

"Could you?" Juliet flashed a smile at Kent, who stood behind her, his arms folded. "We can wait, can't we, please?"

"If you'll care to step into the back," said the woman, "I'll take your measurements—"

"I think not," he said.

Startled by the chilly refusal, Juliet swung fully toward him. Her excitement faded into perplexity, for his features were set into strict lines and his gaze drilled into the shopkeeper.

"Wrap the blue case for Her Grace," he instructed. "That's all we want today."

Disappointment pinched the seamstress's face. Bobbing a curtsy, she plucked the case from Juliet's hand. "As you wish, Your Grace."

As the woman carried the gown into the back room, Kent said in a stiff undertone, "I'm sorry, but I despise buying on credit. Perhaps after the harvest . . ."

Color burnished his cheekbones; regret darkened his eyes. Heat climbed Juliet's throat to scorch her face. Accustomed to purchasing whatever suited her whim, she'd forgotten their lack of money.

"Kent, I shouldn't have . . ." she whispered, her voice faltering. "The gown doesn't matter, really it doesn't."

Eyes hooded, he stared at her. "I'll see about having Augusta sew some things for you. It won't be the same as the wardrobe you left behind, but then, we don't entertain much at Radcliffe."

His image blurred; she blinked back tears. "I don't care about parties and fancy gowns."

He went on as if she hadn't spoken. "You might as well know that I lack the means to spend another night at an inn. We'll go home today."

The reappearance of the shopkeeper cut short the conversation. Watching Kent pay for the small parcel, Juliet realized he must be squandering the last of their coin to buy the trinket. She choked back a protest. It was awful enough to carelessly sting her husband's pride in private; she couldn't humiliate him in front of a stranger.

A week ago she had rarely given a thought to money. Now harsh reality demanded that she count every penny. The shift in circumstance aroused a fiery determination within her. More than any amount of wealth, she wanted Kent holding her close, Kent murmuring endearments in the heat of passion, Kent stroking her hair until she fell asleep.

She studied the noble tilt of his jaw. A sense of injustice stiffened her spine. He needn't suffer penury if she could give him her dowry. . . .

Juliet abandoned the half-formed notion. Papa would never relinquish the money; he must be furious over the elopement.

Under the force of another thought, alarm caught at her chest. What if Papa was waiting for them at Radcliffe?

Chapter 8

The medieval fortress loomed out of the mist. The gray light of late afternoon dulled the age-streaked stone, yet the ancient splendor of the castle caught Juliet's fancy. As the closed landau jolted over the rutted road, she pressed her face to the window and examined the octagonal towers and the crenellated battlements.

From which parapet had Emily fallen?

In her mind she saw the image of a woman stumbling against an embrasure and losing her balance, then plummeting to a rocky death. The joyous anticipation drained from Juliet. Shivering, she drew back and snuggled deeper into her braided jacket.

Kent placed a hand over hers. "Cold?"

Unwilling to share her morbid thought, she merely nodded. The damp chill in the air penetrated her bones; welcoming the warm security of his hand, she turned her palm to his.

"You'll soon be standing before a fire," he promised. "We're home at last."

He spoke softly, almost to himself. His eyes were fixed on the castle, though a clump of cedars now hid all but the jagged tops of the turrets. His intense expression bespoke pride and devotion. Her heart squeezed; she tightened her fingers around his. How he must love this rolling countryside, the heritage of the Radcliffes for hundreds of years.

A heritage that would one day belong to their children.

"Where are the fields?" she asked.

"Beyond that rise." He pointed to a great sweep of parkland that climbed a hill, where a few sheep grazed despite the drizzle. "Another week or two and it'll be haying time. Let's pray this rain stops soon."

"Why? Your crops surely need water."

Smiling, he tweaked her nose. "Don't you know, my Lady Botanist? If there's too much rain near cutting time, the hay can rot in the fields."

"I'd love to learn more about farming. This is my home now, too."

A new look entered his eyes, a blaze of possessiveness that heated her blood. "Yes, it is," he murmured.

He raised her hand and his mouth caressed the back. The warmth of his breath on her skin aroused the memory of those long, dark nights of passion. His masculine scent dominated the musty interior of the carriage. She turned to him, her palms seeking his hard chest and her lips brushing his jaw.

"Oh, Kent, I'm so glad we're married. Thank heavens you tried to end that silly feud. We might never have met otherwise."

The radiance in her eyes hit Kent like a stone. Shame crushed his good humor; dread oppressed his heart. His muscles went rigid under the strain of ruthless deceit. He felt like a fraud, a cheat, yet he couldn't form the words that would ease his emotional turmoil. How could he confess, anyway? The truth would only drive her back to Emmett Carleton.

When she found out, never again would Kent hold her close in bed, never again would he indulge this tug of tender affection, never again would he see love shining in her green eyes. . . .

"If I hadn't come along," he said, striving for a light tone, "you would have married someone else. Like as not, you'd have been just as happy."

"Married whom, Lord Breeton?" she scoffed. "I'd have been bored silly with his prattle of horses and fox hunts."

"Instead you'll be bored with my prattle of corn and hay."

"I'll never tire of you, my love."

She gently touched her mouth to his. The adoration on her face magnified his guilt, yet her honeyed taste and jasmine scent beckoned him as nectar lures a bee. He shouldn't desire her so much; only last night they'd made love . . . again and again. Yet somehow his arms looped around her and he found himself kissing her with all the frenzied passion of a man who'd endured years of celibacy.

She gave a whimper of pleasure and logic fled him. Time and place vanished beneath an explosion of the senses, the swift thrum of her heartbeat, the yielding of her breasts against his chest. Her need fired his own lust. He could lift her skirts, plunge inside the hot silken depths of her body. . . .

And take his wife in a carriage, like a common whore? His vow to avenge Emily's death must have robbed him of all conscience and decency.

Tearing himself free, he rolled his head back against the leather cushion and gulped in air. He was hot for her because she was Emmett's daughter. Yet somehow the thought didn't ring true. Christ, would he never get enough of Juliet Carleton?

Deverell, he corrected himself. *Juliet Deverell.*

"Yes," she said. "I'm a Deverell now."

Only then did Kent realize he'd spoken aloud. Straightening, he absorbed the youthful luster of her face, a luster that made him feel old and jaded, a luster that made him fight the urge to avoid her eyes. Guilt and fear pressed into him again, the mix of dark emotions converging into the resolve to bind her to him.

She'd find out soon enough. . . .

"You'll stay a Deverell," he said. "Forever."

His steadfast words elated Juliet. He hadn't confessed to undying love, but she sensed a need in his heart, a need that might someday overcome his fear of loving again.

The clopping of hooves took on a hollow sound. Glancing out the window, she saw the landau pass over a drawbridge and under the vaulted stone gate of an opened portcullis. Hands shaking with anticipation, she smoothed her hair and skirt. Would his relations accept Emmett Carleton's daughter in their midst?

A moment later, the carriage creaked to a halt and

Ravi helped her down. He stared at her before walking away to help Hatchett unload the baggage. Unwilling to let the servant spoil her eagerness, Juliet turned to inspect her new home.

Immense and deserted, the courtyard bore the fresh scent of the country. Weeds formed clumps of rain-washed green, and a few geese pecked the muddy ground. In one corner stood an old fountain, the nymph statue gone jade with rust, her tilted urn empty. Juliet craned her neck to view the fortress. Ancient buildings adjoined the outer walls; tall arched windows were carved into the crumbling gray stone. Instead of the square medieval keep she'd expected, the structure looked more like a rambling manor house. As the cool mist struck her cheeks, she could see the crenellated battlements and towers that pierced the clouded sky. Without the smoke curling from one of the chimneys, she might have thought the place abandoned.

A distant scream rent the air. Heart pounding, she swung around.

"Peacock," Kent said, stepping closer. "In the garden outside the south wall. My father imported a pair from India."

She shuddered. "It sounded almost human."

"You're not the first to think so," he said dryly. "Shall we go inside?"

A sudden thought made Juliet lift a hand to her throat. "Kent, what if my father is here?"

"I'll deal with him. We're married now, and there isn't anything he can do to change that."

Kent was right, yet apprehension churned in her stomach as he guided her around the puddles in the yard. Just as they reached the vaulted entryway, a massive oak door opened and a woman stepped out.

Tall and thin, she wore a gown of green serge that brought to mind a scrawny stalk of nettle. Her ginger hair had been scraped back into a bun, accentuating the craggy contours of her face. A mole marred her cheek, yet like a lovely bloom on a weed, the hyacinth hue of her eyes saved her from utter homeliness.

She dipped a surprisingly graceful curtsy for a

woman who appeared so ungainly. "Welcome home, Your Grace. May I say, you've been greatly missed."

With a faint smile, he acknowledged the greeting. "Augusta. I trust you received my telegram yesterday."

"Of course." Pivoting toward Juliet, Augusta curtsied again. "Felicitations on your marriage, Your Grace. Welcome to Castle Radcliffe."

So Augusta already knew Kent had wed the daughter of the Deverells' enemy. Her eyes were a blank blue mirror and her mouth retained a civil smile. No animosity there, Juliet thought, yet no warmth, either.

"Juliet," Kent said, "I'd like you to meet my cousin-in-law, Mrs. Augusta Deverell. Augusta, my wife, Juliet."

Augusta stood in deferential silence. Water plopped from the roof in a slow but steady rhythm. Juliet felt as if she were being cataloged, from the top of her fashionably styled hair to the hem of her gold gown. If only she could have worn that exquisite apple-green frock . . .

Quelling the thought, she reminded herself that deeds, not dress, would gain her acceptance. "It's a pleasure to meet you, Mrs. Deverell."

"The pleasure is all mine, Your Grace."

Unable to bear the suspense, Juliet searched for a discreet way to find out if her father was present. "Have you received any messages for me?"

Augusta arched her ginger eyebrows. "Not a one. Were you expecting to hear from someone?"

Relief along with an undeniably bitter disappointment coursed through Juliet. So Papa hadn't cared enough to come after her. "I thought . . . no, I suppose not."

"I've a fire in the Laguerre drawing room," Augusta said to Kent. "Will you join me for tea?"

"Thank you. My wife is quite chilled after our long, rainy ride."

Nodding, Augusta marched inside.

Following with Kent, Juliet entered a great chamber, chilly and dim-lit. A musty scent pervaded the air. The walls were barren save for a few deer trophies and an ancient tapestry depicting a hunt scene. From the tim-

bered ceiling, gargoyles stared down in stony silence.
The vastness of the hall fascinated her; it would swallow more than twice the space of the Carleton foyer.

They tramped along what seemed like miles of
murky corridors. Spine erect, Augusta led the way, her
long strides keeping her a short distance ahead. Juliet
wondered if resentment or a natural stiffness of posture squared the woman's shoulders. Their footfalls on
the stone flags formed a chorus of echoes, the clump
of Augusta's shoes, the ring of Kent's boots, the tap of
Juliet's slippers.

Looking at her husband, she whispered, "How do
you find your way around?"

His smile gleamed through the gloom. "I was born
here. We played tag and hide-and-seek in these halls."

"We? Who did you play with?"

As if frozen by the drafty air, his smile withered.
"Friends . . . and my cousin Gordon came to visit
sometimes."

Augusta halted before a doorway. "I'll fetch the tea
myself," she said. "Can't depend on Fleetwood these
days."

She started to turn away when a blur of movement
erupted from the doorway. The whirl resolved into a
small, short-legged dog with a shaggy brown coat. The
Pekingese planted himself before Augusta, cocked his
squat face at Juliet, and uttered a menacing growl.

"Hush, Punjab," Augusta said mildly. "Come along
now."

She walked off, the dog trotting at her heels.

Amused, Juliet said, "He certainly means to protect
her."

"Don't take Punjab to heart. He reacts that way to all
strangers." Kent waved to the doorway. "After you."

She entered an octagonal drawing room. Like the
rest of the castle, the chamber smelled of damp. Mullioned windows spilled watery light through glass set
in thick stone casements. From the graceful Queen
Anne chairs to the fruitwood tables, the aura brought
to mind the elegance of the eighteenth century, now
gone shabby. Pillars studded the cedar-paneled walls,

the gilt on the capitals chipped. Spread across the high ceiling was a fresco depicting an age-dulled assembly of gods frolicking against a backdrop of clouds.

Kent followed the direction of her gaze. "Painted by Louis Laguerre, late seventeenth century. A pity we can't remove it and sell it."

"Have you sold other art treasures?" she asked, glancing at a wall where a large square shone lighter against the yellowing varnish.

"Only a few. The second duke added most of Radcliffe's furnishings to the entailment, which by law remains intact from generation to generation. At least you'll have a bed to sleep in and chairs to sit on."

His faintly sardonic tone bothered her. Did the treasures mean so little to him, or was he hiding his pain at parting with them? Sympathy swept her. He lacked the luxury of preserving the Deverells' proud heritage; the priceless antiques would be snapped up by the acquisitive nouveau riche like her father. If only she had the means to help Kent refurnish the castle . . .

"We're in one of the towers, aren't we?" she asked.

He nodded, then crouched to add a log to the low-burning fire. "Bosworth Tower. In honor of an ancestor who fought against Richard the Third at Bosworth."

Walking close to him, Juliet welcomed the warmth of the blaze. She glided a finger over a peacock cut into the marble chimneypiece, part of a whimsical Indian motif of strange gods and writhing serpents. "Yet the mantel dates much later."

Glancing up at her, he said, "This was my father's favorite room. Before the family money ran out, he had the mantel added."

Again, mockery shaded his voice. Did it bruise his pride to bring his wife to such dilapidated surroundings? "The castle is charming," she said firmly. "You're fortunate to be master of a place so rich with history."

Straightening, Kent studied her, his expression watchful. She sensed a turmoil of emotion in him, a need for her. She held her breath as he lifted a hand as if to caress her.

"Juliet, I hope ''

The tramp of footsteps came from the hall. To her intense disappointment, his hand dropped to his side and his gaze veered to the doorway. A white-haired retainer entered, his gaunt arms precariously balancing a huge silver tea tray.

Augusta hovered near his frayed sleeve. "Do take care, Fleetwood. That set is an heirloom."

"Yes, madam," said Fleetwood, his tone long-suffering.

The Pekingese trotted behind, so close he threatened to entangle himself in Fleetwood's feet. Unperturbed, the old servant shuffled forward, the china and silver clinking. Juliet found herself sighing in relief as he managed without mishap to lower the tray to a fruit-wood table near the hearth.

Tall and thin as a silver birch, Fleetwood turned to Kent. "Welcome home, Your Grace. Mrs. Fleetwood and I should like to extend our best wishes to you and Her Grace."

With a cool ducal nod, Kent accepted the congratulation. "I brought a pair of field glasses for your bird-watching. And some apricot cordial for your wife. Ask Ravi to fetch them for you."

The butler's wrinkled face broke into a gap-toothed grin. "Bless you, Your Grace, for remembering."

"Run along now," Augusta said, clapping her hands as if chiding a lazy child. "You may take Her Grace's wrap with you."

Juliet considered countermanding the order, but something in those narrowed hyacinth eyes stopped her. Of course, Augusta must resent relinquishing to a Carleton the role of chatelaine. Deciding to exercise prudence for now, Juliet surrendered the braided jacket and sank onto a threadbare settee. A few feet away, Punjab settled onto an old crimson cushion by the fire, his beady black eyes regarding her suspiciously.

"Do fetch Mr. Deverell," Augusta said, as Fleetwood ambled toward the door. "We don't want his tea to go to waste."

"Yes, madam."

"I brought gifts for you and Gordon, too," Kent said, lowering himself to the settee.

"Thank you, but you shouldn't have spent the money." She swept toward the table and stopped, staring stiffly at Juliet. "Would you care to pour?"

As the new mistress, Juliet knew the duty now belonged to her. Yet she shook her head. "Go ahead."

Augusta bent to the task. "There, Your Grace," she said, handing a cup to Kent. "Just the way you like it, without cream or sugar."

"Thank you."

Silently she served Juliet and passed around a tray of cakes; then she sat in a wing chair and reached into a basket of needlework. Punjab leapt up, yapping shrilly.

Augusta set aside her sewing. "Forgive me, my little darling. Did Mama forget you?"

Rising, she poured a saucer of tea, added a dollop of cream, and set it beside the dog, who slurped lustily at the liquid.

Watching her pat the animal's head, Juliet sipped her tea to keep from smiling. Their affection held a certain reassurance, for at least it revealed a chink in Augusta's armor. Juliet glanced at Kent to see his eyes gleaming over his cup; he, too, looked amused by the dour woman and querulous dog.

"Kent tells me you devote much of your time to the needy."

"I do what little I can," Augusta said, resuming her seat and jabbing her needle into a tiny white shirt.

"Don't be so modest," he said. "Augusta clothes half the babies in the district."

"Oh, poppycock," she demurred, though her waspish expression lost some of its sting.

Juliet set down her cup. "May I see?"

As she walked to Augusta's side, Punjab growled.

"Hush," said Augusta, a fond smile touching her lips. The dog quieted, but continued to glower, his bulging eyes fixed on Juliet.

"I doubt I could match your fine stitching," she said, "but I'd like to help in other ways."

"What could a city-bred lady possibly do?"

"Grow vegetables to help feed the poor. Or fruit to make jams and jellies. Our cook has an excellent recipe for gooseberry jam."

Augusta tipped back her head, the mole on her cheek prominent as she regarded Juliet dubiously. "Perhaps you don't realize the work your offer entails, Your Grace. These people live in far humbler circumstances than a lady could imagine."

Smiling, she sat beside Kent. "My constitution is perfectly strong. I assure you, I'm not likely to swoon."

"You do too much," Kent told Augusta. "Let Juliet help you. She can accomplish anything she sets her mind to."

His affectionate regard warmed her far more than the bracing cup of tea. At moments like this, she could believe he hovered on the verge of admitting her into his heart—

"I'd be pleased to accept your assistance, then," Augusta said tonelessly.

Juliet could not read the expression on that unlovely face. What thoughts swirled behind those uncommon blue eyes? What would life be like with the dour Augusta? She felt a sudden longing for Maud's blithe chatter. . . .

A man ambled into the drawing room. His shoulders drooped and his hands hid in the pockets of a maroon smoking jacket. From the untidy state of his thinning brown hair to the pencil stuck behind his ear, she guessed he'd been interrupted at his work. He peered vaguely through thick, round spectacles.

"Hullo," he said, his expression confused. "I observe you've returned to your domicile, Kent." The magnified eyes shifted to Juliet. "And who might you be?"

Kent straightened. "Juliet, this is my cousin, Gordon Deverell. Gordon, my wife."

Augusta frowned at her husband with the same maternal disapproval she'd directed at Punjab. "Don't you remember the telegram I showed you, Gordon?"

He stared, his countenance oddly dreamy. He lifted his shoulders in a sheepish shrug. "If you allege so, my dear, then it must be a certainty. I confess I've been immersed in *The Origin of Species*. Quite the engrossing study—"

"Descended from the apes," Augusta snorted, setting aside her needlework to pour another cup of tea. "Such poppycock is enough to curdle the cream."

He wilted into a chair and fixed his gaze downward, as if the threadbare carpet contained a scholarly dissertation. Was this the playmate of Kent's childhood? Juliet tried to picture Gordon as a boy, playing tag within the castle walls. But she couldn't imagine this deflated man as a robust youngster. He looked so defenseless that she felt compelled to speak out.

"I'm familiar with Darwin's treatise on the fertilization of orchids," she said. "Perhaps, Mr. Deverell, you would be so kind as to tell me more about his evolutionary theory sometime."

He blinked, his eyes owlish behind the spectacles. "Er . . . yes, I should be delighted to expound upon the topic."

"Juliet has great regard for scientific inquiry," Kent said, placing an arm across the back of the settee. "You see, she's a botanist."

"Really?" Augusta's voice held a note of disapproval as she marched past to hand the cup to her husband. "And your parents allowed such unladylike studies? How very singular."

"Yes," Kent agreed with steely softness, "I find her uniqueness laudable. I admire a woman who refuses to be trapped by the narrow-minded precepts of society."

Color washed Augusta's rough-hewn cheeks; she bent to pick up the plate of sandwiches. "Yes, Your Grace. I'm sure you're right. You always did favor newfangled ideas."

She kept her eyes downcast as she passed the plate. Emotions seemed to roil beneath her sour surface. She must resent a stranger coming in and disrupting her tidy world.

Juliet turned her gaze to Gordon. What an odd pair. If Augusta were a nettle, tall and prickly, Gordon was a pennywort, short and meek. Only when he fumbled with his cup did Juliet notice his hands. Her stomach took a sickening plunge. Though Gordon Deverell was barely middle-aged, his fingers were gnarled like an old man's, the joints lumpy and swollen. He managed to lift the cup to his lips, but as he lowered it, his awkward grip splashed tea down his brown trousers and onto the chair.

"Gracious!" Augusta exclaimed, hastening to set down the plate. "Can't you be more careful? That chair is an antique."

Looking bewildered, he stood. "I didn't endeavor to spill, my dear. It just happened."

Juliet snatched up a napkin and sponged at the dark splotch on the faded brocade seat. "I'm sure it'll come clean. If not, I'll write and ask my mother for her stain-removing formula."

"There's no harm done," Kent said. "Take your seats, everyone."

Augusta plopped back down and seized her sewing. "Please don't bother your mother with our rural disasters. I'm sure she must be a busy woman, what with all those society receptions."

A thread of query lifted her tone; she must itch to know more about the Carletons. Let her wonder, Juliet thought uncharitably as she settled back down.

"Mama would be delighted to share her knowledge," she said, ignoring the shaky ground beneath her words. Had Papa's hatred corrupted Mama as well?

"I should like to make the acquaintance of your parents," Augusta persisted. "Will they be coming to visit soon?"

Juliet blinked in surprise. "You can't truly expect my father to pay a friendly call *here*."

"I beg your pardon." Augusta drew herself erect. "Is there a reason he shouldn't deign to visit the household of the Duke of Radcliffe?"

Kent leaned forward. The skin taut over his cheekbones, he stared at her. "Yes, there is a reason," he said quietly. "You see, her father is Emmett Carleton."

Chapter 9

Punjab growled as if the very name incensed him. Augusta's jaw worked like a trout's. The fire crackled in the stupefied lull.

Juliet knew with bitter certainty that Kent's telegram had withheld the identity of his bride. Resentment stabbed her. Why hadn't he warned her that his relatives didn't know who she was?

Astonished hyacinth eyes bored into her. "Carleton?" Augusta sputtered. "*You*, a Carleton?"

Gordon clasped his gnarled hands. "Uncle William wouldn't have endorsed such an alliance, Kent. I advised you so once before—"

"My father is dead," Kent snapped. "And so is the feud."

"Is it?" Augusta said, the mole on her cheek quivering. "Or have you carried William's quarrel into the second generation? Have you added yet another page to his vile volume of hatred?"

A small gasp came from the doorway. "How dare you, Cousin?" spoke a feminine voice.

Turning, Juliet saw a girl standing there, her delicate face framed by a halo of loose sable hair. Her fingers clutched at the lace fichu tucked into the neckline of her modest gray gown.

Rose. Juliet guessed her identity from the family resemblance in the dark coloring. Deep inside, she felt the impact of those large, liquid brown eyes. Yet the girl was staring not at her, but at Augusta.

"How dare you speak ill of my father," said Rose, her features dainty yet determined as she stepped inside the circle of chairs.

Punjab growled again; Augusta sat bolt upright. "I spoke nothing untrue. William Deverell brought about his own downfall by being so obsessed with his own superiority. He couldn't bear to be bested by a commoner."

"You always were jealous of the duke because your own father was a mere knight."

Augusta tipped her sharp nose into the air. "You're one to speak of bloodlines—"

Kent cut her off with a slashing gesture. "Stop this squabbling immediately. You're hardly giving a favorable impression to my wife."

Augusta opened her mouth, then clamped it shut. Rose blinked, her eyes gone glossy with tears.

"Forgive me, Kent," she said. "I . . . I forgot myself. It's just that I can't bear to hear Father's memory sullied so."

His forbidding expression relaxed; he shot to his feet and slid an arm around her slight shoulders. "You're forgiven. Now come, meet my bride."

He looked the caring older brother, Juliet thought as she got up. With her high cheekbones and solemn eyes, Rose was a dainty version of Kent. As he executed the introductions, Juliet saw reflected on Rose's face a veiled curiosity, a wistful interest that promised friendship.

On impulse, Juliet took the girl's smooth hand. "I'm so happy to meet you. I've always wanted a sister."

The slim fingers tensed; she lowered her eyes. "Yes, I'd like that, too," she said, drawing her fingers back. "I had a sister once—"

"Augusta," Kent cut in, "please pour a cup of tea for Rose."

Lips pinched, the woman started to get up.

"You needn't bother," Rose said stiffly. "I've already had mine, in my room."

Her eyes flicked to Augusta and Juliet wondered if animosity had prompted the refusal. The girl's soft, sad demeanor caught at Juliet's heart. So there had been another Deverell sister. A sister who'd died? Judging by the way Kent had interrupted, he clearly considered the matter closed. Propriety precluded her asking any questions on a topic of such delicacy. Yet she couldn't help wondering what else he might be hiding.

"Perhaps I may escort you to the state apartments, Your Grace," said Rose.

"Please, call me Juliet." Weary of battling the undercurrents of hostility, she yearned for escape. "And yes, I'd like to rest before dinner, if everyone will excuse me."

Augusta nodded stiffly; Gordon blinked benignly; Punjab glared balefully.

Kent touched Juliet's arm in an absentminded caress that sent hot chills over her skin. "I'll join you later," he murmured. "I've a few estate matters to attend to first."

His inky eyes seemed distant. Longing swept her, a longing for the dark of night, when she would gain his total attention. Subduing her impatience, she started toward the door.

"Mind you don't light more than one candle," Augusta called. "We can't afford extravagance."

"For pity's sake," Kent said in a low voice.

Juliet missed the rest of his words, for she and Rose entered the shadowy hall. A grimace tautened the girl's milk-pure complexion. "That woman ought to be gagged," she muttered. "What a skinflint she is!"

"Perhaps she only means to look out for Kent's interests."

"Then she should stop embarrassing him with her penny-pinching ways. He can certainly afford a few measly candles." She tilted a keen-eyed glance at Juliet. "Especially now."

"Now?"

"Well, you're an heiress, aren't you?"

The echo of their footfalls filled the stone passageway as Juliet searched for a polite response. "I'm not so certain about that," she said. "My father didn't exactly give his blessing to our marriage."

"You mean because Emmett Carleton couldn't tolerate knowing his daughter has joined the Deverell fold.''

Juliet shivered, as much from the ice in Rose's voice as the chill in the air. She imagined Rose growing up exposed to the same sort of twisted stories about the Carletons as Juliet had heard of the Deverells. What an awful legacy her father and William Deverell had wrought with their rivalry.

"I'm sure my marriage is difficult for Papa to accept,'' she said. ''But I hope, given time, we can all bury the past.''

Rose stared. ''Yes, I'm sure you're right,'' she said, sounding reflective, as if the possibility were appealing. ''You said you haven't any sisters. Do you have brothers?''

"No, I'm sorry to say—''

"Then surely your father won't cut off his only child. At the very least, he'll have to endow you with a rich settlement.''

"Even if he did, Kent would never accept the money.''

"He'll have to,'' she said with a dismissive flutter of her hand. ''My brother always champions his impoverished tenants. He can't in all conscience turn down your dowry. The Deverells will prosper again, as we've done for centuries.''

A wistful smile curved her lips; Juliet didn't have the heart to prick the girl's dream. Much as she, too, wanted to help the estate, she doubted that Papa would dower her. Casting about for another topic, she glanced at the gilt-framed portraits on either wall of the narrow passageway. Stern men in stiff Elizabethan ruffs stared; haughty women in jeweled coiffures glared.

"Are all these people Radcliffe ancestors?''

Rose gave a proud nod. ''Illustrious people form the branches of our family tree . . . aristocrats, diplomats. The Deverells have always had a strong sense of public duty. My great uncle was governor of Bombay.''

"Kent told me the family has a tradition of interest in India.''

"The second duke made a fortune there through the

East India Company. We can even claim royal blood. See there?''

She pointed to a large portrait dominating the base of a stairwell. Lusterless with age, the painting depicted a dapper gentleman with a wealth of dark, curling locks tumbling to his crimson and blue cloak.

Juliet slowed her steps. ''He looks familiar.''

''He should . . . that's Charles the Second. The seventh earl of Ashingham wed one of the king's bastard daughters and became the first Duke of Radcliffe.''

''Expedient,'' Juliet said dryly.

''Perhaps,'' Rose conceded, as she led the way up the age-worn stone steps. ''I've been compiling a family history, and I've come to the conclusion that we're quite the freethinking lot. We've had more than our share of rogues and eccentrics. And the first duke wasn't the only one to wed a bastard.''

Slyness glinted in Rose's brown eyes . . . or was it a trick of the fading light? Graciously Juliet said, ''Oh?''

''Yes, didn't Kent tell you? His first wife was of illegitimate issue.''

Her heart clenched as she recalled Lord Breeton's portrayal of Emily Deverell: *Born on the other side of the blanket, poor thing . . . she was prone to melancholia.*

Was bastardy at the root of Emily's despair? Had a lack of self-honor driven her to suicide? Questions crowded Juliet's mind, but civility kept her from probing the issue until she knew Rose better.

''Yes,'' she said, ''Kent told me.''

Pausing at the head of the stairs, Rose arched her eyebrows. ''And you don't mind?''

''Of course not. Why should I?''

She afforded Juliet a measuring look, then shrugged. ''I suppose I'd expected you to be shocked, having been raised in polite society.''

Pivoting in a whisper of gray skirts, Rose headed down another murky corridor. Clearly she'd been testing her new sister-in-law. Juliet renewed her vow to prove to the Deverells that a Carleton was neither haughty nor prone to holding grudges.

Rose opened an oak door, and they entered a sitting room. The chairs and sofas were upholstered in faded green, the satin on the walls rotting in spots. As in the drawing room, the vaulted ceiling held a painting, this one of nymphs and porpoises cavorting in sea foam.

"This is the Alcove," Rose said, walking across the faded carpet to a gilt-framed door. "And here's the duchess's chamber."

She marched into a huge bedroom, Juliet following at a slower pace, her neck craned in awe. Dominating the gloomy grandeur of the room was the bed with its green and gold hangings of Utrecht velvet; she spied a few moth holes. Across the mattress lay an embroidered counterpane, and ducal coronets graced the bedposts. Even the looking glass and writing desk bore the Radcliffe crest. A great chandelier drew her eyes to the ubiquitous painted ceiling and cobwebbed cornices.

"You've a dressing room through there," Rose said, pointing. "And that door leads to Kent's suite. When we heard yesterday that you were coming, Augusta had the place aired and the linens freshened."

Juliet could scarcely credit that; a smell of mildew pervaded the room. She turned her attention to a series of drawings arranged above the mantel. Strolling nearer, she saw several romantic studies of the castle.

"Don't touch those drawings," Rose said, hurrying over. "I only just hung them this morning."

Wondering at the girl's protectiveness, Juliet said, "The sketches are lovely. They're your father's work, aren't they?"

"Yes, I had them framed and placed here." The pride Rose took in William Deverell's talent glowed in her eyes. "How did you recognize his style?"

"Kent showed me a portfolio of drawings that he found in your London town house."

"Some new ones?" Her voice breathless with excitement, Rose took a step forward. "Did he bring them back here, to Radcliffe?"

"I don't know—"

"I must go ask him immediately. If he shuts himself in the estate office, it'll be hours before he emerges."

She started toward the door. "Oh, I nearly forgot. Dinner is at eight-thirty. When Ravi sounds the gong, just follow the stairs back down and turn left. Do excuse me."

She darted out, her sable hair swaying.

Juliet shook her head and smiled. She didn't quite know what to make of the girl; her mood was alternately furtive and friendly, sly and sincere. Ah, well, she'd get to know Rose better soon.

She poked around, opening the drawers of a gilt desk and peeking into the dressing room. There wasn't a single personal item left from Emily. The knowledge left Juliet with an oddly mingled sense of curiosity and relief.

She wandered to one of the windows, recessed in deep stone. Pushing back the dusty velvet drape, she wrestled with the latch. With a jarring creak, the window swung open. She leaned on the casement and drew in the moist, moss-scented air. The room commanded a breathtaking view of the Avon, now a gray glimmer in the twilight. Great stands of willow and cedar overhung the water, along with clumps of underbrush, unidentifiable in the deepening gloom. Tomorrow, Juliet thought, she'd go exploring and find the south garden and the greenhouses.

A faint shriek pierced the liquid murmur of the river. Though logic told her the sound emanated from one of the peacocks, she shivered. The ancient ambience somehow set her nerves on edge.

Intent on ridding the room of its stale odor, she went from window to window, flinging each wide open. The breeze fluttered the drapes and bed hangings, and chilled the air. Longing for the cheering warmth of a fire, she searched for a bell cord to call a servant, but saw only the frayed end dangling from the ceiling. She subdued her irritation. She could manage alone; often enough she'd watched a house maid light the bedroom fire.

In the grate, coals lay neatly stacked atop a few sticks of kindling. Juliet found a box of matches and knelt to execute the task. Despite try after try, the green wood

failed to ignite. She burned her finger; tears of frustra
tion stung her eyes. Sitting on her heels and sucking
her finger, she felt inundated by a flood of homesick-
ness, a longing for the bright, familiar walls of Carleton
House, for attentive servants and fresh gowns, for
Mama's comforting presence and Maud's cheery gossip.

The thickening darkness of the room added to her
utter isolation. Nothing in her upbringing had prepared her for becoming mistress of such an archaic
household. Nothing had prepared her for coping with
the shrewishness of Augusta, the contempt of Ravi,
the capriciousness of Rose.

Juliet squared her shoulders. This was Kent's home
and hers now, as well. She wouldn't let her own un-
certainties daunt her. The castle was like a neglected
garden; with tender care and devoted nurturing, she
could coax life back into its timeworn walls and happiness into its emotion-scarred occupants.

With renewed vigor, she struck another match and
applied it to the kindling. Long moments later, a tiny
flame licked at the wood. Soon the coals gave off a
blessed, blazing heat.

Shadows snaked in the corners of the antiquated
chamber as she closed the windows. Carrying a single
candle to the dressing room, she found her hatbox on
a rickety dressing table. She tidied herself to the best
of her limited resources, then returned to the bedroom
and sat in a wing chair by the fire to study her lone
botany text. Her attention meandered to the state of
the bedroom. If she had the money, she'd invest in
new wallpaper and bed hangings, a more cheerful decor. . . .

Somewhere in the distance, a gong sounded. Finding her way through the murky passageways, she
joined the others in a cavernous dining room. At the
head of the table, Kent's place lay conspicuously
empty; Ravi entered to report that the sahib had rung
for a tray in his office. Though annoyed, Juliet summoned a smile and asked Augusta about her works of
charity, then engaged in a polite dialogue with Gordon

about his studies of evolution and questioned Rose about the family history. Though the conversation flowed freely, Juliet longed for her husband's presence.

Afterward, the party retired to the drawing room. Kent still failed to appear. Would he often absent himself, sending messages through Ravi? Restlessness drove her to make her excuses and retreat to the bedroom. Minutes ticked into hours. Trying the connecting door, she found it locked. She pressed her ear to the gilded panel. Silence. As she resumed pacing, her irritation slowly dissolved into resentment, then anger. Didn't he care enough to check on how she'd fared with his eccentric relations?

By the time she heard a few faint noises coming from his bedroom, she'd worked herself into a justifiable fury. Marching to his door, she rapped hard.

A key rattled; the door opened. Kent stood with a drink in his hand, his shirt unbuttoned to his broad bare chest. A frown furrowed his forehead; weary lines bracketed his mouth. The black strands of his hair were mussed, as though he'd run his fingers through them. An arrow of concern punctured her wrath and roused the desire to soothe away his weariness.

"What is it?"

His testy tone buried the brief tenderness. "I'd like to speak to you."

"Can't it wait until morning?"

"No; I'll only take a few moments of your time."

Lips compressed, he studied her. "All right, then."

Trailing him, Juliet saw that a single candle illuminated a room as vast and ornate as her own. Lending warmth to the setting were a few scattered mementos, a cluster of framed photographs on the mantel, a collection of books on the nightstand. Sketches of mowers and reapers were tacked above a desk. Beside the elaborate velvet-hung bed stood Ravi, turning down the covers.

At her approach, he looked up, silent and expressionless. She clenched her teeth in annoyance and murmured to Kent, "Might we speak in private?"

"Of course."

He shifted his gaze to Ravi; the servant bowed and left. When Kent turned back, wariness shaded his face. "What is it?"

She took a deep breath. "I wanted to know where you've been all this time."

"Didn't Augusta tell you? I was going over the accounts."

"You couldn't stop long enough to join us for dinner?"

Irritation creased his brow; he set down his drink, then bent his dark head as he worked at a cuff link. "I've been absent for more than a month, Juliet. I couldn't spare the time."

"Not even on my first night here? Didn't you ever stop to think that I might appreciate your presence?"

His hand went still. He looked up, his eyes piercing. "Did someone say something to upset you?"

The concern sharpening his features encouraged her. Stepping closer, she clutched the folds of her skirt. "No, but that's not the point, Kent. You brought me into a strange household, then vanished when I needed you beside me."

He studied her for another moment, then walked away to deposit the cuff link on a side table. Picking up the glass, he took a swallow of the amber contents. "Forgive me. I thought you were quite capable of handling my relations."

Frustrated by his lapse into formality, she tagged at his heels. "It isn't just that, Kent. You've been keeping things from me, and that isn't right."

Like a sword, her words sliced into Kent. He clenched the glass. The uncustomary anger in her eyes jabbed his heart and banished his weariness. Christ, what *had* Juliet heard? Surely not the truth, not so soon.

He was hard-pressed to keep his tone neutral. "Exactly what are you accusing me of keeping from you?"

"For one, that telegram. Why didn't you tell me you'd sent word ahead?"

Deliverance spread through him, a deliverance so sweeping, his knees went weak. He propped a shoulder against the bedpost and sipped his brandy. "I forgot, I suppose."

"You forgot. Is that also your excuse for not telling Augusta right away about my father? You let me assume she knew from the telegram."

"I thought it might be better to let everyone meet you first before breaking the news." Unable to resist, Kent let his fingers slide down her silken cheek. "I know you'll win them over as easily as you did me."

To his dismay, she stepped away and whirled to face him. "That isn't all. Kent, I know precious little about you, about your past. Why didn't you tell me you had a sister who died?"

He stared. What the hell did she mean—? The realization struck with the force of a thunderbolt. *I had a sister once.* . . . Drat Rose and her incautious tongue.

Juliet bit her lip. "Please, Kent, don't shut me out. I'm your *wife*. I want to share everything in your life . . . your sorrows as well as your joys."

Gazing into her green-gold eyes, he felt shaken by the violent urge to haul her against him, to kiss her until he steered her away from this dangerous quagmire of questions. Yet if he put her off, wouldn't she query someone else here? He couldn't always be present to guard her. Perhaps if he fed her a version of the truth, enough to satisfy her, she would cease wondering.

Perhaps, by some great miracle, she might never learn of his duplicity. She might never leave him, might never go running back to her Papa. . . .

He finished the brandy and set down the glass. "All right. Sit down and I'll tell you what I should have told you weeks ago."

Taken aback by his grave tone, Juliet sank into a gilt armchair. Weeks ago? She felt a flash of foreboding, a fear that he was about to say something that would nip their fragile bud of closeness.

Kent sat on the edge of the bed and rested his elbows on his knees, his shirt open to the carved perfection of his chest. "First off, you should know that Rose is my half sister. She's the daughter of my father's mistress.''

Her mind whirled in shock. *"Rose* is illegitimate? No wonder she carried on so about the Deverells being freethinkers.''

"Did she?'' His mouth tilted into a fond smile. "I'm not surprised. Rose knows more about our heritage than I do.''

"She said she was compiling a family history.''

"Yes, the research keeps her occupied.'' A draft stirred the candle flame; shadows wavered over his face. "I suppose it's a way of burying her grief over her sister's death.''

Her thoughts took a great leap. "You mean . . . *Rose* had a sister who died, not you?''

He gave a curt nod. "Rose's mother is Chantal Hutton. Chantal had a love child by another man, long before she met my father. Do you remember the sketch he did of her?''

"The pretty woman, reclining in a boat, in India?''

"Yes.'' A long pause spun out as Kent regarded his clasped hands. "Juliet, there's something else I haven't told you about Chantal's elder daughter. She was my wife . . . my first wife.''

His words struck Juliet with the force of a blow. "Emily?'' she whispered.

He nodded. "After my mother's death, Chantal came here to live. At the time, Emily was five years old and I was nine, so we grew up together.''

And eventually fell in love. The unspoken words echoed through the shadows. So Emily was the childhood friend Kent had played and laughed with. A terrible, unreasoning jealousy tore at Juliet's heart. Unable to control a gnawing restlessness, she rose unsteadily and paced to the hearth. Atop the mantelpiece, in the center of a grouping of photographs, stood the small framed image of an angelic blonde, her smile sweet, her eyes sad.

Juliet knew the woman's identify even before asking, "Is this Emily?''

"Yes.''

That one gentle assertion held a richness of emotion. The fact that he kept her photograph displayed in a place of honor spoke volumes. Her throat closed; she kept her face averted. Now she understood Kent's avowal that he might never love again; he and Emily had been staunch friends as well as devoted lovers. How he must have adored her, to have overlooked the taint of bastardy.

"Chantal still lives here," Kent added, "in the north tower. You haven't met her because she tends to keep to herself."

"I see." Juliet stared down at the cold grate. "Why didn't you tell me all this before?"

"If I've been less than open, it's because the circumstances of Rose's birth, of Emily's birth, have never mattered to me."

Was that the only reason? Or did he love Emily so much, he wanted to keep her sainted memory all to himself?

The thought wrapped Juliet in dark despair. If *she* had carried such a blemish, would he have married her? Would physical passion and a desire for an heir have been cause enough for him to disregard the strictures of society?

"Juliet? What are you thinking?"

His voice sounded tentative, oddly alarmed. Too numb to respond, she kept her back turned. The bed ropes creaked and a clink sounded as he set down his glass; then she heard the tread of approaching footsteps. His warm hands settled on her shoulders and he twisted her to face him. "Tell me what's wrong. Please."

From the breadth of bare chest to the beloved angles of his face, he was perfectly formed: lean, handsome, muscular. Resolution blazed to life inside her. Emily was dead, Juliet reminded herself. She was alive . . . and Kent belonged to her now. He openly admitted his need for her; she could use that physical attraction to win his love. With all the fire and sensuality burning in her blood, she would gently conquer his heart.

"Nothing's wrong, Kent," she murmured. "Nothing but the fact that I'm aching for you."

Reaching up, she began to draw the tortoiseshell pins from her upswept hair. He frowned, his narrowed eyes following the movement of her hands, until the heavy mass rippled to her waist. She dropped the pins atop the mantel.

He caught her wrist. "Juliet, something I said disturbed you. Don't you want to tell me about it?"

Uncertainty clouded his eyes. A sudden, sharp elation buoyed her spirits. Talk had gained her only frustration and heartache. Let him wonder about her innermost thoughts; let a bit of mystery shake him out of his complacency.

"Never mind words," she murmured. "They only clutter up what we both really want from each other."

As she spoke, Juliet massaged the strong fingers that snared her wrist. His grip loosened. Brushing aside his shirt, she spread her hands over the hard wall of his chest. The black hairs tickled her palms and his brandy scent enticed her. She pressed her lips to his warm skin. Sinking slowly to her knees, she let her mouth pursue a downward path to his flat belly.

His muscles jerked and his fingers dove beneath her hair to seize her shoulders. "Stand up," he said, his voice husky. "I want to undress you."

She tilted her head back; the flare of dark fire in his eyes rewarded her. The desire illuminating his face ignited her own breathless excitement. Kent wanted her, needed her. She would see to it that he forgot the past, forgot all but the wife who made him wild with passion.

"In a moment," she murmured. "I'm not yet finished."

Placing a hand over the front of his trousers, she shaped her hand to his heat. The tight barrier of fabric maddened her, kept her from caressing him. Her fingers sought the fly of his trousers and began to work free the buttons.

"Juliet . . ."

The harsh sound of her name shivered down her spine. "I'm here, Kent."

As she curled her fingers around him, the insistent pulsebeat of longing quickened inside her. Kneeling before him was not an act of obeisance, but the offering of an equal. She would give him everything, entice him into loving her.

Goaded by an unthinking urge, she rubbed her cheek against his hot length, her long tresses trailing over him. From there, it took only a slight turn of her head to brush her lips across him. . . .

He hissed out a breath. "What in hell do you think you're doing?"

The shock edging his voice stirred misgivings in Juliet; her own boldness amazed her. Had she done something unnatural? She searched his expression through the dim candlelight. The fever in his eyes restored her exhilaration, encouraged her to follow the tantalizing path of instinct.

"I'm loving you," she whispered. "Loving every part of you." She pressed another kiss to him, this one more brazen, more encompassing.

"Christ, Juliet!"

His grip tensed on her shoulders, yet Kent made no move to forestall her. "Do you want me to stop?" she murmured.

"I'd die if you did."

The certainty of his passion provoked her to greater daring, incited her to accept the lure of forbidden longings. His fingers quivered as they laced into her hair, caressing her, showing her without words how much she pleased him. His deep groans gratified her as she lost herself in learning his taste and scent and texture.

"Enough," he croaked, hauling her to her feet. "You'll have this over without granting me the chance to satisfy *you*."

"There's no injustice in that, my love." Her smile serene yet sultry, Juliet moved her hips against him. "You'd make certain the second time belonged to me."

His eyes blazed through the shadows; his palms

cupped her cheeks. "Every time belongs to you. Whatever I take, darling, I intend to give back."

His words thrilled her as much as the feel of his mouth closing over hers, his tongue reclaiming her warm, wet softness. She kissed him back with all the yearning in her heart, with all the passion burning in her loins. His brandy taste entranced her as her hands burrowed beneath his shirt to find the solid muscles of his back and shoulder blades.

Cool air struck her spine; she hadn't even been aware of him unbuttoning her gown. The instant he yanked down the bodice and unhooked her corset, he focused his attention on her breasts, his fingers plying the nipple of one, his mouth suckling the other. Filaments of fire shot downward, feeding the liquid glow deep within her belly. Her head drooped back, her body wilting like an overripe rose beneath the heat of the sun. Weak and wanton, she reveled in the scorching sensations, the steadily building urgency to touch and be touched, to love and be loved.

When he started to lift his head, she twined her fingers in his hair and arched her breasts to his mouth. "Don't stop," she begged, her voice a husky cry. "Please don't."

"Only for a moment, darling." His smile was endearingly crooked, remarkably affectionate. "I want you in my bed, that's all." He pulled her across the room, toward the shadowy bower within the hangings of rich, dark velvet.

Tipping her head onto his shoulder, Juliet pressed her lips to the sinews of his neck, her hand sliding down his abdomen to the turgid proof of his desire. "I want you inside me, Kent. I don't care where . . . or how."

He uttered a rough exclamation. Stopping beside the bed, he jerked her fully against him, so that she could feel his maleness pressing to her thigh. His hands stroked downward over her breasts and waist to squeeze her buttocks through the flimsy lace of her underdrawers. "My God, you excite me. . . . I've never known a woman like you."

The pure radiance of emotion dazzled Juliet. "I feel this way only for you, Kent. Because I love you."

Naked longing gentled his features; a wild upsurge of hope made her sway in his arms. Then his mouth twisted with a trace of bleak bitterness and his gaze veered from hers. Releasing her, he walked toward the nightstand.

She caught his wrist. "Let's leave the candle burning for once. You look so handsome in the light."

"No." His voice was harsh, almost chilling. Secrets shaded his eyes in the moment before he pinched out the flame with his forefinger and thumb.

Night submerged the room. Disappointment wrenched her insides even as anticipation shuddered like goose bumps across her skin. How could he desire her yet not want to look upon her? Unless it was abnormal to feel this yearning to make love in the light . . .

Against the moonglow filtering through a slit in the window curtains, she could discern Kent's tall, black form. She heard the rustle of fabric, the quiet slither of his clothes as they dropped to the floor. Then his hands, warm and calloused, slid inside her underdrawers.

Any further protest she might have spoken withered on her lips. Instead, a low moan emerged from deep in her throat as he knelt to finish disrobing her, his hands peeling away her silk stockings, then following the flowing line of her legs back up to her bare thighs. His thumbs rubbed in provocative circles, drawing ever closer to the part of her that wept for him. He put his lips to her belly, the moist heat of his tongue laving her skin. With the darkness enclosing them, she could think of nothing save the steady descent of his mouth . . . and then a kiss so intimate and so arousing, she nearly swooned.

"Kent, oh, Kent . . ."

Whimpering, she clutched at his shoulders and felt herself falling, felt the cool embroidered counterpane meet her back. Then he came down on her, his body hard and heavy, gloriously male, pinning her to the bed. His hands cradled her breasts; his leg nudged open her thighs. Before she could so much as lift a hand to his cheek, the plunging pressure of his entry wrested a gasp of delight from her.

"Wife," he muttered. "You're my wife."

His mouth possessed hers in another searing kiss; the desperation in him matched her own reckless need. Her fingers clutched the slick muscles of his back as he launched into the familiar, magical movements. Again and again, he surged into her, the furor ever growing, until she felt like a flower bursting open beneath the radiance of the sun. Even as she tumbled into the white light of ecstasy, she heard his raspy cry, felt him shudder with the force of his own release.

The brilliance faded, leaving her adrift in mindless contentment. Gradually her senses grew aware of the weight of his body, the lingering taste of his brandied kisses, the musky aroma of his skin at the hollow of his shoulder. The pounding of his heart had slowed and his steady breathing told her he'd started on the long slide into slumber.

She drowsed as well, until a chilly draft tickled her arm and the burden of him grew uncomfortable. She tried to turn her head, but a lock of her hair was trapped between their bodies. Feeling a twinge of discomfort, she wriggled to ease the pressure on her legs. Kent mumbled under his breath, and his hand clamped tight to the curve of her hip, pinioning her in place.

Tenderness warmed her; their lovemaking must have exhausted him, too. If he fell into deeper relaxation, she'd never rouse him. "Kent," she whispered, "don't go to sleep this way."

He stirred, the fleece of chest hair abrading her breasts. "Emily?"

The groggy surprise in his voice cut into Juliet, slashing away her happiness. She couldn't think, she couldn't speak. Her heart felt as barren as a rose stripped of its petals.

She managed to say, "Get under the covers before you catch cold."

He rolled clear and she yanked back the counterpane. The icy sheets must have brought him to half awareness, for his arm curled around her waist as she started to swing her legs off the bed.

"Stay," he commanded, his tone slurred, oddly vulnerable. "You promised never to leave me, Juliet."

She swallowed to clear the pain thickening her throat. Calling herself a spineless fool, she posed no resistance as he drew her down beside him, shaping her back to his chest, his hand to her breast.

His breathing settled into an even rhythm that stirred her hair. Gazing into the night, she blinked back hot tears. He'd slaked his lust on her, only to dream of Emily. She'd been deluding herself to think she could win his devotion from the gilded shrine of his first wife.

Wife . . . you're my wife.

He hadn't been referring to her, but to Emily. Doubtless he'd made love to her countless times in this bed, touched her and kissed her, enfolded her in the same erotic embrace.

An appalling idea sprang into Juliet's mind. She tried to fend off the horrid thought, but it clawed at her with relentless talons. He made love to her only in the darkness. Now she knew why.

He wanted to pretend she *was* Emily.

Chapter 10

"What's all this?" Juliet asked.

Standing in her own bedroom the next morning, she stared as Augusta deposited a jumble of gowns on the bed. Juliet had been dressing; uncomfortable at receiving a near stranger in her half-naked state, she folded her arms over her corseted breasts.

Clad in serviceable brown twill, Augusta looked as stiff as the bedpost she stood beside. At her feet, Punjab watched with beady black eyes. "The duke asked me to see to a wardrobe for you," she replied. "He said you'd left home without any baggage."

Curiosity glinted in those hyacinth eyes, clear as the early sunlight pouring past the parted curtains. Juliet lifted her chin and said coolly, "I'm sure you've already surmised that my father didn't approve of the marriage."

"Humph. I rather imagined Emmett Carleton wouldn't." Lips pursed like the wrinkles of a prune, Augusta picked up a primrose-pink gown. "Not the current London fashion, I'm sure, nor as fancy, but the silk's of superior quality and the stitchery is tolerable. Took me weeks to sew all these frocks." She waved a hand at the pastel array on the bed.

Suspicion knotted Juliet's throat, a suspicion so abhorrent, it nearly strangled her. Swallowing, she heard herself asking, "Whose gowns *are* these?"

"Why, Emily's, from her trousseau. Where else would we so quickly find a wardrobe to suit your status as duchess?"

Emily . . .

Numbly Juliet watched as Augusta shook out the

gown, then plucked a bit of lint from the scalloped cuff.
Kent wanted his new wife to wear garments that had
belonged to his dead love? Sickness churned in her
belly. Dear God . . . did his pretense extend beyond
the bedroom? Did he hope to create a duplicate of his
beloved Emily?

Conquering the urge to cry, Juliet seized her own
forest-green gown off the bed. "I won't wear second-
hand clothing."

"You'd waste perfectly good silk? If I might be so
bold as to say so, you haven't room for vanity, Your
Grace." Punjab at her heels, Augusta walked over to
examine a mud stain at the hem of Juliet's gown. The
gold frock had fared a little better; draped over a chair,
the crepe de chine was sadly crumpled after lying the
night on the floor of Kent's bedroom. "You cannot go
about like a common washerwoman. Remember, you
are now the Duchess of Radcliffe."

Juliet bristled at the implication that she lacked the
finesse required of her position. Yet her every instinct
balked at garbing herself in apparel designed for Emily
Deverell. "I've been raised to assume the role of a nobleman's wife," she said in her most chilling tone. "Yet
I've also been raised to respect what doesn't belong to
me."

"Poppycock," Augusta snorted. "Emily would have
been happy to share her gowns—she always did have
an unselfish heart, poor girl. Come here now and I'll
do up your buttons. I can't afford to fritter away the
morning arguing."

So Emily had been generous as well as demure. A
paragon and a saint, Juliet thought uncharitably. She
told herself that she shouldn't feel threatened by a dead
woman. These were only clothes, after all.

Somehow she found herself standing in rigid silence, the gown slithering over her head, guided by
Augusta's impersonal hands. The aroma of lily of the
valley clung to the fabric. Layers of lace flounces
formed the skirt while rosettes of pink ribbon trimmed
the high-necked bodice. Her full bosom strained against

the seams; the old-fashioned bustle made her feel as though she were carrying a spare rump.

Catching a glimpse of herself in the mirror, she decided she looked like a hybrid tea rose on display. If only she had the funds to purchase a new wardrobe . . .

Her eyes as critical as Punjab's, Augusta stood back. "Quite tolerable, if I might say so. You're more endowed than Emily and a few inches taller, but the gown will do for today. After I make my rounds this morning, I'll begin the alterations."

Juliet gave an aristocratic nod. "We'll see. Has my husband gone out yet?"

"Rode to the fields an hour ago. Rather a late start for him, I might add."

Augusta arched a ginger eyebrow at the perfectly made bed, and unexpected humor invaded Juliet. What would such a sour-tempered woman think of the strenuous lovemaking that had tired Kent out? She couldn't imagine Gordon and Augusta doing *that* in bed.

"As the duke is engaged," Juliet said, "I should like to accompany you today. You may show me about the district and introduce me to some of the people."

"I told you, they're mostly tenant farmers and such," Augusta warned. "Hardly high society."

"I understand perfectly. Shall we meet in the courtyard in, say, twenty minutes?"

Augusta glowered, then lowered her gaze in grumpy obedience. "As you like." Stalking to the chair, she seized Juliet's two gowns. "I'll give these to Mrs. Fleetwood to wash."

"Thank you."

The instant Augusta strode from the chamber, Punjab mincing along behind, Juliet let her shoulders droop. She marched through the connecting doorway into Kent's bedroom, straight to the fireplace and the framed photo of Emily.

A sudden fury swept Juliet. "I hate you," she burst out. "Can't you leave us be?"

Those sad eyes rebuked her. Shame trickled through Juliet, along with a nagging bafflement. She didn't resemble Emily in the least. If Kent wanted to recreate

his hallowed love, why hadn't he selected an ethereal
blonde?

She swung her gaze to the velvet-hung bed; the
sheets lay in tangled disarray from her night with Kent.
Her heart felt hollow, empty. She'd entertained such
hopes of winning his love. Instead he wanted to make
her a hybrid, to graft her character with that of his first
wife. Didn't he care about accepting her for the person
she was?

Tears blurred her vision, but she dashed them away.
She could not, would not, go on this way. She would
confront him as soon as he returned home.

As Juliet entered the courtyard, sunlight dazzled her
eyes. Near the stables she spied Augusta sitting erect
in a dogcart. Trust that woman to wait all the way
across the muddy yard, she thought. Yet not for her
entire London wardrobe would she voice a word of
complaint.

Gritting her teeth, she stepped around the puddles
and climbed in beside the surly woman. Augusta
started the horse on a brisk trot over the drawbridge.
Juliet spied a row of lime trees near the corner of the
castle. The strange, contorted branches reached upward like a column of supplicants. "Is that the south
garden?" she asked, pointing.

"Yes."

She spied a flash of movement on the parapet.
Twisting on the seat, she stared. "Is that Ravi up
there?"

Augusta glanced around. "Hmph. Does his praying
there."

"Praying?"

"He's a Muslim. They have some sort of rule about
facing Mecca five times a day."

Ravi's devotion intrigued Juliet; it revealed a hidden
facet of Kent's mysterious servant. Augusta sank into
sour silence, but the countryside was so rich with color
that Juliet soon forgot her annoyance. Parkland
stretched from the castle, a few gray sheep grazing the
sweep of grass. White clouds scudded across an azure

sky; swallows swooped past the brown trunks of cedar and larch.

Her city-bred senses drank in the lush, rain-washed air. As the road dipped to parallel the river, she saw patches of yellow flag iris blooming among the reeds, and green lily pads carpeting the silver-blue water along the shore. A duck quacked over the rattle of wheels. Her London garden seemed insubstantial compared to the wild splendor of Radcliffe.

The narrow dirt lane swung away from the river, winding up and down slopes, past laurel hedges and thickets of oak, past a patchwork of grassy meadows and cultivated fields. Clinging to the open, jolting cart, Juliet shaded her eyes with one hand to search for a tall, dark-haired man on horseback.

Her chest ached from more than the snug fit of her gown. Was he thinking about her today, as she thought about him? Did he miss her, long for night, when darkness would draw them together?

Or did he contemplate still more insidious ways to transform her into Emily?

"The duke's gone to the north end of the estate," Augusta said, her voice gruff over the clop of hooves. "Neighbor's cows wandered through a hedgerow yesterday and got into our wheat."

Embarrassed to be caught with her emotions exposed, Juliet blushed. "I see."

"So do I." Those bland blue eyes held a speculative gleam. "You wed His Grace for love, did you not?"

The blunt question startled Juliet and made her hackles rise. "Of course. Why else would I have left my family, my home?"

"To acquire an ancient title, perhaps. Or perhaps to rebel against your father."

Quelling the painful memory of his slap, she said, "Papa isn't always the tyrant that people around here seem to think."

Shrugging, Augusta returned her attention to the lane. "If you say so."

"What do you know of the feud?"

"That's a question you should put to your husband."

Annoyed, Juliet went on, "Have you ever met my father?"

"In India."

"India? Papa hasn't been there in years."

Augusta clenched the reins. "Gordon and I went there as newlyweds," she said flatly. "William asked him to manage a tea garden in Assam. The plantation lost a great deal of money."

Did she blame Papa for bringing about her husband's defeat?

Juliet had but a moment to wonder when they rounded a bend and came upon a sleepy hamlet tucked into a sheltered fold of hills. Quaint cottages and half-timbered buildings huddled around a village green. Beyond the picturesque appearance, she noticed a few roofs in need of rethatching, a shutter hanging askew, a crumbling wall. Before a cobbler's shop, a wizened old man sat smoking a pipe while a trio of laughing children darted past, scattering the hens scratching at the bare earth.

"Welcome to Wyecote," Augusta said.

She drew the dogcart to a halt before a small cottage ringed by a stone fence. Beyond the house, laundry flapped on a line strung between two spindly yews. Juliet stepped to the dirt lane as Augusta retrieved a covered basket from behind the seat. She marched to the gate, the hinges creaking under a push of her hand.

The fragrance wafted to Juliet even before she walked within the walled yard. She found herself inside a rose garden as lush as the cottage was shabby. A riot of roses climbed and cascaded, tumbled and rambled, in a charming proliferation of yellow and salmon, white and crimson. Delighted, she twirled, arms outspread.

A woman emerged from the doorway, her green eyes vivid against lily-pale skin and a drab black gown. She couldn't have been more than five years older than Juliet, yet weariness haunted that lovely face. At the woman's side, a tiny, fair-haired girl leaning on a single wooden crutch tottered forward, a rag doll dangling from her hand. Her big blue eyes fastened on Augusta.

"Hullo, Mrs. Dev'rell. Did you bring me—" Spying Juliet, she stopped, then awkwardly retreated to the folds of her mother's aproned skirt.

"Good morning, Hannah, Mrs. Forster," said Augusta. "I've brought the new duchess to meet you."

"It's a pleasure to make your acquaintance," Juliet said.

Mrs. Forster's mouth dropped open; she hastily sketched a curtsy. Her daughter attempted to copy the action, but her crutch got in the way.

Watching that small, bright face, Juliet felt her throat go taut with tender compassion. One of Hannah's legs appeared twisted beneath the much-mended gray stocking and knee-length skirt. Impulsively Juliet bent to offer her hand. "I'm pleased to meet you, too, Miss Hannah."

The girl blinked warily, then thrust forth the doll, its tattered state a testament to much loving. "This is Peggy."

"Hello, Peggy."

As Juliet solemnly shook the doll's ragged hand, a shy smile bloomed across Hannah's face, a smile that dissolved Juliet's heart. Would she and Kent ever have such an adorable child?

She looked at Mrs. Forster. "Your garden is beautiful. You must love flowers as much as I do."

"Aye, Your Grace," the woman said, her eyes dreamy. "I work here of an evenin', when it's too dark inside to be at the loom."

"I help," piped Hannah. "Me an' Peggy."

Juliet grinned. "I'm sure you do."

Augusta shifted the basket from one hand to the other. "How is young Master Tom today?"

"Slept better last night," said Mrs. Forster, "thanks to the cordial you brought. Come in, I'm sure he'll want to see you."

One room comprised the cottage. The furnishings were appallingly few: a scarred table with a pair of chairs, a stool beside a butter churn, a glass jar of roses atop a low chest. A grainy photograph of Queen Victoria in Jubilee finery took the place of honor above the hearth. In the corner, near the single window, a loom held a half-finished pattern of blue and tan cloth.

Mrs. Forster went to a wooden cradle beside the hearth, lifted a small, squirming bundle, and brought it to Augusta. "I only just finished feedin' him."

Setting down her basket, Augusta cuddled the baby and felt his forehead. "Fever's gone. Must have been a touch of the ague."

Mrs. Forster wrung her work-worn fingers. "Tom'll be all right now, won't he? I couldn't bear it if . . ." She bit her lip.

"He's as hale as a horse," Augusta said, smiling as a tiny fist clamped around her thumb. "He's already feeling his oats this morning."

As the older woman cooed at the baby, Juliet stared, amazed at the transformation. Those severe features had gone gentle, tender with maternal affection. Why had she never had a child of her own? Sympathy stirred in Juliet. Had barrenness turned Augusta so cross? Or had she lost a baby?

Tugging at Augusta's skirt, Hannah darted an impatient glance at the basket. "Please, Mrs. Dev'rell, what have you brought me?"

"Hannah!" her mother scolded. "Mind your manners."

"It's all right," said Augusta. "Perhaps, Your Grace, you'd care to hold the boy a moment."

Juliet gathered the infant to her breast and relished the unfamiliar sensation. He felt sturdy despite his size. His milky scent and solemn green eyes entranced her, and a flash of memory left her weak. Would the long nights of passion bear fruit? Perhaps she already nurtured Kent's baby inside her. A baby would tie him to her in a way Emily had never succeeded. . . .

"I've something for Peggy," Augusta said. Lifting the cloth from the basket, she drew forth a small parcel. "But you may help her open it."

Balancing on the crutch, the girl tore open the brown paper to find a tiny gingham dress. Her face lit up; she tumbled into Augusta's arms. "A Sunday dress for Peggy," she declared.

"Bless you," murmured Mrs. Forster. "If it weren't for the kindness of you and His Grace—"

"Poppycock," Augusta said, squaring her shoulders. "You just see to these precious babes. We must run now. We've other calls to make."

Juliet handed the baby to Mrs. Forster. "He's beautiful," she murmured. As they walked outside, she couldn't resist touching a perfect salmon tea rose. "This variety is called Adam, is it not? I've seen it displayed at horticulture exhibits."

"Don't know all the proper names," Mrs. Forster admitted. "Emmie . . . the other duchess, I mean . . . she let me take cuttin's from the castle garden." She twined her fingers in her apron. "Beg pardon, Your Grace. I don't mean to sound so familiar. It's just that the duchess and I sometimes played together as children."

Emily again. A pang invaded Juliet's heart. Suddenly she felt isolated, an outsider trying to play a role that belonged to another woman. A woman who had grown up here, a woman who had been loved by these people . . . and by Kent.

"I understand," Juliet said. "And I want you to feel welcome to visit Radcliffe whenever you like."

Mrs. Forster bobbed a curtsy. "You must come back again."

They climbed into the dogcart, and Augusta snapped the reins. The vehicle jolted slowly down the rutted lane.

"Is her husband a farmer?" Juliet asked.

Augusta's jaw tightened; she stared straight ahead. "Tom Forster was killed in a threshing accident last harvest. Mrs. Forster had just learned she was to bear a second child."

Despite the sun warming her back, Juliet went cold with shock. "How will a widow with two small children survive?"

"The duke waived her rent and continued Mr. Forster's wages. Between that and her weaving, Mary and the children will get on.''

''What about Hannah? Surely there must be medical expenses—''

''There's nothing our Dr. Sattler can do. See there?'' She pointed to a clean, whitewashed building near the village green. ''He has a fine new surgery, but there's only so much he can do.''

''What exactly is wrong with her?''

''She was born crippled, something to do with her hip. We can thank God that at least she isn't in pain.''

''But . . . has she seen a specialist? Perhaps a London doctor—''

''We can't afford wild-goose chases, Your Grace. I've told you before, money is short.''

Juliet's frustration flared into anger. ''Something ought to be done for that little girl. We could appeal to a rich patron, perhaps. Or find a doctor willing to take on a charity case. Why have you given up so easily?''

Augusta reined the horse to an abrupt halt before another cottage. ''I've done more than you can imagine,'' she said stiffly. ''We all have our crosses to bear.''

As she stepped down to the lane, the glaring sunlight made her cheekbones appear starker than ever. What sorrows lay hidden behind that severe facade? The absence of her own children to love? The loneliness of a woman wed to an inattentive scholar?

Recalling Gordon's abstracted manner and twisted hands, Juliet felt pity temper her wrath, pity for both him and his wife. All Augusta had was her charity work; all Gordon had was his books.

Getting out as gracefully as her tight gown would allow, Juliet followed Augusta to the rear of the dog-cart, where the woman drew forth another covered basket.

''I didn't mean to imply that you're indifferent to Hannah's plight,'' Juliet said. ''But perhaps I can do something. My friend, the Lady Maud Peabody, comes from an influential family.''

Augusta absently touched her mole. ''Why go so far

afield? You've said your father isn't a tyrant. Perhaps he'll unbend about providing you a dowry."

Juliet knew the answer to *that*. "Kent would never accept Carleton money. He's already told me so."

"Poppycock. If your father puts property in your name, you won't need the duke's permission to spend the income. Nowadays the law allows a married woman control over what's hers."

Juliet frowned. Was Augusta trying to cause trouble between her and Kent? "I've never heard of such a law."

"I'm not surprised. Emmett Carleton strikes me as the sort who prefers to keep his women ignorant of legal matters."

Juliet ignored the slur. "Tell me more about this law."

Augusta shifted the basket from one sturdy hand to the other. "There isn't much to tell. A few years ago, Parliament passed the Married Women's Property Act. A wife may keep any money she inherits or earns. You'll have an advantage *I* never had."

"What do you mean?"

"I was an heiress, too. But William convinced Gordon to use my dowry to pay off Radcliffe's debts. I had no say in the matter." Pivoting, she tramped toward a crumbling cottage.

The caustic words cut into Juliet. Who did Augusta blame, Gordon for his weakness or the old duke for his arrogance? Another thought startled her. Or was it Papa Augusta resented, because she, too, believed he'd precipitated the family's debts?

Slowly Juliet went up the weedy walkway. They visited an elderly couple, then called on the harried mother of nine ill-clad children. Everywhere in the village she saw a privation that firmed her conviction into bedrock. She could accomplish so much . . . if only she could obtain her money.

The notion haunted her during the drive back to the castle. She and Augusta were finishing a late luncheon when Fleetwood shuffled into the cavernous dining room. A salver teetered in his white-gloved hands. "The post arrived during your absence, Your Grace."

Juliet took the letter from the tray. "Thank you, Fleetwood."

The faint aroma of Parma violets wafted from the cream-colored envelope. Her heart lurched as she recognized the elegant script.

"You look rather pale," said Augusta, arching a ginger eyebrow. "I trust that letter isn't from an unwelcome party."

"No, I'm tired, that's all. If you'll excuse me."

Her chair legs scraped the stone flags as Juliet sprang up and darted into the dank corridor. She found herself uttering a fervent prayer as she hastened up the stairs. *Please . . . please.* The letter must hold favorable news. News that Papa had forgiven her. News that the love for his daughter had finally eclipsed his hatred of the Deverells . . .

Entering her bedchamber, she slammed the door. She headed to a window and sank onto the stone seat. Her fingers shook as she ripped open the envelope. She scanned her mother's writing. Phrases leaped out and sliced her heart to shreds.

Your outrageous behavior caused Mr. Carleton to fly into the blackest rage. . . . He insists upon going about as though no one whispers of the scandal. . . . At least you've wed a duke, darling, so no one dares shun us. . . . Your father has disowned you . . . yet you must dress befitting your new station. . . . I shall send a few trunks of clothing, but Mr. Carleton must never, ever find out. . . .

The letter whispered downward to settle at her feet. Clenching the folds of her skirt, Juliet stared at the sheet of pale vellum against the carpet. Tears burned her eyes. A breeze wafted through the opened window and the quack of a duck joined the gentle swish of the river.

The brilliant summer day mocked the bleakness in her soul. She had a sudden, wrenching desire for the security of Carleton House, for the return of familiar routine, for dinner with Mama and Papa, for fresh gowns to wear, for Maud's blithe chatter.

Juliet pressed her cheek to the cool limestone casement. Why had she expected her mother to understand? Mama concerned herself with appearances, not her daughter's happiness. And Papa . . .

Go near that devil again and by God, you'll no longer be my daughter.

Burying her face in her hands, she loosed the sobs that knotted her throat. Searing waves of grief swept over her until she felt void of sentiment, emptied of emotion. As her weeping subsided, she faced the bitter truth: Papa would never change his mind about her chosen husband. His love would never conquer his stubborn pride. He deemed the feud more vital to his life than his only child.

Isolation cloaked her. She'd been cut off from everything, everyone, she knew and loved. She raised her chin. No, not everyone. She had Kent.

On wobbly legs, she walked about the antiquated room. Mrs. Fleetwood must have taken away the pile of old-fashioned gowns. Sunshine highlighted the shabby grandeur of the furnishings and defined every moth hole in the green and gold bedhangings. This was her home now. These rooms would bear the stamp of her character, the echoes of her playing children.

A measure of peace glided into her hollow heart. Pacing past the mirror with its ducal crest, she caught sight of herself and stopped. A chill prickled her skin. A stranger lurked in the wavy old glass. With sad eyes and a wan face, with her body encased in the old-fashioned frilly gown, she appeared so very different. . . .

So like Emily.

For one icy instant, Juliet felt like a rose strangled by a vine. Then she released a shuddering sigh. Absurd.

Walking closer to the mirror, she studied her resolute eyes and determined chin. That odd impression must have been a trick of the light; she didn't look a whit like the modest Emily.

From the ashes of misery sprang the flames of fury. Clenching her fists, she paced the room. The devil take her father for shunning her. And the devil take Kent for trying to metamorphose her into the image of his dead love.

A tightening coil deep within Juliet threatened to squeeze the breath from her lungs, but she ignored the pain. She was the Duchess of Radcliffe. She alone would govern her life; she would demand the rights befitting her position and use them for the good of those who depended upon her.

Your father has disowned you. . . . She'd see about that.

A sense of purpose fed the reckless idea growing in her mind. The time had come to act. She would take steps to obtain the dowry due her. Instead of being squandered on society balls and fancy gowns, her father's money would pay for medical bills and much-needed clothing.

Pivoting on a rustle of old silk, she marched to a gilt writing desk in the corner. Searching the dusty drawers, she found a stack of stationery yellowed with age and stamped with the Radcliffe crest. Before her courage could falter, she took up a pen and began to compose a letter.

Chapter 11

An hour later, Juliet hesitated before the cobbler's shop; the tiny half-timbered building doubled as the Wyecote post office. She could still retrieve the small package she'd just posted to Maud. The package that contained a sealed letter with a daring request . . .

"May I give you a hand in, Your Grace?"

She whirled to see a handsome man of medium height, his tawny mustache curled at the ends. From the fine lines at the corners of his mouth and blue eyes, he appeared to be in his midthirties. His dapper tweed riding suit marked him a gentleman, yet the probing intensity of his stare defied good breeding.

Juliet fixed him with a frigid stare. "Have we met, sir?"

He lifted his bowler hat in a respectful salute, then replaced it on a shock of fair hair. "Pardon my boldness, Your Grace. News of Radcliffe's marriage has swept our gossip-starved district."

"Indeed."

"Perhaps I might introduce myself. Henry Hammond-Gore, Esquire, at your service." He bowed, then added, "My lands lie due north of here."

"Then it was *your* cows who broke through the hedgerow and got into our field?" she said dryly.

"Alas, yes." Henry Hammond-Gore waved a leather glove at a black stallion cropping the grass at the edge of the village green; a small urchin held the animal's reins. "I was just now on my way to assess the situation."

"You've come the long way around, haven't you?"

He shrugged, his grin unaccountably charming. "I confess, catching a glimpse of the new duchess appealed to me more than bridling old Bossie. And diligence has rewarded me. You look quite fetching, Your Grace.''

Again, his gaze traveled over her gown. Juliet felt a flash of annoyance at his curiosity. ''You must excuse me for wearing castoffs. My own trunks have been inadvertently delayed.''

Henry Hammond-Gore gave a sheepish grin. ''Ah . . . now that you mention it, that pink frock does seem familiar. Emily wore it at the May Fair, not long after she wed Radcliffe. She did me the honor of a waltz. . . .'' He blinked and cleared his throat. ''Beg pardon, Your Grace, I'm chattering like a magpie.''

Pain burned inside Juliet. Had everyone in the region adored Emily? Suddenly she felt too impatient, too resentful, to cool her heels waiting for Kent. She would see him now.

''I should like to go with you,'' she said.

Henry cocked his head. ''With me, Your Grace?''

''To 'assess the situation.' ''

''Ah . . . the field. Are you quite sure? You'll be bored to tears.''

''In that unlikely event, I trust you'll be gentleman enough to lend me your handkerchief.''

A blond eyebrow arched and his mouth formed an appealing smile. ''I'm honored to escort a lady of such delightful wit.''

He helped her into the dogcart, then sauntered to his horse and flipped the small groom a coin. Several other boys gathered around; Henry tossed a penny to each. Watching him call out a jest as he mounted, Juliet wondered if Henry Hammond-Gore was really the shallow dandy his manner suggested.

She carefully flicked the reins and the pony began plodding down the rutted road. Henry rode alongside the cart, his pale features and smart figure a flawless foil for the black horse. As they meandered past the river and castle, he entertained her with tales of parties he'd attended with Prince Edward and the Marlborough House set. Somehow Henry managed to leave her shocked, yet amused and intrigued at the same time.

"If I can believe even half of what you say," she said over the clop of hooves, "I can see why we've never met in society."

A corner of his mouth lifted. "I hardly think most papas would regard me as a proper suitor."

"Why aren't you in town for the Season?"

"Had a bit of a misunderstanding with Lord Melton over his daughter, the Lady Marianne. Thought I ought to absent myself for a while."

Juliet had only a passing acquaintance with the Meltons, Lady Marianne being nearly a decade her senior. "What happened?"

"The vixen tried to trap me in a compromising circumstance, but I outfoxed her. Stole a few kisses and . . ." Beneath the curling mustache, his mouth formed a rakish grin. "I shan't offend you with the details, Your Grace. Lady Marianne's handsome enough considering her long stay on the shelf, but she chose the wrong prey this time. I've no wish to marry."

"Why not?"

He idly stroked the horse's silken mane. "Why, indeed? Shall I give up my footloose ways and become a dreary country gentleman with a throng of squawking offspring?"

She smiled. "That hardly sounds dull."

"It hardly sounds exciting, either."

"Perhaps you haven't met the right woman."

"Perhaps," he said, shrugging. "Give me a woman who can carry on a decent conversation, a woman who can see past the nose on her face."

As the lane topped a hill, he commented on the splendid vista. Juliet let his praise of the scenery distract her. This was Radcliffe land, she thought with pride. Cultivated fields of ripening grain abutted green pastureland, the squares bisected by hedges and thickets of oak and elm. The melancholy bleat of a sheep drifted through the warm air.

"There's our destination," Henry said, pointing to the base of the hill.

Juliet gazed over an expanse of wheat, rippling golden in the sunlight. In the pasture beyond, Guernsey cows grazed the lush grass. Workmen scattered the length of hedge bordering the field.

Near a jagged opening in the shrubbery stood Kent. Her heart jolted from more than the bumpy ride. Sunlight gleamed on his raven hair, his broad back. His arms were plunged inside the hedge; from a distance, she couldn't see what he was doing.

What would he say when he learned of the letter she'd posted?

She clenched the reins and looked at Henry, who lazed in the saddle as the horse trekked down the dirt lane. "What are the men doing about that gap in the hedge?"

"They'll reinforce the bushes with wire, then intertwine the branches."

"It'll take weeks for new growth to fill such a large break. That looks like *crataegus monogyna*."

He shifted in the saddle to stare at her. "*Cra*—what?"

At his blank-faced astonishment Juliet felt a flush rise over her throat. "Hawthorn, I mean."

His amused eyes wandered over her. "So you're a scholar as well as a beauty. I like you, Duchess. No wonder Radcliffe succumbed to matrimony again."

As they neared the bottom of the hill, he swung down from the horse. Little did he know, she thought, drawing the pony to a halt, that Kent had succumbed only to the need to replace his dear departed love. Fighting despair, she looked toward the hedge. Several of the laborers had turned to gape, but Kent remained engrossed in his toil.

Henry strolled to the cart to give her a hand down. Striving for lightness, she said, "Mama always insisted that men dislike intelligence in a woman. It scares them."

"Ah, but a quick-witted female knows how to hold a man's interest."

"You sound as though you prefer that sort."

He laughed. "On the contrary, I've been accused of liking all women, the shrewd and the artless, the bold and the timid. . . ." A sudden soberness creased his brow. "I do hope Radcliffe won't neglect *you* in favor of his farming."

"What do you mean?"

His gaze wandered to Kent. "Perhaps if he'd devoted a few more hours a day to Emily, she might not have . . ."

The pensive words startled Juliet. "You believe the rumor that she took her own life?"

"Alas, we shall never know for certain." His fingers tightened on hers. "Be that as it may, if Radcliffe ever makes you unhappy, you can come to me, send a message anytime, day or night—"

"Up to your old woman's gossip again, Hammond-Gore?"

That mocking voice made Juliet jump. Peering past Henry's shoulder, she saw Kent striding toward them, the muslin shirt damp with sweat and adhering to his broad frame. Sunlight glazed his features as he yanked off a pair of thick work gloves. Awash with untimely longing, she pulled her hand free and stepped toward him.

He stopped dead. His glare raked her from breast to toe. His face went taut with a shock so palpable, the greeting withered in her throat.

He jerked his head toward Henry. "Well?" he said coldly. "What are you doing here?"

Henry toyed with the curled end of his mustache. "I met your charming duchess in the village. She displayed an interest in the process of mending a hedge."

"I'm surprised you'd know a hedge from a hedgehog. I'm on to your practice of leaving gaps for your beaters to slip through on the autumn hunts."

"I hadn't thought of that. Capital notion, Radcliffe." He cast a speculative look at Kent. "You're testier than a newly gelded Thoroughbred. I wonder why."

"I'm tired of your bloody cows trampling my grain."

"I've sent a few of my men to help with the hedgerow. What more do you want?"

Kent slapped the gloves against his palm. "Since you ask," he said through clenched teeth, "I'll tell you. I want you to stay away from my property." He gave Juliet a pointed stare.

Shocked, she burst out, "That's absurd! No one dictates whom I associate with."

He cocked an eyebrow. "Except your husband," he

said, his voice too low to reach the laborers. "You're free to do whatever you wish so long as you don't make a fool of yourself . . . or me."

The blood drained from her cheeks as she stared at his taut lips and angry eyes. She could scarcely believe this same man had called her *darling* in the dark of night, had transported her to such glorious heights of pleasure in his bed. But of course, she bitterly reminded herself, he'd been pretending she was Emily.

"I say, Radcliffe—"

He swung on Henry. "Stay the hell out of this. I suggest you hoist your elegant rump onto your expensive horse and ride on."

Oddly, Henry looked more amused than offended. "I shall at that. Adieu, Your Grace."

Tipping his bowler to Juliet, he swung onto the stallion. He cantered away, his coattails flying, dust pluming in his wake.

Kent caught her wrist and drew her to the other side of the cart, out of earshot of the workmen. Furious, she yanked free. "You had no right to speak to me that way," she snapped. "Or to drive Henry away."

"Henry, is it?" He fixed her with a fearsome scowl. "You're on familiar terms for a man you've only just met."

"He's a perfect gentleman—more a gentleman than you're acting right now."

Kent gripped the work gloves so tightly, his knuckles turned white. "Your naïveté is showing. He's the biggest bloody rake in the empire. Give him half a chance and he'll have you on the ground with your skirts above your waist."

His crudeness staggered her. The urge to slap him scorched her. She started to lift her hand, but stopped at the thought of their audience. Instead, she dug her fingernails into her palms, the pain a balm to her numbing fury. Her husband might be rude, but she wouldn't stoop to his level.

Had she been too bold last night, after all? She could think of no other reason why he would insult her so.

The volcano of pain and resentment that had been

seething all day exploded. "Odd, that's exactly what my father warned me *you* would try," she said scathingly. "I suppose I *have* been a fool. Only a fool would be so blind to the fact that you want to shape me into the sort of namby-pamby wife you prefer."

His eyes narrowed. "Shape you—? You're speaking nonsense."

"Am I? You've made your opinion of my character plain enough. It's a shame you married so far below your class."

Pivoting, she grasped the side of the cart to climb in. Kent snared her wrist and brought her back around. His furious frown eased to watchfulness. "Wait a moment," he said. "You've got this all wrong."

His sunlit image shimmered behind a humiliating blur of tears. She yanked at his grip. "Let me go."

"No." Tossing down his work gloves, he touched her cheek, his callused fingers abrasive on her soft skin. "Juliet . . . I didn't mean to be so harsh. More worldly women than you have succumbed to Henry. I only wanted to protect you."

His penitent voice somehow enhanced her misery; his nearness tempted her beyond reason. She could see every handsome angle in his sun-browned face. She wanted to lay her head against his chest, to accept the comfort of his arms. But he offered only empty words designed to placate a dim-witted female.

Swallowing hard, she said coldly, "Protect me? By suggesting I'd sleep with another man, that I'd betray our marriage vows? Is that the sort of woman you think I am?"

"Of course not. I spoke in haste. You see, I . . ." A muscle leapt in his jaw. "I suppose I was shocked to see you acting so friendly with him."

"That's no excuse for what you said, Kent. I don't appreciate being dressed down in public."

"Juliet, I . . ." He lowered his eyes, his expression wary. "I was angry about something else . . . and took it out on you."

Pain stabbed her. When would he open up and discuss his troubles with her? "Angry about what?"

"About the estate problems that mounted during my absence. Oh, nothing critical, just a lot of little things. Juliet, you've never had to face money problems, this blasted waste of time on the hedge . . ."

She sensed he held something back. "And?"

His brooding gaze swept over her. He hesitated, then loosed her wrist. "I suppose I was also surprised to see you in that gown. Where did you find Emily's dress?"

His puzzlement confused her. "Augusta brought it to me. She said you wanted me to have a new wardrobe."

"Augusta," he said in disgust. "She can certainly be a penny-pincher." Kent touched her arm in a brief caress. "I never meant for you to wear ill-fitting cast-offs, Juliet. I wanted her to sew you something new."

The darkness inside her lifted a little. "You mean . . . you don't want to turn me into Emily?"

"Turn you into—" He studied her blankly. "What are you talking about?"

"You don't remember, do you?" She forced the words past the sickness in her throat. "Kent, last night as you were falling asleep you called me Emily."

He opened his mouth, then closed it. A dull flush crept up his cheeks. Sliding his thunderstruck gaze from her, he stared at the field of wheat, the long stalks undulating in a whisper of wind. The breeze sifted his hair, the sun transforming the tousled strands to living sable.

When he looked back at her, his eyes were hooded. "I hardly know what to say," he murmured. "I can't imagine how I could have made such a blunder."

"Because you can't stop thinking about her," she said, forcing herself to voice the tormenting words. "You're obsessed by her. I thought you were pretending I *was* her."

His eyes glittered in the sunlight; his fingers bit into her shoulders. "God, no! I could never look at you and see another woman. I could never hold you in my arms and dream of anyone else." He leaned closer, his hands gentling, stroking. "Much as you tempt me, Juliet, the north pasture is hardly the place for me to delineate all your unique qualities.''

His burning look at her bosom made her knees weak; his earthy aroma made her long for the flavor of his skin against her lips. Yet dismay diluted her desire. She felt a gnawing emptiness, a yearning for him to view her as more than a mere bed partner.

He watched her closely. ''Will you forgive me?''

''I need time to think, Kent. I admit I've been naive, but there's more to marriage than physical pleasure.''

Shadows veiled his eyes; he squared his shoulders to formal stiffness. ''As you wish, then. We'll speak more this evening.''

Steely hands gripped her waist and boosted her into the cart. He guided the pony around; then he lightly slapped the brown rump and the animal began trudging back up the hill.

Juliet scarcely registered the rhythmic tug of the reins in her hands. She couldn't deny a niggling disappointment that he thought he could win her forgiveness by offering her physical satisfaction.

Perhaps her immodest behavior last night inspired his lust but repulsed his love. Yet why shouldn't a wife arouse both ardor and affection in her husband?

As the cart crested the hill, she pivoted on the wooden seat and looked back. Fists planted on his hips, Kent stood in the lane. He raised a hand, then strode back to the hedgerow.

She admitted a deep pride in seeing him work alongside his men. Even if she could share her father's conviction that Kent was a poor businessman, she assured herself he was certainly no pea-brained wastrel planning his next fox hunt.

Only as the pony plodded toward the distant castle did she recall Henry Hammond-Gore's startling charges. Kent had neglected Emily in favor of farming? She'd committed suicide?

Nonsense. No woman could be despondent over bearing Kent's baby, over possessing his love. The death had been a tragic accident. Like Lord Breeton, Henry only mouthed unfounded gossip.

As the stately gray towers of Radcliffe drew steadily nearer, Juliet let her thoughts stray again to the confrontation. Could she trust that Kent didn't want to turn her into a replacement for his dead love? That he valued Juliet for herself? The whirlwind courtship had denied her the chance to learn his every facet.

Yet love glowed within her, mysterious and magical, fiery and fulfilling. She would fight for her husband's affection. She held enough love inside her to embrace the life of an impoverished duchess; enough love to forsake the status of pampered daughter.

Daughter. Pain circled her chest in a tightening band. Kent had warned her that her father would never change; Mama's letter only confirmed Papa's intolerance. Because of the feud, she might never again see them, might never again feel the warmth of her mother's embrace, might never again bask in Papa's proud regard.

The heady scent of meadowsweet drifted from the tall stalks of feathery white flowers bordering the lane. Juliet sat straighter in the cart. She didn't have to accept Papa's stubborn pride. She wouldn't simply give up on bridging the rift.

From the soil of her sorrow thrust a seedling of resolution. If she unearthed everything about the feud, maybe she could reason with her father, force him to see that past hatreds needn't poison future happiness.

Apprehension stirred in her stomach. Of course, the letter she'd posted today would hardly restore her to his good graces. . . .

The dogcart clattered over the drawbridge and into the castle. Late afternoon sunshine bathed the dingy courtyard and gilded the brooding battlements. She made an absentminded note to pull up the ragged clumps of groundsel and dockweed around the forlornly dry fountain. Leaving the pony to the care of a stableboy, she headed for the massive oak door of the entryway.

In the great hall, she encountered Ravi; his mudhued eyes gleamed inscrutably beneath the flat gray turban. "Memsahib," he said, bowing. "I was on my way to deliver this to your room." From a deep pocket of his robe, he withdrew a note.

Juliet unfolded the paper to see an elaborate script flowing across the lavender stationery. *At a time convenient to Your Grace, I would be delighted to have the honor of your presence at tea. Chantal Hutton.*

Excitement rolled through Juliet as she recalled the blond woman in the sketch. William Deverell's former mistress would know the history of the feud. Raising her eyes to Ravi, she said, "I'll join Miss Hutton today."

"Come," he said, turning. "I will show you the way."

The directive needled Juliet. "I'll freshen up first," she countered. "You may call for me in half an hour."

No emotion marred his lean, dusky features. "As Your Grace commands." Bowing again, he glided silently down a dim corridor.

She found the forest-green gown hanging cleaned and pressed in her dressing room. Gratefully discarding the frivolous pink frock, Juliet donned her own gown and tidied her hair. Primping before the age-spotted mirror revitalized her, imbued her with the outer trappings of confidence and the inner resolution to do battle for Kent's heart.

As she joined Ravi in the hall and they started down the worn steps, a thought occurred to her. He must know the particulars of the quarrel, too.

"You served Kent's father, did you not?"

"Yes, memsahib. Since I was sold to him as a boy."

"Sold!" Appalled, Juliet stopped, a hand braced on the rough stone wall. "You mean you were his slave?"

He shrugged. "So it would seem. The old duke offered me a chance to learn to read and write, to serve as his scribe."

As they exited the gloomy staircase, she tried to fathom his loyalty to the Deverells. "Didn't you resent being owned by another man?"

"We are all owned in one way or another, memsahib."

Juliet pondered the statement. Certainly she had obligations to people, had sworn marriage vows to Kent, yet he didn't *own* her. Or did he? Did love bind her to him with silken chains? "Surely Kent has granted you your freedom."

"Of course."

"Then why do you not return to India?"

"Perhaps I shall someday. But England is my home for now. I am happy to serve His Grace."

Their footsteps echoed through the great hall; then they entered a corridor Juliet had not yet explored. Rusted shields and musty tapestries adorned the walls. "How did William purchase you?" she asked. "Wasn't slavery against the law?"

"Perhaps. Yet I begged him to become my master. He owed me that debt because I hid him in the great Mutiny, when many English were slain by my countrymen."

Startled, she met his impassive gaze. "How did you manage to conceal him?"

"In a well, near Cawnpore, where he was visiting friends. Then I helped him flee in disguise to Darjeeling."

"Was Kent in India at the time?"

Ravi shook his head. "The Mutiny raged over thirty years ago, before His Grace's birth."

"Why did you wish to be purchased?"

"I was the eldest of eleven children. My family had little to eat, only rags to wear. That sort of life must be difficult for a lady of your birth to comprehend."

His disdainful look reminded Juliet of his animosity toward Emmett Carleton. Her steps slowed as she asked, "Have you ever met my father?"

He cast her a stony glance. "Yes, memsahib."

"What did you think of him?"

"He is not for me to judge."

Frustrated, she said, "I want to understand this hatred toward my family. How did it start?"

"I am not the one to whom you should address your questions."

Opening a door, he waved her up a flight of winding stairs. He lowered his eyes and assumed the meek demeanor of a servant who could offer no further insight.

Gritting her teeth, she took hold of her skirts and preceded him up the steps.

Around a curve in the staircase loomed a carved mahogany door. Ravi knocked; the panel swung open and Chantal Hutton stood there, limned by sunlight. Fine age lines enhanced her alabaster complexion. She wore her cornsilk hair piled atop her head, adding to her regal height. A white gown swathed her willowy figure and drew attention to her magnificent bosom.

William Deverell's drawing hadn't done justice to his mistress's golden beauty, Juliet thought. Chantal Hutton, the woman who had dared flout society by bearing two bastard daughters, possessed a queenly aspect that no canvas could capture.

"So you are the new duchess," said Chantal, her husky-soft voice edged by formality. She looked keenly at Juliet. "I saw you alight from the landau yesterday—you're even prettier close up. Please come inside so that we may get acquainted."

"Thank you," Juliet murmured.

A strange look passed between Chantal and Ravi; Juliet wondered briefly if he waited upon Chantal, too. The servant bowed, then retreated down the stairs.

The small sitting room had high-arched windows set in stone and a dramatic decor that gave the effect of an exotic bazaar. Cloth in patterns of crimson and black cloaked the walls, while cane furniture and ivory screens abounded. Before the cold fireplace, a maidenhair fern draped a table with antelope horn legs.

Juliet wandered to a window and peered down at the courtyard. What thoughts had Chantal harbored as she'd stood here, watching the woman who had taken her daughter's place as duchess?

"Your apartment is lovely," Juliet said. "This is one of the towers, isn't it?"

"The north tower, sometimes known as the Mortimer Tower." Chantal fluttered her elegant fingers. "I don't recall how the name originated. No doubt Rose could tell you."

"Where is your daughter today?"

"Probably ensconced in a cubbyhole somewhere,

with her nose in a dusty book." A frown creased her patrician forehead; then Chantal made a lavish gesture, her bracelets chiming. "She promised to join us, but we won't let our tea grow cold. She has no sense of time or obligation. Please sit down, Your Grace."

As she swept toward a silver tea service, Juliet settled into a bamboo chair and studied Chantal. The fair coloring and high cheekbones brought a haunting reminder of Emily, yet this woman was no demure violet. Chantal Hutton was an extravagant white water lily.

A fresh scent pervaded the air, a contrast to the mustiness in the rest of the castle. "Sweet woodruff," Juliet said, breathing the distinctive aroma. "And a trace of chamomile."

"Mixing sachets is a pastime of mine," Chantal said, gliding over the Turkish rug to hand Juliet a cup. "Have you an interest in herbs, Your Grace?"

"In all types of plants. I'm a botanist."

"Fancy that! Even so far from London, we've heard of your mother's reputation as a hostess. I'd expected you to be conventional."

Blue eyes narrowed, Chantal paused with one hand poised over her majestic bosom. Could the unorthodox woman disapprove of a lady scientist? A poignant understanding took root in Juliet's mind. Of course, Emily's mother would be shocked that Kent had chosen a wife so different from his demure first love.

She took a sip of tea to allay the dryness in her throat. "Botany is what first drew Kent and me together. We share an interest in growing plants."

"I see." Chantal arranged herself on a cane chair, the back as tall and curved as a throne, the dark wood like a tiara framing her blond hair. "Pardon my ill-bred manners in speaking so plainly, but Kent took all of us by surprise with the suddenness of this marriage."

The speculative look in those celestial eyes told Juliet that her presence greatly disturbed Chantal. "Then you know who my father is."

"Rose told me." She studied Juliet over the porcelain cup. "May I ask what else Kent has said about me?"

Frankness might encourage a like response. "That you and his father had had a romance; that you're also the mother of his first wife."

"I see. Is that all?"

By that probing scrutiny, Juliet had the impression the woman was hiding something. "Is there something he left out?"

Chantal lowered her gaze to her lap. "I thought perhaps you might wonder why I'm still living at the castle."

A seed of sympathy flourished in Juliet. Chantal must fear that a Carleton would cruelly thrust out William Deverell's former mistress. Setting down her cup, she leaned forward. "You're here because Kent and I wish it. This feud has nothing to do with me. As far as I'm concerned, you'll have a home at Radcliffe for as long as you like."

That lovely mouth formed a faintly bitter line. "That's generous of you, Your Grace."

"Please, call me Juliet."

"Thank you, Juliet." She paused in contemplative silence. "Did you know I once played Shakespeare's Juliet?"

"Played? You mean in school?"

Chantal shook her head, stirring the tendrils crowning her brow. "Many years ago, I was the toast of the London theater. I wasn't much older than you when my acting career reached its zenith."

Now Juliet understood the showy gestures, the sense of drama enveloping Chantal Hutton. Perhaps this was the opening to glean more information. "Was that when you met William Deverell?"

"Yes. But he and I didn't become . . . involved until a few years later, in India."

"What made you leave England?"

The blue eyes clouded. "I couldn't bear to stay, so I joined a troupe of traveling players." Rising, Chantal glided to a window. "I'd suffered a broken love affair, you see."

Sunshine silhouetted the sadness on that proud profile. Juliet tried to imagine the pain of losing Kent before ever winning his heart. What awful emptiness she would suffer. "Was he . . . Emily's father?"

"Yes."

Unwilling to pry further into a stranger's sorrow, she said, "Is the heat in India really as oppressive as I've heard?"

The grief fled Chantal's face, as if she were an actress switching roles. Arms outstretched, she laughed. "So hot I longed to peel off my skin and sit in just my bones. During the worst of the summer, most women retired to the hills. Although I, of course, stayed behind."

"Why?"

"Because those elegant ladies cut me dead. I am considered a fallen woman, you know."

"Why did you and William never marry?"

Chantal shrugged. "He would wed only money or position."

Her voice held a hint of caustic pain. A sense of injustice gripped Juliet as she recalled Kent's description of his father: *He held an unshakable conviction about class differences. He believed a man born to the dukedom was superior to other men. . . .* A duke would never bestow the honor of his name on an actress, a woman who had already borne another man's bastard child.

With a twist of guilt, Juliet reflected that she herself had been raised to scorn such females. She could well imagine Mama's horror if she knew her daughter was taking tea with Chantal.

She studied Chantal's elegant form. How could such a proud woman stomach being kept? "You bore William a daughter," she said. "Surely he owed you something for that."

"He gave me a home," said Chantal, with a wave of her beringed hand. A secretive smile touched her lips. "William wanted me close by. Possessive fellows, these Deverell men."

Juliet recalled the quarrel. Yes, Kent was possessive, too. In that respect, he was like his father. . . .

Skirt swishing, Chatal walked briskly back to her chair. "Shall I pour more tea?"

"Yes, please."

Picking up the silver pot, she bent closer, her attention half on Juliet and half on pouring the steaming tea. "Fancy us, sitting here together, speaking so candidly."

Juliet tensed. "You mean because I'm a Carleton?"

"Carleton. I've heard William speak *that* name often enough. No, not because of that . . . because you're a lady. Yet you look at a person directly, without all that silly modesty so many women affect." Chantal tilted her head. "You have the most unusual eyes, too," she went on, her voice soft, meditative. "Green rimmed with gold. A stunning combination."

"I've been told I have my father's eyes."

Chantal turned away to freshen her own cup. "Is that so? What a trick of nature that God would grace a man with such lovely, long-lashed eyes."

A thread of emotion wove through the trifling comment, an emotion that eluded Juliet. Staring at that lissome back, she wondered if Chantal had shared her lover's hatred for the Carletons. "Have you ever met my father?"

"Is he coming here?" spoke a girlish voice from the door. Rose bustled into the room. Windblown sable hair tumbled down the back of her mauve gown, and her cheeks bloomed with color. "Hullo," she said, her voice breathless, as if she'd raced up the stairs. "Well, *is* he?"

"Most certainly not," Chantal said, setting down the pot with a sharp click.

"A pity. I'd like to meet the man Father talked so much about."

Chantal arched a fine eyebrow. "You're late. I was beginning to wonder if you'd gotten lost in the dungeon again."

"Oh, Mama. I'm hardly ten years old anymore." Brown eyes sparkling, she looked from Chantal to Juliet. "I'm so glad you've come to visit. You can hear all about my brilliant idea. I'm going to write a play."

Startled, Juliet said, "I thought you were compiling a family chronicle."

"That's the beauty of it—it's a play about the Deverells. Capturing all the drama of a noble dynasty." Rose twirled closer, ink-smudged hands clasped to her bosom. "Perhaps someday my work shall even be performed at the Drury Lane Theatre."

"An admirable dream, darling," said Chantal, her smile indulgent. "It should prove a challenge to make the dry pages of history appeal to a jaded cosmopolitan audience."

Rose waved the comment away. "My heritage is bound to enthrall even the harshest of critics, Mama. Why, the story of you and Father alone would—"

"Absolutely not, young miss," Chantal said, stiffening. "My private life will not be fodder for public appetite."

Rose hung her head, her eyes suddenly sheened with tears. "But I wouldn't have to use your real names."

Sighing, Chantal folded her daughter in a hug. "Oh, darling. Do you really suppose your father would have approved of such a project?"

"Of course you're right, Mama." A sly gleam in Rose's eye told Juliet she hadn't abandoned the idea. "I wasn't thinking, that's all. I've plenty of other illustrious ancestors."

Chantal nodded. "I'll pour you a cup of tea."

"Thank you." Rose plopped onto a crimson hassock and regarded Juliet. "I stopped by your room this morning, to take you on a tour of the castle, but you'd gone out with Augusta."

"Yes, she took me to Wyecote and introduced me to some of the villagers."

Rose wrinkled her dainty nose. "How could you bear to spend so many hours alone with that harridan?"

"Rose!" chided Chantal, delivering a cup to her daughter. "Augusta has helped many people in the district."

"Yes, Mama. I can admire her without liking her. But still, she doesn't make it easy to warm up to her cross nature . . . her and that dreadful yapping dog."

Though Juliet half agreed, she said, "Maybe Punjab

gives Augusta something to love, since she hasn't any children."

Eyes contemplative, Rose sipped her tea. "Perhaps so. I never saw her in quite that light."

"We all have secret longings," Chantal murmured. "Emotions we're afraid to share. If you're to write a play, darling, you must learn to look below the surface of your characters."

Sympathy unfurled inside Juliet's heart. Did Chantal lead a lonely life in this tower? Did she miss the comfort of William Deverell's embrace, spin dreams about her lost first love?

Juliet set aside her cup. "I thought it indelicate to ask this of Augusta. What's wrong with Gordon's hands?"

"Rheumatism," Chantal said. "He's suffered from the affliction since boyhood."

"Is there any cure?"

Chantal shook her head. "The doctor prescribes medication for the pain."

Eyes conspiratorial, Rose perched her elbows on her knees. "That tonic is why he always seems to have his head in the clouds. Lots of times when I've gone into the library for a research book, I've found him nodding off in his chair."

Another use for her dowry, Juliet thought. A London specialist might be able to treat Gordon's illness. Surely Kent couldn't object to accepting money that would help his cousin.

"If you'd like, Juliet," Rose said, "I'll show you around the castle tomorrow. We have ever so many fascinating heirlooms. Did you know that in the south tower we still have the bed that Henry the Eighth and Anne Boleyn slept in?"

As the girl chattered on, Juliet saw no polite way to divert the discussion back to the feud. Questions churned inside her, making her restless, impatient. Tonight, she reminded herself.

Tonight Kent would provide the answers.

Chapter 12

I t was the only answer.

Deep in numbing thought and warm water, Kent leaned against the back of the copper tub and soaked his work-weary muscles. After travels through Turkey, his great-grandfather had converted a guest bedroom into this richly appointed bath with the white marble floor and mahogany-framed tub so enormous, it required the approach of two steps. That renovation had, of course, occurred before the decline of the Radcliffe fortune.

Before the clash of Deverell and Carleton.

Oh, Christ, it was the only answer.

Willing the tremor from his hand, Kent picked up the glass from the ledge beside the tub and took a swallow. Brandy seared his throat, but instead of easing his anxiety, the liquor nourished the glow burning inside him. The glow that had scorched him ever since that afternoon, when Juliet had ridden out to the fields in the company of that goddamned skirt chaser, Hammond-Gore. Even now, Kent felt a throb of blinding jealousy, the urge to smash his fist into another man's face.

God help him, he'd fallen in love with Juliet.

It was the only explanation for this awesome ache inside him, this insatiable hunger to possess her, this softhearted desire to hold her close for an eternity.

He set down the brandy glass. Nonsense. He craved Juliet only because she was Emmett Carleton's daughter.

The justification rang as hollow as the empty glass. Somehow, through all his vengeful plotting, he'd failed to consider the possibility of loving the woman who had grown up coddled by Emmett Carleton. How had such a treacherous schemer managed to raise a daughter as forthright as Juliet?

Her image swam into his mind, the flashing green-gold eyes, the angry flush of her cheeks, the indignant sway of her hips. Heat pooled in his loins; his mouth went dry until he felt half-sick with longing and remorse.

The hurtful accusation on her face corroded him, became his own pain. His ears echoed with the unmerited implication he'd flung at her: *Give Henry half a chance and he'll have you on the ground with your skirts above your waist.*

Kent sank deeper into the tub. He had charged her with dishonor. He, who had woven a web of deceit so tight, it strangled him with both the need to confess and the fear of admitting the truth.

And, oh Christ, as if his other sins weren't enough, he'd called her Emily. He wanted to drown in chagrin and self-contempt. He didn't know how that blunder could have happened, except that he'd been obsessed with the shadows of the past and determined to resist his feelings for Juliet.

Acknowledging his love made his deception a sin beyond redemption.

Kent dunked his head beneath the water and came up sputtering. Fishing around the bottom of the tub, he snatched up the slippery cake of sandalwood soap. Viciously he began to scrub his hair. From the adjacent dressing room came the quiet sounds of Ravi's movements, the brushing of clothes, the polishing of boots, the closing of drawers.

The routine sounds scraped his raw nerves. Kent thrust his head under the water again to rinse his hair. When he broke surface, the Muslim stood silently beside the tub, a white towel draped over his arm, the candlelight dancing over his dusky face.

By that watchful stance, Kent knew Ravi had something of import to relay. "Well?" he snapped. "What is it?"

The servant placed the towel on the ledge. "Her Grace took tea with Miss Chantal."

"What?" Kent jackknifed to his feet. Water sloshed onto the floor.

"I thought you would wish to know, sahib," Ravi said in his unperturbed, faintly musical voice. "She stayed with Miss Chantal for more than an hour."

"Where is the duchess now?"

"Dining with your cousin. Shall I fetch her?"

"No." Kent brusquely waved Ravi away. "That will be all for tonight."

"As you wish, sahib." Bowing, he glided out the door.

Scarcely aware of his actions, Kent stepped from the tub. Droplets rolled down his body and plopped onto the veined marble floor. As he picked up the towel and rubbed himself dry, alarm and anxiety collided within him.

What had Chantal told Juliet?

Oh, Christ. Why hadn't he had he sense to warn Chantal to guard her tongue? Maybe deep in his heart he wanted Juliet to learn the entire story. To release his conscience from its terrible burden.

A sudden wave of logic deluged him. On second thought, she must not have heard anything damning about him. If she had, she wouldn't be downstairs, calmly dining. Claws unsheathed, she would be at her husband's throat. He smiled with wry tenderness. He knew her well enough to be sure of *that*.

Or did he?

Stalking into the dressing room, he thrust his arms into a silver-gray robe and yanked the sash tight. How certain *could* he be of his wife? Perhaps Emmett Carleton wasn't truly at the core of his fears. What frightened him was that Juliet might leave because she was disillusioned by their hasty nuptials. And enraged that he'd called her by another woman's name.

There's more to marriage than physical pleasure.

His chest tightened, choking the breath from his lungs. God. As a husband, he was an utter washout. He'd failed to give Juliet happiness, just as he'd failed to banish the melancholia from Emily. Had he learned nothing from his first marriage?

Pensively he combed his fingers through his wet hair. Who would have thought he could love two women so dissimilar? Emily had been gentle and shy, shrinking from the physical realities of marriage. Juliet was vibrant and outspoken, eager to share both body and soul . . . so long as she remained blissfully unaware of his true purpose in wedding her.

Bypassing the dinner tray Ravi had left before the bedroom hearth, Kent sought another glass of brandy, then sat before his desk. Candlelight cast shadows over the half-finished drawing for the mechanical thresher, the plan he'd been too distracted these past weeks to finish.

He set aside his drink and picked up a pencil. His gaze wandered toward an opened window. Dusk had succumbed to the dense black silk of evening. Against the perpetual lapping of the river, crickets chirped and frogs croaked. Summer sounds, as timeless and soothing as a dream.

Dreamspinner.

Memory bathed the raw wound inside him. He had sworn to make Emmett Carleton pay for his sins. For years the vow had been the focus of Kent's life; revenge had been a tonic for the heartbreak of grief and the guilt of having failed Emily.

Now, by a peculiar prank of fate, victory left him exposed to a vast vulnerability, to the peril of again losing the woman he loved.

He drank deeply of the brandy, then forced his eyes to the design lying atop the age-creased leather surface of the desk. Instead of the clean lines of the drawing, he saw Juliet's tear-misted eyes. Disgusted with his inability to concentrate, he tossed down the pencil and prowled the shadowed room.

If she left him, where would she go? Because of him, she'd severed her ties with her parents. Oh, God, he couldn't think about losing her. Maybe he was wrong. Maybe she wouldn't abandon their marriage, because she had too strong a sense of honor and commitment.

Yet she also had a powerful need for love. He didn't know if a man so jaded by a life of fruitless hatred, so ensnared by the bitter legacy of the past, could ever satisfy that need in her.

But he wanted desperately to try.

The muffled tap of footsteps came from the adjoining bedroom. Pivoting toward her door, Kent felt his heart jerk under a tightening rope of longing and anxiety. Christ, he felt as uncertain as a youth contemplating his first kiss. He felt suffocated by the soul-shriveling fear of opening himself to the agony of loving again.

He clenched and unclenched his fists. How Juliet must despise him for the way he'd insulted her, for the way he'd denied her the true affection of a husband. God help him if she ever learned how dearly he deserved her hatred. . . .

He didn't know what the hell to say to bridge the abyss in their relationship. Yet he had to try.

Steeling his nerves, he started slowly toward her door.

Tossing a glare at Kent's door, Juliet tried to get her nerves under control. She'd spent the past two hours politely listening to Augusta's complaints about the lack of money for the new vicarage and to Gordon's rambling discourse on evolutionary philosophy. Chantal and Rose were absent; Augusta claimed the two preferred to keep their own company. "That Chantal acts too proud," she'd grumbled. "Thinks we ought to treat her like the dowager, instead of a vulgar tart living here on the duke's sufferance."

Juliet wondered bleakly why Kent hadn't joined them, if neglect would be a habit with him. The strain of keeping a courteous facade only nourished the bud of resentment swelling inside her. Now that resentment was fast blooming into full-blown anger.

After their explosive argument, she'd expected him to at least make the effort to reconcile. Clearly he was arrogant enough to believe her so uncritical and adoring that even his vile insults couldn't rouse her ire.

He'd find out his mistake soon enough.

Just as she stepped toward his bedroom, a low rap sounded; Kent walked inside. Their eyes locked and her heart danced an involuntary reel. The silver-gray dressing gown enhanced his sun-dark skin; the light of the candle on the nightstand caught the disarray of his damp hair. She ached to tidy the dark strands. She ached to slap his aggressively handsome face.

"I didn't invite you in," she said coolly.

"You've every right to shut me out, Juliet. Yet I'd like to have a word with you, if I may."

The gentle contrition in his voice wormed into her heart; deliberately she kept her gaze icy and her tongue acid. "You should have come to dinner, then."

"We didn't finish the hedge until nearly dusk. I was grimy and sweaty. . . ." He paused, his posture stiff, his eyes somber. "I'm sorry about my absence. I'll make an effort to dine with you in the future."

"Don't rearrange your schedule on my account. I can manage to hold a decent conversation with the family."

"I know. Yet you're right, I should have been there." He came a few steps closer, hands plunged in the pockets of his dressing gown. "Speaking of family, I understand you met Chantal Hutton today. What did you think of her?"

An oddly tentative quality skirted his words . . . because he spoke of Emily's mother? Though her heart thumped at his nearness, pain thrust into Juliet. "She was gracious and kind. I can see why your father loved such a woman."

Kent glanced away, his expression moody, as if he was looking into the past. "He was obsessed with her."

"Yet he never married her. Perhaps you Deverell men care little for a woman's happiness."

His sharp gaze sliced into her. "That's nonsense. Chantal has always been happy here. Your happiness is important to me—"

"Is it? Do you intend to neglect me as Henry says you neglected Emily?"

A scowl compressed his face; Juliet knew the bleak satisfaction of striking a nerve. "Hammond-Gore is a meddlesome ass," Kent snapped. "He was in no position to judge whether or not Emily felt neglected. He was no more than a passing acquaintance.''

Goaded by anger, she added recklessly, ''He thinks she took her own life.''

His eyes flashed with darkness, yet when he spoke his voice held no clue to his thoughts. ''He's only repeating gossip.''

''Then why don't *you* tell me about her?''' she said in frustration. ''She needn't be a secret from me.''

Juliet had the impression of Kent drawing back, though he remained perfectly still. ''What do you wish to know?''

''I don't resemble her in the slightest, and I've already guessed I possess none of her virtues. So why would you mistake me for her?''

He brushed past her to gaze into the moonless night, his palms braced on the window casement. ''I told you,'' he murmured, ''I don't know how that happened, except I was half-asleep. Can you ever forgive me?''

''Oh, certainly, Your Grace.'' Juliet swallowed hard and spoke to his back. ''And what of the next time?''

He swung around, his expression as readable as a closed book. ''There'll be no next time.''

''How can I believe that?''

''You have my word on the matter.''

The quiet strength of his tone shook the firm ground of her anger. ''I won't have you pining for the past,'' she said, struggling to keep her voice steady. When he started to protest, she put up a hand. ''I can live with crumbling walls,'' she went on. ''I can admire your devotion to farming because I know how much you love Radcliffe. I can even face the fact that our marriage isn't going to be as I'd envisioned. But there's one thing I won't tolerate, Kent Deverell. That's being judged against the standard set by another woman.''

Her frankness left Kent at a loss for words. The candleglow illuminated her lovely face, though her skin shone paler than normal. She kept her chin tilted at the determined angle so rare in a woman, yet so appealing in Juliet. Her proud character gleamed like a ray of sunshine in the dark secrets of his life.

Thank God, she hadn't announced her intent to leave him. Yet.

Relief left him weak-kneed. He wanted to take her into his arms, but fearing his reception, he walked slowly to her and touched only her smooth cheek.

"You're wrong to think I find you lacking," he murmured. "In you, I have everything a man could want in a wife."

Her shoulders squared beneath the green silk of her gown. "Everything? What exactly does that mean?"

"You're forthright . . . strong . . . loving."

She watched him closely. "Yet from what you've said, Emily was very different from me. And you loved her."

My love for you is greater. The realization screamed inside his head. Never had he reacted with such violent jealousy to seeing Emily with Hammond-Gore. Shaken by the unexpected power of his feelings, he fumbled for words.

"You're each unique. Each of you owns a piece of my soul." He lowered his voice to a whisper. "How can I compare the sun and the moon?"

Yearning gentled her face. "Oh, Kent, I want to believe you."

"Then do." Though he feared to declare his love, he could show her how precious she was in the best way he knew how.

He started to gather her into his arms; she stiffened and drew away. Her green-gold eyes regarded him with a resolution that made his heart stumble over a beat.

"That isn't all I have to say, Kent. I want some answers, too."

"Answers?"

"About the feud."

The night breeze that fluttered the draperies felt like a blast of bitter air. "What do you want to know?" he said warily.

"How did the quarrel begin? What happened to make Deverells and Carletons hate so deeply?"

Christ. What could he say to *that*?

Pushing his fingers through his hair, Kent walked to

the bed and perched on the edge. He had to compose a credible reply; he was fast learning that when his wife had that unflinching look in her eyes, she wouldn't be easily put off.

"All right, then," he said, his mind concocting a version of the truth. "Sit down and I'll tell you."

He patted a spot beside him, but Juliet knew better than to seat herself on the bed. The suspicion that Kent wore nothing beneath that robe provided far too much temptation, especially when she still reeled from the implication that he cared so deeply for her. *How can I compare the sun and the moon?*

Boneless with longing, she sank into a wing chair near the hearth. "I'm listening."

He leaned forward and stared at his clasped hands. "The story began more than forty years ago, when my father and yours attended Harrow together. Emmett resented being a commoner, present only by grace of scholarship, while most of his classmates were nobly born. Apparently my father made a pointed remark about Emmett's heritage, and a fist brawl ensued. From then on, the two were rivals."

"There must be more to it than a boyhood squabble."

Kent shrugged. "Of course. Emmett coveted all the privileges my father had inherited. His envy goaded him into trying to prove he was the better man, whether it be in the classroom or on the cricket field."

Juliet bristled. "I admit that Papa is ambitious, but don't blame the feud entirely on him. William played a part, too."

"Of course," he said easily. "My father was guilty of believing himself superior because of his birth."

"How did the feud grow into a business rivalry?"

"For generations, the Deverells had interests in India—spices, tea, indigo. Apparently Emmett vowed to outdo my father, and struggled to build his own enterprises from nothing. He resented the fact that my father had the leisure to live like a gentleman." Eyes stony, Kent regarded her. "He tricked my father into buying a tea estate just days before the market crashed. My father lost a huge sum of money on the transaction."

"Papa told me about that. He said it was a fair bargain, that he couldn't control the market."

"A shrewd businessman can predict trends. Unfortunately my own father wasn't so shrewd. He didn't realize he was dealing with Emmett until it was too late. You see, Emmett had hired an agent to act as the owner. He knew it was the only way to lure my father into the purchase."

She gripped the chair arms. "Papa wouldn't do such a thing." Yet even as she spoke, the memory of that slap rang in her ears. Her father had proven he was not the man she had grown up to revere. He had a dark, unforgiving side.

"That isn't all," Kent said. "My father was caught bringing stolen opium into England. He suffered great distress when an anti-opium society made him the focus of their campaign against the drug."

"Surely you can't blame *that* on Papa."

"My father didn't hide the opium there. Nor did anyone else in my family. The leader of the fanatics admitted that Emmett Carleton had urged them to use my father as their scapegoat."

Her mind closed against the terrible accusation. Yet the words taunted Juliet, threatened to further corrode the tarnished image of her father. He hated the Deverells enough to renounce his only daughter. Was he also capable of the unprincipled act of framing a rival?

Wracked by uncertainty, she paced to a window. Kent sat with his hands clasped. Candlelight threw shivering shadows over his lean features. She scanned his face for a clue to his thoughts, but his dark eyes betrayed nothing.

Desperate for reassurance, she said, "And you? What do you believe?"

His gaze faltered, but only for an instant. Rising, he came close and planted gentle hands on her shoulders. "I believe the feud isn't ours. I believe we should forget the past and concentrate on the future. Our future."

Sincerity rang in his deep voice. Yet his sidestepping of the question told Juliet the truth: he thought Emmett Carleton guilty. "You still mistrust my father," she said. "Yet you wanted to end the feud. Why?"

"I've told you, I saw no reason to perpetuate my father's quarrel." His smile heartbreaking, he combed back a stand of hair from her brow. "Once I'd met you, I knew I'd made the right decision."

"Oh, Kent, I never believed Papa capable of such awful things. How could I have grown up so blind to his faults?"

"Tell me how you saw him."

Wistful memory washed through her. "He worked long hours, yet he always found time for me each evening. He told me tales of his stay in India, riding elephants through tiger-infested jungles, meeting maharajas in their jeweled palaces." She swallowed. "He called me his princess . . . and sometimes his little dreamspinner."

His hands convulsed around her shoulders. For a moment he only stared at her. "I'm sorry to be the one to shatter his image," he said roughly. "Perhaps I shouldn't have told you the truth about him."

Though her heart rebelled, Juliet knew she must acknowledge the probability of her father's dishonesty. Tears blurred her eyes. "I want to make amends with Papa," she whispered. "But I don't know if I can ever forgive him."

Pulling her close, Kent settled her against his chest. "Then at least forgive me. I'm sorry for losing my temper today, for hurting you."

The humble contrition in his voice roused a warm ache inside her. She pressed her cheek into his palm and kissed his callused fingers. "I do forgive you, Kent. I do." Yet a sudden thought barred her contentment. "There's something I forgot to tell you. I received a letter today from my mother."

His embrace tightened protectively. With his thumb, he tilted her chin up so she met his probing eyes. "And?"

"She said Papa was furious over our elopement, just

as we knew he'd be." Juliet took a hurtful breath.
"He's disinherited me."

His fingers began to rub the tension from her neck.
"Believe me, Juliet, I deplore seeing you cut off from
your parents. But we don't need Emmett Carleton's ill-
gotten gains."

The aloofness in his voice shook her. For an instant,
she agonized over confessing about the letter she'd
posted. Yet why invite his anger when the scheme
might never bear fruit? She'd lost her parents; she
couldn't chance losing Kent, too.

Wetting her lips, she regarded him warily. "My
mother also said she was sending a few trunks of my
clothes."

His hand ceased its mesmeric massage. "I trust you
wrote back and refused them?"

"As a matter of fact, I didn't." Reluctant to harm his
pride, she chose her words carefully. "If I'm to make
a place for myself here, I should dress as a duchess. It
seems more practical to use the wardrobe designed for
me, dresses I like, than to put us in debt over the purchase of cloth."

A frown tightened Kent's face. She had the impression of turbulent emotions in him, as if he withheld
something vital. The lonely hoot of a barn owl drifted
into the silence.

Then he dropped his arms to his sides. "As you
wish, then," he murmured. "I won't object to the
gowns."

"I'm glad. Because I'd intended to accept them re-
gardless."

He stared; Juliet held her head high. Then his lips
quirked into a wry smile, his finger catching a tendril
of her hair. "You do act the duchess, don't you?"

The esteem in his gaze drenched the last embers of
anger left by their quarrel. Putting her hands to his
chest, she slid her palms upward over the polished silk
of his robe, over hard muscle and taut sinew, until her
fingers meandered into the still damp strands of his
hair.

Soft and sultry, she asked, "How else would you have me act, Your Grace? I'm yours to command."

His eyes gleamed. "You're managing perfectly well on your own, Duchess. Nevertheless . . ." Shaping his hands to her lower back, he pressed their hips together. "Ah, now that's better."

Through the layers of gown and petticoat, she felt him rise against her. The sensation ignited the fuse of her own passion; the familiar fire began deep in her belly and radiated outward to her thighs and breasts. Wanting more, she moved her hips with restless urgency.

His grin vanished and his eyes went unfocused, half closing as he gazed down at her. "Darling Juliet . . ."

She had but a moment to revel in the emotion enriching his voice; then he was kissing her with such tender violence that she swayed from the force of her feelings. Her hands caught the breadth of his shoulders; the warm circle of his arms held her steady. She loved the feel of her softness against his solidity, her slenderness against his strength. He tasted of brandy, smelled of sandalwood. His tongue plundered her mouth until she felt dazed and trembly, craving the ultimate joining yet savoring the eternity of his kiss.

His lips nuzzled her temple and trailed down her cheek to the sensitive hollow below her ear. She felt his fingers at her back, unbuttoning her gown to the waist. "Tell me how to make you happy," he murmured. "Tell me how to make you forget the past, to start anew. I want to be everything to you."

She felt a twist of longing, the ache to be first in his heart. Hiding the sensation, she echoed his words, "You're managing perfectly well on your own, my lord duke."

His arms flexed as he drew down her bodice. "Forgive me for behaving like a jealous fool," he whispered, unhooking her corset. "I never meant to imply you'd break our marriage vows, that you'd ever deceive me about anything."

Her heart sang at the confession that he cared enough to want her all to himself. Then, sharp as a thorn, the memory of that audacious letter pricked her joy. Dear God, she should tell him. She should—

His mouth closed around her nipple and a floodtide of desire drowned the guilty thought. Half-delirious, she arched her spine to offer more of herself. The pleasure-pain of his suckling set her afire. His hot breath bathed her breasts; rivers of excitement rushed through her veins. The room suddenly tilted as he lifted her in his arms and set her down on the bed. Gown and hairpins fell away under the swift work of his fingers.

She wrestled with the tie of his dressing gown until the garment gaped open. Tracking the ridges and valleys of his muscles, her hand stole downward along the arrow of dark hair on his belly until she found the purpose of her quest.

"Ah, God, Juliet," he groaned, "when you touch me like that, I could die from the pleasure."

"Then perhaps I should cease," she teased, stilling her hand. "I shouldn't like to be widowed so soon."

"Minx. I'll prove how alive I am."

He caressed the wetness between her legs. Even as she gasped in ecstasy, her heart leapt from the memory of his words: *Whatever I take from you, I intend to give back.*

The words surged from deep within her: "I love you, Kent. I love you so much."

The declaration slid over Kent like the finest silk. He wanted to drown in those words, to let them heal the self-loathing that eroded his heart. Oh, God, he didn't deserve the trust shining in her eyes. . . .

He rolled away and stretched an arm toward the candle. Juliet leaned over to catch his wrist in her fingers.

"Please, don't," she begged. "Not tonight, Kent. I want to look at you while we make love."

Her hair draping him in a cinnamon waterfall, she kissed his chest. The gesture made his belly constrict with the need to kindle a hundred candles, to take her with his soul opened in honesty and their bodies bathed in brilliance.

Yet how could he gaze into her radiant eyes and hide his guilt? How could he risk revealing the secret that would splinter her soul and extinguish the light she'd brought into his life?

Sick with fear, he reached for the candle again.

"Kent?" she said in a small voice. "Does my boldness disgust you?"

He sat back. Her chest rose and fell, her breasts gilded by candleglow. Her eyes were shadowed by a pain that perplexed him.

"Disgust me?" he said blankly.

She shifted her gaze to a point past his shoulder. "You must think me unladylike. Last night—"

"Last night you excited me beyond comprehension. I thought I made my feelings on that perfectly clear."

She sighed; her expression was tentative, as if she didn't dare believe him. "Then why do you never leave the candle burning? Don't married couples ever make love in the light?"

A cold sweat broke out on his palms; his lips felt suddenly parched. With great effort Kent kept from averting his face from hers. "Of course," he said, casting about for an explanation, "but I prefer the darkness . . . when the senses come alive. It's a quirk of mine, that's all."

He held himself still under her solemn regard. Like dawn stealing over a garden, a soft glow entered her eyes. She leaned past him and blew out the candle.

Night whispered through the room. His heart faltered; his breath abandoned him. Juliet had believed another of his lies. The knowledge that she would so sweetly indulge him left Kent too staggered for speech. He'd married her for all the wrong reasons. So why did it feel so right to love her?

He heard a rustle as she shifted position, felt the silken slide of her thigh against his. "Kent?" she whispered. "Tell me what you're thinking."

Through the darkness, his unsteady hands found the precious shape of her waist. Clasping her close, he put his lips to the fragrance of her hair. "I was thinking," he said slowly, "that if you weren't already my wife, I'd ask you to marry me."

Chapter 13

"Pleasin' to look on, you are," said the cobbler, the last rays of sunset illuminating his wizened face. "Radcliffe'll finally get himself an heir."

Juliet bit back a startled laugh. "We're hoping to be so blessed, Mr. Peek."

"Bide your tongue, Alf." Round as a cowberry, Mrs. Peek unfolded her dewlapped arms to swat at a fly. "Beer's gone to his head, Your Grace. We ain't had a haying supper here at the castle since the other duchess's passing, God rest her poor soul."

Peek winked at Juliet. "But you've put the smile back on the duke's face, you have."

Contentment and love swelled inside her. The Peeks were right. Since their reconciliation nearly a month earlier, Kent had seemed lighter of heart, more affectionate. Her stomach tightened at the thought of their long nights of loving, of lying in velvet darkness. . . .

Seeking his tall form, she looked over the gathering of tenants and their families. The south garden bordered the outer wall of the castle, the ancient turrets outlined against the amethyst sky of dusk. But Kent was nowhere in sight.

"Come along, Alf," said Mrs. Peek. "I hear Dickie tuning his fiddle, and you promised me a reel."

"Hold your bloomers on, Cora." The cobbler raised his pewter beer mug. "First, a toast to our new duchess. May she bloom at Radcliffe like a rose in springtime."

A few people standing nearby raised their cups as cheers echoed through the overgrown rose garden. Touched by the salute, Juliet accepted the toasts with a gracious smile. She held herself proudly as more than

one admiring glance took in her ivory silk gown
trimmed with gold ribbons. They expected their duchess to look and act the noblewoman; she was eager to
fill that role.

Suddenly a pair of strong hands came from behind to
circle her waist. His breath warm in her ear, Kent murmured, "You've scored quite the triumph, Duchess."

Smiling, she turned to look at him. "Everyone seems
to have accepted me."

"Radcliffe is your home now," he said staunchly,
"as it always shall be."

As he took her arm and guided her through the
crowd, they exchanged greetings with tenants and their
families, and renewed old acquaintances. The scents of
honeysuckle and roses perfumed the air. Giggling children darted over the newly trimmed stone flags. Near
the greenhouses, long tables of food had been set up,
laden with everything from meat pies to gooseberry
tarts, from Stilton cheeses to pickled ham. On an open
stretch of grass, couples, young and old, danced to the
polka played by a makeshift orchestra, a fat man saw-
ing at a fiddle, a gangly youth rattling a tambourine, a
skinny pensioner plying a mouth organ.

Juliet spied a peacock strutting at the fringe of the
garden, its regal head bobbing, iridescent tail feathers
dragging. A tiny, fair-haired girl on a crutch hobbled
after the colorful bird.

Kent grinned. "Hannah Forster has been trying to
catch that peacock for the past hour."

For the hundredth time, Juliet thought of the letter
she'd written, the secret she'd kept from Kent. Frustration twisted inside her. Now that nearly a month
had passed, she'd resigned herself to the probability
of failure.

"Oh, Kent, I wish we could help her."

He pressed his hand to hers. "The harvest promises
to be bountiful. Maybe we'll have the money to find a
cure for Hannah."

"I pray we will. Did I tell you I've become friends
with Mary Forster? Twice now she's come for rose cut-
tings."

His midnight eyes softened. "It must be difficult for you, without your London friends. Especially when your husband works such long hours."

Juliet smiled. "When would I find time for boredom? Between Rose showing me around the castle and Augusta taking me on visits, I tend the vegetables in the greenhouse."

"My dear Lady Botanist." Bending, he snapped a crimson moss rose off a rambling bush; then he brushed her cheek with the satiny petals. "Do you know what I'd like to do right now?"

The rough velvet of his voice left no mistake about his meaning. Breathless, she said, "Shall we take a stroll down to the river? You've never shown me your favorite fishing spot. . . . We could lie on the bank. . . ."

His eyes gleamed. "You tempt a man with absurdly small effort. However—" he glanced over his shoulder at the party "—duty calls."

As the dusk grew thicker, Fleetwood shuffled down the pathways and lit tall rush torches. Beyond the yellow glow, two people walked in the gloom beneath the row of lime trees. She nodded toward the couple. "Isn't that Ravi and Chantal?"

"It would appear so."

"I wonder what they're talking about."

Slowing his steps, Kent smiled. "He's been giving her lessons in Hindustani. Perhaps he's making her practice."

"How intriguing. I wonder why she'd wish to learn a foreign tongue."

"It's all the rage, I understand. The queen herself is learning Hindi from her *munshi*."

The mention of Victoria seized Juliet with guilty apprehension. Quickly she said, "*Munshi*? What's that?"

"Teacher. The queen has an Indian servant whom she greatly favors."

"I see." Juliet looked back at the shadowed figures, each of equal height. Against the darkness Chantal's blond hair gleamed as pale as Ravi's turban. "Odd, how they both seem disinclined to mingle with anyone else."

"They're both different from the people here. Perhaps they find comfort in each other."

She stopped. "Kent, do you suppose they're lovers?"

Chuckling, he tweaked her nose. "Duchess, your mind is in the bedroom."

"But I wonder if they're lonely—"

"Obviously not anymore. Now, if you'll excuse me for a few moments, I shall go rescue the curate from Gordon's long-winded discourse. Just remember, the last dance is mine."

Juliet watched him skirt the edge of the throng, pausing several times to speak to tenants before joining his cousin. Passion and tenderness glowed in her heart, both feelings so tightly entwined, she wanted to burst with joy. She could scarcely wait until she and Kent could retire for the night. . . .

She turned back to the lime grove, but Ravi and Chantal had vanished. Restless, Juliet wandered toward the trio of greenhouses. The cracked panes glistened on the one she'd commandeered for her planting.

She spied Rose near a cask of wine. Resplendent in an old-fashioned gown of mauve silk, the girl hurried toward Augusta, who directed Mrs. Fleetwood and several other servants.

Juliet reached them in time to hear Rose say, "The ale is nearly gone. I've sent Hatchett to fetch another barrel from the cellar."

"Poppycock," Augusta snapped, her mole quivering. "There's plenty of plain cider left to drink. With a harvest party next month, we can scarce afford to host this haying supper. If you ask me—"

"No one has," said Rose. "Kent wanted me to help see to the comfort of our guests. And that's precisely what I've done."

Punjab waddled from beneath a table and growled, planting his squat body before his mistress. Augusta spared a gentle glance at the dog, then glowered at Rose. "You're overstepping your bounds. One would think you were a trueborn Deverell."

Rose gasped. "How dare you say such a wretched thing! I, at least, have the blood of kings flowing through *my* veins—"

"That's quite enough," Juliet said firmly, stepping between them. "We'll open the additional barrel."

Augusta stiffened. "But we haven't the money—"

"If the harvest is as bountiful as Kent hopes, there'll be no difficulty in supplying more ale. But more to the point, it is Kent's wish."

"Yes," said Rose archly, "the Duke of Radcliffe will never let his people go hungry or thirsty."

The smug tilt of that dainty chin bothered Juliet; Rose had no business being so coy. "Yet from now on," she said, "I'm certain you'll want to consult me before ordering more refreshments."

Her mouth settling into a pout, Rose folded her arms across her lace fichu. "But my brother always lets me—"

"Do whatever you please," finished Henry Hammond-Gore.

A rakish smile on his face, he emerged from the shadows between the greenhouses. In one hand he held a pair of kid gloves dyed green to match his tweed jacket.

Rose's disgruntled expression melted into bland welcome. "Why, Henry. This is most unexpected."

Augusta's ginger brows descended. "This is also a party for the estate folk. Did the duke invite you?"

Henry whipped off the bowler hat and held it to his chest. "I must confess, he didn't. Yet I couldn't bear to pass up the chance to converse with my three favorite ladies."

He graced a charming grin on each of them in turn. The wary blush on Rose's milk-pure complexion intrigued Juliet. Did friendship or ill will exist between those two?

She noted in amusement that the strict line of Augusta's mouth softened into tolerance. "I'll fetch you a glass of that burgundy you like," she said, then strode off, Punjab at her heels.

Rose tidied her modest fichu. "Since you've met our new duchess, I won't bother to introduce you, Henry."

"Indeed." He arched a fair eyebrow at Juliet. "The news of Radcliffe's marriage took this pastoral district by storm. It's like the tale of Romeo and Juliet, the two feuding families brought together by love."

"But I hope," Juliet said, "to forgo the tragic conclusion."

Rose clapped her hands. "Oh, Henry, that reminds me. I haven't yet told you. I'm writing a play about the Deverells."

"A stage play?"

"Yes, in my research I've uncovered so many fascinating stories about my family. Perhaps one day I'll tell you a few of them."

"Perhaps." A frown flitted over Henry's brow so swiftly that Juliet thought she'd imagined the instant of worry. With a flourish of his bowler hat, he bent to kiss Rose's hand, then Juliet's. "Imagine, Radclife has two beautiful bluestockings ensconced in his castle."

"Why, thank you," Rose said, smiling demurely.

He straightened, his gaze lifting past her shoulder. Under his breath, he muttered, "Speak of the devil, there's the lucky fellow right now."

Juliet turned to see Kent striding out of the crowd. Her spine tensed at his unsmiling face. His lordly demeanor threatened an explosive scene.

But as he came to her side and slid an arm around her waist, he merely gave a civil nod to Henry. "Hammond-Gore."

"Ah, Radcliffe, old chap. Seen any of my Guernseys lately?"

"Thankfully, they've kept to their own side of the hedge." Kent paused, then cocked an eyebrow. "Unlike their owner."

Augusta marched into the circle and handed a glass of red wine to Henry. "Sorry to take so long," she said gruffly. "The vicar asked me to prepare a plate for him."

"You're a dear."

His appealing grin made Augusta blush. Then she

pursed her lips and bent to feed Punjab a slice of cherry cake.

Eyeing the dog, he added, "Do fetch the old fellow his saucer of tea." Turning to Kent, Henry savored a sip of wine. "Surely you won't begrudge me a drink, too. All in the spirit of neighborliness, of course."

"Of course," Kent said dryly. "Next you'll be trying to convince me you're starved for feminine companionship."

Henry slapped his gloves against his buckskined thigh. "By George, you're astute, Radcliffe. For nigh on a month now, I've been rattling around that old house of mine, talking to no one but myself."

"Poor soul," Kent said. "Imagine having only *you* for company. Next time, don't get yourself banished from London."

"Banished?" Rose asked, brown eyes rounding. "How positively inspiring. Do tell us what happened."

"A minor inconvenience, nothing to include in your stage play." Henry raised his glass, torchlight glinting through the burgundy contents. "I propose a toast to you lovely ladies."

Rose patted her halo of sable hair. Augusta smoothed her drab brown skirts. Juliet coughed to conceal a laugh.

"Henry," she said, "you're welcome to take tea with us any afternoon. We'll give you your fill of scintillating conversation."

"With such a truly gracious lady present, London has lost its allure." Henry paused, peering into the raucous crowd. "Speaking of truly gracious ladies, who the devil is *she*?"

Juliet craned her neck to see past Kent's broad shoulder. The music stopped. A buzz of murmurs rose into the starry night. For one frustrating moment, she glimpsed only a lavish pink ostrich feather bobbing above the throng of guests.

The crowd parted. The feather led downward to a fashionable, begonia-hued hat atop a headful of upswept fair hair. Below the wide straw brim, girlish blue eyes peered through a pair of gold-rimmed spectacles.

Juliet gasped. "Maud!"

Kent gave a start of surprise. "What the devil—?"

Catching sight of them, Maud surreptitiously whipped the eyeglasses into a blue case, which she thrust in her pocket. She picked up her skirts and sailed closer, a vision in elegant shell-pink voile. "There you are," she declared. "I wondered why no one answered the coachman's knocking."

Juliet couldn't stop an astonished grin. "Whatever are you doing here?"

"You said in your letter that I should visit sometime. So I took the afternoon train from Paddington."

"I meant . . . well, it doesn't matter now." Thrilled at the sight of her friend's dear face, Juliet swept Maud into a tight hug. "I'm delighted to see you."

"Welcome to Radcliffe," Kent murmured.

"Hear, hear," said Henry, his eyes gleaming as he lifted his glass. "My lady, I'll be happy to offer my services should you require an escort around the district."

Maud squinted avidly. "I don't believe we've been introduced."

"Allow me," Kent said. As he presented her around, Rose looked quietly curious, Augusta dourly attentive, Henry openly admiring.

Grasping Maud's gloved hands, Juliet bubbled over with questions. "Why didn't you write that you were on your way? Did you come alone? Does your mother know you're here?"

"I didn't know till this morning, so I couldn't very well post a letter in time. Miss Fane accompanied me; she's waiting in the station hackney." With an impish grin, Maud drew her hands free. "And yes, Mother knows that I've gone . . . by now."

"You mean you left without telling her?"

"She was waiting on the queen at Windsor, so I sent a note." Shrugging prettily, Maud tilted a myopic glance at Kent. "Your Grace, didn't you receive the telegram?"

"Telegram?" he said, frowning.

"From Sir Ponsonby. I'm *sure* Mother said it would arrive this afternoon. But I didn't have my glasses—" Glancing at Henry, she blushed as pink as her gown. "Well, somehow I must have misread her message."

"Ponsonby," Henry mused. "Now, why would the queen's private secretary be wiring you, Radcliffe?"

Dizziness swept through Juliet. Her mouth tasted dry as dust. She hadn't expected her letter to precipitate this turn of events.

Augusta said, "Perhaps Her Majesty heard gossip of the elopement."

"Of course, the scandal," Rose exclaimed. "Victoria would be livid to hear the Duke of Radcliffe had run off with the Carleton heiress."

Kent said nothing. He turned to gaze at Juliet.

His black brows were quirked at an inquisitive angle. She stood paralyzed under his scrutiny. Only her heart gave evidence of life, thumping wildly in her ears. She wanted to turn and flee, but her legs remained firmly rooted to the grassy ground.

Abruptly she caught herself short. She had done nothing wrong. Nothing but keep the existence of that letter from him.

"I'm sorry," Maud whispered to Juliet, "it took nearly a fortnight for Mother to find the right moment to pass your note to the queen. You see, Her Majesty has been in mourning over poor Frederick's death—"

"Note?" Kent murmured, his eyes gone steely.

Maud squinted from him to Juliet. "Egad. I believe I've made a muddle of things."

"A muddle," said Kent, "of precisely what?"

She hesitated. He glared.

"Oh, fiddle," Maud said. "The queen commands your presence at Windsor Castle day after tomorrow."

He stood still. Music and laughter swirled from the party. "Does she, now?"

He spoke to Maud, but his stony gaze penetrated Juliet. Again she felt that peculiar swimming sensation.

"What an honor," said Rose, clapping her hands. "Kent meeting with Victoria herself!"

"At the cost of a rail ticket," Augusta muttered. To Maud, she said, "Your ladyship, I'll see about preparing rooms for you and your maid." She tramped toward the castle gate, Punjab trotting in her elongated shadow.

"I trust you won't be retiring just yet, my lady," Henry said, twirling his wineglass. "Your absence would sap the very life from this rustic gathering."

Maud fluttered her lashes. "Goodness, no. I haven't journeyed so far merely to act unsociable."

"Yet Her Grace and I must be just that," said Kent, taking ungentle hold of Juliet's arm. "If you will excuse us."

He marched her along the outskirts of the garden. A few people turned to look, but most remained engrossed in merriment. She braved a glance at Kent's face; his features might have been set in granite. As they followed a gloomy path along the castle wall, the heavy scent of honeysuckle wafted from the shadows.

"Where are we going?" she asked.

"Where no one will overhear us."

His curt reply arrowed into Juliet. He was angry already and he didn't even know the full extent of what she'd done. . . .

The sounds of conviviality faded as they went through the narrow postern gate and into the darkened courtyard. Fingers firm on her arm, he drew her to a room off the entrance hall.

He struck a match; an oil lamp flared yellow light over the simple furnishings of the estate office. Neat rows of account books lined a shelf beside a pair of plain oak chairs. A stag trophy stared balefully from over the stone fireplace.

Settling on the edge of a scarred desk, he folded his arms. "You're white as a sheet," he said coldly. "Sit down."

She sat. "Kent, I can explain—"

"I expect as much. You may begin with your note to Victoria."

Though her stomach roiled, Juliet held her chin high. "I'd heard from Maud's mother, the Lady Higgleston, that our queen champions the rights of women. So I asked her to intercede in obtaining my dowry."

His eyes narrowed; the skin over his cheekbones went rigid. "Against my express wishes."

"I meant for Her Majesty to contact my father, to command him to give me the money. I never expected her to request *your* presence."

"Undoubtedly she believes I pressured you into writing to her." His voice lowered to an ominous murmur. "That I duped a gullible heiress into marrying me and now seek to steal her father's fortune."

"That isn't true!" Yet, too late, Juliet could see how the queen might draw such a conclusion. Striving to vanquish her guilt, she said, "I'm sorry to put you in the position of having to explain yourself. But I asked only for what's rightfully mine. My father would have settled that money on me had I married anyone but you."

He slammed his palm onto the desk. "Precisely. He wants no part of giving me the money and I want no part of receiving it."

Anger blazed to life inside her. "You'd refuse the wealth that can only help the people who depend on you? What about Hannah? She might not be crippled if only we had the means to pay for a London physician."

"I'll grant you, I've been remiss in seeing to the girl's well-being. But we'll seek a cure for her by using our own resources."

The slight thawing of his icy self-control encouraged Juliet to lean forward. "Hannah represents only a fraction of what money can provide for us, Kent. We could repair the castle, safeguard the heritage of our children. You could even fund the development of your inventions."

"I'll survive as I've always done, on my own wit and toil."

"Why? Why simply survive when we can do some good?" Frustrated, she leapt up to pace the room. "Why pass up this chance to help your tenants?"

"I've told you before, I want no part of Emmett Carleton's ill-gotten gains."

"If you truly believe my father cheated the Deverells out of your wealth, then you should welcome the opportunity to get some of that money back."

He straightened. "No. The subject is closed, Juliet."

The shadows cast by the lamplight cut stark hollows in his cheeks. Studying his taut features, she felt the happiness of the past weeks slipping from her grasp. "You keep saying you want to end this feud," she said slowly. "I'm beginning to doubt your sincerity."

His gaze faltered; when he looked at her again, all emotion had fled his dark eyes. "Doubt me if you must. But I will never accept a farthing of Carleton money."

His harsh statement shattered her last fragile hope. "Then it's a blessing the dowry isn't yours to refuse," she said, matching his frigid tone. "The law gives a married woman the right to manage her own wealth."

Fury thinned his lips. "So. You're determined to shove this money down my throat, no matter what my feelings to the contrary."

"Your feelings are distorted by ancient hatreds," she snapped. "I'm finally beginning to see that you're as obstinate and narrow-minded as my father."

He reared back as if she'd struck him. "Don't you dare compare me to Emmett Carleton."

"Don't blind yourself to the truth. Hatred has bred hatred in him, just as in you. So long as you tie yourself to the past, Kent Deverell, our marriage hasn't much hope for the future."

His face went white; the faint strident sound of his breathing broke the stillness. He took a step toward her. "Juliet, you'll not leave me—"

"I'll make you no promises," she said, resisting the tears closing her throat. "I'll tell you my plans when you return from Windsor."

Whirling, she stalked from the office and took bleak delight in slamming the door.

Chapter 14

~~~ ∽◯◯◡ ~~~

Their steps echoing on the marble floor, Kent followed a liveried footman down the Grand Corridor of Windsor Castle. Royal busts, gray with age, stared from pedestals set against either wall. The mullioned windows along one side overlooked the rain-soaked upper ward. Drafts of damp air gusted from doorways along the passage.

The chill cooled his sweating skin. He detested having to face Victoria's forbidding presence and explain that he hadn't orchestrated the meeting. Yet his fury already had burned down to the cinders of guilt. Juliet only meant to help his tenants. How could he charge her with deceit when a far greater secret weighted his own shoulders, a secret that could shatter her heart?

Unless her heart was already shattered by his angry outburst.

He hungered to be back at Radcliffe. At this very instant, Juliet might be packing in preparation to depart.

Unless she'd already gone.

His pace slowed. *I'll make you no promises.* God. Would she truly abandon their marriage? Recalling the disillusionment shadowing her face and his own denouncement of her father, Kent feared the worst.

After that bitter argument, she had kept to her room, only emerging the next day to bid him a dispassionate farewell. No fervid kiss, no whispered words of love, no warmth gentling her face. He'd longed to apologize, but how could he? How could he beg a forgiveness that hinged on accepting tainted money from Emmett Carleton?

Squeezing his eyes shut, Kent tried to envision a future without her lively conversation, without her passionate loving, without her radiant smile. He saw only darkness.

When he opened his eyes, the footman had vanished. In his place, a man strode back and forth along the end of the corridor. Kent's stomach twisted with involuntary aversion.

Emmett Carleton.

A silk hat topped his silver-streaked hair; a formal black frock coat rode his broad shoulders. Yet beneath the finery, he looked older somehow, grayer. A nervous quality pervaded his gait; he reminded Kent of a prowling lion.

An aging lion who had lost his pride to a younger challenger.

Yet Kent felt no sense of triumph, only a niggling sympathy that tasted both bitter and foreign in his mouth. Deliberately he made his footfalls louder.

Emmett pivoted. He jerked in surprise. His eyes widened, then narrowed. Green eyes rimmed with gold.

God, Kent thought. Juliet's eyes.

Hatred has bred hatred in him, just as in you.

Was she right? Had malice spun an eternal web of darkness? A darkness so dense, he'd lost sight of all that was clean and light?

Entombing his disturbing doubts, he inclined his head in a cool nod. "Emmett."

"You bloody bounder!" he sputtered. "What are *you* doing here?"

"Exactly what you are. Answering Victoria's summons."

The lips went taut beneath the handlebar mustache. "Why would the queen invite *you* to my—"

"To your what?" Then Kent knew, and said with mocking softness, "Ah, did you think she meant to award you that knighthood?"

The leonine face contorted. "I hope the queen strips you of your title. I'd buy a ticket to *that.*"

"On the contrary, Juliet will stay the Duchess of Radcliffe."

Emmett knotted his fingers into fists. "If you've harmed my daughter," he spat, "I swear before God I'll kill you."

"You're the one who harmed her. You slapped her. . . . The bruise on her cheek lasted a week."

Emmett stood still. His glare faltered, and for an instant Kent had the powerful impression of guilt in him, a guilt so human, Kent felt a startling stab of compassion.

Unable to resist, he added a lie. "Besides, Juliet has never been happier in her life. But then, you haven't bothered to find that out."

Emmett bristled. "Why, you—"

The door opened. A distinguished, bearded man in scarlet-trimmed uniform regarded them.

"Ponsonby," Kent said.

"Your Grace." The secretary bowed to Kent, then nodded to Emmett. "And Mr. Carleton, I presume. Her Majesty awaits."

Ponsonby took their hats, then led them into a small reception room. "His Grace, the Duke of Radcliffe, and Mr. Emmett Carleton."

Queen Victoria stood with her back to a rain-streaked window. Small and plain, her bell-like figure was swathed in black, her gray hair covered by a white widow's cap. She might have been a dowdy hausfrau except for the aura of command she emanated.

"Your Majesty." Kent kissed her age-mottled hand.

Emmett followed suit, his movements jerky with awe.

She gazed at Kent. "You're looking fit, Radcliffe. Marriage must agree with you."

"Indeed so, ma'am."

"Yet the ancient title of Radcliffe is being bandied about by every newspaper in London. The gossips have been saying that vengeance induced you to elope with Mr. Carleton's daughter."

Kent chose his reply carefully. "Not vengeance,

ma'am, but love. Juliet and I knew that he would grant us neither his permission nor his blessing."

"Scandal doesn't become you, Radcliffe. I would have expected such disgrace of William, but not of you."

Her regal glare had reduced many a smooth-tongued statesman to babbling incoherence. Only with effort did Kent keep his gaze steady.

"As for you, Mr. Carleton," she said, turning to Emmett, "why would you not bless this union? Your daughter has made a brilliant match, far better than could be expected for a commoner."

"I . . . I had another man in mind for her. . . ." His words trailed off as she fixed him with a cool stare.

"This feud," she went on, with a wave of her beringed hand, "can yield nothing but more detestable gossip. I shall not tolerate it. I command you both to settle your differences."

Given no choice, Kent nodded. "Yes, ma'am."

Looking overwhelmed, Emmett mumbled, "As you wish."

Victoria reached into a pocket of her voluminous gown and drew forth a sheet of stationery. "Mr. Carleton, I understand from your daughter's note that you've disinherited her. How deplorable that a man of such wealth would condemn his only child to poverty." She arched an eyebrow. "As a token of your good will, I should like you to grant her a suitable endowment."

Emmett shot Kent a murderous glance. "I knew Radcliffe was after my money."

"I didn't marry Juliet for money," Kent said quickly. "And I knew nothing of her request. I seek only the right to live with my wife in peace."

Emmett snorted in disbelief. "That is a lie—"

Victoria silenced him with a cold look. "Your daughter has wed a duke. Will you leave her without the means to support her position?" Lifting the note, she studied it for a moment. "She seeks the betterment of the Radcliffe tenants. Houses wanting repair, a crippled girl in need of an operation. Quite an admirable goal for so young a duchess, don't you agree, Mr. Carleton?''

Kent veered from the peak of pride to the depths of humility. How badly he'd underestimated Juliet.

"I . . . yes, ma'am," Emmett said.

A rare smile imbued her homely face with unexpected charm. "Then we shall expect this settlement to be generous. I would never consider knighting a man who would disown his daughter." Folding the note, Victoria turned to Kent. "And financial security will grant you the time to occupy your seat in the House of Lords."

Chagrined, Kent said, "Of course, ma'am."

"Excellent. We expect every Englishman to do his duty." She sent Emmett a piercing look. "And without delay. *Salamty se jao.*" With a wave of her pudgy hand, the queen dismissed them.

Go with peace. Kent sardonically translated the Hindustani. Peace was impossible with Emmett Carleton following so close behind.

The instant the door shut, Emmett growled, "You conniving bastard. I should have expected you to go crying to the queen."

"I'd like nothing better than to toss your cursed money back in your face."

He uttered a snarl of impotent fury. "You plotted this. You tricked my Juliet into marrying you to get your greedy hands on the fortune I earned."

"The fortune you swindled from my father."

"Liar! Your father couldn't manage a penny without losing a crown. God, the thought of you with my Juliet! You badgered her into writing to the queen."

The misinterpretation galled Kent. "She's my Juliet now," he snapped. "And you badger far better than I. It was your hounding Emily over buying Dreamspinner that drove her to take her own life."

Rage darkened Emmett's face. His broad chest rose and fell rapidly. "You dare imply—" Drawing back a fist, he started to lunge.

"Gentlemen?" An impassive footman appeared with their hats.

Emmett froze; his arm dropped to his side.

As Kent accepted his hat, a dark instinct overpowered him, prodded him into a taunting smile. "Goodbye . . . *Papa.*"

Papa . . . Papa . . . Papa . . .

Emmett Carleton splashed straight whiskey into a tumbler. Tilting back his head, he gulped down the alcohol, his parched throat working. The drink failed to expurgate the tormenting memory of Juliet's voice. *Papa . . . Papa . . .*

"Mr. Carleton."

He swung around to see Dorothea scurrying into the library. His chest squeezed. In her face, still exquisite despite her forty-two years, he saw echoes of Juliet's youthful beauty. God, he missed his daughter.

"Potter told me you'd returned," Dorothea said breathlessly. "Why didn't you come tell me about your interview with the queen? Did she indeed dub you a knight?"

Crystal clinked as he refilled his glass. "No."

"No?" Surprise slackened her aristocratic jaw. "After all your philanthropic deeds? Oh, my dear! How disappointed you must be."

"Never mind, Dorothea. It was nothing important."

"But Mr. Carleton, a man doesn't receive a summons from the queen every day. Was it a business matter—?"

"I said, *never mind.*"

Blinded by the need to be alone, he stomped past her and into the hall. He didn't grasp his direction until he found himself upstairs, standing before Juliet's bedroom door.

He twisted the knob and walked slowly inside. The room was dim and forlorn, the drapes drawn shut. An aura of emptiness pervaded the air, though the French gilt furniture stood just as she'd left it. The clean aroma of beeswax couldn't disguise the faint scent of jasmine. Juliet's scent.

Juliet . . . ah, God, Juliet. His beloved daughter on whom he'd pinned his hopes and ambitions. The unconventional sprite who'd brought such joy into his life. Stolen by a Deverell. Damn that blue-blooded devil to hell!

Emmett hurled his glass at the hearth. Shards spewed over the white marble; whiskey drenched the empty grate.

His rage vanished beneath a tidal wave of grief. With the slow steps of an old man, he walked to the bed and leaned against the post. Juliet had stood in this very spot the day he'd slapped her. . . .

He passed a hand over his face. "I'm sorry, Princess," he muttered. "I'm sorry for driving you away."

It galled him to think he'd played right into Kent Deverell's vengeful game. It galled him to think of having grandchildren with Deverell blood. Was she truly as happy as Deverell claimed? What if he spent his spite on her!

No, Emmett assured himself, Kent Deverell's way was more subtle, more devious. He'd simply neglect Juliet, drive her to melancholy. And there was nothing Emmett could do except what the queen had commanded. At least money of her own would give Juliet the means to protect herself.

Fingers trembling, he reached into his breast pocket and drew forth the filigreed locket. The mantel clock ticked into the silence as he studied the two photographs inside. A revelation struck hope into his empty chest. There *was* someone at Castle Radcliffe who might be persuaded to watch over Juliet, to telegraph him the instant she showed the slightest sign of misery.

Snapping the locket shut, Emmett stalked to the rolltop desk and sat down, the dainty gilt chair creaking under his weight. Eyes watery, he drew forth a sheet of stationery and began to compose a letter.

Dear Juliet . . .

Anxiously she scanned the familiar handwriting on the scented paper, the post that Fleetwood had just delivered. Spying the return address, she'd splashed tea onto the tablecloth in her haste to rip open the envelope. She glanced down to catch the gist of the message. Her head reeled in shock as she returned to the opening paragraph and devoured every dismaying word.

From across the breakfast table, Maud craned her neck to see around a vase of yellow tea roses. "Oh, fiddle, I can't bear the suspense! What does it say?"

"It's dreadful," Juliet said, dropping the letter onto the table. "Mama says that Papa received a summons to see the queen, too. That means both he *and* Kent were at the audience."

"Egad. Mother didn't warn me about *that*."

"It gets worse. Papa thought the summons meant he was to be conferred a knighthood."

Slathering apricot jam onto her toast, Maud stared owl-eyed through the gold-rimmed glasses. "He must have been in quite the steam when he learned the truth."

Juliet's stomach wrenched. How disappointed Papa must have been. "No doubt," she said on a sigh. "Mama must have posted the letter before he went to Windsor yesterday afternoon."

"I wonder what the queen said to them."

"We'll find out soon enough. Kent should return today."

"The duke certainly seemed in an ill humor when he left." Licking her fingers, Maud blinked guiltily. "I do hope I didn't get you into too awfully much trouble."

"I'm happy you're here." Juliet reached out and patted Maud's hand. "And the situation is hardly your fault. I'm the one who wrote that letter in the first place. I'm still convinced I did the right thing."

Toying with her teacup, she tried to focus on the good her money would accomplish for the people of Radcliffe. But her thoughts kept flitting to the dark fury on Kent's face, to the harsh words they'd flung at each other. She felt a sick stirring inside. Once again, she'd acted bolder than the mousy Emily. She'd gone against his wishes and jeopardized their growing closeness.

I'll tell you my plans when you return from Windsor.

Grand words, she reflected, as a breeze from the open window scudded the letter against a silver salt cellar. Even were she intent on leaving Kent, where would she go? Her father wouldn't welcome her, not with the taint of the Deverells upon her.

Slowly she folded the letter and stuck it in her pocket. The truth was, she *wanted* to remain mistress of this crumbling castle with its shabby furnishings and walls seeping a mildewy dampness. Over the past weeks, this old place had become intrinsically wound up with her love for Kent.

Augusta clumped into the breakfast room, Punjab close behind, his paws clicking on the flagstones. Gordon followed, vagueness on his thin face, his suit in its perpetual untidy state.

"Good morning," Juliet said. "Did you sleep well?"

"Tolerably."

The woman headed to a sideboard laden with covered dishes; Gordon shuffled in her wake. The instant their backs were turned, Maud stuck her eyeglasses into the blue holder, then contorted her face into a comically accurate rendition of Augusta's dour expression. Juliet lifted her napkin to smother a laugh.

Augusta marched to the table, her plate piled with poached eggs and grilled bloaters. The rubbery yolks and soft-fleshed fish increased Juliet's queasiness. Averting her gaze, she poured a fresh cup of tea and added a dollop of cream.

"Not eating?" Augusta inquired, eyeing the untouched piece of toast on Juliet's plate.

"I wasn't hungry."

The ginger brows arched; then Augusta poured a saucer of cream-laced tea and placed it on the floor. "There you go, my little darling."

Tail swishing, Punjab settled down to slurp at the liquid, his snorts of satisfaction filling the silence.

Augusta's hyacinth gaze shifted to Maud. "And you, my lady? Did you find breakfast sufficiently filling?"

"Marvelous," Maud gushed. "I was just about to sample the kidneys. I need to sustain my strength if I'm to go riding with Henry this afternoon. He seems a man who could make demands on a lady's constitution." She joined Gordon at the sideboard.

"Humph." Augusta chased her spoon after a slippery lump of egg. "I do so dislike seeing good food go to waste."

Pungent aromas wafted from the dishes Maud and Gordon carried to the table. Juliet sipped at the tea to settle her churning belly. The shock of that letter following the argument with Kent must have upset her more than she'd thought.

Gordon's gnarled hand fumbled with the silver; his knife clanked to the floor. "Beg pardon," he mumbled.

Augusta gave a long-suffering sigh. "Yesterday's rain settled into his bones. He had one of his spells."

"Have you ever tried an infusion of meadowsweet?" Juliet asked him. "It's said to ease aches and pains."

"Meadowsweet." His brown eyes went unfocused behind his thick glasses. "Derived from the Anglo-Saxon *medu*. In medieval times the plant was used to flavor mead. The flower heads contain salicylic acid—"

"Please, dispense with the lectures this morning," Augusta said. "Your Grace, the doctor keeps him adequately supplied with proper medication."

"I was merely trying to help," Juliet said patiently.

"I've got it!" Maud waved a forkful of beef kidneys. "The queen suffers from aching joints. Mother could prevail upon Victoria to allow Mr. Deverell access to her own Dr. Reid—"

"Deverells do not accept charity," Augusta stated. "Lady Higgleston has done quite enough prevailing on behalf of *this* family." She paused. "Still, Carleton money will certainly be welcome, if indeed the queen awards the dowry."

She speared a chunk of silvery fish and popped it into her mouth. Bile rose in Juliet's throat. She focused her eyes on the vase of yellow roses, but the food smells saturated her in a sea of nausea.

She started to rise, the chair legs screeching on the flagstones. A swimming sensation made her sway. Squeezing her eyes shut, she grabbed at the table.

From a distance came Maud's voice: "Egad, Juliet! You're white as a ghost."

"Are you unwell, Your Grace?" asked Augusta.

"I've a remedy for pain, a tincture of opium," said Gordon.

His voice faded as darkness sucked at Juliet. The firm familiarity of the table evaporated. Unable to catch herself, she plunged into a whirling inky pit.

She awoke to see Ravi looming over her. His dusky features looked solemn, his muddy gaze penetrating.

Baffled, Juliet tried to sit; black spots cavorted before her eyes. "Where's Kent?"

"The sahib has not yet returned. Lie back now."

She sank against a pillow. As Ravi moved away to stand sentinel by the door, she took in the faded green canopy of her bed, then the women who hovered alongside. Her skin felt clammy, her stomach unsettled. "What happened?"

"You fainted," Augusta said. "Straight into your chair, thank God, else the hospital fees might have cost us a month's kitchen money."

"A genuine swoon," said Maud, her eyes agog behind the spectacles. "Alas, it wasn't nearly so picturesque as those bogus faints that Bea Lyndon affected to weasel out of schoolwork."

Rose placed a cool palm against Juliet's forehead. "I was coming down the hall and heard the commotion," she said, withdrawing her hand. "I've sent Hatchett to fetch the doctor."

"Doctor?" Juliet elbowed into a sitting position; this time her head felt steadier. "But I'm perfectly fine. I've never fainted before in my life."

Augusta peered intently at Juliet. "If my guess is correct, Your Grace, I would say you're breeding."

"Breeding?" Maud echoed, her nose wrinkled. "Why, of course Juliet has breeding. Her mother is a Beckburgh and her father is one of the richest—"

"Augusta means a baby," Rose cut in. Focusing unsurprised eyes at Juliet, she added thoughtfully, "Her Grace carries the Radcliffe heir."

The possibility flabbergasted Juliet. Her monthly time was overdue by more than a week, but she had attributed the delay to the upheaval in her life. Wilting into the pillows, she placed a hand over her stomach and tried to absorb an upsurge of joy.

"A baby!" Maud clapped her hands. "Won't the duke be pleased! We must order the layette from Paris. I'll help you start drawing up a list of prospective nursemaids—"

"Slow down," Juliet said, laughing weakly. "We should at least wait to hear the doctor's verdict."

Fleetwood shuffled through the doorway. Precariously balanced in his hands was a tray with a porcelain teapot. "A tisane, Your Grace. Marigold and honey, Mrs. Fleetwood's finest restorative."

Rose took the tray and set it on the desk. "Thank you. We could all use a cup."

"Fleetwood," said Augusta, "do stop in the library and tell Mr. Deverell that Her Grace is recovering."

"Yes, madam." The old retainer ambled out of the room.

Ravi bowed to Juliet. "Memsahib, please ring if I may be of further assistance."

As he vanished into Kent's bedroom, Juliet stared after Ravi and wondered what he thought of Carleton and Deverell blood mingling.

"That foreigner makes me shiver," Maud whispered, plopping onto the bed. "Why didn't he go with the duke?"

"Kent needed him to supervise the start of the harvest."

Maud fluffed her aquamarine skirts. "Well," she declared, "this whole place is spooky. Last night I heard the most peculiar moaning outside. Do you suppose there're ghosts?" She shivered in delicious fright.

"Poppycock," snorted Augusta. "Most likely you heard the wind whistling around the eaves. Or one of the peacocks crying out."

As Rose distributed the cups, she cast a sly glance at Augusta. "Or Punjab howling from a bad dream."

"Punjab never howls." Despite her icy words, Augusta perched gingerly on a chair, as if she were anxious to stay but uncertain of her welcome. Juliet wondered how the older woman felt, knowing if the baby was a boy, he would usurp Gordon's place as heir.

"Still," Maud confided, "I was glad for Miss Fane sleeping on the cot in the dressing room. Heaven knows what poor, unhappy souls haunt these ancient walls."

Rose sank onto a footstool and studied her tisane. "This family has suffered many tragedies. My own sister was one of them."

Juliet nearly choked on a swallow of bittersweet tea.

Maud leaned forward so far, she almost tumbled off the bed. "Juliet told me about your relation to Emily. What exactly happened to her?"

Rose lifted eyes gone liquid dark with sorrow. "It was three years ago, August eleventh. There's a door from my mother's tower apartment leading onto the north parapet. Emily went out there, apparently to get a breath of fresh air. No one really knows how she fell. Kent found her lying on the rocks."

Maud shuddered. "That's the most gruesome tale I've ever heard."

"My brother went half-crazy over her death," Rose said, a faraway frown wrinkling her brow. "He didn't want to believe . . ."

A moment of silence spun out. Juliet felt her heart thumping faster. "Believe what?" she asked.

"That she killed herself," Rose whispered.

Augusta stirred, her face grim. "Precisely. His Grace was so overwrought that he accused us all of murder."

Chapter 15

M *urder.*
⁢⁢⁢⁢⁢Tilting her face to the warm sunlight, Juliet found the notion too alien to ponder on such a perfect afternoon. Yesterday's rain had washed the slanted glass roof of the greenhouse so that she had a clear view of the castle, the south tower looming like a gray guardian. The rear of the hothouse abutted the fortress, and with prudent use of the potbellied stove, winter crops would thrive in the sheltered spot.

Ancient vines twisted over wires strung along the glass walls. Despite years of neglect, the vines bore clusters of small green grapes that nestled like tenacious jewels within the bower of leaves. Already the fruit was beginning to turn a rich purple. The grapes would be ready in September to harvest for jam making, Juliet calculated.

Drawing on a pair of white cotton work gloves, she glanced down the long row of seed boxes. A mist of green covered the trays; new leaves like delicate fans unfurled to the sunshine. A miracle, like the tiny life growing within her.

Pregnant. Another alien word . . . alien yet exhilarating.

After a somewhat embarrassing physical examination, with Augusta acting as baleful chaperone, the doctor had confirmed Juliet's impending motherhood. "Been examined three times myself," Augusta admitted afterward. "For babes I miscarried." Her eyes held a haunted look of grief as she'd left on her rounds.

Poor Augusta. Perhaps she'd find it easier to smile once a baby occupied the Radcliffe nursery.

With a lightened heart, Juliet set to work thinning the seedlings for her garden. Cauliflower, asparagus, broccoli, cabbage, leeks, all would bear bounty come autumn. Would Kent be thrilled to learn she would bear his baby come spring?

Surely he would. Every man wanted an heir.

Even from a wife who was too brash for his tastes? She paused, dirt clods clinging to her gloves. He'd been enraged over the dowry; he'd acted aloof upon leaving for Windsor. How he must resent her for causing his humiliation before the queen.

Emily would never have taken such bold action. Emily, who hadn't had a rich dowry. Emily, who had died with Kent's unborn child in her belly . . .

Murder.

Juliet yanked out a weed as the word again stirred uneasiness inside her. Not because she thought Emily had been killed—the notion was too absurd to contemplate—but because it confirmed that Kent had adored his first wife. Desperate to clear his beloved of the blemish of suicide, he'd grilled each resident of the castle, not resting until each had been exonerated.

Augusta made no secret of the fact that she held a grudge over the unjust accusation; Rose had been quieter, as if the memory saddened her.

A baby would bring happiness to this troubled household.

Joy bubbled inside Juliet, like a ginger beer bottle shaken, then uncorked. She and Kent must settle their estrangement. Their child would have a home filled with laughter and love. She envisioned reconciling with Kent, kissing him, loving him, then seeing his face light up when she told him about the baby. . . .

In the meantime, the doctor had given her leave to go about her normal tasks, so long as she took regular rest periods and ate well. Despite her morning nausea, she felt vital, alive.

Tranquillity came from inhaling the lovely scent of earth, from feeling the mysterious softness of dirt beneath her fingers, from seeing the rich fruit of her labor. If she held her breath, she could almost hear the plants growing, stretching toward the sunshine.

Juliet tipped her head back to relish the life-giving rays. Far above, on the parapet adjoining the south tower, she glimpsed a pale flash framed by a stone embrasure. The spot vanished as fast as a blink.

Had someone been watching her from the lofty perch?

Nonsense.

Yet a chill invaded her warmth. Frowning, she turned her eyes to the odd gray object resting on the brink of the opening.

The block moved, teetered. Leaving a gap in the parapet, the chunk of stone hurtled straight toward the glass roof.

Her scream splintered the air. She dove frantically toward the tray of seed boxes and rolled. Petticoats entangled her legs. Earth showered her. Gravel abraded her cheek.

A single coherent thought blazed across her mind. *The baby. Oh, Kent, our baby.*

Mounted on a station hack, Kent rode toward Castle Radcliffe. The brilliance of an enameled blue sky hurt his eyes. A few puddles scattered the ruts in the road, but the sun had dried much of the moisture from the fields. He passed shorn pastures with only brown stubble left from haying time. If luck brought fair weather for the next few weeks, the single day of rain needn't slow the harvest.

At the top of a rise, he looked across the fertile valley toward the castle occupying a knoll above the Avon River. The gray stone gleamed in the afternoon sunshine like a time-battered jewel. The sight grabbed his throat and held hard.

Would Juliet still be there?

I'll make you no promises.

As he'd done several times already, he nudged his bootheels into the horse's sides. For a score of yards, the dun accelerated to a trot, then settled back into its dull, plodding pace. The ancient cob was more suited to pulling a plow than bearing a duke.

So much for haste.

Clenching the reins, Kent decided this horse must be a penance visited upon him for his sins. For making love to Juliet while shrouded by dark secrets. For reaping joy from her smile when he deserved her contempt. For denying her the right to use her own money to help the people of Radcliffe.

Not Carleton money. Not Deverell money. *Her* money.

Thinking about the dowry that way made the glut of pride slip easier down his throat.

A clump of cedars hid all but the jagged teeth of the turrets. He stared at the age-darkened stone and again prayed Juliet abided within those walls.

The money would give her the independence to leave him.

He pushed the sobering thought from his mind. No, he couldn't let her go. He wouldn't. Somehow he'd breach the bulwark of her anger, make amends for his arrogant behavior. He'd back down and apologize.

The lane stretched like a brown ribbon through the green parkland that swept toward the castle. The mournful bleat of a sheep drifted across the steady clip-clop of hooves. A jackdaw swooped from the cloudless sky and into a thicket of larch.

The tranquil setting lulled Kent; he let his thoughts spin dreams of an ardent reception from Juliet. . . .

A far-off scream shattered the peace, then a muted crash. The sound rang hollow, discordant, like glass pulverizing.

Glass? He straightened, staring at the distant row of lime trees that bordered the south garden. The greenhouses?

Where Juliet worked most afternoons.

Terror drenched him in sweat. He plunged his heels into the horse. The dun obliged with a burst of speed. Just as the animal began to lag, Kent slapped the reins.

"Go, for Christ's sake. Go!"

The pointed ears pricked. The dun maintained a trot,

the breeze lifting the matted mane. Kent muttered a frantic encouragement. Some buried instinct of youth must have awakened in the cob, for the beast launched into an unsteady canter.

The castle loomed steadily nearer. Kent strained to see past the limes. For the first time in years, he uttered a heartfelt prayer.

Dear God, You can't let it happen again. Please don't take my love from me. And then he prayed she'd left him for that would ensure her safety. . . .

A figure darted from the postern gate, followed by another. Ravi? Chantal? Behind them scurried the beanpole shape of Fleetwood.

"Go, damn you!"

Like a racehorse sighting the finish line, the dun stretched his neck. His gait expanded to a teeth-jarring gallop. Yet the motion felt as sluggish as a nightmare.

"No . . . no . . . no . . ."

The wind snatched away the desperate denial. The dun lurched into a final spurt of speed and vaulted a hedge of roses.

Kent spied the trio of hothouses. A jagged hole gaped in the end of one roof. Metal window frames twisted grotesquely. Juliet's greenhouse.

Too late again . . . too late . . . too late . . .

Horror-stricken, he yanked on the reins. The horse skidded to a halt. He leapt from the saddle just as Rose came hurrying down the walkway.

"I heard a crash," she said breathlessly. "What happened?"

He didn't answer; he couldn't answer.

Already running, he pounded toward the greenhouse. Tears of panic fogged his eyes. The door of the long chamber hung askew and cracks threaded the fanlight window.

He plunged inside. Dust blurred the air. The smells of crushed plants and damp soil swirled about him. In the center of the room Chantal hovered, wringing her hands. Beyond her, Ravi and Fleetwood and Augusta pulled at a heap of debris lying atop a crumpled form.

Juliet.

He sprinted down the path. "No . . . no . . . no."

She lay curled into a ball, her back to him, her hair atumble. Dark splotches spattered her lemon-yellow skirts. Blood. Oh, Christ, blood.

Gravel flew from beneath his feet. A litany played over and over inside his skull: *Please let her live . . . please . . . please. . . .*

Thrusting Chantal aside, he dropped to his knees beside Juliet. A splintered board tilted drunkenly against her shoulder; he shoved it away. Dirt smeared the pale oval of her face. He cupped her bloodied cheek. So warm. So fragile.

Nightmarish memories siphoned him toward spinning darkness. Only his hands on her body anchored him to reality. "No," he muttered. "Not again. This can't happen again.'

Augusta bent toward him, touched his shoulder. "You're overwrought. Let me see to Her Grace."

"No." Shaking off her hand, he searched Juliet's throat for a pulse. The gentle throb of her precious life rewarded him. "For God's sake, wake up. *Wake up!*"

She stirred. Her hand lifted to swat at his. She turned onto her back and her eyelids fluttered. She squinted into the brilliant sunshine and her green-gold gaze bathed him in relief.

"Kent," she said, sounding surprised. "You've come home."

Joy blazed like a comet into his heart. "Yes, love, I'm home."

He fought the urge to grab her, to cradle her beloved body. Seeking injuries, his gentle hands roamed the length of her. "Are you in pain? Does anything hurt?"

"I'm fine." She struggled to sit.

"Lie still," he murmured. "You may have broken a bone."

"No, I haven't."

"Sssh. Let's make sure."

"There's nothing wrong with me." Abruptly Juliet sat. Clumps of dirt rolled from her skirts. Not blood, thank God, but dirt. "Oh, no!" she exclaimed. "Look at all my plants . . . my poor lovely grapes—"

"Forget the damned grapes."

Kent buried his face in her disheveled hair. She smelled of jasmine and earth and life. Her arms came around him, clinging tightly. "Praise God," he muttered. "Praise God you're all right, darling."

"Are you certain you're having no pains?" Augusta said.

Juliet drew back and rubbed her arm. "I bumped my elbow, that's all."

"You might have been killed," said Rose in a quavery voice.

Chantal peered closely. "I don't understand what happened."

"I will show you," said Ravi.

The servant stepped carefully through the rubble and shattered glass. Bending to pluck something off the floor, he turned, extending his robed arm. Resting in his bronzed palm were two large chunks of gray rock.

Augusta looked dubious. "Could a few bits of stone wreak so much damage?"

Ravi nodded. "If it gathered speed by falling a great distance, then broke apart on impact."

"It fell from the parapet," Juliet said, her voice shaky as she leaned against Kent and peeled off her cotton gloves. "I spied the rock hurtling toward me just before I dove under the seed boxes."

All tilted their heads back to gaze at the battlements.

"Thank heavens," said Chantal, "you had such presence of mind."

Rose shuddered. "How could such a calamity happen?"

"Ahem," said Fleetwood, squaring his sloping shoulders. "If His Grace will permit me to speak."

"Go on," said Kent.

"I have recently visited the southwest parapet to observe a nest of starlings. The stone there is crumbling. Perchance a portion broke loose?"

"Humph," said Augusta. "That doesn't surprise me. This castle is falling to pieces."

"Just think," Rose said, goggle-eyed, "we nearly added another tragedy to the family chronicles."

Chantal arched a blond eyebrow. "It's truly a miracle that Her Grace survived such an accident."

Accident, thought Kent. His mind teetered on the brink of a dark well as he stared at the litter. *Had* the incident been an accident?

It must be. *It must be.*

And yet . . .

Dust motes danced in the sunshine, incongruous with the hideous questions clashing within him. What if he'd been wrong about Emmett Carleton's role in Emily's death? What if he'd been right three years ago? What if Emily *had* been murdered! What if the killer now stalked Juliet. . . .

"Egad!"

Holding Juliet close, he whipped his head around to see Maud squinting from the doorway. Garbed in a sapphire riding costume, her hat waving a single white egret plume, she scurried down the path.

Henry Hammond-Gore hastened in her wake. "Your Grace!" he gasped, focusing on Juliet. "Whatever happened?"

Smoothing her hair, she gave a quick accounting of the incident.

"Good heavens!" Maud said. "You might have been killed!"

She drooped artfully against Henry; his arm curved around her waist and his shrewd blue eyes focused on Kent.

"An accident, old chap? Always did think this old ruin would tumble around your ears someday."

"Oh, dear," Maud said. "I suppose the doctor shall have to come straight back and examine you again, Juliet."

Shock lanced Kent. Had there been another accident?

Wheeling, he took Juliet's arms. "Again?" he said hoarsely, his eyes drilling hers. "Were you hurt earlier?"

"Of course not. I'm . . ." A faint blush stained her milk-pale face. Looking oddly nervous, she touched her scraped cheek and frowned at her friend.

Maud clapped a hand to her mouth. "Oh, fiddle. I've spilled the beans, haven't I?"

He glared. "Spilled what beans?"

Blinking, she fell uncharacteristically silent. A moment of suspended breathing stretched out. Releasing Juliet, he looked around the sunlit gathering. Ravi stood impassively beside Chantal. Rose fussed with the fichu. Augusta pursed her lips. Fleetwood took sudden interest in his shoes.

By God, if they meant to hide another murder attempt from him . . .

Juliet touched his forearm. "Let's go inside and discuss this in private—"

"I'm not going anywhere until I get an answer." Fear made his voice harsh, dry. "Why did the doctor see you?"

The pink tint to her cheeks deepened. "Kent, please. I'd really rather not talk about it here."

"You *will* talk about it here and now."

"Don't you dare bully her." Her fair features screwed into a belligerent expression, Maud marched in front of him. Lowering her voice, she said, "You see, Your Grace, you mustn't upset her, for she's breeding."

Stupefied, he gaped at Juliet. The unwavering softness of her eyes confirmed the report. A baby, a creation of their love. His heart took a joyous leap; his stomach took a sickening dive. She could have lost the baby. She could have been killed. Just as Emily had died with his child in her womb.

Oh, God. *Oh, God.* He could lose Juliet, too. The ruined greenhouse gave mute testimony to the possibility. By marrying her, he had set in motion a scheme that had turned his life into an emotional morass. He had plunged her into a mire of danger.

Everyone stared as if awaiting his response. "I . . . I'm pleased, Juliet. Very pleased."

Their faces swam in and out of focus. Behind which one lurked the demented mind of a killer? Kent tried to tell himself he was mistaken; the incident today had been no more than a chance misfortune.

Yet how could he be sure?

Dreamspinner. Emily's last word. Damn, what had she been trying to tell him?

The plan grabbed him, a plan so improbable, it just might succeed. A plan to flush out the killer . . .

He scooped Juliet into his arms. "You're coming with me."

She wriggled against him. "Put me down."

"No."

"For pity's sake, Kent. I'm perfectly capable of walking."

"I'll decide that."

The grim ducal tone rankled Juliet. But judging by the lowered slant of his eyebrows and the rigid set of his jaw, she'd best withhold further protest.

And why resist when the fright of the awful accident still weakened her limbs? She loved being cradled in the security of his strong arms, loved being nestled against his hard chest. He smelled faintly of horses and sweat and the indefinable essence of man. She started to snuggle her cheek into the crook of his shoulder, then caught herself. Ill feelings still seethed between them, feelings that must be settled before she could lie content in his embrace.

As he strode toward the door, she caught a glimpse of Maud gawking. "Your Grace!" she squeaked. "Where are you taking her?"

"To bed," Kent said, "where she belongs."

Amid the row of startled faces, Henry grinned. "Good show, old chap. You always let your women know who's in charge."

The air smelled pure after the settling dust of the greenhouse. A peacock strutted the garden, its fan spread. Kent's heart thrummed against her breast; his muscles shifted rhythmically as he walked.

A flash of brownish gray caught her eye. Tilting her head, she saw a horse cropping the weeds beside an overgrown bank of rosebushes. "Where did that nag come from?"

"That nag," Kent said, with a glint in his dark eyes, "could win a steeplechase." Swinging around, setting her head to whirling, he called to Fleetwood, "Fetch a stableboy. I want this horse to have a good rubdown and a hearty serving of oats."

The postern gate stood ajar; Kent passed under the stone archway. Gordon wandered across the dusty, sunlit courtyard. He stopped and blinked, his eyes dreamy behind thick spectacles.

"Why are you holding her, Kent? Is she dead?" His thin voice elevated. "Is Emily dead?"

His confusion shocked Juliet and stirred her compassion. "It's me, Juliet," she said gently. "And I'm perfectly fine."

"She suffered an accident in the greenhouse." Kent narrowed his eyes on his cousin. "Where have you been?"

Gordon waved a misshapen hand at the manor. "Researching Machiavellian theory in the library. Heard a crash, then shouts and tramping feet and the like. Disturbed my cogitation . . ." His voice faded, as if he'd lost the thread of thought.

"If you'll excuse us," Kent said.

"Certainly." The glaze suddenly left Gordon's eyes; he looked remarkably lucid. "Er . . . felicitations on your happy condition, Juliet."

"Thank you."

The great hall lay in gloom. His bootheels ringing on the stone floor, Kent carried her down a winding corridor.

"How oddly Gordon behaved," she said.

"He's absentminded, that's all. Don't worry about him. You need to concentrate on watching over yourself."

His high-handed manner annoyed her. "Yes, Your Grace."

Though she kept her eyes downcast, she felt his gaze prickle her skin. She stared at his white shirt, where a few curling black hairs escaped his unbuttoned collar. As if she weighed no more than a spray of roses, he bore her up the steps. Was it the curving of the staircase or his tantalizing nearness that made her so deliciously dizzy?

Pushing open a doorway, Kent walked through the alcove and into her bedchamber. He settled Juliet on the vast canopied bed and propped two pillows behind her. Then he disappeared into the dressing room, returning a moment later with a wet cloth. The mattress dipped as he sat down on the bed. He brushed aside her tumbled hair and began to cleanse her brow.

"Are you certain you're all right? The doctor should take a look at you."

"I told you, I'm fine." Only then did she recall her dishevelment. An inexplicable wave of shyness inundated her. "Although I must look a fright."

His eyes briefly met hers. "The sight of you alive and well is all that matters."

Yet his tone held a distracted quality; she had the impression his thoughts ranged far from her and this ancient bedroom. She swallowed an upsurge of frustration and dismay. The uncompromising set of his face proved he hadn't forgiven her for appealing to the queen.

For trampling his pride and seeking what was rightfully hers.

He cares more for the feud than your love.

Her scraped cheek stung beneath a swipe of damp linen; she winced.

His hand stilled. "I'm sorry. I didn't mean to hurt you."

His formality smarted more than the wound. "It's only a scratch. Believe me, I've suffered worse pain."

His gaze sharpened. For an instant he seemed on the verge of speaking; then he tightened his lips and looked back at her cheek. He gently angled her jaw as the cool cloth glided over her skin.

Tears pricked her eyes; blinking, she prayed he'd attribute it to the abrasion. This was hardly the romantic scenario she'd envisioned, being placated with soft words of forgiveness, wooed with tender kisses of reconciliation. Instead, she faced a cold-eyed stranger who seemed more inclined to silence than peacemaking.

His callused fingertips lightly inspected her cheek. "It's only a minor scrape, thank God. Ought to heal without a scar." Taking firm hold of her wrist, he wiped the grime from her palm. "I want you to rest until dinner. I'll give orders that no one's to disturb you."

Resentment burst inside her. "You're good at giving orders."

His fingers tensed; his gaze shot to hers. "What's that supposed to mean?"

"It means," she said, tugging her hand free and sitting up straight, "That you've been gone for nearly three days. Doesn't it occur to you that I might be interested in hearing what happened with the queen?"

Something flashed across his features. Guilt? Regret? Annoyance? "Of course I intended to tell you about the audience. But you're too shaken right now."

"Kent, I'm fine. How many times must I say so?" She bit down hard on her lip. "Mama wrote that Papa received a summons, too. Was he there?"

He bent his head to examine a small scratch on the back of her hand. "Yes, Emmett was there."

"And?"

"Her Majesty commanded him to dower you properly. I expect you'll be hearing from his solicitors within a fortnight."

His reticence maddened her more than her father's capitulation pleased her. "Is that all?"

"It was a brief meeting."

"Did . . ." She held a long breath, then expelled it slowly. "Did Papa ask after me?"

The relentless severity of his face softened; tossing the wet cloth onto the bedside table, Kent tunneled a hand into her hair. "Yes, darling, he did. I told him you were happy."

His quiet words ended on the faint uplift of a question. A question she could not honestly answer. The murmur of the river drifted into the silence. A breeze billowed the velvet draperies and wrapped the bed in the fresh scent of summer sunshine. Against her neck, his hand lay heavy and warm. His aggressively handsome features bore a vulnerability that arrowed into her heart. He was waiting, she knew, waiting for her assurance.

Not yet . . . not yet.

"Do you still oppose my accepting the dowry?"

His steady gaze faltered, but only for an instant. "No. You've the right to use the money for the good of the people here and whatever else you please."

"You're not angry anymore?"

"No." His mouth thinned into a grimace. "After what happened today, I can see how dearly we need money to safeguard this place for our child."

She knew the pride the admission cost him, yet wariness thudded in her stomach. "Are you truly pleased about the baby?"

He exhaled in a hollow rush. "For Christ's sake, Juliet. Of course I am. Did you think I wouldn't be?"

The tender curve of his lips distracted her. "I wasn't sure *what* to think . . . after that awful quarrel—"

His sudden taut embrace scattered her doubts like the feathery seeds of a dandelion. She reveled in the flex of male muscles, the possessive steel of his arms, the sandalwood scent of his skin. Beneath her hands, his shoulders were solid and warm. His mouth caught hers in an open kiss that spun into a long, lush outpouring of passion. He pressed her against the bed; she lay back willingly. When at last he moved his lips to her brow, his heart beat a swift tempo against her breasts.

"I was so afraid," he muttered. "Afraid you might not be here when I returned. Then when I saw the greenhouse, I was even more terrified that you *were* here and hurt."

She cupped his smooth cheekbones. "Don't think about the accident anymore, love."

"How can I not?" His grip tensed; his voice lashed almost angrily: "You might have been killed, Juliet. You and our baby. Just like . . ."

In a blinding slap of awareness, she knew he was recalling Emily. The old wound ached, but Juliet shoved it away. "We weren't, Kent. I'm here for you."

"I can't lose you. Not now. Not before we've had a chance at the future . . . children . . . happiness."

Naked need blurred his features, a need that shot a shiver of longing through her. She wanted him now, with the birds twittering outside and sunlight filtering past the curtains. The depth of her yearning made her fingers quiver as she smoothed the black strands of hair edging his collar. "I've missed you terribly."

His night-dark lashes lowered; his broad palms weighed her breasts. "And I, you."

"Then make love to me, Kent."

Abruptly he sat up. "No, we can't."

She blinked. "Can't?"

"You've had a shock, and you're pregnant. You need to rest."

"Oh, for pity's sake. Are we back to *that* again?" She leaned toward him, her breasts finding the delicious solidity of his chest. Smiling seductively, she said, "The doctor told me that I could continue my normal schedule of activities."

A muscle in his jaw leapt. Indecision hovered in the flexing of his hands on her shoulders, in the swift rise and fall of his breathing. "Later," he said, pressing her against the pillows. "I want you to take a nap, get your strength back."

"Nap! I haven't taken a nap since I was three."

"Darling Juliet, we do have tonight."

Of course, she thought crossly, he made love to her only in the dark of night. Yet the flame in his eyes melted her annoyance. The truth was, she *did* feel a weakening wash of fatigue.

"I won't sleep," she warned.

Smiling, Kent pushed up from the bed. "I trust you'll try. I want you to feel well enough to attend dinner tonight."

"I will. I'm hardly an invalid."

Bracing a hand on either side of her, he planted a hard kiss on her lips. "Grant me a favor."

"I tried to grant you a favor a moment ago."

His eyes gleamed. "Wear the white gown to dinner. The one you wore at the ball when we first met."

"Why?"

"Because you look lovely in it."

"Is that all?"

"You'll find out soon enough, Duchess." Kent gently ran his knuckles along her cheek, where the scrape still burned. That odd preoccupied quality again shadowed his face. "I'll be right next door if you need me."

He strode from the bedroom and left the door ajar. Tonight she'd make certain he thought only of her. Rolling onto her side, she hugged the pillow and started to plan precisely how she would entice him into a declaration of love. . . .

She opened her eyes to the dusky light of sunset. For a moment Juliet couldn't recall how she'd come to be lying fully clothed, gazing at the green and gold canopy of her bed. She felt stiff, her muscles aching from the fall. Then a quiet rap sounded on the door and Mrs. Fleetwood trotted inside.

In contrast to her husband, she was short and stout; Juliet found the woman an efficient lady's maid. She soon sat garbed in the gown of white tulle before the dressing table. A pair of candles dispelled the gathering darkness. The gray-haired woman chattered freely as she coiled Juliet's hair atop her head.

"His Grace has a big to-do planned tonight," confided Mrs. Fleetwood. "He's ordered everyone to dinner."

"Everyone?"

"Even Miss Chantal and little Rose." Clutching the hairbrush, she leaned forward. "Not that he hasn't asked 'em before, but that Miss Chantal is usually too snooty to come out o' her tower."

"Perhaps she doesn't feel welcome."

"Humph. Lordin' it over the rest of the family, when she's only a—" Catching Juliet's frown in the mirror, Mrs. Fleetwood hastily patted the coiffure. "There now. You'll do the duke proud, you will."

She was carefully dusting a bit of face powder over the scrape on Juliet's cheek when the door opened and

Kent strode inside the dressing room. Mrs. Fleetwood bobbed a curtsy and scurried out.

Juliet rose. Tall and breathtakingly handsome in black evening garb and white cravat, her husband walked toward her. He was smiling, though the aura of concentration still hovered about him. She wondered if he could tell how fast he made her heart beat.

Taking her hands, he kissed her. "You've a sparkle in your eyes again. And you look ravishing."

From beneath her lashes, she cast a cunning glance at him. "Then perhaps later you'll ravish me."

Chuckling, he swiveled her toward the mirror. Reflected in the rippled glass, their images complemented each other, he so tall and dark, she so slender and radiant.

"I've brought a trinket to brighten your gown," he said.

Out of the corner of her eye she saw him draw something from his pocket, something that shimmered like a living entity in the candlelight. Reaching in front of her, he placed a necklace around her, the gems cold against her skin.

As he fastened the clasp, the surprise of his gift and the magnificence of the jewels dazzled Juliet into silence. A thick rope of emeralds hung from her neck. Above her breasts lay a splendid peacock worked in more emeralds, its tail fan winking with rubies and diamonds and sapphires. From its ruby beak dangled an emerald the size of a dove's egg.

Now she knew why he'd asked her to wear the simple white gown—to set off this superb piece of jewelry. But where could he have gotten the money to purchase it? Was it a peace offering?

She met his eyes in the mirror. "It's stunning," she breathed, touching the glossy emeralds.

"Alas, it doesn't shine as brightly as your eyes," Kent said, running his fingertips along her cheek. "Nevertheless it's in honor of the heir to Radcliffe."

Her throat tightened. Turning her head, she pressed a kiss into his callused palm. "And what if the baby's a girl?"

He smiled. "An heiress will do nicely."

"Is the piece an heirloom?"

"It's become one. My father acquired it in India. In Hindustani, it's called *Khwabon ke raja.*"

The exotic words entranced her. "What does that mean?"

A breeze made the candle flame dip and gutter; shadows danced across his face. In the mirror his eyes appeared demon-dark, as hard and glittering as the gemstones circling her neck.

"Dreamspinner."

Chapter 16

"Dreamspinner!" Juliet whirled to face Kent. "But . . . that's what my father used to call me when I was a little girl."

Kent cocked a black eyebrow. "So you've said."

"He was referring to this necklace? Why didn't you tell me?"

"It was another legacy of the feud. He and my father once had a dispute over which man had the right to own Dreamspinner."

The jewels suddenly hung heavy and cold from her neck. Stroking the smooth emerald drop, she sank onto the dressing table stool. "A dispute. Did they come to blows?"

He stood unmoving, watching her. "Yes."

"William won," she guessed.

A certain controlled emotion guarded Kent. "And Emmett never forgave him for the humiliation."

"Papa must have had a reason for thinking the jewels belonged to him."

"Shortly before the family fortune trickled away, my father purchased Dreamspinner from a maharaja, a prince of Kashmir. Emmett Carleton claimed the necklace had been promised to him. My father denied all knowledge of that fact."

"I see." So the necklace was tangible evidence of their animosity. Juliet wondered which man had told the truth, William or her father. Her throat closed around a lump of sadness. She would likely never have the chance to ask Papa for his version of the story. "Kent, why did you keep the necklace all these years?

It must be worth a small fortune. Couldn't you have sold it and used the money for Radcliffe?"

"My father made me promise never to let Dreamspinner leave the family. And I do keep my vows." He hauled her against his lean length. "Including my vow to make my wife happy. I'm sorry I left for Windsor in such a rage."

"I'm sorry I kept such a secret from you."

She sensed a sudden tension in him. His hands skimmed her bare arms; his lips brushed hers. The display of affection weakened her knees, yet Juliet was uneasy. He had something on his mind, something that put distance between them.

He must be shaken by the accident, she told herself. He claimed to be pleased about the child. Perhaps he feared to admit outright how much he cared for his wife. . . .

From far off drifted the boom of the dinner gong. "Shall we?" Kent said, offering his arm.

Juliet took his smooth sleeve. Strolling beside him, she said, "I understand Chantal and Rose will be joining us."

Through the gloom of the corridor, he glanced at her, his lashes half-lowered. "I thought it high time the family supped together."

The odd edge to his voice discouraged further inquiry. Later, when they were alone, she'd dig below the surface of his reserve and unearth whatever he was hiding.

In silence they made their way to the drawing room. Everyone was gathered near the massive marble chimneypiece. A silver candelabra on a rosewood table augmented the failing light of dusk.

Augusta perched stiffly next to Gordon on the settee. Punjab lolled at her brown hem. Directly opposite, Rose sipped a glass of sherry. Chantal wore a flowing fuchsia gown as regal as the Queen Anne chair she occupied. From beside an indolent Henry, Maud appeared to be directing the conversation with the grand gestures of an orchestra conductor.

She squinted toward the doorway. "Hullo!" she

said, waving gaily. "Juliet, I was just telling everyone about the time we sneaked a bottle of champagne into school to celebrate your seventeenth birthday."

As she and Kent walked closer, Juliet smiled. "Please, Maud. You'll ruin my dignified image."

Maud giggled. "Oh, fiddle. Don't play the stuffy duchess with me."

Suddenly Juliet noticed the others staring at her. The amusement withered inside her, bewilderment blooming in its stead. Augusta looked furious, Gordon startled, Rose awestruck, Henry worried.

Chantal sprang up, a tall purple iris in the elegant gown. "Dreamspinner," she said, the word hissing like an oath. She made a dramatic sweep of her hand, her sleeve swaying. "Kent, how could you let her wear that . . . that *thing?*"

His forearm tightened beneath Juliet's fingers. "I beg your pardon," he said, his voice cool as steel. "I see no reason why my duchess shouldn't wear the Radcliffe jewels."

Augusta snorted. "They're too extravagant for a simple family dinner."

"I've apprised you before," Gordon said, blinking fretfully at Kent. "Uncle William wouldn't have abided a Carleton donning Dreamspinner."

"Yes," said Rose, her brown eyes brimming with resentment as she set aside her glass. "Father meant for Dreamspinner to be worn only by a *true* Deverell."

The blaze of passion shocked Juliet; Rose had more of a fixation on her heritage than Juliet had thought.

Kent spread his warm palm against her back. "My wife *is* a true Deverell. Now, I want all of you to forget the feud. Is that clear?"

Juliet detected a faint tension in his fingers. She glanced up to find him studying the dinner party. His keen scrutiny disturbed her more than the ill feelings weighting the air.

He had *expected* controversy to erupt over Dreamspinner. Dismay dashed her hopes. Now she knew the cause of his preoccupied mood. Yet why did he deliberately wish to arouse hostility?

Rose looked stricken; her eyes were liquid with un-shed tears as she twisted the lace fichu draped around her shoulders. "I only meant we shouldn't forget to honor Father's wishes. . . . Just because he's gone . . ." She clapped a hand over her mouth to contain a choking sob.

"I understand how you feel, Rose," Kent said, his voice gentle. "Yet the queen ordered an end to the quarrel. We mustn't cling to Father's hatreds, especially now, with a baby on the way."

"Hear, hear," said Henry, elevating his sherry glass. "May I propose a toast to the imminent heir?"

Only he and Maud, Juliet noted in distress, sipped their wine.

Maud jumped up to peer myopically at Juliet. "My goodness. It's truly a remarkable piece."

"It's indecent," Augusta sniffed. "An English lady wearing a peacock designed for a heathen princess! It's no wonder William squandered a fortune, if he'd waste the last of the Deverell money on such barbaric non-sense."

"Never mind the money," snapped Chantal. Her fine features all fiery emotion, she swooped toward Kent. "It's the curse that alarms me. Have you forgotten so quickly that Dreamspinner caused Emily's death?"

Juliet swayed. Only the bracing strength of Kent's hand held her upright. She touched the necklace, the gemstones feeling warm, uncannily alive.

"Dinner," intoned Fleetwood from the doorway, "is served."

Kent pressed insistently against her back. "Shall we?"

She planted her feet firm. "First you'll tell me what this is all about. Emily's death? A curse? Surely you don't expect me to eat while my head is spinning from all these secrets."

"We can discuss it at the dinner table."

Despite his curt words, his pitch-black eyes held a haunted quality, the watchfulness of a cornered wild animal. Defiance fled from her. With sudden searing instinct Juliet sensed that he somehow needed her support.

Taking his stiff arm, she walked with him into the vast dining room. The others followed, Punjab trotting behind, his claws clicking on the stone floor. Twin candelabra cast shadows over the faded tapestries on the walls. Kent seated her at one end of the long, linen-draped table as the others filed into their chairs, Maud and Henry and Chantal on one side, Gordon and Augusta and Rose on the other. It was the first time, Juliet noted dimly, that the entire family had eaten together.

She rued the social convention that dictated her husband sit at the opposite end of the dinner table. She wanted him beside her, wanted to ferret out the hidden emotions seething inside him.

Fleetwood began to serve an asparagus soup. Clad in robe and turban, Ravi moved around the table, pouring white wine into crystal glasses.

Juliet shifted uneasily. "The necklace, Kent. You said we'd speak of the necklace."

"What Chantal is referring to," he said in a conversational tone, "is the tale of a curse on whoever possesses the necklace."

Juliet's fingers froze around her silver spoon. Was it only her fancy or did a feral gleam touch his eyes?

Maud gasped. "Egad! A real curse?"

Henry's hand covered hers on the table. "Come now," he scoffed to Kent. "Surely you aren't going to dredge up *that* old fable."

"It's no fable." Chantal leaned forward, the candle flames striking her cheekbones with gold. "Dreamspinner is bad luck. First William died of influenza, then Emily fell from the parapet."

"Father's death had nothing to do with the necklace," Rose objected.

"Can you be so sure, young miss?" Chantal said. "The necklace can only bring more disaster to this family."

"Poppycock," snapped Augusta. "Although I *would* argue for selling the piece and putting the money to better use."

"An unparalleled notion," said Gordon, a soup-spoon grasped awkwardly in his clawlike hand. "Yet the dowry is imminent."

"I will not break my vow to Father," Kent stated. "Understand this, all of you: Dreamspinner remains in the family. And Juliet's money is her own."

Shaken by the savage edge to his voice, Juliet forced down a swallow of creamy soup. "I should like to hear more about this curse," she said. "How did such a story come about?"

"Ravi can tell you," Rose offered. "He acted as Father's agent in purchasing Dreamspinner."

Everyone turned to look at Ravi, who stood silently in the shadows by a sideboard. At Kent's slight nod, the servant stepped into the circle of candlelight.

"It is true," he said. "*Khwabon ke raja* belonged to the maharani of Kashmir, favored wife to the maharaja Ranbir Singh. One day the maharani sat in a grove of oranges, in the gardens of the palace. A man crept past the guards, a man crazed from smoking the hookah. Wanting her jewels, he choked her to death with the necklace."

A collective gasp swept the table. Juliet's throat tightened under the weight of the emeralds. Prodded by a sense of unreality, she touched the peacock and tried to imagine the maharani's breathless terror.

The servant held everyone spellbound, she noticed. Everyone but Kent, who pondered each person in turn. Again she wondered why he was so absorbed by their reactions.

"The thief was flayed alive," Ravi went on in his musically foreign tone. "And the maharaja was so heartbroken over his beloved wife that he cursed the necklace. Whoever possessed it, he swore, would suffer the same sorrow."

"William should never have purchased Dreamspinner," Chantal said bitterly. "I warned him not to. Just look at the calamity it wreaked on our lives."

Maud shivered. "How utterly frightening."

"How utterly barbaric," mocked Henry, twirling his wineglass.

"The Hindus are indeed a barbarian people in many ways." Gordon reached up a knobby finger to adjust his spectacles. "The goddess Kali, for instance, is often depicted dancing with a necklace of human skulls, her tongue dripping blood—"

"For pity's sake, Gordon! Do spare us another of your lectures." Frowning, Augusta bent to feed Punjab a tidbit. "I, for one, don't believe such superstitious blather as curses."

"But Emily herself believed it," Rose whispered. "Ask Kent . . . the last word she uttered was 'Dream-spinner.' "

For one protracted moment Juliet's heart ceased beating. Emily again. Always Emily.

She gazed down the expanse of table, past the silver candelabra, to Kent. He leaned back in his chair and sipped his wine. His eyes were hooded, his thoughts impenetrable.

"Is it true?" she said, pushing the words past dry lips.

"Yes, but if there were really a curse, then I myself should have died years ago. So you see, I'm living proof you've nothing to fear." He glanced around at the others. "There's been enough said about the necklace. I'd like to eat the rest of my dinner in peace."

His directive seemed to shatter the spell; Maud began narrating the latest court gossip. Fleetwood cleared away the soup dishes and brought a course of poached mackerel in gooseberry sauce. A spidery daze spun a web around Juliet's senses. She ate without tasting, smiled without feeling, listened without hearing. Suspicion hovered at the rim of her mind, knotting her insides.

Buried misgivings surged forth. Kent's secretiveness about Dreamspinner had something to do with Emily's death. Not with any hidden joy over his coming child, not with any guarded love for his new wife. She'd been so elated when he'd put away Emily's photograph weeks ago. . . .

Dinner ended at last. Juliet started toward the drawing room with the rest of the party.

Kent slipped an arm around her. "My wife has had a long day," he said smoothly. "We'll forgo any further socializing tonight."

His grip firm at her waist, he guided her up the dim curving stairs. Pain pushed at her throat. Her stupor began to lift, blown away by the winds of resentment.

The instant they reached her bedchamber, she wheeled on him. "I demand to know exactly what you planned to accomplish tonight."

"Planned?" His eyes were piercing, though he casually peeled off his coat and tossed it over a chair. "What do you mean?"

"Don't be coy. You gave me Dreamspinner on purpose because you wanted to see everyone's reaction. Your scheme had something to do with Emily, didn't it?"

The mantel clock ticked into the silence. As if gauging her mood, he studied her. His reticence set her teeth on edge.

"I want the truth, Kent."

He turned away to throw open a window. Then he leaned a shoulder against the stone wall, the draperies undulating under a rush of cool night air.

"Perhaps it's best you know," he said slowly. "I believe Emily was murdered, that someone pushed her from the parapet. Someone in this household."

The dreadful certainty in his voice sliced into her heart. "Who would do such an inhuman thing?"

"I don't know." His gaze went unfocused before sharpening on her. "Dreamspinner is connected somehow to her death. I wanted you to wear it tonight in hopes that the murderer might give himself away."

She bit back a moan. Though she sensed the powerful grief that drove him to assume murder, her own misery overwhelmed compassion. He didn't love her; he was still obsessed with his dead wife.

Her fingers quivered on the necklace clasp. Dreamspinner slithered toward the valley between her breasts. She caught the jewels; they lay like a dead weight in her hand. Then she hurled the necklace straight at Kent. "Take your meaningless gift."

It struck his chest. His hand shot out to catch the emeralds, the gems glinting dark green against his white shirt. "What the devil—"

"You used me." She meant to be firm; her voice emerged a reedy whisper. "You couldn't give a gift out of love for me or pride in our baby. All you wanted was to absolve Emily, to keep her from being branded a suicide."

His black brows slashed into a frown. "That isn't true—"

"Don't try to placate me. I'm tired of your devotion to a dead woman." Blinded by anguish, she stumbled away from him, toward the door.

He caught her hand on the knob. His fingers dug into hers, holding fast and firm. He pressed her to the door, his chest wedged against her spine, his arms straddling her.

"Juliet, for Christ's sake, let me explain."

She stood still, trapped as much by his body as by her own foolish yearning.

"You're wrong about this, about me," he said. "I gave you Dreamspinner because I wanted to protect *you*."

His words made no sense, yet perfect sense. *Protect*. Not love. Not cherish. Just hollow emotion when her own heart ached with love. His nearness tempted her to forgo reason, to turn around and lose herself in the steady warmth of his embrace. Laying her forehead against the hard oak of the door, she steeled herself against giving in.

His fingers moved restlessly up and down her bare arm. "Don't you see, darling? I gave you the necklace because I'm afraid the murderer is after *you*."

His words took a moment to penetrate. She twisted violently to face him. "Me?"

"The accident today revived my suspicions. If indeed it *was* an accident."

His voice rang with grim conviction, a conviction echoed in the harsh set of his features. She wanted desperately to believe his concern was solely for her.

But . . . murder? "It can't be true," she murmured. "It just can't be."

"Look at the facts. I *heard* what Emily said. She must have been trying to tell me something about her killer."

"Was she wearing Dreamspinner at the time?"

Kent shook his head. "The necklace was in the library safe."

"She must have been confused, then, in shock. Perhaps she merely meant the *curse* had caused another tragic misfortune."

He frowned into the distance. "That's what I had to conclude three years ago. But it never made sense. What was Emily doing on the battlements to begin with? She was too timid to venture out there alone . . . unless someone was with her. Someone she trusted."

"But how does Dreamspinner fit in?"

Kent pushed his fingers through his hair. "I don't know. God, I just don't know."

Despite his warm proximity, Juliet felt the icy ball inside her thicken. "Why would anyone want to kill her . . . or me?"

He swung away and began a restive pacing of the bedroom. "Emily carried my child," he said, his tone hollow yet heavy. "Now, on the very day you discover your pregnancy, a rock falls on the greenhouse and nearly kills you. Perhaps someone doesn't wish an heir born to me."

Shaken, she put a protective hand over her belly. "You can't mean Gordon . . . or Augusta?"

"I've known Gordon all my life. I simply can't imagine him or his wife stooping to murder. Besides, if he wanted to be duke so badly, why hasn't he tried to kill *me*?"

Juliet thought for a moment. "Augusta gave up her dowry to Radcliffe. Perhaps she thinks the castle ought to be hers."

"She spends her days helping people. I can't picture her in the role of murderess."

"Who else, then? Chantal? Rose?"

"Chantal wouldn't have killed her own daughter. Nor would Rose have killed her half sister."

Juliet caught her breath. "Maybe Ravi?"

Kent decisively shook his head. "When Emily was a child, he pulled her out of the way of a rearing horse. That isn't the act of someone who'd want her dead. I'd trust Ravi with my life."

But it isn't your life at stake. "Kent, there's something I almost forgot. Right before that rock fell, I happened to look up at the parapet and saw something pale."

He rounded on her. "What? What did you see?"

"It may have been a face." She shivered, remembering. "At the time, I thought it was a trick of the sunlight."

A sinister fury entered his gaze. Kent went to stare at the necklace that lay on the night table, the emeralds glowing like evil eyes in the light of a single candle. Abruptly he slammed his fist onto the table, making the jewels leap and clatter.

"Dammit, I thought Dreamspinner might help me identify the killer. But I couldn't tell anything conclusive. *Nothing!*"

"We'll find the killer, Kent."

"Oh, no, not *we*." He resumed his swift circuit of the carpet. "You're taking the first train to London in the morning." His mouth twisted bitterly. "You'll be far safer under your father's protection than mine."

Juliet stared. "I'm not leaving you."

"Yes, you are. It's far too dangerous for you to stay. At the very least, another of these 'accidents' could cause you to lose our baby."

"You might have consulted me—"

"You're going, and that's that."

His arrogance stirred her to unreasoning anger. The words emerged without thought: "And which do you care more about protecting, me or your heir?"

Prowling the room, he shot her a glance. "Don't be absurd. Of course I care for you."

A devil of resentment nudged her toward him. "Do you? Perhaps all this talk of murder is a convenient excuse to send me away, to rid yourself of a wife who insists on having her dowry."

"A convenient excuse!" Kent swung toward her, his

expression arrested. "Are you mad? Do you really think I would cast you off—" His voice faltered, as if words deserted him. He brushed his fingertips across her scraped cheek. "My life will be empty without you. But your safety is at stake."

"Is it, really? Perhaps what happened today *was* an accident."

"Don't be ridiculous." His mouth looked vulnerable. "Juliet, I love you too much to risk losing you."

Her heart leapt. Sincerity radiated from him, and the faint tremor of his hand displayed the force of his emotions. But did he truly care or did he merely mean to placate her?

Desperate longing swirled through her, a longing so acute, it left her breathless. Yet she'd been hurt too many times. "Oh, Kent, I want to believe you. . . ."

He pulled her close, nestling her to his chest. "Then do. Nothing will be the same without you here."

His mouth came down hard on hers; he kissed her until her head spun and her loins ached. The sleek strands of his hair sifted through her fingers. Greedy for the ecstasy his kiss promised, she slid her hands inside his starched collar and pressed her hips to his groin.

His low growl of appreciation gusted against her mouth. "I want to make love to you," he whispered. "But dare we? I don't want to hurt our baby."

Uncertainty shaded his voice, an uncertainty that sparked a flame of curiosity in Juliet. "The doctor said it's safe to make love while I'm expecting. Don't you know . . . from Emily?"

He drew back to stare moodily at her. "Juliet, I should tell you . . . we were more friends than lovers. Emily grew up without a father's guidance, so she looked to me to take care of her. Her dependence brought me a quiet joy. But with you . . ." His hands cradled her neck, his thumbs gently rubbing her jaw. "With you I've discovered the consuming fire of love. I never dreamed a wife could be so passionate until I shared a bed with you."

Elation throbbed heavily in her belly. She lay her

head on his broad shoulder. "I need you, Kent. Forever. For always."

"I need you, too," he whispered, unbuttoning her gown. "It's been four lonely nights since I've held you in my arms."

He drew off her dress and corset, and cool air kissed her skin. His urgency vitalized her; she felt an unbearable hope for the future, a hope that would be torture to abandon. If arguments couldn't dissuade him from sending her away, perhaps lovemaking would.

"There'll be no more waiting," she said, her fingers seeking his trousers. "No more nights spent apart."

Indecision haunted the aggressively male contours of his face; yearning softened the austerity of his mouth. "Darling, you can't stay here. It's impossible—"

He stiffened as she took his heat into her hand and began stroking him. "Ah, Juliet." Tension melted from him and he buried his face between her breasts, his hands cupping the undersides while his thumbs drew circles around the silk-draped nipples. A gush of liquid fever threatened to drown her sanity.

"There'll be no more secrets between us, either," she murmured. "From now on, we'll both be honest with each other."

Abruptly his head swung up; his eyes clouded with a strange and savage intensity. "Here's honesty, then: I want you. Now."

Without bothering to finish undressing, he pulled her toward the bed and snuffed out the candle. Night enclosed them in intimate darkness, a darkness as soft and primal as the earth, a darkness as familiar and exciting as the insistent pulse of desire within her. Catching her by the waist, he guided her down onto the bed until she lay atop him. His breath blew hot and harsh against her throat; his hands coasted unerringly beneath the layers of her petticoats and up her bare legs. He probed the parting in her underdrawers and found her moist and ready.

Moaning, she spread her legs to encompass his trouser-clad thighs. She rocked her hips, the better to feel his hardness. He eased upward in a slow, sweet movement and joined their bodies. She bent to kiss his shadowed face, her hair tumbling like a curtain around them, her breasts heavy and loose inside the silk chemise.

He guided her hips. "Move with me, Juliet. Love me. Love me."

She didn't answer; she couldn't speak for the exquisite pleasure tightening her throat, a pleasure born as much from the surety of his love as the passion of their bodies. He pressed deeper into her, thrusting upward with the rhythm and rush of passion. She clutched at his shoulders, her petticoats billowing around them. An exhilarating tension lured her on the relentless ascent to bliss. The pressure burst at last, convulsing her body with the sweet-sharp spasms of ecstasy. Even as she collapsed against his slick skin, he cried out her name in the throes of his own release.

Unable to move or think, she lay sprawled over him. Beneath her cheek she felt the quick rise and fall of his chest and the solid thrum of his heartbeat. His hand drifted over her hair, the hypnotic movement making her drowsy.

"Juliet."

The quiet agony in his voice snapped her fully awake. She pushed up against his chest, but darkness obscured his expression. "What is it?"

"I should never have brought you here. I should never have exposed you to such danger." Guilt and horror burdened his words.

She touched his cheek, the stubble abrading her fingers. "Danger?" she said, trying to lighten his mood. "Since when is making love dangerous?"

He laughed a little, then sobered. "These feelings I have for you, Juliet. . . . It frightens me to think of losing you."

More determined than ever to stay and explore their newfound closeness, she searched for a convincing argument. "Maybe we're wrong. Maybe there *is* no killer."

His arms tightened. "There is. I'm certain of *that*."

"Then this person could follow me to London. What then?"

"I'd know if anyone left the castle."

"Can you be certain? What if Augusta said she was going on her rounds? She could board a train and have a knife at my throat before you realized the truth."

"Don't be absurd."

"Don't be illogical. Gordon stays in the library for hours on end. Chantal is usually alone in the tower. Rose devotes her time to writing that play. And Ravi . . . who knows what *he* does all day? The culprit could even slip out during the night. Or hire an assassin. Can you account for everyone and oversee the harvest at the same time?"

"Damn the bloody harvest!" His hands clamped around her arms. "You're going back to your father, and that's that."

"If you try to force me, I'll just come back. I'm perfectly capable of taking a train from London. So you see, I'll be much safer right here, under your protection."

The triumph in her voice almost made Kent laugh in spite of his despair. She meant every word, by God. What had he ever done in his sin-filled life to deserve a devotion as rich as Juliet offered? Now she even nurtured his child in her womb. . . .

There'll be no more secrets between us. . . . From now on, we'll both be honest. . . .

Oh, God. What could he say to *that*? He dared not tell her the truth, dared not reveal the link between Emily's murder and today's attempt. If he told his wife, not even the depth of his love would earn him her forgiveness.

"Kent? Tell me what you're thinking."

He drew her down, smoothing her petticoats and banishing the awful image of her lying broken, lifeless. "I was thinking that you debate as well as Gladstone himself."

"Then you won't send me away?"

Torn between caution and passion, he pressed his

lips to her fragrant hair. Perhaps she *would* be safer by his side. . . .

"Darling Juliet, I'm yours to command."

Her sigh bathed his throat in warmth, and she snuggled against him. Long after her breathing slowed to the even rhythm of sleep, frustration kept Kent staring into the darkness. He'd been dead wrong about Emmett Carleton. His revenge had hinged upon a lie. He'd wed Juliet for all the wrong reasons. Now his sin had reaped a dreadful punishment: the possibility of her death.

A sudden thought gripped him. Good God. He *did* have a lever to force Juliet back to London.

It would mean sacrificing his own happiness in exchange for her safety. Yet how happy could he be so long as she faced danger?

Wanting to hold her forever, yet knowing he dreamed the impossible, he tightened his arms around her precious form. Yes, it was the only answer.

Tomorrow he would tell her his secret.

Chapter 17

"A secret murderer!" Peering saucer-eyed through her spectacles, Maud swiveled on the dressing table stool and stared at Juliet. "Whoever would want to see *you* dead?"

"I wish I knew."

Sickness stirred inside Juliet, a mixture of anxiety over yesterday's events and aversion to the remains of Maud's hearty breakfast on a nearby tray. Seeking a distraction, she parted the moth-eaten blue curtains and peered outside.

The single window in the guest dressing room overlooked the vast lawn that swept toward a thicket of oak and larch. In the distance rippled the ripe gold of the fields, and a breeze wafted the summer scents of grass and sunshine. The fine morning seemed to mock such an unreal notion as murder.

"Egad! I have it."

Juliet swung back toward Maud, who sat brushing her unbound honey-blond hair. "Have what?"

"The killer's identity, of course." She leaned forward so far, she almost fell from the stool. "Augusta."

"Augusta?"

"Precisely." Maud wagged the silver-backed hairbrush. "It's simple enough. If Kent has no children, Gordon could inherit someday, and Augusta will be Duchess of Radcliffe. She must have pushed his first wife from the parapet and now she's after you."

Another lurch of nausea assailed Juliet. Did the merciless mind of a murderess lurk behind those hyacinth eyes? She recalled Augusta embracing little Hannah

261

Forster; maternal affection had softened that severe countenance. . . .

"I'm not so sure," Juliet said slowly. "Augusta's obsession with money doesn't fit your theory. Why would she try to kill me *before* I received the dowry? If she waited a few more weeks, Kent—and Radcliffe—would gain the money upon my death."

"Unless she's a madwoman."

"Don't be absurd. You've been reading too many penny dreadfuls."

Maud crinkled her nose in concentration. "I know! Rose. She must be madly jealous because Henry flirted with you at that haying party."

"Why me, then? *You're* the one who's smitten handsome Henry."

Pleasure and alarm chased across Maud's features; she clutched the frilly cambric dressing gown to her throat. "Egad! That means I could be next on her list."

Smiling wanly, Juliet shook her head. "I'm afraid you'll have to come up with a more solid motive."

"And so I shall," Maud declared. "Henry knows everyone here at the castle. We must pay him a call this morning and interrogate him." Leaping up, she scurried to the wardrobe and flung open the double doors. "Shall I wear the pistachio silk? No, the azure walking dress, I believe." She batted her fair lashes. "Henry prefers me in blue. He says it enhances the color of my eyes."

A troublesome thought invaded Juliet's worries. "Maud, I don't mean to meddle, but Henry has quite the reputation with the ladies. Do be careful that he doesn't lead you astray."

"Just let him try to dishonor me." An unholy gleam entered Maud's gaze. "You see, I know a man's tenderest place. Discovered it by accident when that beastly Roger Billingsgate grabbed me in the garden at Lady Winkel's ball. As I ducked to elude his grasp, my elbow struck his . . . well, suffice to say I left him doubled over and in no condition to pursue."

Perched on the stone casement, Juliet swallowed a giggle. "You never told me that story."

"It happened after you eloped." Maud sighed. "I didn't want to tell anyone, but that's partly why I came to visit. Father has been supporting Roger's suit, and I thought it prudent to absent myself for a while."

"You and Henry," Juliet said, recalling his exile from London, "make quite a pair. At least promise to take Miss Fane along today as chaperone."

"Oh, but aren't you coming?"

Her stomach turned at the thought of riding in a swaying carriage. She shook her head. "I don't feel up to visiting today."

"Dear heavens!" Maud raced to Juliet's side. "You aren't going to swoon again, are you?"

"It's only a bit of nausea, and now that we know the happy cause, I don't mind. I'll lie down in my room for a while."

"You do look a trifle pale. Oh, dear, you shouldn't go back alone, and here I am in my dressing gown. Let me see if Miss Fane is returning yet with the laundry."

Before Juliet could speak, Maud darted to the door and peeked out. In a flash she slammed it shut again. Gasping, she stood clutching the folds of her robe, her eyes round behind the gold-rimmed spectacles.

"Ravi," she hissed. "He's lurking in the hall. Waiting to pounce on you, no doubt. Oh, merciful heavens, I should have guessed that mausoleum would be the murderer."

"That's Muslim," Juliet chided in exasperation. "Kent had to leave unexpectedly this morning to repair the mechanical reaper, so he asked Ravi to stay near me."

"And you trust him?"

"Kent does."

Maud missed the slight hesitation. "I keep remembering that frightful tale Ravi told us last night," she said, shuddering. "The duke must be awfully brave to ignore the curse. I do hope you aren't going to wear Dreamspinner again."

Dreamspinner. No longer did the name conjure fond memories for Juliet. She swallowed the queasiness creeping up her throat. "Not anytime soon."

She slipped into the hall. Ravi stood gazing out an

arched window at the end of the corridor. As she passed, he fell into pace behind her. He said nothing; she heard only the whisper of his robe and the tap of his slippers. She wondered if the sounds would awaken her if he were to sneak into her chamber at night. . . .

Ridiculous. Kent slept beside her. Kent would protect her.

As they reached the door, Ravi stretched out an arm to stop her from entering. "Your pardon, memsahib."

"What are you—"

The quiet command in his manner silenced her. He stepped into the alcove sitting room, looked around, then went into her bedchamber. Following, she saw him examine the dressing room and glance behind the draperies. Then he produced a key from the folds of his robe and locked the outer door.

"All is safe," he said. "I will wait in the sahib's room."

He started toward the connecting door.

"One moment." Disquiet sent Juliet marching after him. "I'll hold that key, please."

His mud-hued eyes bored into her. Bowing, he dropped the key into her outstretched palm. "As Your Grace commands."

He left the connecting door slightly ajar. She tightened her fingers until the hard metal teeth of the key dug painfully into her flesh. Having grown up with Ravi, Kent might be blind to evil in the servant. Though she couldn't fathom why Ravi might profit from her death, until she felt certain of his loyalty, she must stay on guard.

Her stomach churned; pocketing the key, she walked unsteadily across the rug. The windows were open to the cool breeze. Mrs. Fleetwood had tidied the room, for the tangled sheets and embroidered counterpane had been straightened. Cheeks warm, Juliet recalled the activity that had produced such disarray.

Only upon reaching the bedside did she notice the small book lying on her pillow. The unadorned cream cover blended with the yellowed linen.

Mystified, she picked up the slim volume. Handwriting filled a few ruled pages . . . governess hand-writing with perfect lettering. Flipping through, she realized the book was a diary. Along the spine, ragged bits of paper indicated where pages had been torn out. She held the volume to her nose; a musty odor mingled with a trace of lily of the valley. Odd, she wouldn't have connected the sturdy Mrs. Fleetwood with such dainty work.

Juliet hesitated. She ought to return the book. Yet it had been left on her bed. Feeling like a spy, she glanced down.

Several lines on the first page caught her eye:

October 6, 1883. Something dreadful happened last night; Mama had the most terrible argument with the duke. They thought my sister and I asleep, and in truth Rose was indeed abed. . . .

My sister . . . Rose?

Dear God, this must be Emily's diary. *Mama* was Chantal; *the duke . . .* William?

Dizziness swept through Juliet; she wilted onto the bed. Her fingers gripped the slender book. Who had put the journal here, on her pillow? And why? Why now, right after her life had been endangered?

Her mind felt drugged, unable to sort through the mystery. She felt guilty for reading something so personal, yet the neat script drew her gaze, and she couldn't stop herself from reading on . . .

The slamming of a door jolted me awake. I knew it must be the duke, for he only comes to visit Mama late at night, when he needn't encounter me. Mama tries to shield me from his scorn, but she can't hide the way he showers Rose with presents fit for a princess, gives her pretty gowns, and invites her to share dinner each evening with him and Kent. Rose thinks me envious of all her finery. But I long only for a father to hold me close and tell me tales of his youth, a father to listen to my hopes and dreams, a father to kiss me good-night. Impossible yearnings! For cruel circumstance forbids me to openly receive my own papa.

Unable to sleep, I donned my wrapper and crept into the

drawing room to find the copy of Black Beauty which Papa sent last week for my sixteenth birthday. Long ago he ceased sending gifts of any great value because the duke sold the pony, the elegant jeweled combs, even the fine gold locket with Papa's photograph inside.

In the darkness the draped walls and cane furnishings danced with shadows and gave me the shivers, but Mama adores the exotic from her years in India, and I cannot bear to criticize her small joys. My hands were closing around the book when I realized her bedroom door stood ajar, spilling a thin bar of lamplight. The duke's voice boomed through the opening.

"Chantal, be reasonable. Cassill's Academy for Ladies will give her the training to find work as a governess or companion."

"Nonsense. I won't see Emily waste her life herding a brood of whining children. Nor will she enslave herself to some querulous old countess."

I shrank against the wall. Me . . . they were speaking of me.

"What else do you propose she do?" the duke demanded. "No man of consequence will ever marry a bastard-born commoner. Rose at least has the noble blood of the Deverells." His heavy footsteps paced the floor. "No, Emily must prepare for the future, for a time when you aren't around to coddle her. She's going away to school, and that's final."

"It isn't your decision to make."

"You'd defy me on this matter, then?" Rage trembled in his voice. "How swiftly you forget all that I've given you. I took you in and gave the both of you a home. I could have sent her away long before this."

"I've forgotten nothing, yet I will not let you banish Emily." Mama lowered her tone to a placating murmur. "Oh, William, she's my daughter, a part of myself. If you truly care for me, why can you not show her a fragment of affection—"

"Affection! I can't bear the sight of her—and you know why! Do you truly expect me to embrace that bastard—"

I couldn't bear to hear any more. Tears blinding my eyes, I rushed from the room and slammed the door. My *slippered feet sped down the spiral staircase of the tower, and for once I plunged without fear through the shadows that cloaked the castle. My heart ached with desolation. Scarcely aware of anything but the need to put distance between myself and that awful scene, I ran and ran down the echoing corridors until the estate office loomed ahead, the candleglow from within beckoning like a sanctuary.*

Pushing open the door, I saw through blurry eyes that Kent sat behind the desk. His dark head was bent over the ledger that lay upon the scarred oak surface.

He looked up, then tossed down the pen and stood. Concern etched his features. "Emily! What's wrong?"

Sobbing, I flew into his arms. Ever since I'd come to the castle as a timid child of five and met Kent, four years my elder, he had been my protector, my refuge, someone who listened to my dreams of having a normal family, someone who teased me out of melancholy. His warm presence comforted me, made me feel less alone. Gradually my weeping diminished to a few hiccuping sniffles.

"Here now," he said gently, pressing his handkerchief into my fingers. "Wipe those pretty eyes and tell me what's the matter."

Dabbing the moisture from my face, I struggled for composure. "Mama and the duke were talking. . . . He wants to send me away."

His arms tensed. "Away? Where?"

"To a finishing school." Suddenly I knew why the prospect was so disheartening; I longed to remain right here, within the safe circle of his arms. "Oh, Kent, I don't want to go. I can't bear to leave you."

He stared down at me. His soft brown eyes seemed to change, to deepen with tenderness. "My dear Emily . . ."

Before I realized his intent, he took my face into his hands and kissed me. Surprise held me immobile, but the pressure of his lips felt strange yet pleasant, and gave me the sense of being cherished. Seeking the haven he offered, I wound my arms around his neck and let his warmth flow into me.

I was devastated at what happened next.

"What's the devil's going on here?"

The duke's brusque voice snapped me out of the reverie.

With a gasp, I turned to see him filling the doorway. As always, his high starched collar and burgundy smoking jacket were immaculate, his side whiskers neatly trimmed. In the cheekbones and dark eyes he resembled Kent, though William Deverell had a haughty way of gazing down his aristocratic nose at me. From the lowered slash of his graying eyebrows to the ruddy hue of his cheeks, he glared with fury.

Recoiling against Kent, I realized how compromising the scene must appear. Clasped by the duke's son, I wore only a dressing gown. My legs felt wooden, too paralyzed for escape.

Surprisingly the duke said nothing about the kiss. "How dare you frighten your mother by running off like that. And you were eavesdropping as well."

He must have heard the door slam. "I meant no harm. . . ."

Kent's hands pressed reassuringly into my shoulders. "Emily was upset, and rightly so. She has no wish to leave here."

The duke glowered. "Her wishes are immaterial. It's long past time she accepted her lot in life."

"Emily has accepted more than enough. She can't help the circumstances of her birth."

"She can't aspire beyond her bloodlines, either. I've made her a generous offer, to pay for her schooling and give her a productive life." His shrewd gaze shifted from Kent to me. "Unless, of course, she prefers to live under the protection of a gentleman."

Appalled, I realized he meant I could live as Mama did. I could sit up at night and wonder if my lover would come to me; I could weep bitter tears and wonder if he would ever grant me the honor of his name.

"Emily will live under my protection," Kent said.

The duke cast a thoughtful look at me; then his eyes gleamed with sly satisfaction. "An admirable notion. I wonder why I never considered such an arrangement before."

Kent flexed his fingers around my shoulders. "I don't believe you understand," he said quietly. "As soon as Emily comes of age, I intend to marry her."

Astonishment made me gasp. I twisted to gaze up at him,

*but he was staring at his father. My mind whirled to grasp
his meaning. Surely he merely needled the duke; his very
bravery in doing so alarmed me. At the same time, the prospect of becoming his wife held an unimaginable happiness,
for at last it would give me a place here. Everyone else at the
castle had a niche: Augusta her almsgiving, Gordon his research, Mama her role of mistress, Rose her rank as honored
daughter. At last I needn't feel unwanted, never truly accepted by the others.*

*A choked sound came from the duke and his cheeks flushed
redder. "You would dare . . ." he sputtered. "You, my son,
my heir, would wed this . . . this . . ."*

"Emily will make a perfectly suitable duchess."

*"Her . . . Duchess of Radcliffe!" Repugnance inflamed
his face as he took an angry step forward. "I won't stand for
it, Kent. I won't see you bring disgrace to the Deverell
name."*

"You'll have to. I've made up my mind."

*"I won't tolerate grandchildren with tainted blood." He
pointed at me. "She'll never wear Dreamspinner—"*

Juliet stared at the ragged edges where the remain-
der of the diary pages had been torn out. Lifting her
head, she saw that she still sat beside the pillow. Dust
motes danced in the sunbeams. The bedchamber
looked the same, all faded grandeur and musty elegance, yet inside she felt changed, different somehow.

She clutched the journal in her lap; slowly she forced
her fingers to relax. The glimpse into the past left her
drained, numb, unable to react, but seething with
questions.

Why would someone want her to read about Emily
and Kent? Who had left the diary? Chantal? Rose? Augusta? Gordon? Could Ravi have slipped back here
while she'd been visiting Maud?

Juliet got up to study the trio of framed drawings
over the fireplace, all romantic renderings of the castle
sketched by William Deverell. How could a man so
sensitive to beauty treat a defenseless girl so harshly?
How could he sell her pony and her precious locket,
and seek to deny her the happiness of marriage?

Suddenly she knew what had changed. Through the intimate outpourings on paper, Emily had lost the lifelessness of a shadow figure. She had taken on the form and substance of a real person who had known both heartache and happiness. She was just as Kent had described her, meek, kind, and unimposing. Her lot had been difficult, barren of a father's love. How well Juliet could understand the sorrow of losing a father's devotion.

Tears of pity blurred her eyes. It was hard to imagine anyone hating Emily enough to kill her. Could William's cruelty have driven her to suicide? Yet Emily had been about to fulfill her dream of having a family. She wouldn't have taken her own life.

Could her death have been an accident? Could Kent have overreacted last night? Perhaps the greenhouse incident *had* been mere mischance, a natural result of ancient stone decaying.

Juliet felt the burning need to discern the truth. Perhaps there was a way to erase the doubt from her mind. Yet in case she was wrong, she didn't dare take Ravi with her.

Going to the outer door, she reached into her pocket and withdrew the key. As she turned it in the lock, metal screeched on metal.

She froze. No sound came from Kent's room; Ravi must not have heard.

Carefully she eased the door open and slipped into the alcove. Tiptoeing out, she glanced around to make certain the corridor was empty. Not until she reached the bottom of the stairway did she release the breath from her lungs.

In the great hall she met Augusta coming inside, Punjab trotting behind. Augusta clasped a basket in her sturdy hands. Her thick ginger eyebrows drew into a frown. "Shouldn't you be resting, Your Grace?"

Juliet's stomach jumped. "I'm going for a short walk, that's all. To get a breath of fresh air."

"Do have a care. In your condition you might have a fainting spell. You could fall and harm yourself or the babe."

She forced a wooden smile. "Don't worry, I feel in the pink of health. If you'll excuse me."

She escaped into the castle yard. Did Augusta resent her for bearing a baby? Juliet shoved the thought from her mind. Dear God, she hated feeling so wary of everyone; she and Kent must solve this mystery swiftly.

The brilliant sunlight made her blink. She looked around to be sure the place was deserted. Then she headed for the staircase leading to the south ramparts.

The steps were steep; she held her skirts with one hand and braced the other on the uneven stone of the curtain wall. Her feet dislodged an occasional pebble, which tumbled back down to the courtyard. She kept her eyes focused on the battlement above, away from the dizzying downward view.

As she gained the top, relief washed over her. A narrow walkway ran the length of the wall between the south tower and the eastern one. A strong breeze tugged at her hair and gown. Her head spun as she noticed one side of the walkway falling in a sheer drop to the ground. She hastened to the safety of the wall.

Across the courtyard a glint caught her attention. She shaded her eyes to see a man, thin as a silver birch, leaning over the north parapet.

Fleetwood. The old retainer didn't see her; his back was turned as he peered through the field glasses Kent had brought from London. Fleetwood seemed to be studying the waving fronds of a willow just outside the castle.

Juliet grinned. No doubt he had stolen a moment from his duties to observe a nest of birds.

Her smile died under a numbing thought. Emily had fallen from the north parapet; Fleetwood made a habit of frequenting the battlements. Could he be the one? Could he hide a dark motive for wanting both of Kent's wives dead?

Her gaze shifted to the north tower. Sunlight rendered the arched windows opaque. Did Chantal or Rose stand inside, watching? A door led onto the parapet, the door Emily had used that fateful evening. Juliet felt a fierce desire to unearth the truth about the death.

Marching to an embrasure, she leaned against the toothlike opening. She caught her breath at the beauty below. The river gleamed like a blue satin ribbon woven through the shaggy green of willow and cedar. Lush water meadows stretched beneath an azure sky; she felt as free as a swallow soaring beneath the white clouds.

Then she looked directly down.

Giddiness swamped her in nausea. Blinking, she forced herself to focus. Far below lay the rose garden, and to the left, the trio of greenhouses. A jagged hole marred one roof.

A protective hand over her belly, she buried the cowardly urge to retreat to her room. A cool wind blew hard, whistling in her ears and restoring her equilibrium. Keeping her gaze trained on the stone flags, she walked slowly southward, searching for any indication that someone had been up here yesterday.

Her shoes kicked small chunks that had crumbled from the wall. It proved easy enough to locate the embrasure directly over the greenhouses. The age-streaked stone had eroded there, leaving pieces of rock littering the opening.

She spied something pale wedged into a crack. Her fingers worked at the chalky limestone until the small object broke free. It was an ivory button, a man's shirt button, still shiny.

As she put the button into her pocket, agitation twisted her stomach. A man had been here recently. Fleetwood? Gordon? Did Ravi have buttons anywhere on his robe? Juliet couldn't remember.

She leaned against the opening and glanced down. Fighting dizziness, she tried to imagine someone standing here, peering at her as she worked. Had he positioned a block of stone on the brink? Waited for a suitable moment and then pushed—

A hand clamped on to her shoulder. Gasping, she turned her head to see a man's strong fingers. A whimpering cry burst from her as she spun to face him.

Chapter 18

Heart hammering, Juliet stared at the man looming over her. His hand bit into her shoulder and his eyes bored into hers.

"*You,*" she said, her voice faltering. "You followed me."

"You should not have come up here alone."

His sharp words needled her. Anger burned away the knee-weakening alarm. "How dare you speak so after giving me such a fright," she snapped. "Kindly remove your hand."

Ravi complied, stepping back. The wind whipped the gray robe around his lean form. His swarthy features showed no sign of emotion, yet his dark eyes still held a trace of censure.

"The stone is crumbling, Your Grace. I meant only to keep you from falling to your death."

"You nearly startled me into falling."

"The sahib wishes me to guard you. I cannot do so without your compliance."

Juliet regarded him keenly. Having read the diary, she was burning with questions. Questions Ravi might answer. "Kent says you protected Emily, too, that you once saved her life."

He shrugged. "I did only what anyone would have done."

"Tell me what happened."

"She was a mere child, new to the castle. The old duke kept a fine stable, and she wandered into a paddock where a nervous mare awaited breeding. When the mare reared, I pulled Miss Emily away."

"I see." She braced her spine against the stone wall.

"I've been wondering about William, too. He disapproved of Kent marrying Emily, did he not?"

Ravi narrowed his eyes to slits. "Because of her bastard birth."

"Of course. What other reason could there be?"

He shrugged. "What, indeed?"

She sensed hidden emotion in him, emotion that perplexed her. Suddenly she recalled her second day at the castle, when she'd seen him on the parapet, praying to Mecca. A chill struck her. Ravi, too, frequented the place where Emily had fallen. . . .

Reining in her fear, she said, "When did William die?"

"Four years ago. He succumbed to influenza."

"Why did you stay on? If you were loyal to William, why did you serve Kent after he'd disobeyed his father's edict about marrying Emily?"

"Because I have attended the Deverells for thirty years."

Trying to pry a reaction from him, she said, "Then you must have despised the Carletons for as long. Doesn't it bother you to have to guard me?"

Irritation flickered in his dark eyes. "You are the master's wife. He has solicited my protection. That is enough for me."

Juliet studied his frown. Dare she believe Ravi? Or could he harbor a fanatical devotion to William's memory, a devotion that might drive him to murder Emmett Carleton's daughter and grandchild? Therein lay another possibility. Perhaps Emily's death had been an accident, but the attempt on Juliet had not been.

Fleetwood had departed the north rampart. She and Ravi stood alone on the battlement. In his hand she'd detected a wiry strength. He could easily overpower her, push her over the embrasure. Her fingers would scrabble for purchase on the decaying stone. Screaming, she would plunge to the rock-strewn ground. . . .

A dizzying shudder seized her. With great effort, she raised her chin and coolly regarded Ravi. "I wish to return to my room."

He bowed. "I will lead the way, memsahib."

Turning, he walked to the stairs. She started down the stone steps, bracing a hand on the wall to steady herself. He stayed close, glancing back to watch her descent. If he really wanted to kill her, wouldn't he have followed? A slight shove and . . .

She forced away the morbid thought. She had to stop the wild speculations and start solving the mystery. Fingering the button in her pocket, she examined Ravi's garments, the turban and the robe. She could see no fastenings other than the wide sash cinching his waist.

Impatience prodded her. Perhaps Kent would recognize the button. When they reached the base of the stairs, she said, "I've changed my mind. I'm going to see the duke."

"The sahib wishes you to rest."

"The memsahib wishes you to accompany her. Otherwise she'll go alone."

A gleam entered those murky eyes. He bowed. "Come with me, then, Your Grace."

They veered toward the stables, where he directed a stableboy to hitch a pony to the dogcart. Ravi helped her onto the seat, then took the reins. The wheels clattered over the drawbridge, the horse's hooves clopping.

As the lane dipped and rose through copses of oak and meadows shorn from haying, misgivings rolled through her. Perhaps it had been a mistake to drive alone with Ravi. If he chose to attack, she had little defense. Yet he'd ignored other opportunities.

Clutching to the side of the swaying cart, she forced herself to ponder the other suspects. Had Gordon or Fleetwood lost a button yesterday? She couldn't recall. Perhaps she was wrong in thinking the button belonged to a man. How did Augusta fasten her cuffs? Or, for that matter, Rose? Chantal? Juliet resolved to pay greater heed to such details.

Beyond a small stream she spied a half-mown field. Sickles swinging, a row of men labored at cutting the wheat. Another group followed to tie the grain into sheaves, which dotted the stubbled ground.

She drew in the dusty-warm scent of sunshine and harvest. Contentment settled inside her as the vehicle rattled over the narrow wooden bridge. At the edge of the field, Kent crouched beneath the spreading boughs of a chestnut tree. He tinkered with the long rakelike object lying before him.

As Ravi halted the dogcart, Kent looked up. Grease smeared one fine cheekbone and streaked his half-open shirt. He got up, wiping his hands on a rag. Alarm tautened his features as he approached, stuffing the rag into his pocket.

Juliet scrambled down. "What's wrong?" she asked, peering past him. "That's not the threshing machine in the sketch you showed me."

"It's a horse-drawn reaper, but the axle broke." He slid his hands around her shoulders. "Never mind that," he said hoarsely. "What are you doing here? Is something wrong?"

His concern warmed her. "Of course not, love. I needed to speak to you, that's all. Could we have a moment alone?"

He glanced at Ravi, who sat impassively in the dogcart. "We'll walk to the brook."

Fingers braced at her back, Kent guided her a short distance down the stream. Water gurgled merrily over the rocks. Clumps of reeds lined the bank, along with a few stalks of yellow loosestrife. A fat bumblebee buzzed among the tiny blue stars of a forget-me-not bush.

Longing to savor a moment alone with her husband, she paused beneath the dappled shade of a willow. "Do you ever fish here?"

"No, usually in the river." He drew her around to face him. "You didn't come all this way to speak of fishing. What's so important that it couldn't wait until I came home to you?"

His eyes expressed a deep, abiding love, an emotion so honest, she nearly swayed from giddy joy. How could she ever have found his handsome face difficult to read?

Striving for composure, she lowered her gaze to his

open collar, where the dark mat of chest hair was visible. The warmth of the day had caused him to half unfasten his sweat-dampened shirt. . . . Her eyes sharpened.

"You!" she gasped, then burst into startled laughter. "It was *you!*"

Puzzlement etched his features. "Me? What are you babbling about?"

She took a breath to contain her relieved amusement. "The button," she said, plucking it from her pocket and eyeing the loose threads on his shirt. "I thought this belonged to the killer."

"The killer?"

"I found this button on the parapet, wedged into the wall above the greenhouse—"

"You went up there?" He seized her arms so swiftly that the button went bouncing down the embankment and plopped into the water. "Are you mad? My God, Juliet, you could have fallen . . . died. . . ."

His horror raised a sense of guilt. "But I didn't, love. I thought only to find a clue—"

"You might trust me to do what's necessary," he snapped. "I checked the parapet myself this morning."

"Did you learn anything?"

"Only that the place is crumbling around our ears. I'm astonished that Ravi would escort you to such a dangerous place. I shall have a word with him."

"Don't blame Ravi, please. I slipped away without his knowledge."

An ironic smile touched his mouth. "I might have guessed. You do have a way of taking matters into your own hands."

The reference to the dowry annoyed her, yet she held her head high. "I behave according to what I believe is right."

"This is one case where you're wrong. You'll leave the investigating to me."

The directive rankled. "If I hide in my room like a mouse, we'll never solve this mystery."

A shadow passed over his face. Abruptly he loosed

her arms and stepped back. "We'll speak later, as soon as I've finished out here. I've something important to tell you."

Intrigued, she said, "About the mystery?"

His eyes slid away for a moment. "Yes, but it's too involved to go into right now. In the meantime, I want you to promise you'll not venture out again without Ravi or me."

Unable to refuse the entreaty, she nodded slowly. She debated telling him about finding Emily's diary, then decided its mysterious appearance would only cause him undue worry, when his mind should be on the harvest. There would be time later to show him the journal, to speculate on who wanted her to know about Emily's thoughts and fears.

Abruptly he walked away and returned a moment later with a sprig of forget-me-not. His smile seemed almost melancholy as he tickled her chin with the brilliant blue flowers. "Remember the time I brought you a spray of these?"

"On our wedding night. If I recall, you identified the Latin name before I could."

"If I recall, you set me on fire with wanting you, my Lady Botanist. Perhaps I should show you again."

Her legs felt on the verge of wilting. Breathlessly she teased, "Perhaps I don't kiss a man who has grease on his cheek."

"Have I?" Cocking a sheepish eyebrow, he rubbed a hand over his face. "Where?"

"Here, let me wipe it."

Juliet pulled a rag from his pocket and stroked at the spot. He smelled faintly musky, uniquely male. His breath stirred her hair; his nearness stirred her blood. She wanted to shape her hands to the powerful muscles of his shoulders, to undress him, to lie in the sunshine and feel him inside her. . . .

Glancing up, she saw Kent watching her with that odd nervous intensity. What could he have to tell her? "I'd best take you back," he murmured, "before I ravish you right here."

"I wouldn't mind."

His mouth tilted into a half smile. "I told you once before, I won't chance any other man seeing what's for my eyes alone."

Placing the rag in his hand, she let out an exaggerated sigh. "Your wish is my command, Your Grace."

He tucked the stem of forget-me-nots into her bodice, his callused fingers brushing her breasts. Cupping her cheeks, he brought his lips down hard on hers in a sudden violent outpouring of emotion. Willingly she melted into him, welcoming the keen pleasure of his kiss. Time spun away as she tasted him, caressed him, pressed her hips to his. He held her tight as if he could not bear to let her go.

"I love you, Juliet. Don't ever forget that."

Joy thrummed inside her. To hear him speak such passionate words in the light of day brought a sense of boundless contentment. Last night had been no illusion, no isolated confession brought about by his fear for her life. He truly loved her.

An arm at her waist, he walked her back to the dogcart. "I shouldn't be much longer than another hour or two." He looked at Ravi and added, "Guard her well."

"Yes, sahib."

Kent brushed a distracted kiss across her cheek; his mind must already be combing the list of suspects again. As the vehicle jolted down the lane, frustration eroded her heart. He must have thought of a vital clue; that must be the reason for his pensive mood. A pity the shirt button had proven to be a false sign. Her hand stole over her midsection. She wanted nothing to mar her happiness with Kent, nothing to harm their child.

Inside the castle, she and Ravi met Gordon emerging from the library. His shoulders drooped beneath a frayed burgundy jacket. An odd gray pallor shadowed his face, and despite the dank coolness of the air, beads of sweat glistened on his brow.

"Have you seen my wife?" he asked. "She was to procure my medication from the physician."

Gordon must be in pain from his rheumatism, Juliet

thought in sympathy. "I saw Augusta come in a couple of hours ago. Would you like me to find her?"

Confusion chased across his nondescript features. "No . . . no. She's in our apartments, I would surmise."

With a wave of knotty fingers, he shuffled down the corridor. As she and Ravi continued upstairs, Juliet wondered if Gordon could be the one. Could he really wish to prevent the birth of an heir? Did he possess the strength to push Emily over the parapet? Could he heft a heavy rock in his deformed hands?

She shook her head. Kent knew far more about the people here; later they could put their heads together and arrive at a culprit and a motive.

Ravi locked the bedroom door and placed the key on a table. "If you should need me—"

"You'll be next door."

The corners of his mouth quirked slightly. "Yes, memsahib." Bowing, he retreated into Kent's bedchamber.

Juliet freshened up in the dressing room, then wandered through the vast bedchamber and stopped by an open window. Leaning on the casement, she gazed down at the river, blue-gray and calm. Its lapping harmonized with the quack of a duck and the murmur of a wood pigeon. The outing had dissipated the nausea and left her restless. She longed to plunge her fingers into warm earth, to find peace in the mundane tasks of trimming rosebushes and pulling weeds. A dismal sense of loss eddied through her. All those beautiful seedlings. And the clusters of glossy green grapes, ready to darken to a rich purple. All destroyed. Of course, she might salvage something from the wreckage.

But Kent had asked her to remain here. Out of love he'd begged her to be cautious. Even without the directive, she wasn't certain she possessed the courage to work in the greenhouse, to know that someone might be leaning over the parapet, peering down at her. . . .

Shuddering, she took a deep breath. She refused to

go through life fearing every shadow, seeing danger around every corner.

There must be something she could do to chase away the specter of peril. Perhaps she should reread the diary, more slowly this time, to search out a hidden clue.

But the cream-covered journal had vanished from her pillow. In its stead lay a thin sheaf of papers.

Someone had been in the bedroom during her absence. The notion unleashed a prickly sensation over her skin. The intruder could be anyone here in the castle. Even Ravi had had the opportunity to invade her private chamber.

Hand trembling, she picked up the stack. One edge was ragged; the pages must have been torn from a diary. Yet these sheets were slightly different, of a finer-quality stock; they must have come from a different journal. Emily's feminine handwriting unrolled across the ruled lines. The hand was firmer, less girlish.

August 11, 1885. The day she had died.

The third anniversary was four days away.

Juliet swallowed. She had a sudden, peculiar urge to throw down the pages. Was the person who'd left the diary a murderer? Did the journal hold a clue to the mystery of Emily's death?

She dragged a wing chair to a shaft of sunlight. Curling her legs beneath her, she began to read.

Papa came to visit this afternoon. When Mama slipped me his note yesterday, I had no notion of the grief his call would wreak upon my heart and upon my marriage. Only joy and excitement danced inside me. His brief letter was the first response I'd received since writing to him about my marriage, then the coming child, his grandchild. For the first time I would see Papa in my own home and, as the Duchess of Radcliffe, receive him. I prayed my newly respectable rank had inspired him to at last acknowledge me as his true daughter. Perhaps I'd taken the one step that would win his esteem.

He did not shun me altogether. When the old duke was alive, Mama arranged a trip to London once or twice a year, ostensibly to purchase new gowns. (Rose preferred to remain at Radcliffe with her father.) Mama would contrive a meeting between me and Papa, while she went to the dressmaker.

Those stolen hours were short, but achingly sweet and the only time I felt truly secure. Sometimes Papa took me for a walk along the Embankment or to the Punch-and-Judy show on a street corner. We explored the echoing nave of St. Paul's Cathedral and took tea in a tiny shop near Covent Garden. Once he bought me a baby doll from the penny-toy man, a doll still tucked away in my wardrobe.

When I was eleven, Papa pointed out the street where he'd been born, a dingy lane near the fearsome edifice of Newgate Prison. Filthy children played chase along the kerbstone, and women sat gossiping on stoops. Though he wore an unassuming dark suit and I a simple dress, the cut of our clothing marked us as superior to the poor souls here. Amazed at the news that my papa hadn't always been rich, I clung tightly to his hand and admired him all the more.

For a long time, he gazed up at the brick tenement. Then he spoke: "My mother worked herself to death taking in the laundry of gentlemen. I swore then that I would never suffer as she did, that I would never act as any man's servant. That I would become one of the privileged myself."

An inexpressible sadness colored his strong features and compelled me to speak. "And you did, Papa, you did."

He looked startled, as though he'd forgotten my presence. Suddenly he seized both my hands and said, "You must never worry about money, Emily. I cannot help you as long as your mother insists upon living with that . . . devil. But upon my death, you'll be well provided for."

The thought of losing him made me shudder. Bursting with love, I pressed my cheek to the fine fabric of his lapel and drew in the scent of his expensive cigars. "Oh, Papa, how I wish we could be together."

His arms held me tight for an instant and his mustache brushed against my brow. Then he pulled stiffly back. "Don't waste your time on foolish dreams. Come along now."

Choking back tears, I regretted the rash outpouring of

*my heart. I should not have forgotten my status as bas-
tard. Though I tried to content myself with the stolen moments, I was bitterly aware that we never went places
where persons of Quality might recognize him and wonder
about the thin girl with the straggly blond braids. We never
rode the elephant at the zoological gardens or saw the
Egyptian exhibit at the British Museum or fed the swans
at St. James Park. Those places Mama took me, and Rose,
too, when she came to London with us.*

*As hurtful as it is to admit, I know Papa is ashamed of
me. He's ashamed to acknowledge his dark secret because
it would bring down the wrath of Society on himself and
his legitimate family.*

*I recall vividly the time Mama let the truth slip. It was
a gray November day when I was thirteen. Papa and I had
spent a precious hour roaming the toy stalls at the Lowther
Arcade; then he left me in front of the millinery where
Mama had spent the morning. As the hansom cab rattled
away down Regent's Street, she emerged from the shop
and swept to my side. Her lovely features were pinched
into a frown.*

*"He won't even let you ride in his own carriage," she
said, her tone caustic. "And he won't be seen speaking to
me."*

*It was always in those sad moments when leaving him
that I was most apt to leap to his defense. "But look what
he bought me." I reached into a parcel and drew forth a
trinket. "When I wind the key, the rabbit's paws beat the
drum."*

*She made a sweeping wave of her arm, her cloak billow-
ing. "A pittance, a salve for his guilty conscience. Imagine
what he must spend on her."*

"On who, Mama?"

*A pink flush crept up her alabaster cheeks. Then her
breath formed a fog in the chilly air. "I suppose you're old
enough to know, darling. Your father has another daughter, born of his marriage to a noblewoman."*

*My heart seemed to cease beating. Shoppers surged
around us, but I felt trapped in a glass-enclosed island,
where sights and sounds failed to penetrate. At last I managed to ask, "How old is she?"*

"Near Rose's age, I believe. Probably eight or nine."

"This other girl . . . she's my half sister, then."

"Yes." Taking me by the shoulders, Mama studied me closely. "Are you quite sure you're all right, Emily? Perhaps I shouldn't have told you."

Guilt and worry tightened her regal cheekbones. The pall over my senses lifted slightly. I knew she hadn't meant to hurt me, only to help me see the reality of the world.

"I'm fine, Mama. I'm relieved you told me about her."

She nodded, and turned away to hail a cab. I badgered her for more facts about my legitimate sister, but she refused to speak of her again. The shocking news ate away at me, kept me awake at night wondering about the daughter fortunate enough to share every day with Papa. I didn't even know her name, yet I couldn't erase her from my mind.

The morning before we were due to depart for Radcliffe, I could no longer contain my curiosity. Never have I been the venturesome sort, but this once the need aching inside me overwhelmed any natural caution.

The Oxford omnibus conveyed me from our modest hotel in Soho to a point near the elegant address where my father lived. Fog hung in the air and a few icy raindrops spattered my face. Wrapped tightly in a cloak, I trudged the few remaining blocks and wondered what I would say if anyone challenged my presence in this elite neighborhood. Of course, I was being foolish and fanciful; no one would take notice of a nondescript girl.

On a quiet street near St. George's Church in Mayfair, I located the terrace house. As I paused across the road, beneath the bare branches of an elm, my hands trembled as much from nervousness as the cold. Why had I done such a foolhardy thing as to come here? Suddenly I wanted to run as fast as possible, but my legs felt stiff and frozen.

The house lacked the immensity and majesty of Castle Radcliffe, but it was certainly more luxurious and well kept. Four stories high, the redbrick residence towered over its neighbors. Despite the damp weather, the brasswork on the door gleamed and the tall windows shone. There was no sign of life anywhere, not even a servant sweeping the porticoed porch.

So I had seen where Papa lived. Now what? Agitation

and indecision engulfed me. Lacking another plan, I walked slowly down the street, then back again.

A brougham stopped in front of the house. My heart began to pound faster. I shrank against a wrought-iron fence and hoped the hooded cloak concealed me. Perhaps I might glimpse these visitors, see the noble folk who associated with my father.

But the footman remained perched on the rear page-board; no one got out of the carriage. Puzzled, I stared until realization struck—this must be Papa's carriage. Just then, the front door opened and a girl emerged from the house.

She stood somewhat taller than Rose, with a mass of reddish brown hair curling over the miniver collar of her coat. Dainty high-buttoned shoes peeked from beneath her knee-length dress, and her hat sported a cluster of pink hothouse roses.

Papa stepped outside and took her gloved hand. He looked elegant in his top hat and double-breasted coat, more elegant than when he took me on outings. Smiling, she tilted her head up at him and said something which made him laugh. The jolly sound carried across the street.

Even from the distance of years, I can still feel the jumble of emotions that choked me. Pain, anger, and yes, even envy, for I yearned with all my heart to be her. This was Papa's other daughter. The pampered daughter who shared every day of his life. The legitimate daughter he proudly presented to society. But for a trick of fate, I might have been the sun in his universe.

He helped my half sister down the steps and into the carriage. Neither noticed me gawking shamelessly. As the brougham rattled away, hot tears coursed down my cold cheeks. Did she realize her good fortune? Of course not. Such a well-bred girl would have no knowledge of anything but privilege and luxury. In her wildest fancies, she would never dream that Emmett Carleton had another daughter. . . .

Chapter 19

The handwriting blurred before Juliet's eyes. She had the dizzying sensation of sinking into a mire of disbelief.

Her father and Emily's father were one and the same? Impossible!

Papa would never engage in such a sordid affair. He was too proper, too gentlemanly. He couldn't have a secret life. A life he'd hidden for so many years.

There must be another man named Emmett Carleton.

Logic scoffed at the wild thought. Another Emmett Carleton in London society? An Emmett Carleton who had lived near St. George's Church, in a terrace house exactly like the one in which Juliet had grown up? An Emmett Carleton who hated William Deverell?

A cold weight pressed into her chest, squeezing the breath from her lungs. Her limbs felt leaden, numb.

Emily . . . Emmett. Dear God, she must have been named for him. Emily . . . his first daughter—

A quiet rap broke the stillness. The sound jolted Juliet. Obeying a half-rational impulse, she wedged the diary pages behind the chair cushion.

The door opened. "Memsahib?"

Ravi. It was only Ravi. Drawing in a deep breath, she laced her trembling fingers in her lap. "Come in."

Carrying a silver tray, he walked into the bedroom. "I have brought your luncheon."

He set the tray on the dressing table. She watched, only half comprehending as he uncovered plates and poured a cup of tea. A part of her mind cataloged the odors of shepherd's pie and warm, crusty bread. Her stomach felt empty, but the notion of eating held no appeal.

Ravi straightened. "I have tested the dishes, so you need not fear dining."

"Tested?"

"For poison, Your Grace."

She stared. The fact that someone wished her dead seemed eons distant. Her thoughts were scattered pieces of a puzzle that didn't fit together. Emily. Papa. Kent. Murder.

Ravi peered intently at her. "Do not look so worried, memsahib. I will keep you safe."

Juliet managed a nod, more because he seemed to desire a response than because she understood him. He departed, leaving the door slightly ajar.

How much did Kent know?

She couldn't think. She couldn't see a way out of the dark chaos in her mind.

Without conscious intent, she pulled out the diary pages. Her eyes brought Emily's feminine handwriting into focus.

. . . *Emmett Carleton had another daughter. I tried to tell myself that Papa loved me, that I should be grateful for all he had given me, that only the selfless need to protect his second child prevented him from acknowledging me as his own. Yet the circumstance still caused me deep pain, even as I grew older and wiser in the ways of the world.*

I was thrilled to learn that at last he would come to the castle. So what if his intent to declare me his daughter was linked to my new position as duchess? He loved me in his own way, and I was willing to accept him on any terms.

In the note I received yesterday he asked me not to tell Kent of the call. At the time I thought Papa only meant to resolve our situation before informing my husband. I implored Mama to let us hold the secret rendezvous in her sitting room.

"No. I don't care for the idea of him coming here," she said stiffly. "Kent might not regard the feud with as much vehemence as William, but he is the duke. He deserves to know that an enemy is about to breach his walls."

I took her smooth hand. "Please, Mama, don't be melodramatic. I'll explain things to Kent later, at the right moment."

"Emmett will only upset you. What if you lose the baby?"

"He won't harm his own grandchild."

"Can you be so certain? Darling, you don't know how hatred can fester inside a person's heart."

"Yes, I do," I whispered. "I've seen what the feud has done to you, to Kent, to the old duke. Even Gordon and Augusta resent Papa."

"Precisely." Pulling free, she pointed at my slightly rounded belly. "That child represents the mingling of Deverell and Carleton blood. I can't imagine Emmett acting the doting grandfather to a Deverell. William would never have done so, either."

Uncertainty whirled inside me, but yearning overpowered doubt. "Please, Mama. I have to see him."

Studying me, she pursed her lips. At last a bitter sigh escaped her. "You've asked me for so little, darling. I suppose I can grant you this one request."

A sudden, great premonition of disaster overwhelmed me, that something would happen to prohibit the meeting. "Don't tell anyone," I begged. "Not even Rose."

Mama nodded reluctantly. When the appointed hour arrived, she admitted Papa through the postern gate and spirited him up into the tower sitting room. Whatever words they had spoken remain a mystery to me, for she merely gave me a tight smile and vanished into the bedroom.

I hadn't seen him in nearly a year. Money had grown scarcer since the old duke's death, when Kent had discovered the extent of his father's mismanagement of estate funds. To save the expense of London dressmakers, Augusta had generously volunteered to sew my trousseau. Today I wore the finest of those gowns, a pale blue silk that brought out the color of my eyes.

Feeling shy, I let Papa kiss my cheek. "You look well, Emily. News of your marriage came as quite a surprise."

"I wanted to invite you to the wedding," I hastened to say. "But Kent insisted on keeping the party small."

"Never mind that."

His eyes flitted to my belly. Anxiously I put a hand there. Already I felt a fierce love for my baby, a love that would endure even if he had twisted limbs like the poor infant, Hannah Forster.

"You're happy about the baby, aren't you?" I asked.

"I didn't come here to speak of babies." Lips thinned beneath the handlebar mustache, he prowled the room. *"There's something else I came to discuss today. Since you're now the duchess."*

His air of agitation puzzled me as much as his dismissal of my child hurt me. Not even in our clandestine visits in London had I seen him look so anxious, so reluctant to meet my eyes. My breast constricted under the force of a startling thought. Was he worried that I might not wish him to acknowledge me as his daughter?

Going to him, I lovingly touched his cheek. *"Whatever it is, Papa, you may speak freely to me."*

"All right, then, I'll get straight to the point. I want Dreamspinner."

I sank into a bamboo chair. Dreamspinner? That gaudy peacock necklace gave me the shivers. Ravi had related the tale of the curse, and the memory made me tremble. Though the piece was worth a king's ransom, I had never felt the slightest inclination to wear it.

"But why?" My voice emerged a feeble whisper. *"Why would you want Dreamspinner?"*

"Because William Deverell cheated me out of the necklace. But you're the duchess now, Emily. Dreamspinner belongs to you."

I still reeled under the numbing knowledge that this cold-blooded bargain was the purpose of his visit. Would he never forget the feud? *"I can't simply give away jewelry of such value."*

"I'm not asking you for charity. Name your price and I'll meet it."

I shook my head. *"Kent would never allow me to sell the necklace. It meant too much to his father."*

"You're in desperate need of my money. Look at this place." He waved a hand. *"It's falling around your ears."*

"Kent says the harvest will—"

"His paltry harvest will never buy you the luxury you deserve, Emily." Leaning down, he gripped my shoulders. "I want to help you, but he's as stiff-necked as his father; he'll not let you accept gifts from me. But if you sell me Dreamspinner—"

"Take your bloody hands off my wife."

Gasping, I turned to see Kent standing in the doorway. His eyes were black with fury, the skin taut over his cheekbones. The loose white shirt and faded breeches gave proof that he'd just ridden from the fields.

Papa straightened, his fingers tensing into fists. "Emily is my daughter. I've every right to visit her."

Kent let out a disbelieving chuckle. "If you really want to lay claim to Emily, why don't you take her to London, declare her your daughter before all of society?"

Papa's mouth opened and closed. "Why don't you launch her into society?"

"Because I can't spare the time for such useless pursuits as balls and soirees."

"The time . . . or the money? Admit it, Deverell. For all your exalted rank, you can't even provide for your own wife."

Tears blurred my eyes; I couldn't bear to see the two men I loved fling insults at each other. "Please, I don't need money."

Neither seemed to hear me.

Staring at Papa, Kent walked closer, hands on his hips. "If we Deverells lack your wealth, it's because our money swells your bank account. Money you stole from my father."

"Any Deverell money I possess, I earned fair and square."

"You don't know the meaning of the word fair. Today you had to sneak in here when you thought I was gone. Because you wanted to get your greedy hands on Dreamspinner."

Papa glowered. "I'm doing you a favor by offering to buy the necklace. It's only gathering dust in a vault."

"And there it shall remain. I intend to honor my father's wishes. So you see, this time stealth has gained you nothing."

Papa's chest rose and fell with suppressed fury. For a moment I feared they would come to blows. Then he pushed past Kent and stalked toward the door.

Pain lanced my breast; he was leaving me again. I leapt up and ran after him. "Papa! Don't go yet."

He seized my hand. "Come away with me, Emily. You're old enough to live on your own. I'll buy you a fine house with servants of your own, a carriage, a fashionable wardrobe. . . ."

Temptation tugged at me. As much as I loved Kent, I'd yearned forever to hear my father make such an offer.

"But will you claim her as your own?" Kent said softly.

Silence stretched out. Through teary eyes, I gazed at Papa's beloved face. "Come, Emily," he repeated urgently. "Leave him. I'll give you everything you need."

"But will you acknowledge me?" I whispered.

His eyes shifted from mine. My dearest hopes crumbled to dust. Drawing my hand free, I backed away, his image like a blurred figure seen through a rain-washed window.

He hesitated a moment, then turned and went down the stairs. Back to the daughter to whom he'd devoted his life, the girl he was grooming for a grand match.

Kent still stood with his hands planted on his hips. He made no move to take me into his arms, to stop my tears. Unlike the tender man I loved, he was a cold-eyed stranger.

"I'm sorry you're hurt," he said, "but it's high time you saw him for the greedy man he is. You should never have invited him here."

"How did you know—"

"Rose warned me. And it seems provident that she did, else you might have sold him Dreamspinner in hopes of gaining his favor. You're so naive where he's concerned."

"But why don't we sell it?" A shudder coursed through me. "I've no wish ever to wear the necklace."

"I promised Father to keep Dreamspinner out of Emmett Carleton's possession. I don't ever want that scoundrel coming near you again. Perhaps now you'll see that he'll never treat you like a princess, the way he does his legitimate daughter."

He strode from the room. Left alone, I buried my face in my hands and wept bitterly. Even Kent, who never spoke an unkind word to me, was furious. As my sobs slowed, a curious fluttering sensation stirred inside me. Joy shone through the darkness of my sorrow. The first movements of the baby. Papa's grandchild.

Despair clutched at me again. I feared never again seeing my dear papa; that cursed necklace had come between us. I fancied it lying alone in the family coffers, the emerald peacock glowing with malevolent satisfaction at the trouble it had wrought. Dreamspinner. A preposterous name for a necklace that symbolized so much bitter hatred, so many broken dreams.

How could I face a future torn asunder by a feud? How could I ever win back Papa's love?

Trying to get my thoughts in order, I went to my room to write in this journal. The action has eased my pain a little. Many of the incidents I've recorded here were too painful to write about before today. But the exercise has given me the courage to defy Kent for the first time, to do what must be done.

Juliet slowly looked up from the final diary page. Her head aching, her eyes clouded with confusion, she stared across the bedroom. The luncheon tray still lay untouched on the dressing table. The bar of sunlight had barely shifted; no more than an hour had passed since she'd sat down. Yet an emotional earthquake had realigned the landscape of her life.

She tried to put her disjointed impressions in order. How had Emily intended to defy Kent? Certainly not by committing suicide when she so eagerly anticipated a baby.

Whatever she'd planned had triggered her murder.

I had a sister, Juliet reflected. *A sister who was murdered.*

Disjointed thoughts spun through the black mist of her mind. Emily. Papa. Kent. Murder.

Abruptly the pieces formed a cohesive whole.

Dear God. Emily was Papa's firstborn daughter. Emily must have been murdered because she carried Emmett Carleton's grandchild.

Horror deluged Juliet. The pages scattered as she

flattened her palms over her stomach. Now *she* bore a baby with Deverell and Carleton blood. And the murderer had tried to kill again.

Nothing must happen to her child. She imagined herself cuddling the infant. Who could want to harm an innocent babe?

Shakily she got up. Something fell from her bodice. Bending, she picked up the sprig of forget-me-nots and unthinkingly brushed the tiny petals across her chin.

Kent. Dear God, he had known.

He'll never treat you like a princess, the way he does his legitimate daughter.

He had known she was Emily's half sister. He had known when he'd first approached Juliet at the ball. He had known when he'd asked her to marry him.

He'd known while making love to her. While whispering of his love for her. Lies. All lies.

Pain lashed her, a pain so terrible, she crumpled to the floor, her skirts forming a pool of emerald silk around her. Pressing her brow to the musty-scented chair, she tried to deny his complicity, to find an excuse for his actions.

Yet the relentless truth hammered at her.

Kent had deliberately wooed and wed her. Not for passion. Not for companionship. Not for love.

For revenge.

The time had come to tell her the truth.

Willing away the tremor in his hands, Kent splashed cold water on his face and methodically cleansed himself of the grime and sweat of a hard morning's work. If only he could cleanse himself of guilt so easily. He groped for the towel hanging from the washstand hook. Despair cudgeled his brain.

If only there were another way. If only he could conceive another plan to compel Juliet to leave the castle and return to her father's house, where she'd be safe.

But she was determined to stay. To stay with the husband she loved and trusted. She didn't realize the danger. She didn't know the bond between her and

Emily. She didn't know what Kent had done because of that bond.

And when she did . . .

Oh, Christ. The love shining in her eyes would darken to hatred. The light she'd brought into his life would vanish forever, leaving him in joyless shadow.

In a hell he richly deserved.

He trudged into the bedroom and found his brandy glass. Swallowing the liquor without tasting it, he knew the confession was long overdue. He should have admitted the truth weeks ago. He should never have deceived her in the first place.

But then she wouldn't have married him. He wouldn't have so many precious memories: the sound of her laughter brightening the air; the sight of her guileless smile; the gratifying sense of expectation, of never being certain what she would say or do. His throat tightened. The sweet contact of hands and lips and bodies. The peace afterward of falling asleep in each other's arms.

And she wouldn't be nurturing their child within her womb, a child formed from the essence of their love. A child he desperately wanted. The promise of a real family and a closeness unmarred by hatred.

He could blame no one but himself for the loss.

Hand shaking, he took a final gulp of brandy and set down the glass. He mustn't delay any longer; he must secure his wife's safety once and for all. If he told her now, she might still catch the late train to London.

On leaden legs, he walked to the connecting door and pushed it open. Sunlight illuminated some papers scattered around a chair near the window. An untouched tray of food rested on the dressing table. The bed linens lay smooth, unslept on.

She was gone.

"Juliet!"

Panic sent him dashing for the outer door. He wrenched at the knob. Locked. She must have relocked the door from the other side. Where the hell was she?

He pictured her lying in a puddle of blood. Oh,

Christ, he shouldn't have left her, not even for an instant.

He spun around, rushing for his bedroom and the hall door.

A flash of color yanked his gaze to the dressing room. She stood watching him from the shadowed doorway, the emerald silk of her gown enhancing the green-gold of her eyes.

Veering in midstride, he clutched her close and buried his face in her hair. The familiar scent and warmth of his wife drenched him in relief.

"Thank God," he muttered. "Thank God you're safe."

She said nothing. Her arms hung at her sides; a strange stiffness pervaded her body. Baffled, he drew away, his hands grasping her slim shoulders.

"Juliet?"

She stared back, unblinking. He had the disquieting notion that she viewed him as a stranger. A stranger she despised.

He cocked his head. "What's wrong, love? Why are you—"

"Don't call me that."

"Call you what?"

She stepped out of his grasp. "Love. You can't possibly comprehend the meaning of the word."

Accusation hardened her delicate features. A part of himself withered and died. *She knew. Oh, God, she knew.*

He swallowed the wild urge to utter a denial, to banish the loathing in her eyes. "Juliet, I do love you. I wanted to tell you the truth—"

"Another lie. I should have expected as much. You lied even as you spoke our wedding vows. To cherish me . . . to honor me . . ."

The agony in her voice stabbed his chest. He braced a hand on the doorframe. "Who told you?"

"Emily."

Unreality shrouded him. As Juliet walked to the chair by the window, he shook his head to clear the fog. Sunlight limned her slender form; she bent to pick up the papers there. Already she'd drawn away from him.

He'd never see the belly rounded with his child; he'd never watch her suckle their baby. He'd never again see affection softening her smile.

His cruel deception had wrought this change in her.

Marching back, she thrust something at him. Numbly he gazed down at a sheaf of pages; then shock assailed him. "This is Emily's handwriting. Her diary. After she died, I looked all over for it. Where did you find it?"

"Someone left it on my bed. Someone who wanted me to know that you lured me here without telling me I'd married my own brother-in-law."

Words failed him. With effort, he found his voice. "She was your half sister. An illegitimate relationship that only a handful of people even knew about."

"Oh?" She arched her brows. "Is that supposed to *excuse* what you did to me?"

"Juliet, I couldn't tell you. You wouldn't have married me. From our first meeting, I wanted you to be a part of my life—"

She cut him off with a slash of her hand. "Don't equivocate. You wanted revenge on Papa. That's why you sought me out in London, slinked in through the garden, pretended to be infatuated. You never meant to end the feud. You deliberately set out to bewitch a naive girl into running off with you."

Too shamed to meet her eyes, he walked to the nightstand and set down the diary pages. Logic told him that nothing could repair Juliet's shattered illusions, yet he felt compelled to say what was in his heart.

Slowly he forced himself to look at his wife. "There was a reason for what I did. You have to understand what happened back then . . . the day Emily died. Your father came to see her—"

"I know. She recorded the episode in her journal."

"She was despondent over the visit. He demanded Dreamspinner in an attempt to avenge himself on me for marrying her."

"Revenge again! Everything revolves around the feud. No doubt you deluded Emily into marrying you, same as you did me."

"You're wrong about that. I loved her—"

"Love." Juliet gave a scathing laugh. "That's impossible. She was Emmett Carleton's daughter, too."

"She was a girl who needed me." Kent extended his hands, palms up. "Juliet, at first I didn't think it possible that you could grow up in his shadow and fail to be corrupted like him. I was certain he'd raised you as a spoiled society beauty, as tainted as he is. It wasn't until I got to know you that I realized how wrong I'd been, that you're nothing like Emmett."

"If my father is corrupt, then you're two of a kind."

She regarded him with icy contempt. He lowered his hands. God help him, she was right.

"I wed you for all the wrong reasons," he murmured. "But I love you, Juliet. I love you."

"That's your misfortune."

He leaned heavily against the wall. He couldn't bear to hear scorn spill like venom from lips that had once spoken only of love. "Let me finish telling you about Emily," he said. "I didn't want to believe it, but I had to conclude she'd committed suicide. For God's sake, her last word was Dreamspinner! I thought Emmett had driven her over the edge, demanding she take money for the necklace when all she'd ever wanted was his love."

"But he *didn't* cause her death! She was murdered . . . by someone here, someone who hates the Carletons even more than you do."

Did he still loathe Emmett with such vigor? Kent wondered. Or had his love for Juliet somehow diluted his capacity for hatred? "I know now that Emily was murdered," Kent said. "That's why I tried to convince you to leave."

"Don't affect any concern for my welfare, Your Grace. It's no longer necessary to keep up the pretense."

He deserved that . . . he deserved to be flayed for his petty and unconscionable plot. Still, her words pained him. "I'm only trying to explain what I believed back then, why I acted as I did. I vowed to avenge Emily's death by stealing what Emmett treasured most."

"I wonder why you bothered marrying me, then. Why not simply ruin me?"

He said nothing. Horror widened her eyes.

"That *is* what you first intended," she whispered, her gaze dark with the revelation. "Isn't it? That day at your town house, you asked me to go upstairs to your bedroom. You were going to seduce me, then let all of society know that Emmett Carleton's daughter had whored herself to his enemy."

He wanted to deny it. Staring at her beloved features, flushed with anger, he said, "Yes."

Her breasts rose and fell beneath the emerald silk. For an instant, he feared she would swoon. As he took a step forward, Juliet sank onto the edge of the bed.

"I wish you had," she murmured. "Then I would have had done with you. I would never have come here. I would never have married you."

The bleak words lashed him. This was what he'd planned, Kent reminded himself. To make her hate him so much that she would go running back to Emmett.

Her stiff-shouldered dignity affected him more than weeping and railing. Oh, God. He'd turned an innocent girl into this disillusioned woman. He felt his eyes blur with tears, and he turned toward the connecting door before she could accuse him of trying to reap her sympathy.

"I'll ring for Mrs. Fleetwood," he said. "She can pack your things. Hatchett will drive you to the rail station."

Silence hung as heavy as his grief. At the door, he risked a glance at her. She sat still, staring intently at him.

"You planned this," she said slowly. "You *wanted* me to find out about my father. *You* left the diary because you couldn't face the task of telling me yourself."

"No! Last night I'd decided the truth was the only way to convince you to leave here. I never meant for you to find out from anyone but me."

Her mouth pursed with mockery. "You've lied to me before. Why should I believe you now?"

"Juliet, I . . ." He stopped, helpless to convince her. Feeling the sting of tears, he clenched his jaw and seized the doorknob. "I'll make the arrangements and leave you to gather your things."

"No."

He swung back. "No?"

Sliding off the bed, she walked toward him. "You heard me. I'm staying here."

"Why?"

"Emily was my sister, my flesh and blood. I intend to find her murderer. And whoever wants to kill me . . . and my child."

"You'll be safer in London. I'll make certain no one leaves here."

She tossed up her chin and placed her hands on her hips. "We've been through this argument before. I won't live the rest of my life in fear of an assassin."

"Your father will protect you. He'll hire a bodyguard."

A somber smile touched her lips. "Will Papa really welcome me with open arms? Will he raise my child in his house, a child with Deverell blood?" She shook her head. "Once this is over, I'll find another place to live. But until then, I'm staying."

Oh, God, what a tangled web he'd woven. Yet Kent recalled the gray look of concern on Emmett's face when he'd asked after Juliet. "He'll take you in. He still cares about you."

"It doesn't matter," she said coldly, shaking her head again. "I despise what you've done to me, Kent. Our marriage can never be what I thought it was. But I refuse to leave."

Dumbfounded, he could only stare. Never had she looked so beautiful, so tempting . . . and so resolute. With a sinking heart, he knew that her staying was the greater punishment. To see her every day yet not touch her. To endure the contempt in her eyes.

To live with the constant fear that she could die.

Chapter 20

"**H**enry thinks it's Ravi," Maud confided to Juliet the following afternoon, as they sat in the Laguerre drawing room after luncheon. In a stage whisper, Maud added, "And *I* must agree with Henry."

Kent looked up from the desk, where he was tying a fishing fly. "Agree with what?"

"Henry said Emily was terrified of Ravi. He was always giving her the Evil Eye." Perched on the edge of a Queen Anne chair, she rounded her own eyes behind the spectacles.

"Henry Hammond-Gore is talking through his bowler hat," Kent said. "If Ravi wanted her dead, he wouldn't have saved her when that horse reared."

"Where was he when she fell from the parapet?" Juliet asked.

"Transcribing some letters in my office."

"Aha!" Maud said, wagging a finger. "Just as I suspected, he has no alibi."

"Fleetwood saw him there," Kent said, using a bit of floss to form the tiny wing of a bluebottle.

"But can we trust Fleetwood?" Maud asked. "Perhaps he and Ravi are in cahoots."

"For what purpose?" he said dryly. "Neither of them has anything to gain."

"That is precisely what Henry and I intend to find out," Maud declared, springing to her feet. "By the by, have either of you seen my book? I could have sworn I left it right here last night." She pointed to a fruitwood side table.

"What book?" Juliet asked.

"*A Study in Scarlet*. A smashing new murder mystery. There's a detective named Sherlock Holmes who solves the most uncanny crimes—"

"Mrs. Fleetwood was tidying here this morning," Juliet said, too weary for a rendition of the plot. "Perhaps she put the book in the library."

"I'll check." Maud started toward the door, then spun around to squint at Juliet. "Egad! You don't suppose the *killer* took it? He could be hoping to learn a unique murder method."

For the first time since reading the diary, Juliet felt a glimmer of true amusement. "I rather doubt that. I'm sure the book's around here somewhere."

"Probably right under my nose and I'm not seeing it." Maud smoothed her cobalt riding skirt. "Ah, well, don't wait tea for me. Henry and I shall be using our powers of deduction."

"Don't trust that rake," Kent warned. "If you leave the castle, take Miss Fane along."

"I will. Don't worry, Your Grace, I can handle Henry."

Like a ship intent on a battle course, Maud sailed out the door. Juliet ruffled the pages of the botany text lying beside her on the settee. Yet her mind failed to register the varieties of the figwort family; her gaze strayed to Kent.

His attention focused on his work, he carefully wound a strand of iridescent blue thread around the shank of a fishhook. She wondered if he frowned out of concentration or because he, too, seethed with memories of their bitter quarrel.

No longer did she delude herself into thinking she could read his expression. No longer was she the naive debutante swept off her feet by a noble stranger. No longer was she the contented wife looking blithely forward to a lifetime of happiness.

Thankfully Maud had been too intent on her own theories to notice the estrangement. But now, without her lively chatter to diffuse the tension, Juliet was keenly aware of the barrier between her and Kent.

I vowed to avenge Emily's death by stealing what Emmett treasured most.

He had used her. She meant nothing more to him than a tool of vengeance, a cold-blooded method of retaliation. She held herself partly to blame. She had been an easy target, ripe for romantic dreams and ready to believe his lies.

They had scarcely spoken to each other since the quarrel, even though he'd insisted upon sharing her bed last night. The threat of murder had kept her from objecting. In that one respect she still trusted him; he would protect her. In the darkness they had lain far apart, and by his tossing and turning she guessed he'd slept as little as she.

A guilty conscience for him. A broken heart for her. Meager leavings for the banquet she'd thought their marriage would be.

I love you. Don't ever forget that.

His words haunted her. Why had Kent bothered to proclaim his love when he'd already accomplished his revenge? When he could so easily rid himself of his wife and unborn child?

Unless he really *did* love her. Unless he really *did* value her life more than his own happiness.

Grief threatened to crush her hard-won composure. She took a breath and held it, exhaling slowly. No, she couldn't indulge in the folly of believing in him again. His words were meant only to pacify her. He had singled her out to be his whore. The fact that he'd married her didn't alter his dishonorable intent.

And yet . . . yesterday she could have sworn that tears sheened his eyes. That he truly regretted his actions. That he couldn't bear to lose the precious closeness of their marriage.

As she regarded his strong profile, sadness seemed to sharpen his cheekbones, to drag down his mouth. She had the sudden keen longing to comfort him, to lie in his arms, to stroke his hair. . . .

Angry with her foolishness, she clapped the book shut. ''I'd like to talk about the suspects.''

He paused in the midst of tying off the blue floss. "Fair enough. Where shall we start?"

His cool self-possession irritated her. She got up and shut the door, then turned, bracing her back against the oak panel. "You must have investigated everyone's whereabouts when Emily died. Tell me what you found out."

Shrugging, he turned his gaze to the mock bluebottle. "Gordon was alone in the library. Augusta had left the castle to visit a sick neighbor."

"Then the neighbor can corroborate Augusta's story."

"Alas, no. Old Mrs. Jennings died a few days later, before I thought to question her."

Juliet pursed her lips. "What about Chantal?"

"She was napping in the tower."

"You have only her word on that?"

He nodded.

"And Rose?"

"She was off tending Father's grave, as she does once a week. In summer she often goes in the early evening, when it's cooler. Mrs. Fleetwood saw her leave just after tea."

"Rose might have crept back in, then."

His midnight eyes bored into her. Abruptly he swept an arm across the desk, scattering the small piles of wires and fibers and cock's hackles across the faded rug.

"Christ! My own sister—Emily's sister—can't be the killer. Neither could Chantal have murdered her daughter. And Gordon? He couldn't harm a trout. Nor could Augusta. She spends her time saving lives, not taking them."

Frustration snapped through his voice; the outburst of emotion reached across the rift and touched Juliet. How devastated he must be that one of the people he loved was a killer. Resisting the urge to console him, she pressed her spine against the door. "We must consider everyone, Kent, no matter how unlikely."

Slouching in the chair, he passed a hand over his

brow; the gesture conveyed an inutterable weariness. "I know."

She forced her mind back to the mystery. "What about Fleetwood? And Mrs. Fleetwood?"

"Except for the few minutes Fleetwood went to the estate office, he was polishing silver in the pantry. Mrs. Fleetwood was in the kitchen, cooking dinner."

"So no one has an ironclad alibi."

He shook his head regretfully.

"I see." In a circuit of the drawing room, she absently fingered a small brass elephant. Now she could better appreciate why he had brought out Dreamspinner; faced with a dearth of evidence, he'd grabbed at any chance, however remote, to unmask the culprit. Before more murders occurred. Her own . . . and their baby's.

Suppressing a shudder, she turned toward him. "You read Emily's diary last night. Did you see any clues I missed?"

"No, but the fact that she had a plan confirms that her death couldn't have been suicide." His mouth twisted. "I wish I'd read the journal earlier. After her death, I tore the place apart looking for it, but I never found it."

"That last entry recorded the meeting with Papa, that you'd sent him away. She said she'd decided to defy you."

"Maybe she intended to visit him no matter what I said." Kent leaned forward, head bowed, elbows resting on his knees. "I shouldn't have forbade Emily to see her father. I was resentful of her obsession with him."

The open admission touched Juliet. "She had a deep need for Papa's love. That wasn't your fault."

"But I hurt her. I was so furious over seeing Emmett that I walked out on her, never dreaming I wouldn't have the chance to apologize. Now it seems my arrogance may have prompted her to do something rash."

Seeing his guilt, she felt a twist of compassion. Unthinkingly, she stepped around the litter and stopped beside him. "For pity's sake, Kent, don't blame yourself. All husbands and wives quarrel sometimes. You couldn't have known she would die.''

''But I do know not to make the same mistake again.'' He took gentle hold of her wrist. ''I'm sorry, Juliet. Words can't possibly make up for what I've done to you, yet they're all I have to offer. I want to spend my life making it up to you.''

His gaze was steady, soft with regret. His thumb massaged the inside of her wrist and sent shivers over her skin. His masculine scent drifted to her. As she stared at his familiar rugged face, a magical intimacy leapt between them, an undeniable joining of mind and body and soul. The sensation enticed her. . . .

Damn, she was doing it again. Pain and resentment flared hot. The instant he'd sensed a weakening in her reserve, he'd exploited it. Kent Deverell was a master at manipulation.

Pulling free, she walked to a chair and gripped the back. ''We were speaking of Emily's murder.''

He lowered his eyes to the vise holding the iridescent fly. When he looked at her again, his expression was empty of emotion. ''That we were,'' he murmured.

The moment of closeness might never have happened. It was better this way, she told herself. Better to stay away from him rather than endure the torture of desiring a man who had decided her fate as a means of revenge.

''I've been wondering who might have left the diary,'' she said. ''Who has Emily's things? There's nothing of hers left in my bedroom.''

''She never used that room.''

''Never?'' Juliet said, surprised.

''She didn't feel comfortable in such a grand setting. She wanted a smaller room down the hall, and I saw no reason to deny the request.''

An odd arrangement for husband and wife. Yet by Kent's own admission, they'd been more friends than lovers. ''Perhaps we should look in Emily's room, then. We might find a clue to whoever put the journal on my bed.''

"I may have a quicker method for getting to the bottom of this," he said. "Come with me, please."

He strode to the door and flung it open, then waited for her to precede him. As they walked down the hall, she stole a glance at him. He might have been the man she'd first met, enigmatic and aloof, his face revealing nothing of his thoughts. She wondered if the days ahead would follow this dismal pattern of polite reserve. What would they talk about until the mystery was solved?

She imagined endless dinners with civil conversation about crops and household matters. Endless nights without a loving husband to share her innermost dreams and desires. The prospect dragged on her spirits. For the hundredth time, she mulled over the idea of returning to London. Her mother would surely welcome her with open arms, but Papa . . .

She'd eloped with his enemy. She'd caused his humiliation before the queen. Recalling his callous dismissal of Emily's unborn child, Juliet couldn't imagine him accepting a grandchild with Deverell blood.

The thought sparked a blaze of fierce protectiveness. Her baby would not suffer from this nonsensical feud. Two generations had already been ensnared in the trap of hatred. For the next generation, she intended to see the threat of danger vanquished, the hostility ended. Soon she would have the money to leave here, to establish a comfortable home somewhere for her child. Why did the thought make her feel so empty?

She suddenly realized Kent was leading the way up the winding stairs of the north tower. "You think Chantal left the diary?"

He case an oblique glance at her. "It's one possibility."

They reached the small landing outside Chantal's apartment. The muffled sound of an upraised female voice penetrated the oak door. Kent hesitated only an instant; then he rapped hard.

The door opened. Ravi stood with a hand on the knob, his dusky features taut. He bowed, and when he raised his turbaned head, his irritated expression had smoothed into blank deference. "Sahib. Were you looking for me?"

Kent shook his head. "We're here to visit Chantal."

"Come in," she called. "Ravi, do invite my guests inside."

He stepped silently away to allow them entrance. Juliet followed her husband into the bazaarlike decor of the sitting room. Despite the sunshine flowing through the narrow windows, the crimson wall hangings created the impression of a cave, mysterious and secluded.

Garbed in a loosely gathered gown of garnet-hued cotton, Chantal sat in a tall cane chair, the dark wood framing her blond hair. Rose stood near the mantelpiece. Her lower lip jutted sullenly and her arms were crossed over her lace fichu. Juliet had the impression that they were interrupting an argument.

"If you'd like," she said to Chantal, "we could return at a more convenient time."

Their hostess swept her arm in a grand gesture of cordiality that made her silver bracelets clink. "Of course not. Please, do sit down."

As she and Kent settled into chairs, Juliet subjected Chantal to a surreptitious scrutiny. A buffalo horn necklace drew attention to her splendid bosom. Despite the age lines furrowing her alabaster complexion, she was still a handsome woman, exotic and queenly. Her beauty had an untamed quality, unlike the disciplined elegance of Juliet's mother.

Papa had had a love affair with Chantal; the notion was both painful and jarring. Juliet couldn't imagine her staid and proper father having such a mistress. Yet this woman had shared a past with him, a hidden past that excluded his legitimate family, a secret past that included a bastard daughter, Juliet's half sister. Like a bone-deep laceration, the knowledge of his betrayal throbbed within her.

Ravi came forward, his robe rustling faintly. "If you will excuse me, I will return to my duties."

Kent gave a distracted nod.

As the door closed, Chantal waved at a small bundle

on a bamboo side table. "Ravi was kind enough to deliver a batch of the Calcutta newspapers. They came in today's post. News of India always brings back memories of a happier time."

Rose let out a disgruntled huff. "Indeed, Mama. A time when you were content with Father's love. Now you think nothing of betraying his memory by consorting with that . . . that dark-skinned servant—"

"That's quite enough, young miss." Chantal slashed a hand downward. "Ravi is a dear friend. I'll not hear you malign him."

Rose scowled. Uneasy at witnessing the private quarrel, Juliet said quickly, "I haven't seen you since the dinner party, Rose. Writing your play must be keeping you busy."

The girl's fractious expression eased. "Yes, I've had to do a good deal of research into the family chronicles."

His gaze keen, Kent leaned toward his half sister. "You wouldn't happen to have come across Emily's diary, would you?"

The color faded from her cheeks and she twisted her fichu into a knot. "Emily's—? What do you mean?"

"I suspect you know perfectly well what I mean."

Staring at the floor, Rose said nothing.

Shock stung Juliet. *Rose* had left the diary?

"What's all this about?" Chantal asked.

"Someone left the journal in Juliet's room yesterday," he said. "The pages contained a description of Emily's father."

Chantal went pale; her bosom rose and fell. Clenching the arms of the chair, she gazed first at Juliet, then Rose. "Why . . . what a wicked, malicious act. What induced you to do such a dreadful thing?"

Rose hung her head. "I never meant any harm," she said stiffly. "I merely thought it was unfair that you've both kept such a secret from Juliet. She deserves to know of her sister."

"Half sister," Kent corrected. "And if you felt so strongly on the matter, you ought to have discussed it with me."

"I'm sorry. I . . . I didn't think."

Her voice sounded subdued, but her face remained tilted down, and the rich mass of sable hair half concealed her expression. They were the same age, Juliet reflected suddenly. Yet Rose, with her schoolgirl hairstyle, seemed much younger, almost childlike. When she lifted her head, tears misted her brown eyes.

"I suppose I was considering only myself," she added. "Even though we're not related, Juliet and I shared a sibling. That makes us almost sisters, doesn't it?"

Struggling between sympathy and suspicion, Juliet studied the girl. Had she really meant no harm? Rose was such a fey creature, impetuous and emotional. She might well have responded to impulse in leaving the diary. Her actions could have been spurred by the need for a sister to ease her loneliness.

Compassion crowded Juliet's throat. What was it like to lose a beloved older sister to tragedy? She ached to solve the mystery, not only to protect herself, but also to avenge Emily. The diary had sparked a loyalty to the sibling she had never known.

"Next time," Kent told Rose, "I trust you'll think before you act. You ought not to have interfered."

Her lower lip quivered. "You always scold. Father never treated me so harshly."

She put a hand to her mouth and choked back a sob. Hair swinging, she darted out and slammed the door.

His breath came out in a hiss. Gripping the chair arms, he started to rise.

"Let her go," Chantal said, gracefully lifting a hand. "Perhaps I was too hard on her—"

"You said nothing that shouldn't have been said. That willful girl! Sometimes she reminds me of . . ." Her eyes went unfocused, as if she were pondering a distant problem; then she fluttered her fingers. "Ah, well, never mind. The truth is out and there's no retracting it."

At Chantal's unperturbed manner, Juliet felt a stirring of resentment. "Don't you mind me knowing that you were my father's mistress?"

"Our association ended a long time ago. How comfortable would you have felt here had I been candid?" Turning to Kent, she said, "Would you like a brandy?"

"Thank you."

He looked moody, withdrawn into his thoughts. As Chantal glided to a cabinet inlaid with mother-of-pearl, Juliet wondered if she was the only one who seethed with hurt and bitterness. Of course, the truth came as no surprise to *them*. She was the only one who'd been kept in the dark.

Chantal handed the glass to Kent. "Would you care for any refreshment, Juliet? A sherry, perhaps? Or I could brew a pot of tea—I have Darjeeling."

"No, thank you," she said coldly. "I should like to talk about my father."

The older woman arranged herself in the tall chair and smoothed her garnet skirt. "As you wish."

"This must relate to the feud," Juliet said. "First you had an affair with Papa, and then with his arch-rival. That can't be a coincidence."

Kent frowned. "Perhaps Chantal finds that topic too painful to discuss."

"It's all right," she said, flicking her wrist in dramatic compliance. "I believe I told you, Juliet, that I was once a celebrated actress. It was at the height of my career that I met your father. He was, of course, not married at the time."

Juliet recalled the first time they'd talked here in the tower. Feeling suddenly ill, she put a hand to her mouth. "I remember now," she whispered. "You played the lead in Romeo and Juliet. He *named* me for you."

Chantal shrugged. "It would seem so. Yet his feelings for me weren't strong enough to offer marriage." Her lips twisted into a bitter line. "He had a plan for his life that didn't involve an actress with questionable bloodlines."

The hostile tone startled Juliet. Had Chantal hated Emmett enough to punish him by killing his daughter? She would have to be a madwoman. . . .

"But Papa came from a poor background, too."

"Perhaps that's why he craved respectability. When I learned of his betrothal to your mother, I walked out on him, even though I knew I was to bear his child. He offered to buy me a house, to give me a generous allowance." Chantal frowned at her elegant hands. "But I was young and foolish and hurt, so I refused him. After Emily was born, I left her with an aunt and fled to India, to escape the intolerable memories."

"And you met William Deverell there."

She nodded. "I'd already encountered him in London. You see, he tried to court me, too." Casting a glance at Kent's reserved expression, she added, "But I feared his interest stemmed from the rivalry. It wasn't until later that we fell in love."

Juliet regarded Chantal with suspicion. There had to be more that she wasn't telling. "How could you love two men who were so very different?"

"Different?" Tossing back her blond head, she uttered a brusque laugh. "William and Emmett were more alike than you can imagine. Both stubborn, both proud, both intriguing. It was a challenge to find the gentleness beneath the arrogant exterior. Kent, don't you agree?"

Sipping his brandy, he gave Juliet an intent look. "I wouldn't know about Emmett, but Father did have a kindhearted side. He had a sensitivity that he seldom showed anyone outside the family. You can see it in his drawings."

The image so jarred with Juliet's view of William that she sprang to her feet. "Sensitive! A man who would sell Emily's pony, even her locket . . . out of spite?"

"William never touched a penny of that money," Chantal said. "He gave it all to me, to purchase Emily's clothing and to provide for her future."

"How generous," Juliet mocked. "William denied her his love and forbade her to seek the love of her natural father. For heaven's sake, Chantal, he made my sister's life miserable."

"Emmett is as much to blame—"

"Papa wanted to take care of her," Juliet said hotly. "He wanted her to keep his gifts. He would never have abandoned his own daughter. Emily herself wrote that he said so.''

Chantal arched a fine brow. ''So you would excuse Emmett, but not William? The situation was Emmett's fault in the first place—he denied both Emily and me the honor of his name.''

An angry retort seared Juliet's throat. Abruptly she caught herself. Why was she defending Papa? He wasn't the gentleman she'd grown up to admire and love. He'd hidden a mistress and a sister from her. He'd denied poor Emily the right to a father's love and protection. And all the while, she herself had enjoyed luxury and contentment. She had had everything while Emily had suffered Papa's neglect.

''Perhaps,'' she murmured, dropping into the chair, ''Papa isn't as perfect as I used to believe. He renounced me easily enough.''

Kent set his glass down sharply. ''You can't know that for certain. I'm sure he'd welcome you back for a visit.''

''You're leaving?'' Chantal asked, her keen eyes on Juliet.

''No. At least not for a while.''

She looked at Kent; his lips were taut, his gaze grim.

''There's something else you should know,'' Chantal said. ''I received a letter from Emmett the other day.''

Juliet swiveled to stare at her. ''What on earth did he say?''

''He asked me to watch out for you, to let him know the instant you're unhappy here at Radcliffe.'' Her lips quirked with biting humor. ''So you see, even Emmett can care in his own stiff-necked way.''

Juliet's mind plunged from high hope to deep anger. He'd taken the time to write to his former mistress, but not to her. ''If he loved me, then he would have come after me.''

''Emmett has far too much pride,'' Chantal said with a brusque sweep of her arm. ''He'd want the world to think he'd washed his hands of you. Coming here would be tantamount to admitting he approved of his daughter marrying a Deverell.''

"This ridiculous feud,'' Juliet burst out. ''When will it ever cease?''

"When old men fail to pass on their disputes to the next generation,'' Chantal said dryly.

"Yet some good came of the past,'' Kent said. ''I'm sorry you were hurt, Chantal, but I must say I'm glad that Emmett married Dorothea.''

Because of you, his eyes added to Juliet. The tenderness on his face trembled inside her heart. She took a steadying breath. If emotion kept clouding her logic, she'd never decipher the truth.

She looked at Chantal. ''I wanted to ask you about something puzzling in Emily's diary—''

"Rose should never have given you that diary. She should have brought it to me.''

"I'm glad I had the chance to read my sister's thoughts. On the day of her death, she mentioned that she'd devised a plan to defy Kent. Did she tell you what the plan might have been?''

Chantal cocked her regal head. ''No. I've no idea.''

"Did you speak to her after Papa left?''

"Only briefly. She said she wanted to be alone, to think, so she returned to her bedroom in the family quarters. Emily was never one to distress others with her private suffering. I should have . . .''

"You should have what?'' Kent said.

She shrugged. ''I should have gone after her, talked to her.''

Juliet had the strange impression that wasn't what Chantal had intended to say. ''So you didn't see her again?''

"No.'' Her composure suddenly crumpled and she looked old, her mouth sagging. ''But, oh, how many times since then have I regretted respecting her wishes! I knew she was despondent—I should have insisted upon comforting her. Perhaps I could have stopped her from taking her own life.''

Tears glistened in her blue eyes. Sympathy tugged at Juliet, but she forced herself to remember that Chantal was an actress, capable of staging a superb performance to throw off suspicion. But was she capable of killing her own daughter?

Kent got up to touch the woman's shoulder. "I don't mean to upset you, but the diary has reawakened distressing memories. Juliet's accident has finally made me realize there may be some truth to the curse." He paused, looking keenly at Chantal. "I've been thinking of selling Dreamspinner."

Startled, Juliet stared. His gaze remained fixed on Chantal.

She sprang up and paced toward a window. Her grieving expression became tight-lipped resentment. "That abominable necklace! But are you sure, Kent? You'll be breaking your vow to William."

"I'd sooner do so than risk another tragedy."

She nodded sagely. "A wise decision. We must keep disaster from striking this family again."

A pensive quality underlay her voice. Sunlight silhouetted her majestic figure and cast her expression into half shadow. Yet Juliet sensed with shuddering certainty that she herself was the focus of that speculative regard.

Did Chantal realize a murderer lurked somewhere in the castle?

Or was she herself the one?

Chapter 21

Which one?

Prowling his bedroom, Kent let his thoughts travel the dark road of suspicion. As always, the journey proved both frustrating and painful. Everyone here had cause to dislike Emmett Carleton. But in which person had animosity degenerated into a twisted excuse for murder?

He thought about the interview they'd left an hour earlier. Chantal had delivered no surprises. And he'd been right about Rose leaving the diary. In her usual childish way, she hadn't considered the consequences; she'd wanted only to let Juliet know they'd shared a sister. Rose was so sheltered, she'd never learned how to make friends. Guilt niggled at him. Since their father's death and then Emily's, loneliness had shadowed his sister. When all this was over, Kent vowed, he'd spend more time with her. Perhaps if he took her to London for the Season, she could find a husband.

His mind veered back to the mystery. Hidden emotions seethed inside so many people here. He had the nagging sense that he was missing something. A vital clue. Something to do with the feud?

Oh, God. He was the one who had perpetuated the quarrel. It was hard to believe that he'd once felt justified in using Juliet for vengeance. He'd taken the gift of her love and pulverized it beneath the heel of hatred.

Remorse engulfed him. Snatching up his glass from a table, he took a gulp of brandy. The liquor burned untasted down his throat.

Grimacing, he set down the glass with a sharp click.

Drinking the afternoon away wouldn't erase his sin. Or protect his wife.

Drawn by an urge stronger than logic, he moved to the open doorway. Stepping quietly inside, he looked to her bed. Empty.

His heart lurched, then calmed as he saw Juliet sitting before the gilt desk in the corner. Brow furrowed, she wrote on a sheet of stationery. Sunlight illuminated the purity of her profile and set fire to the red highlights in her upswept hair. She looked slender and soft, the image of a perfect wife. His wife.

He recalled her angry words: *I despise what you've done to me. Our marriage can never be what I thought it was.*

Memory hammered at Kent. He hungered for a return of their too brief interlude of happiness. Oh, God, what if he failed to protect her?

Deliberately making his footfalls louder, he stepped into the room. "Shouldn't you be resting?"

She tilted a cool face to him. "I wasn't sleepy."

"Do you feel all right?"

"I'm fine. The nausea comes only in the morning."

Returning her attention to the letter, she continued writing. Only the ticking of the mantel clock and the faint scratching of her pen marred the silence. A few days ago, she would have abandoned her work and come running for his kiss.

No more.

Unable to bear the encroaching darkness of despair, he said, "Who are you writing to?"

"My mother."

Shoving his hands into his pockets, he paced to the desk. "Didn't she ask you not to contact her?"

"Yes, but matters between my father and me could hardly be any worse than they are now."

The chill in her voice discouraged further dialogue, yet a self-punishing impulse made him go on. "Are you telling her about the baby?"

"Yes, I've already written that part."

"What are you writing about now?"

"Hannah Forster. As soon as I receive the money

from Papa, I intend to take her to a London physician.
I'm asking Mama's advice about making the appointment."

"I see."

Christ. How wrong he'd been to oppose her about
the dowry. He'd viewed the money as contaminated;
she viewed it as a benefit to the people of Radcliffe.
The legacy of his father's hatred had blinded Kent to
her goodness. She was right; he was as rigid and self-
seeking as Emmett Carleton.

Her womanly fragrance drifted to him. He ached to
reach across the chasm separating them, to fold her
into his embrace, to kiss away the pain and distrust
and betrayal. To prove he wasn't altogether a scoundrel.

Impossible.

"Did you say anything . . . about what's happened?" he asked.

Juliet set down the pen. Her green-gold eyes looked
as cold as Emmett Carleton's. "Shall I tell Mama that
you married me for revenge? That you were once wed
to her husband's bastard child? That you blamed him
for driving his own daughter to suicide?"

The truth shriveled his soul. Would he ever grow
accustomed to seeing repugnance where love had once
bloomed?

You sowed the seeds of vengeance, he reminded
himself. Juliet's hatred is the bitter harvest.

Wrenching his gaze away from her lovely face, he
went to a window and braced an arm on the stone
casement. Dizziness swept him, as if he teetered on the
precipice of black damnation.

Far below, the river flowed serene and blue-gray,
lapping against the ancient wall. A trout's fin flashed
against the water. He concentrated on the familiar view
of hills and fields. Doom ebbed slowly, driven away by
the calming sight of his castle, his lands.

He had Radcliffe. His heritage . . . his child's heritage. It offered at least a token hope for the future,
even if she raised their child far from here.

He turned back to Juliet. Her frigidity had thawed to

a guarded coolness, as though she took pity on his suffering.

Pity. Not love.

He returned her stare. "No, I don't expect you to tell your mother anything distressing. Yet I wonder if you ought to let your father know about the greenhouse incident."

"One of you badgering me to leave here is quite enough."

"So you believe he still cares?"

Her gaze faltered; then she sat up straight. "I don't know what to think anymore. Except that I want to find the murderer so we can . . ."

We. She'd used the word unconsciously, of course. Yet for a moment he could only look at her and yearn for a future together. Would he ever again be singed by the flame of her love?

The mantel clock chimed four times. She turned away, and his fantasy faded into dreary reality.

"Since you're determined not to rest," he said, walking to her, "do you mind finishing the letter later?"

"Why?"

"I sent a note to Augusta, asking her to join us for tea at five o'clock. I'd like you to be there. But first, I'd like to speak to Gordon."

"About what?"

"Dreamspinner." Frustration gnawed at him. "At this point, the necklace is our only clue. I'd like to see if he—or anyone else here—reveals strong feelings about it leaving the family. Will you come with me?"

Hesitating only a second, she rose to face him. "Do you suppose Chantal resents the fact that your father never gave the jewels to her? Could she have turned that resentment on Emily?"

"No," he said, emphatically shaking his head. "I've known Chantal Hutton for almost twenty years. She keeps her emotions close to the surface."

"But she was an actress, Kent. Can you be so sure she isn't playing a role?"

An arrow of misgiving pierced him. What if he was

wrong about Chantal? He'd certainly been wrong about *someone* here.

He gazed at Juliet. Pregnancy had enhanced her natural beauty with the glow of health, and sunshine shimmered upon her cinnamon hair. Her dainty features were so dear that he ached just looking at her. From their first meeting she had brought an unexpected radiance into the darkness of his heart. The absence of that light left him dismal and empty. "Juliet . . ."

She tilted her head to study him. "Yes?"

He yearned to touch the rose-kissed ivory of her cheek, to savor the warm affirmation of life. Instead his fingers formed a cold fist at his side.

"I'm no longer sure of anything," he murmured.

She blinked, but gave no acknowledgment of his irony. He escorted her out the door, and the gloomy chill of the hall enveloped them, as if the very air held a premonition of peril. A fury born of fear flared inside him. He would kill the person who threatened his wife.

She tipped a curious look at him. "You aren't serious about selling Dreamspinner, are you?"

He opened his mouth to say no. Then the notion blazed with a sudden, enormous appeal. "Yes," he said firmly. "I am."

The resolution on his face fascinated Juliet. As they walked down the age-worn stairs, she glanced at his imperious profile. Was it possible that he could shed the hatred learned at his father's knee? That he could forget the feud and accept love as the cornerstone of his life?

Longing seared her soul. She wanted to see his harsh expression soften into a smile again. She wanted to hear his husky voice murmuring tender words of affection. She wanted to lie naked in the dark and feel his hands and mouth arousing her body to vibrant life.

So he could betray her again? So he could whisper more lies? Ever since their quarrel, he'd avoided touching her. He didn't love her; he'd only said what he thought she'd wanted to hear. Now that she'd learned his secret, there was no need for pretense.

Angry at her gullibility, she walked rigidly at his side until they reached the library. He grasped the tarnished knob and pushed open the huge oak door. The room formed an H, with long branches stretching to either side of the entrance. The scents of old leather bindings and musty parchment hung in the air.

Kent directed her straight ahead, down a short corridor that led to a second set of wings. There, he turned left. A yellowed globe on a wooden stand occupied a cobwebbed corner. Several armchairs sprouted stuffing from holes in the faded burgundy upholstery. A fire snapped in the hearth. At the end of an age-scarred table sat Gordon.

His head was bowed over an open book, his face hidden, only the top of his thinning brown hair visible. He looked as though he were peering closely at the pages. Even the tap of their footsteps failed to penetrate his concentration.

Had Gordon always been so frail, so scholarly? Juliet tried to envision him as a healthy youngster, frolicking and playing. Gordon must be nearly ten years older than Kent. How close had they been as boys?

Stopping beside his cousin's chair, Kent gently shook the maroon-coated shoulder. An incoherent mutter escaped Gordon. Like a trout shooting to the surface, he sat abruptly straight, his thin mouth working in protest and his pale eyes magnified behind the spectacles.

He blinked hard at Juliet. "You look rather familiar," he said, the words slightly slurred. "Do enlighten me with your appellation."

His dreamy tone startled her; he must have been sound asleep when they walked in. "It's me, Juliet. Kent's wife."

Leaning onto the book, he cocked his head. "Ah, yes . . . the other Carleton girl. Ought to have discerned so from the eyes. Quite singular. Identical to your father's."

Uncertain if he meant the words as a compliment, she said, "Thank you."

"I hope we're not disturbing you," said Kent, withdrawing his hand from the stooped shoulder.

Gordon listed awkwardly in the chair. "Ah, Cousin. Didn't apprehend your presence."

"I wanted to show my wife where the safe is located."

"Needn't procure my consent for that," he said, waving a clawlike hand. "This domicile belongs to you."

His red-rimmed eyes drifted shut and his chin began to sink toward his chest. Odd, she thought. His medication must make him drowsy.

Kent gave a faint nod, asking her to follow him. Pursing her lips, she complied. Above the rows of bookshelves hung a collection of ancestral portraits. Many were so darkened with age that she could make out little more than the pale glow of face and hands, the white of ruffs and collars.

Someday she'd see to cleaning the pictures. Then she caught herself, her heart aching. No, she was leaving here.

Kent stopped before a more recent painting that occupied a prominent place at the end of the room. This one depicted an unsmiling man in modern garb, a starched neckcloth and navy blue coat.

"My father," he said.

Of course. She should have spied the resemblance in the cheekbones and devil-dark eyes. William Deverell's chin was tilted at a haughty angle, giving the impression that he looked down his nose at the rest of the world. That stern, condescending gaze seemed to bore into her. So this was the cruel man portrayed in Emily's diary. The rigid man who'd hated her father. Somehow she felt only pity that he'd let enmity ruin his life.

Gripping the gilt frame, Kent lifted the portrait and propped it against a chair. The removal revealed a metal door in the stone wall. Pulling a ring of keys from his coat pocket, he inserted one and unlocked the safe.

The hinges squawked loudly into the dusty air. She glanced at Gordon, but he was nodding over the book.

Curiosity induced her to move closer to Kent, to stand on tiptoe and see inside the repository.

Only a forest-green velvet pouch occupied the shadowed interior. Even as he withdrew the bag and untied the drawstring, she guessed the contents.

Dreamspinner.

The emeralds glinted dully in his hand. Without the softening luster of candlelight, the peacock looked merely vulgar. *Glowing with malevolent satisfaction . . .*

Emily's description made Juliet shiver. Had this necklace motivated someone to murder?

She raised her head to find Kent staring at her. Angry desperation tightened his jaw and burned in his eyes. The impulse to embrace him throbbed like a physical pain inside her.

His fingers abruptly clenched around Dreamspinner. Wheeling, he stalked toward his cousin.

"Gordon."

The word snapped him from the stupor. Blinking, he looked up and frowned. "Ah, Kent. What brings you here?"

His disorientation startled Juliet; she walked slowly to the other side of the table. Kent gave no sign of noticing the lapse.

"I've come to fetch this." Bracing one hand on the table, he held forth the necklace. "I'm selling Dreamspinner."

"Selling—?"

"Yes, my wife doesn't much care for the piece. Do you, Juliet?"

Numbly she shook her head.

"So you see," he continued, "it's foolish to keep the jewels when the estate could reap a small fortune from the sale."

Gordon stared at the necklace. His benign expression slipped away. He struggled to his feet, his gaunt form swaying. "You mustn't sell Dreamspinner. You *can't!*"

"Why not?"

His mouth opened and closed. The hand he pressed

to his lapel trembled visibly. "Because . . . you pledged so to Uncle William. You can't break a vow!"

Kent shrugged. "I no longer feel bound by a vow based on hatred. As I said before, my feelings about the feud have changed."

"Changed?"

"Yes. Since I married Juliet, I've come to realize how little I care for past quarrels."

The falsehood hurt . . . because he'd voiced what she so dearly wished for, an end to hostility and a beginning of peace. He couldn't even bear to look at her as he lied; his fierce gaze remained focused on his cousin.

Gordon shook his head in childish befuddlement. "I cannot comprehend this transformation in you. I never conceived you would ever sell Dreamspinner."

"The prospect seems to alarm you. Why is that?"

Gordon wilted into the chair, his hands worrying the book pages. "Uncle William would be most aggrieved," he said, his tone plaintive. "That necklace meant the world to him. You, of all us Deverells, must perpetuate tradition."

"Tradition be damned. We're better off without this cursed necklace." Kent let the emeralds slither back into the velvet pouch. "I should have gotten rid of it long ago."

Gordon blinked wildly. "You must reconsider—"

"No. Ravi will make inquiries at a few London jewelers. I expect to have a buyer within a fortnight."

Gordon fell silent. His shoulders drooping, he supported his head with his gnarled hands. He gave the impression of retreating from a reality too painful to bear.

Reluctant sympathy gripped Juliet. How different he seemed, how pitiable. On impulse she touched his arm; the feel of wasted flesh beneath the maroon coat appalled her. "Would you care to take tea with us, Gordon? We're joining Augusta in the drawing room."

He didn't seem to hear the invitation. After a moment Kent guided her away. Through the mullioned window she glimpsed the intricate walkways of the rose garden. By craning her neck, she could see the ruined greenhouse abutting the outer wall.

A chill prickled her skin. Had Gordon watched her at work there? Had he plotted her murder?

She couldn't reconcile that notion with the defeated man slumped at the table. Yet she'd seen a spark of desperation at the notion of selling Dreamspinner. Perhaps such a powerful emotion could give him the strength to attack. . . .

The instant the library door closed with a quiet click, she said, "How strangely he behaved. What's disturbing him?"

Kent stared at the pouch in his hand. "Gordon has his own demons to fight. For some reason he wants me to keep Dreamspinner."

"Maybe he has a fanatical attachment to it. Maybe he truly does want to honor William's wishes."

Kent shook his head. "He and my father weren't close. I've know Gordon since boyhood, and he's always shown far more interest in books than people. I can't imagine him harming anyone."

"You aren't privy to his secret thoughts. Even someone you know well can have a hidden side."

By the darkening of his gaze, she knew he'd applied her words to their own painful schism. A muscle in his jaw leapt; then he looked away. "I deserved that," he murmured.

In spite of his lies and betrayal, she found a bittersweet joy in his nearness. Protection, she told herself. That was all Kent Deverell offered her. That was all she wanted from him.

"There's another reason for Gordon's odd behavior," he went on, as they started down the dim hall. "My cousin is addicted to opium. He started using the drug many years ago, to counteract the pain of his rheumatism."

Horror and pity dried her mouth. Of course, drugs would explain so much . . . the hazy mannerisms, the lapses of rationality, perhaps even his gray pallor yesterday, when he'd been searching for Augusta and his "medication." If opium could make him act in an irrational manner, could it turn him into a devious maniac?

Before she could speak, Kent added, ''Juliet . . . believe me, I wanted to tell you earlier. It's just that Gordon prefers people not to know, and I've tried to honor that wish.''

He looked so earnest and anxious that she touched his sleeve. ''People are entitled to their privacy. It's just a shame we can't do anything to alleviate the progress of his disease.''

The tap of hurrying footsteps echoed down the corridor behind. ''Kent, wait!'' called Rose. ''I must speak to you.''

Turning, Juliet spied the girl hastening after them. Sable hair swinging loose about her shoulders, she clutched her gray skirts, the upraised hem revealing the fringe of a modest white petticoat.

She scowled at her brother. ''Mama told me the news! How could you even think such an awful thing?''

''Think what?'' he asked.

''Selling Dreamspinner, of course!'' Her gaze dropped to the pouch in his hand, and she gasped. ''Why have you taken the necklace from the safe? You can't have found a buyer so quickly.''

He watched her closely. ''And if I have?''

Her brown eyes widened. She clutched the lace fichu over her bosom. Abruptly she rounded on Juliet. ''This is all *your* fault. I tried to believe otherwise, but you're just as greedy as your father. You'd peddle a family heirloom instead of thanking my brother for granting you the honorable role of his duchess.''

The burst of passion startled Juliet. ''Kent made the decision on his own. I have no need for money, what with my dowry coming.''

''Yes, the money your father stole from mine.''

''That's quite enough,'' Kent snapped. ''You'll apologize to my wife for your rudeness.''

Her lower lip quivered. ''I only meant—''

''Apologize, Rose.''

Head lowered, she muttered a grudging ''I'm sorry.''

Then she turned to stare at the pouch in Kent's hand. "You must tell me . . . who's buying Dreamspinner?"

"No one as yet. Ravi will take it to London for appraisal."

She raised a forlorn face. "Father let me try it on once. May I see it one more time?"

His mouth tightened, but he reached inside the bag and withdrew the necklace. Spilling over his broad palm, the emeralds appeared dull in the shadowed corridor. Even the diamonds and rubies in the peacock's tail had lost all their sheen.

Rose didn't seem to notice. As if saying good-bye to an old friend, she lovingly caressed the jewels.

"Oh, Kent," she said, blinking tear-misted eyes. "Have you forgotten how much Father revered Dreamspinner? Won't you please reconsider?"

His expression gentled. "Perhaps no one will offer an adequate price."

She nodded, the words clearly comforting her. Juliet wondered at the girl's mercurial moods. Was her attraction to the necklace a response to her bastardy? She must feel the same emptiness Emily had. Yet instead of seeking love, Rose clung to proof of her heritage. Dreamspinner was a link to her beloved father.

"We're taking tea in the drawing room," Kent told his sister. "Why don't you join us?"

"No, thank you. Mama has a headache. I promised to fetch her one of Mrs. Fleetwood's tisanes."

With a rustle of starched petticoats, she scurried toward the kitchen.

The jewels clacked faintly as he dropped them back into the green pouch. "Well. So far only Chantal is in favor of selling these. And we can't even be certain of her true feelings."

His weary tone affected Juliet more than she cared to admit. How awful to suspect your own sister of murder.

"Let's talk to Augusta," she said. "Perhaps her response will give us a stronger clue."

His obsidian eyes bored into hers; then his expression went as blank as a closed book. Slipping the pouch into his pocket, he escorted her down the long corridor.

In the Laguerre drawing room, Augusta sat near a window. Her capable hands glided a needle in and out of the fine lawn of a baby's gown. Lolling beside the empty hearth, Punjab scrambled up and uttered a shrill yap.

"Hush, darling. Do behave, else you shan't have your tea."

With a complaining wheeze, the Pekingese settled onto his cushion.

Turning in her chair, Augusta said, "Good afternoon."

"I trust we haven't kept you waiting," Kent said.

"Time is never wasted when I have my sewing."

Juliet walked closer to see the miniature garment. "That looks too small for Hannah's brother, Tom. Is there another new baby in the district?"

"Of course. The coming heir will need a proper layette."

Touched, Juliet reflected that she hadn't yet had time to appreciate expecting the baby, to ready a nursery, to look forward to future happiness. Instead, suspicion tainted her joy. "You're very kind to think of my baby."

"It's my duty," Augusta said gruffly. "Unless you'd prefer to order a layette from London."

"Of course not."

She set aside her needlework. "I shall ring for tea straightaway. Fleetwood can be terribly slow."

She clumped to the corner to tug on the bell cord. Juliet looked at her husband; he observed Augusta while collecting the fibers and wires he'd knocked from the desk earlier while constructing his fishing flies. A breeze rustled the curtains and eddied the freshness of summer into the musty room. With Kent tidying his fishing flies and Augusta resuming her sewing, the scene appeared tranquil and domestic.

Yet someone in the castle plotted death.

Augusta? Then why would she be stitching garments for the baby? Unless her action was the calculated ruse of a madwoman.

Determined to unearth the truth, Juliet sank shakily to the settee. "I've written to my mother and asked her advice on a physician for Hannah."

"Humph," said Augusta. "You needn't bother a society lady with our rural tragedies. She's likely too engaged with her recitals and soirees."

"You don't know her. Mama takes great interest in aiding people in need. The moment we have the funds available, I want Hannah to have the chance to walk normally."

A spasm of pain and affection twisted Augusta's features. "You're generous to consider the girl. I'd have used my own dowry to help her, but the funds were squandered long ago on this castle and William's follies." With ill-concealed anger, she stabbed her needle into the fine lawn.

"When I take Hannah to London, perhaps you'd care to come along. She would feel more at ease in your company."

Augusta looked up in surprise. "I should be happy to do so, Your Grace."

"I must add a note to Mama's letter, then." Watching her closely, Juliet went on, "I'll inquire if we can all stay in my father's house."

"Nonsense," she said with an unladylike snort. "Emmett Carleton might unbend long enough to let his daughter come to visit . . . even a darling waif like Hannah. But he shan't welcome someone who's been a Deverell as long as I."

The words sounded more matter-of-fact than malicious. Could she bear Papa a hidden grudge?

"Perhaps he's changed," Kent said. Standing by the desk, he held the tiny bluebottle fly to the sunlight. "Perhaps his daughter's marriage has softened Emmett."

"Poppycock. He's as deranged by the feud as William was."

"How do you know that?" Juliet asked.

"He duped William into buying that tea estate. He's

cut from the same cloth as William—too proud for his own good."

"Yet I've changed," Kent said, "so why not Emmett?" Tossing down the hook-fly, he withdrew the jewel pouch from his pocket. "You might as well know, Augusta. As a token of my willingness to end the feud, I'm planning to sell Dreamspinner."

Her jaw dropped. The ruddy color vanished from her cheeks, leaving the mole prominent against her whitened skin. "*Sell?*" she said, her voice faint. "Why would you do that?"

"We've no need for it. You said so yourself at dinner the other night." He tossed the bag from hand to hand; the jewels clanked dully. "Didn't you?"

Eyes following the bag, she sat still, the needle and thread poised over the little gown. Her mouth hung open in astonishment . . . and with palpable alarm, Juliet thought.

Silence hung as thickly as the dust motes dancing in the sunlight. Lowering her eyes, the older woman resumed sewing, her movements jerky. "I never thought you would take my words so seriously, Your Grace. Especially now."

"Now?" Juliet prompted.

"With your dowry coming. We hardly need the extra money, so it makes no sense to rush out and find a buyer. Better to put the jewels away as a nest egg for your children. God knows William left us with little enough."

"I think not," said Kent. "Dreamspinner is a symbol of hatred that we're well rid of. I'm dispatching Ravi to London with the necklace very soon."

Augusta plied the needle with quick, mechanical strokes. Blood suddenly welled from her fingertip. Vacantly she watched a red droplet drip onto the white linen.

"You've pricked yourself," Juliet said. "Shall I fetch you some sticking plaster?"

"No, it wouldn't help." Augusta lurched to her feet. The sewing basket overturned, spilling threads and thimbles and pins. "Do pardon me. I must put this to soak before the stain sets." Clutching the tiny gown, she scurried from the drawing room.

The Pekingese started to pad after his mistress. He paused to look hungrily at the empty tea table, then returned to his cushion.

"How oddly she acted," Juliet mused, absently observing the dog. She lifted her eyes to Kent. "Something isn't right. First Gordon and Rose want you to keep the necklace. Now even Augusta is opposed to selling it."

"Curiouser and curiouser." He tossed the bag into the air, then deftly caught it and aimed a glower at the green velvet. "She's hiding something."

"Yet she doesn't hate Papa."

"Unless that's another lie."

Fear slithered down her spine. "Kent, perhaps we're mistaken to think Emily's murder—and the attempt on me—had anything to do with the feud. Perhaps . . ."

"Go on. What?"

Shuddering, she shook her head. "I can't say . . . it's too horrible."

"Tell me, Juliet. We can't keep casting into a stream and failing to catch any fish."

She drew an aching breath. "Perhaps the *baby* sparked the murder attempts. Augusta admitted to miscarrying several times. Perhaps she was madly jealous of Emily's pregnancy. Now she may have turned that jealousy on me."

Shadows lurked in the dark depths of his eyes. "Dreamspinner doesn't work into your theory."

"Her dowry went to repair the castle and to pay William's debts. She might view the jewels as rightfully hers."

"It's possible," he said slowly. "But she's so devoted to children. My God, she's even been sewing for our baby."

"The greenhouse incident happened the very day I learned I was carrying your child."

He stood silent and somber. Weeping inwardly, Juliet felt his desperation as her own. He, too, wanted to exonerate the people here, the family he loved.

Abruptly he slammed the pouch onto the desk so hard that she caught her breath.

"This damned necklace," he said through gritted teeth. "The sooner we're rid of it, the better."

The explosion of violence stunned her. Even as she stared at Kent, Fleetwood entered, bearing a large silver tray in his white-gloved hands.

Punjab waddled forward and nearly entangled himself in the servant's feet. China clinked and spoons rattled. Unperturbed, Fleetwood shuffled across the antique rug and deposited the tray on the table.

Thin as a silver birch, the old retainer straightened. "Good afternoon, Your Grace. I've brought the tea Madam ordered."

Kent gave a curt nod. "Thank you."

As the butler began to leave, Juliet jumped up, fingers twisting her turquoise skirt. "Fleetwood?"

"Your Grace."

"What would you say if the duke were to sell the necklace, Dreamspinner?"

Astonishment creased his ancient brow. "What would *I* say?"

"Yes."

"Er . . . I would say . . . er . . ." He glanced uncertainly at Kent. "I would say best wishes, Your Grace."

No furtiveness marred that puzzled countenance. She smiled. "Thank you, Fleetwood. That will be all."

He hesitated by the door. "The Lady Maud Peabody questioned me about the necklace earlier today. It isn't missing, I trust?"

"No, why do you ask?"

"After the dinner party, Mrs. Fleetwood found the necklace on the night table. I'm certain she gave it to Ravi for safekeeping—"

"Nothing's happened to Dreamspinner," Kent said, gesturing at the pouch. "As a matter of fact, it's right here on the desk."

The butler's expression cleared. "Ah, so it is."

Bowing, he departed. Kent focused a frown at her. "You don't really consider *him* a suspect."

Her skirt rustled as she walked to the tea table.

"Probably not. But I've seen him on the north parapet."

"Looking for a red-breasted snipe, no doubt."

"Perhaps," she said, spooning tea leaves into the steaming water. "Yet someone pushed Emily from that very battlement."

Hands planted on his hips, he watched her. "And that same someone threw a boulder at you."

By the starkness of his expression, she knew he regretted plunging her into peril. She fortified her heart against a treacherous weakening. He *should* suffer. Unwitting or not, he had set off this dreadful chain of events by embroiling her in his scheme for vengeance.

Punjab loosed an earsplitting series of yaps. Eyeing the tray, he sat up, tail wagging. Juliet filled a saucer with weak tea, added a generous dollop of rich dark cream, and placed the dish on the floor. The Pekingese lapped noisily at the liquid.

Mrs. Fleetwood had outdone herself today. An array of sandwiches crowded a chipped porcelain platter. Chunks of Stilton cheese and stalks of celery lay beside thick slices of apple cake. Realizing the hours since luncheon, Juliet gazed longingly at the feast.

"I wonder what's keeping Augusta. I never knew a baby could make one so nauseated in the morning and so hungry the rest of the day."

Striding to her side, Kent pressed a plate into her hand. "Don't wait, love. Your health is more important than etiquette."

His gentle tone and unexpected closeness unnerved her. She lowered her gaze to the open collar of his shirt. Her appetite drowned under a surge of bittersweet yearning.

The echo of a girl's foolish fancies, she told herself.

Setting down the plate, she raised cool eyes to his face. "I'll eat in a moment. May I pour you a cup of tea?"

He made an impatient gesture. "Never mind the damned tea. I'm more concerned about your welfare."

"Let's catch the murderer then. What shall we do next?"

"That's the frustrating part. We'll need to find another approach. The necklace raised more questions than it answered."

Harsh lines of worry bracketed his mouth. Pouring herself a cup of tea, she wondered how far he would go to protect her. "You could sell Dreamspinner to my father."

His eyes went as black as night. A muscle clenched in his jaw. "I fail to see what that would accomplish."

"Perhaps it might enrage the killer, force his . . . or her hand."

"With you the focus of that fury?" He shook his head decisively. "I think not."

For all her outer indifference, she felt a spasm of pain grip her chest. She added cream to her tea and slowly stirred. "Are you certain that my well-being is all that's stopping you?"

"What do you mean?"

"Perhaps you wouldn't sell Dreamspinner to my father under any circumstances. You've made it plain that you care more for the feud than for your own wife."

Wariness haunted his eyes. "Now isn't the time to discuss my feelings for you, Juliet. I'm already breaking a vow by selling the necklace. Must I also betray my father's memory by giving it to his enemy?"

"His enemy . . . or yours?" Raising the steaming cup, she studied him over the rim. "Could you in all honesty shake Papa's hand in forgiveness?"

He stared. She sensed the turmoil raging inside him, though his face remained barren. He lifted a hand to cradle her cheek. At the touch of his warm, callused palm, she felt helpless, mesmerized. Her heartbeat accelerated under an absurd rush of hope.

"Juliet, if it meant—"

"What's the matter with Punjab?"

Augusta's horrified voice shattered the moment. Brown skirt swishing, she dashed into the room.

Juliet spun around to see the dog staggering toward his cushion. He stopped, swaying. Stiffening, he collapsed onto the hearth rug, his body quivering and stretching. Foam flecked his mouth.

"What the devil—" Kent muttered. He snatched the teacup away from Juliet and set it down. "Christ! Don't drink or eat anything."

Augusta dropped to her knees beside the Pekingese. She ran her hands over the furry form. "Oh, dear sweet heaven! Punjab, Punjab! What's wrong with you, darling?"

His face grim, Kent knelt to examine the animal. "He was fine a moment ago."

"I'll ring for help," Juliet said.

She ran to tug on the bell cord, then hastened back. Fingers worrying the silk of her skirt, she watched Augusta and Kent try to rouse the dog.

Their efforts proved fruitless. Suddenly his small body gave a fierce convulsive shudder and went still.

"No!" Augusta whispered. She frantically rubbed Punjab's chest in an attempt to revive him. The animal lay unmoving. With a finger that trembled visibly, she lifted his eyelid and peered into his face.

"Dear God!" she gasped. "He's been poisoned."

Chapter 22

Juliet clutched the back of a chair. Horror swept her in sickening waves. Her mind chased in confused circles, trying to find the sense in such a shocking development.

"Poisoned?" she murmured. "How is that possible?"

Kent kept his gaze trained on Augusta. His bronzed face gone white, he crouched on his heels. "You're certain?"

She gave a jerky nod. "The pupils contract from an overdose of morphine. Doctor Sattler warned me. In case Gordon ever . . ."

Her voice caught in a sob. She bent over Punjab, her sturdy back bowed with grief as she stroked a silken ear. "Oh, my poor baby. My poor darling."

Ravi appeared in the doorway. His narrowed eyes flitted from the fallen dog to Kent. "Sahib? I was in the kitchen and heard the bell."

"Fetch Gordon immediately," he snapped. "Then get everyone else in here."

Nodding his turbaned head, the Indian hastened away.

Kent lay a comforting arm around Augusta's shoulders. The handkerchief she crushed to her mouth muffled her weeping.

Punjab had been like a child to her . . . she, who'd never been blessed with her own baby. Juliet's heart ached in sympathy and shock. "Perhaps it isn't too late to revive him. Mrs. Fleetwood knows a bit about herbs. I'll fetch her."

Turning, she started toward the door.

"Don't you dare!" Before she could go three steps,

Kent lunged to snare her wrist. "You're not to move an inch from my sight. Do you understand?"

"But Punjab—"

"Is gone." Lowering his voice to a rough whisper, he added, "Dead from poison meant for you."

Her body went cold. Recalling the way he'd wrested the cup from her, she glanced at the saucer the dog had licked clean. "The tea?"

Kent gave her a terse nod.

"Who would do such an awful thing?"

Sinister fury hardened his face. "That's precisely what I intend to find out."

Someone here harbored enough malice to execute such a cruel act, Juliet thought. Someone who cared little about harming others, so long as she died. The threat suddenly took on chilling proportions.

"Dear God. I shouldn't have poured Punjab the tea. If only I'd waited, he'd still be alive—"

"And we wouldn't have known." His arms supported her in a desperately tight embrace. "You nearly drank the tea and died. Along with our baby."

Fear carved a cold, empty place inside her. Shaken, she wilted against his muscled chest and tried to absorb his warmth and life. Steady and strong, his heart drummed against her ear. "And you, Kent. You, too."

"Not necessarily."

Drawing her to the table, he picked up the creamer. The liquid bore an amber tinge; he held the dish to his nose.

"Sweetish odor, like opium," he murmured. "The drug was added to the cream. Everyone here knows I drink my tea black."

"Tea?" Augusta said in a quavering voice. With the sluggishness of an old woman, she tilted up a haggard face. "I don't understand, Kent. Did you say someone poisoned my darling's tea?"

The hyacinth eyes reflected a misty bafflement. If the poisoning had been a horrid error on her part, she hid it well, Juliet thought. Against her waist, she felt tension cord his arm. He was staring at Augusta, his features drawn by both compassion and mistrust.

Shuffling footsteps came from the hall. Blinking behind thick spectacles, Gordon ambled into the drawing room, his hands plunged into the pockets of his frayed smoking jacket.

"Hullo," he said. "Ah, teatime. Ravi might have told me so when he bustled me from my research. The fellow was quite overbearing. Deserves a reprimand, Cousin."

His earlier incoherence had vanished. Had the effects of the opium worn off? Juliet wondered. Perhaps he'd feigned that rambling manner. So that no one would suspect him of slipping into the kitchen and tampering with the cream . . .

Releasing her, Kent turned to his cousin. "Never mind what Ravi deserves," he said. "Someone's poisoned Punjab."

Gordon's high forehead furrowed. "Poisoned?"

"I've lost my baby," Augusta murmured, wringing the handkerchief. "Oh, Gordon, he's gone!"

Her husband walked closer and peered at the dog. "Dear me. Dear me, indeed. Yet we needn't leap to an erroneous hypothesis. Poor beast was getting on in years. Perhaps he suffered cardiac arrest."

"My Punjab was *killed!*" she cried. "Oh, who would have done such a wicked thing?"

Tears dampened her sallow cheeks, and her eyes flashed wildly, as if she teetered on the brink of hysteria. Shifting from one foot to the other, Gordon hesitated. Then he gathered her close and his clawlike hand awkwardly patted her back. They made a curious couple, he the shorter of the two, and as gaunt as a skeleton beside her robust frame. Their closeness softened Juliet's heart.

"There, there, my dear," he said. "A tragic misfortune, to be sure. Fleetwood must have put out rat poison, and Punjab lapped it up. Arsenic ingestion can generate symptoms of acute—"

"Not arsenic," Kent said. "Morphine."

Gordon gave a start of surprise and dropped his arms to his sides. Peering again at the dog, he adjusted his glasses. "Indeed? How very singular. An overdose of morphine produces narcosis, then a coma and respiratory failure.''

"How swiftly would the drug work?'' Juliet asked.

His pale eyes focused on her. ''A lethal amount administered to the adult human could kill within an hour. For such a small creature, the end might well occur more rapidly.''

Augusta dabbed her eyes. ''Must you go on so clinically? We must find the person responsible!''

He placed a gnarled hand on her broad shoulder. ''Beg pardon, my dear. I had no intention of causing you further woe.''

"Someone here hated my poor darling. . . .'' Her watery gaze shifted to the door. ''Someone . . .''

Chantal and Rose hastened into the room. They were a study in contrasts, the regal blond in the flamboyant garnet gown and the girlish brunette in modest gray silk.

"Ravi said that Punjab has taken ill.'' Spying the still form, Chantal brought a hand to her bosom. ''Mercy! Is he all right?''

"He's dead.'' Augusta aimed a shaking finger at them. ''And one of you must have poisoned him!''

"That's absurd,'' Rose said, lifting her chin. ''Kent, tell her to stop making such unfounded accusations.''

He remained silent, watching the group. Fear wormed into Juliet's bones. One of the people here could be the killer. . . .

"Unfounded?'' Augusta said. ''You've always resented me. You and your actress mother. I have a *legitimate* place in this household.''

A furious flush pinkened Rose's cheeks. ''But you haven't the noble blood of the Deverells flowing through *your* veins. Do you?''

"That's enough,'' snapped Chantal. ''You're hardly behaving nobly at the moment.'' To Kent, she said, ''Will you be so kind as to tell us what's happened? Was Punjab really *poisoned*?'' Bewilderment lifted her voice.

"Yes. And I intend to find out who—''

Maud burst into the drawing room, her cobalt skirt swishing, the feather on her hat bouncing. Henry followed, the Fleetwoods and Ravi close behind.

Maud squinted at the dog and swung away in wide-eyed alarm. "Egad! Someone has committed a heinous crime!"

Henry thrust his bowler hat at Fleetwood, then strode to Augusta and pressed her hand. "My poor lady. You have my very deepest condolences."

Her jaw quivered, but she held herself stiffly upright. "Thank you, Henry. You're most kind."

Maud tugged on his tweed sleeve. "This is exactly like in my book. I told you . . . the one that was stolen!"

"Dash it all, darling," he chided. "This is no time to be prattling about your penny dreadfuls. Besides, I found the book, slipped behind a chair cushion."

"But it can't be a coincidence. The same thing happened to the dog in *A Study in Scarlet*." She lowered her voice. "The villain employed a poison used by South American natives on the tips of their arrows."

Kent aimed a withering look at her. "This was morphine." To his cousin, he added, "You keep a supply for times when you're in acute pain, do you not?"

Gordon blinked, then walked slowly away. "Yes, but I cannot comprehend how a dog could have gotten—"

"The poison was secreted in the cream." Kent stared at each person in turn. In a savagely soft voice, he went on, "I believe it was meant for Juliet."

A hush settled over the gathering. With an inward shiver, Juliet studied the others. Chantal wore a dramatic posture of shock. Rose clenched both hands to her fichu. Maud half swooned against a grim-faced Henry. Augusta pressed the handkerchief to her mouth. Gordon sagged into the desk chair. Fleetwood stood frozen beside his wife, who clasped her pudgy hands in prayer. Only Ravi exhibited no sign of surprise.

A clamor of voices exploded.

"I don't understand—"

"This can't be true—"

"You must be mistaken—"

"Who would harm—"

"Quiet, everyone!" Chantal stepped forward, fluttering her voluminous sleeve. "Are you saying someone tried to *murder* Juliet?"

"That's madness!" Augusta said, staring "You mean the poison *wasn't* meant for my Punjab?"

"Precisely," Kent stated.

Lacking her usual grace, Chantal began an agitated circuit of the room. "But . . . why?"

"That's what I would like to find out."

Mrs. Fleetwood approached him, her hands gripping the white apron around her bulky midsection. "Yer Grace, if I might have a word."

"Go on."

"The cream came from ol' Bessie, it did. Skimmed it just this mornin' and poured it into the creamer me-self." Doubt pervaded her thick country accent. "I didn't see no poison! I run a clean kitchen, I do!"

"No one's accusing you," he said gently. "Was anyone else in the kitchen while you were preparing the tea tray?"

"Lots of folks traipsed in an' out. Madam brung in a baby gown to soak in the scullery. Mr. Ravi fetched a cup o' tea. Mr. Henry even popped his head in to say hello."

"Did you ever see anyone near the tray?" Juliet asked.

Mrs. Fleetwood shook her head vigorously. "Come to think, though, I did step out for a few minutes." A blush stole over her doughy features. "Had to tend to a call o' nature, I did."

Maud hissed out a breath. "Then we must deduce that's when the killer seized his chance!"

The butler noisily cleared his throat. "Begging your pardon. I remained close by, Your Grace, yet I heard nothing. I was in the pantry, cleaning the silver service for dinner."

Kent looked at Rose. "What about you? You went to fetch a tisane for your mother."

"Me? I peeked into the kitchen, but when I saw how busy Mrs. Fleetwood was, I decided to return later." Her brown eyes glossed with tears. "Surely you can't suspect *me.*"

"I must consider everyone," he said quietly.

"Well, *I* didn't do it. Father would never have

doubted me." Whirling, she flounced toward a window and folded her arms over her breasts.

His mouth compressed into a strict line, he stared after Rose before turning to her mother. "And where were you, Chantal?"

"In the tower, of course."

"Alone?"

She gave a royal nod. "Of course, you have only my word on the matter."

Could she have stolen down to the kitchen? Juliet wondered. Dread formed an icy knot inside her. No one here could prove his innocence. Which left the killer free to strike again.

"I don't suppose the medication was locked up," Kent said to Gordon.

He raised himself from the desk chair, his Adam's apple bobbing. "No. Someone must have pilfered my capsules!" Hands thrust into his pockets, he cast a glance at the door, as if longing to flee back to his books. "Oh, dear me. This state of affairs is my fault. My failing."

Augusta's shoulders sagged. "And my poor darling is the victim."

Silence hung like a pall. Ravi left and returned a few moments later with a blanket. Kneeling before Punjab, he wrapped the small body.

By unspoken agreement, everyone gathered close, their faces sober. Maud tiptoed to Juliet's side and squeezed her hand.

"That might have been you," she whispered, her blue eyes big with alarm. "But don't worry. Henry and I are working on a theory."

"Just be careful." Sickness churned inside Juliet. She placed a protective hand over her belly and prayed for her baby's safety. Who knew what trick the murderer might try next?

Augusta hovered over Ravi. "Do have a care," she murmured, coiling the handkerchief in her stout fingers. To Kent, she added, "If you'll excuse me, I'll see about arranging a proper burial."

As Ravi carried the precious bundle from the room, she trudged at his side.

A minute crept by in solemn stillness. Standing by the chimneypiece, Kent frowned at the peacock cut into the center of the marble. His face might have been carved from the same stone. Juliet wondered if he was as baffled and frightened as she.

With the drama of an actress stealing center stage, Chantal marched inside the circle of chairs. "If you ask me," she said, her blue eyes piercing, "what happened today is the fault of the curse. Dreamspinner has caused yet another tragedy." Skirts swishing, she stalked from the scene.

Gordon drifted after her; Rose trailed him. One by one, the others slipped out.

Fleetwood went to the tea tray. "Shall I dispose of this, Your Grace?"

He made a distracted wave. "Yes, yes."

The butler bore the silver tray out, leaving Juliet alone with Kent. Aware of a sudden frailty in her knees, she collapsed into a chair. "I don't know whether to be joyful that I'm still alive or saddened for poor Augusta."

He wheeled around. A grimace of anxious fury compressed his mouth. "You're damned lucky, that's what you are. There wouldn't have been an attempt if you'd gone to London as I told you."

Stubbornness shot strength into her spine. "The matter has already been decided. I'm safe *nowhere*."

"We can both go away, then. To the Continent . . . to America . . . to India, wherever suits your fancy. We'll venture so far afield that no one will ever track us down."

"And how would we live?"

"Off your dowry."

"For how long, Kent?"

"Forever, if need be."

The concentration of his stare unnerved her as much as the prospect of shedding danger and darkness. He was willing to live as a kept man, dependent on her money. He'd abandon his ancestral home, his family, his beloved fields. For her sake and for the safety of their child. Resisting a quick leap of hope, Juliet lowered her lashes. Because he loved her? Or because he felt guilty . . . obligated to protect the wife he'd wronged so terribly?

She raised her eyes to his impossibly handsome face. The words choked her throat. "You've orchestrated my life from the very start, Kent. I'm staying until we find Emily's murderer."

The intensity faded, leaving his features barren of emotion. He turned slightly to gaze out the window. Though a bar of sunlight illuminated his strong profile, she had the impression he stood wrapped in shadow.

"And then?" he murmured. "What will you do afterwards?"

"I haven't decided."

That much was the truth. As Kent walked slowly away, she recalled how the reassuring warmth of his arms had chased away the horrid image of him dead from drinking the tea. Now the rift was back between them, as vast as ever. Could she stay at Radcliffe and endure a lifetime of polite distance? See him every day and know that she could never trust him, that he might be secretly contemplating another way to get revenge on her father?

He claimed to want to end the feud. But he'd lied to her about that many times before.

An inutterable weariness dragged on her heart. Soon she would have the funds to set up her own household wherever she pleased. A town house in London. Or a peaceful cottage in the country, where she could grow a garden and watch her child play and thrive.

Kent's child, too.

As he went to the desk, she couldn't stop her gaze from following his familiar form, the shoulders honed hard and brawny from physical labor, the black hair and bronzed skin that formed so stunning a contrast to his white shirt, the narrow waist and firm male hips that inflamed her blood. . . .

"What the devil—" he muttered. Pivoting sharply, he drilled her with a furious, baffled glare. "The necklace is gone! Someone's stolen Dreamspinner."

Chapter 23

"What do you suppose it means?" Juliet mused.

She glanced up at Kent, then gazed again in perplexity at the note in her hand. The firm script flowed across the sheet of scented stationery. Just moments ago, someone had slipped the envelope under her bedroom door. Kent had hastened into the hall, but whoever had left the message was gone.

Standing at her elbow now, he bent closer to reread the words. So close she caught his sandalwood scent. She kept her eyes fixed on the letter.

Juliet, I've something of grave importance to tell you. Please come to see me at once. Chantal.

"There's only one way to find out what she means," he said, straightening. "I know this is addressed to you, but I'd like to accompany you if I may."

"I'll freshen up first."

Stalking into the dressing room, she closed the door and blew out an exasperated breath. His request was a mere formality, for she knew he wouldn't allow her to go alone. Was it his constant presence that made her feel on the verge of exploding?

Three tedious days had passed since the poisoning attempt that had culminated in Dreamspinner's disappearance. Three sleepless nights of lying beside Kent and wondering how much longer she could bear living like this, so close yet so far apart.

Crumpling the note, she flung it onto the dressing table, where it rolled to a stop among the ancient bottles and jars. She scrutinized her reflection in the mirror; the wavy glass held little evidence of her agitated mood. Wistful eyes stared back from a pale face. A gown of fashionable topaz silk skimmed her still slender figure. No one would guess from her appearance that she would bear a baby come spring. She looked like an ordinary woman with an ordinary wish for happiness.

Only the dark smudges beneath her eyes hinted at hidden sorrow and unmitigated strain.

Sighing, she smoothed her chignon and dabbed perfume at her wrists and throat. Obeying a sudden strong impulse, she opened a drawer and drew forth the pearls her father had given her on the occasion of her debut. His gruff voice echoed in her ears and the memory of his quick embrace brought a phantom warmth.

I can't wait to show you off, Princess . . . the jewel in my crown of achievements.

She swallowed a lump of grief. That enchanted night seemed as if it had happened to another girl. She was a woman now. A woman who had chosen a path for her life and must now follow it.

Juliet, if it meant . . .

What had Kent been about to say the afternoon of the fateful tea? That he would do anything, even shake hands with Emmett Carleton, if it meant repairing the damage to their marriage? Or had he been about to say that she asked the impossible?

He hadn't broached the topic again, and neither had she. To herself, she admitted to mistrusting either answer. It was less painful to remain in the dark

Fastening the strand of pearls around her neck, she dragged in a steadying breath. The moment alone had fortified her, and she felt strong enough to face her husband again.

He waited by the outer door. His midnight eyes surveyed her with disconcerting directness before he turned to open the door. A quiver stirred inside her. A quiver that took great effort to subdue.

He fell into step beside her. To fill the oppressive silence, she said, "I wonder if Chantal knows what's happened to Dreamspinner."

"I pray to God she does. I could kick myself for failing to watch everyone more closely that day."

Juliet shared his frustration. "We were all distracted by Punjab. Anyone could have slipped over to the desk and stolen the jewels."

"Yes, anyone. That's the damnable crux of the matter."

"Maybe we're wrong to look for one person. Maybe it's two people working together."

Kent arched an eyebrow. "Anything's possible."

As they passed a casement window, she glanced at the overcast sky and mentally reviewed the facts she and Kent had gone over many times. Gordon seemed the most likely culprit since he'd sat by the desk. Yet the others couldn't be discounted. Chantal had paced the drawing room. Rose had distanced herself from the group. Even Augusta might have moved away for the moment necessary to pocket the jewel pouch. And neither she nor Kent had kept a close eye on the Fleetwoods or Ravi.

Maud and Henry had been unable to cast any light on the enigma, either. The pair spent every waking hour with their heads together, but Juliet suspected they were too distracted by their own budding romance.

In the uncertain hope of gleaning a reaction from someone, Kent kept the disappearance of Dreamspinner a secret. One by one, each suspect had asked when Ravi would be leaving for London; Kent had been deliberately vague. Otherwise, Gordon hadn't ventured from the library. Rose ensconced herself somewhere to work on her play. Chantal kept to her tower apartment. Devastated by the loss of her beloved dog, poor Augusta took to her bed.

The castle seemed quieter than ever. The waiting rubbed on Juliet's nerves and left her feeling so chilled, she couldn't contain a shiver.

"Would you care to go back for your shawl?" Kent asked.

"No, thank you. I want only to find out what Chantal knows."

He nodded, then politely supported her arm as they mounted the winding steps of the north tower. Reaching the small landing, he rapped on the door. The knob rattled and the oak panel swung open.

Her heart skipped a beat. It wasn't Chantal who stood there, framed by dreary gray daylight.

It was her father.

Behind her, Kent uttered an exclamation, then fell silent.

Emmett held himself as proud and erect as a lion, his impeccable garb befitting his status as a prosperous businessman. Yet he'd aged in the long weeks since he'd locked her in her bedroom and out of his heart. An overabundance of silver streaked his groomed hair. Lines of tension dragged at his mouth, sweeping his mustache downward.

Wary and oddly hesitant, he regarded her. "Princess, you're . . . looking well."

An unbidden throb of affection paralyzed her. His gaze dipped to her belly; he must have heard about the baby. The Deverell baby he would never acknowledge. The acid memory of his hatred burned away the brief tenderness.

"So the note was a ruse," she said coldly.

"I was afraid you might refuse to see me." Knuckles white, he clenched the door. "I wanted you to know your dowry is settled. But that's not the real reason I came. Chantal wrote to me about your finding the diary. I'd like to explain why I never told you—"

"There's nothing you can say that can make me forgive all your lies."

In a whirl of topaz skirts, she stalked toward the stairs. Kent caught her wrist and drew her back.

"He's come a long way," he murmured. "At least give the man a chance to speak."

Juliet strained to read the emotion in the striking planes of his face. His eyes reflected only a dark dispassion. Suddenly she saw the choice looming before her. Would she perpetuate the feud, or take the first step toward healing a sundered family? Confused, she let him lead her into the apartment.

Emmett seated himself in a cane chair. Despite his stiff boiled collar and sedate frock coat, he looked oddly at home against the exotic decor.

She walked to the window and turned, bracing herself on the casement. "Where is Chantal?"

"She and Rose went to visit the cemetery," Emmett said. "Today is . . ." His voice faltered and his gaze fell to his clasped hands.

August 11th. Juliet swung her eyes toward Kent, who stood with his shoulder propped against the chimneypiece. The bleakness in his expression told her he hadn't forgotten the date. Anguish flooded her, an anguish made more acute because she didn't know whether it arose from grief over her sister or the ugly, niggling thought that he cherished his memories of Emily over the wife he'd chosen as his instrument of vengeance. She would live forever with the gnawing pain of his deception.

And her father's deception. Both men had woven a conspiracy of silence.

She pressed trembling fingers against the cold stone behind her. "Today is the third anniversary of Emily's death. The sister I never knew."

Emmett's head jerked up. "I wanted to tell you about her. So many times. I used to imagine the two of you playing together, sharing girlish confidences. But how could I admit the truth? If word had slipped out that I had a bastard daughter, the scandal would have caused you and Dorothea needless suffering."

"You mean *you* would have been hurt," she retorted. "You care only about your own reputation. You couldn't bear to lose the chance at your cherished knighthood."

His brawny shoulders squared. "There's no wrong in a man wanting to better himself—"

"Even at my expense? You denied me the love and companionship of an older sister. You subjected Emily to years of miserable longing for your love."

"Princess, you were only fifteen when Emily died. Too young to understand why I'd had an affair before I married your mother."

"Emily knew about *me*. In her diary she wrote that she'd waited in front of our house until she saw us together."

He passed a hand over his face. "I didn't know. She never breathed a word about that to me."

Juliet swallowed hard against an upsurge of tenderness. "I'm not surprised. She wouldn't have jeopardized what precious little time you gave her. More than anything, she wanted your love."

"She had my love, my support," he said roughly. "I've always carried her image close to my heart. See here?"

Reaching into his breast pocket, he drew forth a locket and fumbled with the clasp. Juliet found herself walking on numb legs toward him. Over his shoulder she saw that one side of the locket held a portrait of herself; the other bore a photograph of Emily, a miniature of the sad-eyed angel once displayed in Kent's bedroom.

She turned her gaze to her husband; he stared back, his arms folded. His expression remained oblique, offering no clue to his thoughts. He was leaving the choice to her. . . .

Pacing away, she spun toward her father. "You were looking at that locket on the night of my debut."

"Yes, I was wishing Emily could have been there, to meet you. I regretted that she'd never had the opportunities you had. She never had a come-out ball, or the chance to wear a grandmother's pearls."

His sorrow shook the firm ground of her anger. Recalling her naive happiness on that long-ago night, Juliet touched the glossy strand circling her throat. "Jewels can't replace a father's company. All Emily ever wanted was for you to declare her your own."

"Can't you see—? If I'd acknowledged her before society, the stigma of her bastardy would have touched you as well, Princess."

Was it true? *Had* he meant to protect her?

"*I* could have borne the shame. It's a small price to pay for having a sister to love."

"I'm sorry, Princess. I don't see the situation that

way." As he clicked the locket shut and tucked it away, he cast a guarded glance at Kent, then back at her. "You're a married woman now, with a child of your own on the way. I'd hoped you could understand the delicacy of my position. Whether you believe it or not, I wanted to do my best for both my daughters."

She reflected on the girl she'd been, blithe and trusting, with a blind belief in eternal love and perfect faith. The death of her dreams ached like a raw wound. Perhaps Papa was right in that; perhaps she had once been too innocent to comprehend that people could love, yet still hurt each other.

No more. Still, too many painful questions roiled inside her to allow room for forgiveness.

"Your best obviously wasn't enough for Emily," she said. "If you loved her so much, why did you demand Dreamspinner from her?"

Leaning heavily on the chair arm, Emmett kneaded his brow. "I resented the fact that she grew up here, in the Deverell stronghold. I resented His Grace for marrying her. When I learned she was to bear him an heir, I could think only of punishing him by getting the necklace back."

His expression darkening, Kent pushed away from the mantelpiece. "Back? Dreamspinner never belonged to you in the first place."

Emmett surged up to confront him. "When William learned I meant to buy the necklace as a wedding gift for Dorothea, he sent his agent to the maharaja and beggared himself to make a higher bid. A peer of the realm ought to have had more respect for a gentleman's agreement."

"What he did was no more underhanded than you selling a tea garden at an inflated price."

Her father's chest swelled. "That sale was perfectly legal. It isn't my fault that William couldn't spare the time to examine the property or consider that the market was due for a crash."

"He most certainly would have made the effort had he known the supposed owner was acting as *your* agent."

"I wasn't the only plantation owner looking for a buyer. William never had a lick of business sense. Nor any scruples. Look at the way he stole that opium."

Kent clenched his fists. "*You* hid the drug. Isn't it long past time you admitted that?"

"How dare you accuse me of dishonesty!" Emmett paced forward. "You, the man who stole my daughters!"

"Stop it, both of you!" Disappointed and angry, Juliet stepped between the two men. "I won't stand by while you drag out old quarrels. Kent, this was William's feud, not yours. Can't you ever let it go?"

"I have to honor my father's memory—"

"With more spite? When is this worthless cycle going to end? It's already caused Emily's death. And damaged our chance at happiness."

He stared at her. Gradually the rigid line of his mouth eased. The black fury in his eyes gave way to shameful regret. "Old habits die hard," he murmured.

"I've no sympathy for nasty habits. You've let hatred become too much a part of yourself." She rounded on her father. "And you're no better. You let your precious place in society overrule everything. Why couldn't you have been pleased at the prospect of Emily bearing your grandchild? Why did you have to view it as another battle lost?"

He crumpled into a chair. "William took everything that mattered from my past. With the baby, the Deverells would have owned the future, too."

"So you'd strike out at Emily. My God, Papa, she was innocent of the feud! And so was her baby."

"You're right," he said, burying his face in his hands, his voice ringing hollow. "I've been so obsessed with besting the Deverells that I sacrificed my most priceless assets, my own daughters. I've had to live with the knowledge that Emily died without. . . ."

"Without what?"

"Without me telling her that I was an old fool for objecting to her marriage. And for refusing to accept a Deverell grandchild."

Juliet held a painful breath, then slowly expelled it.

Could she believe him? "What about *my* baby?" she said softly. "Will you be a true grandfather to it?"

He looked up, his proud features edged by unhappy grooves, his eyes beseeching. "Oh, Princess, yes. If you'll allow me."

The wall around her emotions broke. She suddenly saw her father as a man, a man with flaws and feelings, a man who had struggled and sometimes made the wrong choices. How difficult it must be for him to humble himself, to discard the enmity of a lifetime. To ask, instead of demand. To treat her as an adult, capable of making her own decisions.

Tears blurred his image. Crossing the room, she knelt before him, shaping her fingers around his broad hands. "Oh, Papa. I do want you to be a part of my baby's life . . . and my life, too."

A husky sob broke from him. Somehow she found her cheek pressed to his chest, his familiar scent of cigars embracing her as warmly as his arms. He wept like the vulnerable man he'd hidden inside himself all these years.

"Princess," he muttered. "How I've missed you. My daughter." His sigh gusted against her temple. "Emily was my precious secret, but I'm glad you know at last. Will you forgive me for keeping silent for so long?"

"I have, Papa. I have."

Watching them, Kent felt the shadows inside him shifting, lifting, like mist rising from a deep flowing river. Juliet nestled against Emmett, her cinnamon hair afire against his graying head, her fine features aglow with joy. Father and daughter. The similarities were striking in the eyes, in the stubborn set of the chin. Emmett Carleton had sired two fine women, each unique and noble, one inspiring an abiding affection, the other a vivid passion and consuming love.

His throat ached. Emmett loved her, too. No man could feign those tears, that quiver of emotion in his hands.

You've let hatred become too much a part of yourself.

Kent searched himself for the animosity that had

ruled him for so many years. He found only a fathomless longing for light. The light Juliet had brought into his life.

Gloom settled over him. Shoving his fists into his pockets, he stared at her. She had pardoned her father, but his own sin had been the far greater one. With ruthless arrogance, he had abused her trust, duped her into marriage, and transformed a guileless girl into a disillusioned woman. He'd intentionally set out to destroy her father. She'd never forgive him. Never.

She sat back on her heels. "I've no wish to reawaken sad memories, Papa. But I must know. On the day Emily died, did you see her again? After that one encounter, I mean."

He shook his head. "I went straight back to London. Dear God, I should never have demanded Dreamspinner. Through my own selfishness, I drove her to suicide."

The grief on his face reached inside Kent. "No, you didn't," he said, striding forward. "I was wrong to blame you for her death. Emily didn't take her own life—"

"How can you say that?" Emmett burst out. "God forgive me, I tried to condemn you for the deed, to ease my own guilt. But I should never have badgered her so, not when I knew about her spells of melancholia."

She clutched his hands. "Papa, don't torture yourself. Emily was murdered. The same person who killed her wants to kill me."

The color drained from his face. "What?" he choked out. Leaping up, fists clenched, he swung on Kent. "Tell me this isn't true, Your Grace."

"It is." In a brief, stark statement, he related the incidents of the greenhouse and the poisoning.

Agitated, Emmett prowled the room. "But who would want to harm my daughters? Unless it's someone who hates me."

"We've found precious little evidence," Kent said. "The culprit could be anyone in the castle."

Emmett shot an accusing look at Kent. "How could

you have let Juliet stay here? Haven't you any care at all for your own wife?"

The accusation cut deeply into Kent. He arched a sardonic brow. "Oh, yes, I care a great deal. If you can convince her to leave Radcliffe, you have my blessing."

Stalking to her, Emmett seized her hands. "Princess, you heard him. We must leave at once for the train station. You can have your things sent on later—"

"No. I'm staying until I can bring my sister's killer to justice."

"Don't be ridiculous. I'll not let you risk your own life."

"It isn't your decision to make, Papa. I'm a woman now, and neither you nor Kent will change my mind."

He opened his mouth, then clamped it shut. As if seeing her for the first time, he studied her resolute expression before swinging toward her husband. "Then I intend to remain, too. If you've no objection, Your Grace."

Kent gazed at the man he had despised for too long. Emmett stared back with the frank expression of a man looking at his equal. Cautious sincerity eased the lines on his face, the green eyes rimmed with gold. Juliet's eyes.

In breaking the chains of hatred, he and Emmett could forge a deeper bond . . . the bond of love for her and the bond of protection for the coming child.

He stepped forward and held out his hand. "Only if you'll call me Kent."

Emmett gazed at the extended hand, then slowly reached out to join the salutation. The firmness of his clasp echoed the candor in his gaze. "As you wish . . . Kent. I want you to know I never planted that opium . . . although when I got wind of the incident, I did call out those crusaders. I did a lot of things I shouldn't have done. This feud has gone on long enough."

Thoughtfully Kent nodded. "Perhaps it isn't too late to start anew. We've both harbored mistaken opinions."

Standing to the side, Juliet marveled at the sight of

her husband shaking hands with her father. Dare she believe that Kent had renounced the feud forever? Dare she hope he'd done it out of love for her? Or if he and Papa should disagree someday, would his ingrained feelings explode again?

Old habits die hard.

Studying the handsome features of her husband, she felt the weakening urge to trust him. But trust had broken her heart once already. Trust meant opening herself to the terrible risk of betrayal.

Emmett stepped back, his face grim. "We must find the scoundrel who would dare threaten my daughter. We'll need to scrutinize everyone here."

"I've a private matter to discuss with my cousin first," Kent said. "In the meantime, gather your thoughts on the suspects. We'll pool our impressions in an hour, over tea. Is that agreeable?"

"All right. Perhaps I'll even poke around myself."

"Go anywhere you wish. We'd like you to feel at home here."

As they started down the winding stairs, Juliet felt the power of Kent's gaze. Warmth stirred deep in her stomach, hunger for him.

Suppressing her dangerous yearnings, she hastened ahead and took her father's arm. "How is Mama?"

"Well, except she misses you." He patted her hand. "I know you've been corresponding with your mother, Princess. She thought to hide it from me, but her maid told my valet that Dorothea had sent along your wardrobe. I should have settled a dowry on you sooner."

"You've been very generous." Juliet felt a sudden wistful longing for her mother, for the familiar scent of violets and the comforting dullness of gossip. "Did you tell Mama you were coming to see me today?"

"No . . . I didn't dare. She would have wanted to accompany me."

"What will you tell her now?"

He shot her a troubled glance as they entered a long corridor. "I'll send word that I've been detained on a business matter. But don't condemn me as a liar, Princess. I see no sense in ever hurting Dorothea merely to unburden myself of guilt.''

Their footsteps echoed through the stone corridor. Mullioned windows let in a watery gray light that reflected off the ancient shields on the walls. He was right, Juliet reflected; sometimes the omission of a painful truth could serve as an act of love.

She angled a glance at Kent, who walked at her side, his dark head bowed in contemplative silence. In the days since their confrontation, his attempts at reconciliation had dwindled. She shuddered to think that the ending of the feud had come too late to save her marriage. Could he deliberately hold himself aloof as an act of love, because he wanted her to feel free to leave him?

I love you. Don't ever forget that.

The memory of his words made her throat tighten. Yet he'd told her so many lies. . . . Or had his concealment of Emily's identity been less a lie than another act of love?

The noble answer gave Juliet pause. Perhaps it *had* been the desperate deed of a man wanting to shield his wife from a painful truth. A truth sure to sever the tender bonds of their marriage.

I couldn't tell you. You wouldn't have married me. From our first meeting, I wanted you to be a part of my life . . .

A knot formed in her chest. If only she could separate fact from falsehood, trust from doubt. If only she could verify that Kent loved her . . .

The pressure of her father's hand on her arm brought her back to reality; they'd reached a guest bedroom near the ducal suite.

Longing shone starkly in Emmett's eyes. ''Juliet,'' he said, ''will you tell me everything Emily wrote about me in the diary?''

A wave of tenderness rolled over her. He *had* loved Emily, in his own fashion. ''Later you can read it for yourself.''

''Watch over her well, Kent. The sooner we find the murderer, the sooner we can get on with our lives and our friendship.''

"I won't let her out of my sight."

Kent directed her back to the stairs. Now that they were alone, tension throbbed between them, a tension aggravated by her unresolved emotions. Her every step felt stiff and unnatural. She wondered at his aura of distraction, as if he were embroiled in deep, disquieting thoughts.

"Why do we need to see Gordon?" she asked.

His dark eyes glided over her. "I've been thinking about people and their obsessions. I've been blind about something . . . or at least I think I've been. We'll find out in a moment."

They reached the library, where he pushed open the massive door. The dim daylight dulled the barren bookshelves and antiquated furnishings. Speculating on his purpose, she followed Kent down the short leg of the H, to the second set of wings. A faint sweetish odor tainted the air, and now that she knew the source of the smell, her stomach churned with pity.

Gordon sat at the end of the long table, his shoulders slumped beneath the maroon smoking jacket. He looked blessedly lucid, his eyes alert behind thick spectacles. To Juliet's surprise, Augusta occupied the seat to his left. The weariness of spent grief drew down her mouth. From the tense way she gripped his flawed hands, it appeared that husband and wife had been involved in a heated discussion.

"Pardon us for interrupting," Juliet said.

Augusta released his hands and sat back, her face pale but composed. "It's quite all right, Your Grace."

Bracing both palms on the scarred oak, Kent stared down the length of the table. "I've come to ask you a question, Gordon."

"Most assuredly, Cousin." He tugged nervously at his cravat. "How may I accommodate you?"

"By giving me an honest answer. What do you know about the opium Father was accused of stealing?"

He went still; only his gaze shied away. "The opium? Emmett Carleton did that to discredit Uncle William."

"I know. But I've just had an interesting talk with Emmett."

Augusta's jaw dropped. She turned to stare at Juliet. "Emmett Carleton is *here?*"

Kent gave a curt nod. "As my honored guest. He claims no responsibility for the incident. A few months ago I would have called him a liar. But we're through lying to each other now. Well, Gordon?"

"I . . ." He swallowed, the dry gulp audible.

"Tell him," Augusta said flatly. "There've been too many secrets here. It's cost this family too much."

Gordon glanced around as if seeking an escape route. Then he sank lower in the chair, his high brow propped against his knobby hands. "So be it," he mumbled. "I concede my culpability."

The confession stunned Juliet. So Papa *was* innocent. And William, too.

"You lied to my father," Kent said, his tone incredulous. "I remember him asking you straight out if you were involved, and you denied it."

"I was afraid—"

"Afraid! You let your crime besmirch Father's good name."

"I never meant anyone any harm," Gordon said brokenly. "I located a source of exceptionally pure opium. It wasn't pilfered, either. I paid an outrageous sum to an agent of the East India Company. You see, I needed—"

"You needed." Kent thumped his fist onto the table. "Christ! You let the wrong man shoulder the blame."

"I never meant to impugn his character. Uncle William charged the deed to Emmett Carleton, and it seemed . . . simpler to concur. What was one more wickedness attributed to that knave?"

"What, indeed?" Kent said, his voice heavy with irony. "I loved you as a brother. I thought I could trust you."

"I'm sorry," Gordon muttered, hanging his head. "So utterly sorry."

"I wish you'd said that twenty years ago."

Kent walked away to stare out the diamond panes of the window. Disillusionment darkened his strong features. The incident had been a keystone in his hatred for her father, Juliet thought, a hatred grounded in falsehood. How dreadful he must feel to know his blood kin had perpetrated such a lie.

"Your Grace," Augusta said, "that isn't all we have to confess. Gordon and I had just decided it was time we admitted the truth about Dreamspinner."

Juliet felt her every nerve come alert.

Kent spun on his heel. "What do you mean?"

"We thought we must speak out before Ravi left for London." With bleak hyacinth eyes, Augusta glanced at her husband; he stared at his hands. She focused her gaze on Kent.

"You see," she said slowly, "the necklace is a forgery."

Chapter 24

Silence wrapped the library. Juliet saw a blankness in Kent's eyes, then a struggle to assimilate the incredible news. He remained perfectly still, the cloudy afternoon light framing his lordly features, the broad shoulders and lean hips.

"Counterfeit?" he said. "But my father had the necklace appraised by a reputable London jeweler."

"And shortly thereafter," Augusta said, "I sold the real stones and had them substituted with paste."

"But why?" Juliet said. "Why would you do such a thing?"

She lifted her chin. "For the good of the Radcliffe tenants. I had no other resources to help them. The old duke took everything."

"It's my fault," Gordon said, his shoulders hunched in misery. "Uncle William convinced me to expend her dowry to pay the debts he'd incurred over the opium incident. I could scarcely refuse."

Augusta's mouth twisted into a grimace. "That was in the days before the law recognized a wife's right to control her own money."

Kent stared, his hooded eyes masking his emotions. "Dreamspinner was worth a small fortune. How did no one ever notice you spending the money?"

"It was my nest egg for nigh on fifteen years, Your Grace. I used a little bit here, a little bit there. A new roof for the church. A university education for Alf Peek's eldest boy. The biggest expense was building the surgery for Dr. Sattler."

"I assumed the rents had paid for that."

Augusta shrugged. "So did everyone. William took

such scant interest in the estate that he never guessed, either. The money ran out just before you inherited the dukedom. Unfortunately, before I could help Hannah Forster.''

She sat straight, the tight ginger bun crowning her head. No remorse for the misdeed colored her plain features, only a deep conviction and a quiet honesty.

Compassion formed a warm pool inside Juliet. She stepped to Augusta's side and touched her sturdy shoulder. ''Forgive me for ever suggesting you neglected Hannah. With my dowry, we'll get her the finest medical care.''

''I know.'' A shadow of a smile crossed the older woman's face; then she looked soberly at Kent. ''You took me by surprise, Your Grace, the day you said you meant to sell the necklace. After I left the drawing room, I resolved to confess the truth. But when I came back, my poor Punjab . . .''

Her composure crumpled and she blinked hard, looking away.

Gordon reached out to pat her hand in awkward tenderness. ''There, there, my dear. I wish I could assuage your tribulation. Yet I only seem to ruin everything I touch.''

''Oh, poppycock,'' she murmured halfheartedly. ''I wish only to find whoever is responsible for the poisoning. Because that same person is deranged enough to harm Juliet and her precious babe.''

''It must have been a tragic accident,'' Gordon said, shaking his head in befuddlement. ''Murder is simply inconceivable. Who could it be? Ravi is too loyal. Little Rose is too much the scholar. Chantal is . . . well, she is . . .'' He paused, blinking.

''She's your likely culprit,'' Augusta said with conviction. ''Always did think there was something peculiar about a woman who'd be content to live off her lovers.''

Juliet's stomach turned over. Could Augusta be right?

Harsh weariness etched Kent's cheeks and jaw.

"That's neither proof nor motive. Does anyone else here know of the forgery?"

Augusta wiped her eyes. "Not a soul. Your Grace, please believe that I never meant to deprive you of your inheritance. When William took my money, I felt Dreamspinner was only my due."

"I've no quarrel with you. To be honest, I find it gratifying that the cursed necklace has accomplished so much good."

His words seemed to comfort Augusta; she squared her shoulders as he took Juliet's arm and guided her out of the library.

Their footsteps resounded in the empty hall. Her gown swishing, she scurried to keep up with his long strides. He scowled into the gloom ahead, and she had the impression his thoughts ranged far from her.

"Do you think they took it?" she asked.

Kent shifted his frown to her. "Pardon?"

"Dreamspinner. Would Augusta or Gordon have stolen it to prevent Ravi from taking a false necklace to London?"

He shook his head. "Surely she would have admitted as much. On the other hand, I scarcely know what to believe anymore."

"At least we know Augusta acted out of humanitarian reasons."

"Yet for so many years my own kin deceived me." Through the shadowy light, his eyes glowed with an obsessive savagery. "I'm getting a proper lesson in how betrayed *you* felt."

Self-derision made his voice gritty. She wanted to comfort him, to ease the hurt he must be feeling. But their estrangement loomed between them, a barrier widened by suspicion and broken dreams.

As he led her through a maze of corridors, toward the kitchen, she said, "I thought we were going to take tea with Papa."

"I'd rather not," he said. "I have to escape these walls for a while. Will you come with me?"

A haunted quality dimmed his expression. He, too, felt the sting of shattered illusions. Again she felt the hopeless longing to kiss away the unhappiness shading his mouth. Looking down, she nodded.

They passed the empty servants' hall and entered a room she hadn't seen before. The small chamber was stuffed with rusted coal scuttles and fire irons, cricket bats and croquet mallets, cobwebbed shovels and abandoned trinkets. The air smelled of damp stone and mildewed wallpaper.

From a corner he fetched two fishing rods and a wicker creel. Hefting the items in one hand, he touched her arm and nodded to the door. An intense awareness prickled her skin and clenched her stomach. Quickly she turned and walked out.

They left the castle through the postern gate. Clouds hung low, presaging an early dusk. Passing through the south garden, Juliet found her mind wandering not to the ruined greenhouse, but to the haying party, when she had been deliriously in love, when her trust in Kent had been untainted by doubts. Oh, dear God, if only she could return to that untrammeled innocence . . .

The cultivated area gave way to the untamed beauty of the meadow and a colorful splash of wildflowers: yellow loosestrife, white comfrey, blue forget-me-nots. A brace of hares bolted from the green undergrowth and bounded off. Bees buzzed the fluffy white seedballs crowning stalks of water mint.

Brambles choked the path and caught at her skirt. Kent took her hand, his fingers strong and warm as he led the way down the gentle slope to the river. Tall reeds grew thickly near the water, and the ground was spongy. Yet still he drew her onward, through copses of oak and cedar, until they reached a cluster of willows.

The long, leafy fronds formed a cool bower beside the river. Setting down the creel and rods, he waved at a broad, flat rock overhanging the water. "Behold . . . my favorite fishing spot."

His somberness distressed her. The atmosphere felt strained, the tension tangible. Her stomach squeezed tight. Once, they'd laughed and chatted easily; once upon a time he'd been her knight in shining armor, the man she'd adored without reservation.

As he sat on the hard stone, she sank beside him, her topaz skirts whispering. "How long have you been coming here?"

"Since I was a boy."

A heron swooped out of the reeds, flying low with slow beats of its great wings. Grasshoppers fiddled and leaves rustled. In search of flies, a fish sucked at the surface of the water.

Only her doubts and dreams disturbed the peace. Kent made no move to open the creel. Arms hooked around his knees, he gazed toward the lily pads matting the opposite shore. She suddenly saw him as a lad, solemn and tousle-haired, stealing from his studies to laze away the summer hours. A bittersweet longing crept inside her.

She took a deep, hurting breath. "I wonder if our son will come here someday."

He shot her a sharp glance. "I thought you meant to leave Castle Radcliffe."

Her heart tripped. "Do you want me to go?"

"What I want isn't the issue anymore."

The rigidity in his expression shut her out of his thoughts. Uncertainty sparked an abrupt anger. "Yes, it is," she insisted. "We're married, with a child on the way. We both have a responsibility to decide his future, even if we live apart."

"I want you to do whatever makes you happy."

"I won't be happy until you give me an honest answer. Do you want me to go?"

A breeze stirred the willow fronds. He stared at her, and that fierce look gentled to tender despair. "Dammit," he growled, "of course I don't want you to go."

"Why not?"

"Don't you know—?" He started to reach out; then his hand halted in midair and settled between them, palm flattened on the stone. "Because I love you. And because I want what we had before . . . the closeness . . . the trust. . . ."

"We never really had trust," she felt compelled to point out. "I only thought so."

His lashes dipped slightly, though he held her gaze. "You're right. Perhaps our marriage can never be what you thought it was."

The desolate words blended with the murmur of the river. She saw the watery gleam of tears in his eyes; then he lowered his gaze to a tiny red ladybird trundling over the barren rock.

The harshness fled his face, unveiling an unhappiness and a loneliness as acute as her own. Her heart overflowed with the need to touch and be touched. The distance separating them suddenly seemed remarkably short.

Her fingertips skimmed the back of his hand, the dusting of black hairs, the bronzed flesh and strong bones. "It's better that we don't return to the past," she said.

He didn't look up, only nodded.

"You see," she went on softly, "I'm no longer the naive girl, dreaming of the perfect love. And you're no longer the embittered man, dreaming of the perfect revenge. We've both changed."

Turning his palm up, he seized tight to her fingers. "I'm sorry, love. I did you a terrible wrong. Believe me, I'll live with that guilt for the rest of my days."

"I don't want you to, Kent. I'd rather you let the past go, so we can begin anew. We can make something better."

The leaves whispered overhead. His eyes came alive, bright with disbelieving hope. "Are you saying . . . you'll stay?"

"Yes. This is my home now. I belong here."

His hand gripped hers with a taut and steady warmth. She could feel the roughness of each callus. Slowly he reached out and settled her against his chest, so that the uneven thrum of his heart beat against her cheek.

"My darling wife . . ." His voice choked to a halt, and for a moment he rubbed his hands over her spine.

"You won't regret your decision. I want the chance to win back your love."

She drew away to touch his cheek. "I love you more than ever, Kent. At first I had a girl's fascination for a mysterious duke. But the man I've come to love so deeply is human and fallible, full of doubts and fears. A man capable of infinite tenderness."

"Juliet."

Her name emerged on an exhalation of breath. His lips brushed hers, tasting as he might savor a rare wine; then a shudder ran through his powerful frame and he gathered her tighter. His tongue drove inside her mouth to drink deeply of her sweetness. The hard, hungry kiss released a burst of passion inside her, a melting fire that leaped in her loins. She slipped her arms upward, her palms relearning the broad contours of his shoulders, the flex of muscle and the heat of flesh.

His lips found the delicate whorls of her ear. "I've dreamed of touching you again. But I was afraid you'd never trust me."

"I was afraid, too," she whispered. "Afraid that you only felt guilty, that you didn't really love me."

His eyes darkened, but the glow there was warm, rife with promise. He began to pluck open her buttons. "I couldn't find the words to bring you back to me. I had only fantasies and memories—poor substitutes for my wife."

"What are you doing?" she teased, breathless. "You told me once that only peasants made love in the open countryside."

He cocked an eyebrow at the wall of willow fronds enclosing the grass. "This place is as private as our own bedchamber."

"Are you quite certain, Your Grace?" She shaped her fingers to the hard thrust of his arousal. "Oh, yes, I see you are. Yet I wouldn't want another woman to view what's for my eyes alone."

"The devil take the outside world. It's been forever since we came together in love."

He bent to kiss her again, a long and luscious joining. Then his mouth moved downward, his tongue tasting her throat and drifting along the neckline of her gown. With a small whimper, she arched her neck and closed her eyes, the better to focus on the sensations of touch and smell. An awesome erotic ache surged inside her, demanding the appeasement only Kent could give her.

He drew the gown to her waist, then wrestled with her corset hooks and muttered a curse. "The devil take all the clothes you women wear, too."

A smile trembled on her lips. "Don't bother with my gown. Just love me. Love me now."

Kent would have smiled back if he'd possessed the strength. The gift of her forgiveness still staggered him; the offering of her body excited him beyond belief. He paused only long enough to wrest the stiff corset from her, then half carried her the few feet to a patch of soft marsh grass. Lying atop her, he dipped his mouth to the scented valley of her breasts. As he tasted one rosebud peak, she writhed and moaned, her sinous movements sparking a liquid fire that pooled in his groin. He slid shaking hands up the silken length of her stockings, delving beneath petticoats and skirts to push aside her undergarments, where his fingers found the hot, slick folds of her flesh.

"Oh, Kent . . ."

She clutched his waist; her sighs warmed his throat. Her eyes were closed, the lashes dark against her ivory skin. Her face reflected a radiant pleasure he'd never viewed by light of day. His chest tightened with fleeting regret and burgeoning wonder. God, she was beautiful. His wife.

"Look at me, Juliet," he commanded, his voice low and unsteady. "Look at the man who loves you."

She opened her eyes, green eyes rimmed with gold. The adoration shining there almost sent him over the edge.

He couldn't speak; he couldn't move. Greater than physical passion, love flowed between them, warmer and richer than ever, a river without depth or end. She was right; they'd both changed, and miraculously the bond between them had been strengthened by their separation.

"Come inside me," she whispered. "I've missed you so."

Keeping his gaze locked to hers, he pressed slowly into her until his full length fitted her snug velvet sheath. The blood beat hot and savage through his veins, but he reined in the urge for release, determined to prolong the moment.

"Ah, you feel good," he muttered. "I could stay right here for the rest of my life."

"As you wish." Her lashes lowered slightly; her lips formed a slumberous smile. "I'm yours to command, Your Grace."

They kissed again, slow and openmouthed, until her taste intoxicated him and her caresses tempted him beyond control. She was soft and eager, all lush, womanly curves and warm, healing sunshine. His willpower fled before the need to move with longer, stronger thrusts. Her legs tightened around him and her breath came in panting sobs. Teetering on the verge, he reared back slightly to stroke her into tumbling over the brink with him.

"Come with me, love," he said hoarsely. "Come with me into the light."

She shivered in ecstasy and moaned, the sound infusing him with exultation. Her name a fierce cry of homage on his lips, he succumbed to the pulsing brilliance of fulfillment.

Oblivion slowly released his senses. His limbs felt drained and torpid. A breeze cooled his sweat-dampened shirt. Juliet lay beneath him, her shuddering breaths slowing, her hands clinging limply to his shoulders.

He opened his eyes to the cinnamon hair haloing her face and the dreamy satisfaction of her smile. To think he'd so long deprived himself of savoring her sweet sated expression . . .

"I thought," she said, touching his chin with a fingertip, "that you only liked to make love in the dark."

His chest constricted. Somehow he found the

strength to pull away from her warmth. He crossed his arms beneath his head and stared up at the lacework of green leaves and brown branches. As he inhaled a lungful of air, her jasmine scent blended with the aroma of crushed grass and the musk of their lovemaking.

"Oh, Christ," he said. "You deserve the truth about that."

Wondering at the heaviness in his voice, Juliet pushed up on an elbow to scan the magnificence of his body, then his face through the waning light. She couldn't imagine why he looked so solemn after the joy they'd shared. "The truth about what?"

"The darkness. That was something else I lied to you about."

She lay still. "You mean . . . it isn't a preference of yours?"

He shook his head. "So many times I wanted to make love to you in the light. But I couldn't bear to look into your eyes and know I was deceiving you. I couldn't bear to leave you alone, either."

A grasshopper sang into the silence. Regret glowed on Kent's face, along with a heartwarming vulnerability. Plucking a blade of grass, she rolled onto her stomach and tickled the inflexible line of his jaw.

"I think," she said, "that shows your true character. You're a good man, Kent Deverell, a man with a conscience."

He caught her hand, the grass blade fluttering away as he kissed her palm with gentle fervency. "Juliet, I was lost before I met you. All I felt was grief and rage. You brought me out of the shadows, into the light of forgiveness and love."

Joy coursed through her. "And you gave me love in return," she said softly. "So it means we're a well-matched pair."

"There'll be no more darkness," he promised. "Tonight I intend to light a hundred candles while I love you."

"Augusta will be appalled at the expense."

His eyes gleamed. "Augusta has no say in how I choose to revere my duchess."

He drew Juliet astraddle his hard body and subjected her to a long, languid kiss. He felt deliciously solid beneath her, and desire began a slow burn inside her again. But when he broke the kiss, the deviltry had left his expression.

"God help me," he said. "I'd die if I lost you . . . or our baby."

A rush of reality doused the heat. Bracing a hand on his chest, she sat up on the grass and fought off her own despair. "Do you suppose it's safe to exclude Augusta and Gordon as suspects?"

"I'd like to think so, but who the hell knows anymore?"

"We're going to find the murderer, Kent. Papa will help us. I'm so happy you two are going to work together."

"The reconciliation has been long overdue." His mouth slashed downward into a determined scowl. "I just hope Emmett's thought of something we've missed."

As they dressed, Juliet found herself praying for the time when they'd be free of fear, when they could live and love without danger. Tidying her hair, she saw Kent frown as he tucked his shirttails into his trousers. What frustrated fury he must feel, to know that someone close to him, someone he'd known for years, had killed Emily and now plotted to kill again.

As he gathered up the creel and rods, she said, "You never got to fish."

"I may have found a better use for this place."

"*May* have?" she said, trying to tease away his moodiness.

With a distracted grin, he kissed her forehead. "All right, Duchess, I *have*. I'll never come here again without remembering today."

Taking firm hold of her hand, he led the way down the brambled path. In the gathering dusk, bees hummed over the cornflowers and a jackdaw pecked at the ripening blackberries. A barn owl, disturbed by their approach, swooped through the air.

When they spied the castle, a stark silhouette rising against the gray sky, curiously she felt no dread, only a deep, abiding contentment. Knowing he loved her made everything bearable again. She paused to smooth her wrinkled, grass-stained skirt. "Do you suppose anyone will guess what we've been doing?"

Smiling, he plucked a twig from her hair. "Does it matter? I want everyone to know how much I love you."

Rubbing his stubbled cheek against hers, he kissed the tender skin below her ear. Juliet lowered her lashes; she adored the feel of him, his woodsy scent and his arousing kisses. Desire flooded her belly, a desire so acute, she wanted to lie down in full view of the castle—

"Yoo-hoo! Yer Grace!"

He straightened. She turned in his arms to see Mrs. Fleetwood galloping down the garden path, aproned skirt clutched in her beefy hands, anxiety pulling at her doughy face.

Huffing and puffing, she ran up to Kent and bobbed a curtsy. "Please, Yer Grace. You got to come quick, you do."

"Calm yourself and tell me what's wrong."

"It's Mr. Carleton," she gasped. "He's been coshed over the head, he has!"

Chapter 25

Juliet's knees threatened to buckle. Kent put a steadying arm around her and snapped, ''Where is he?''

''In his room. 'Twas the Lady Maud who found the poor gent lyin' in the hall.''

''Is he conscious?'' she whispered.

Mrs. Fleetwood nodded vigorously. ''Aye, but groggy. I sent Hatchett after the doctor.''

''Excuse us,'' Kent said.

Veering past the housekeeper, he strode toward the postern gate, keeping Juliet close to his side. Horror pressed at her throat and squeezed her rib cage. Someone had tried to kill Papa. The same malicious someone who hated all Carletons.

Her breath came hard and fast as they hurried into the castle and down the dim corridors. ''Easy, love,'' Kent murmured, slowing as they mounted the stairs. ''You mustn't overtax yourself.''

''But Papa—''

''Will be there even if it takes us half a minute longer.''

Nodding, she took a calming gulp of air. The baby. She must think of the baby. Clinging to his reassuring warmth, she walked up the age-worn steps.

In the guest bedroom, they found Augusta bending over Emmett, who was stretched out, fully clothed, on the bed. His eyes were shut as she applied a damp rag to his brow. Maud and Henry stood on the opposite side of the massive bedstead. Fleetwood hovered nearby, holding up an oil lantern, its yellow glow augmenting the dusk light filtering past the window curtains.

Juliet rushed to Augusta's side. "Papa, are you all right?"

"Princess?" Opening his eyes, he squinted against the brilliance and waved an imperious hand. "You, there. Move that infernal light away."

"As you wish, sir." The butler shuffled off, setting the lantern on a side table before departing.

Rising on an elbow, Emmett swayed.

Juliet caught his arm. "Papa!"

"Lie back down," Augusta said crisply. "You need to rest."

"I've had enough coddling," he grumbled. "I'll be fine once I sit up for a moment."

"Humph. Suit yourself, then." Mouth pinched, Augusta marched out of the room.

Appalled at her father's paleness, Juliet said, "Augusta's right. You should lie down."

"I'll live." Swinging his legs off the bed, he yanked away the wet cloth and gingerly felt the side of his head. "I've taken harder knocks than this in my youth."

She swallowed. A patch of blood stained the silver strands of his hair, where a lump was visible. Taking the rag, she daubed at the blood. "Thank goodness the doctor is on his way."

"I don't need a cursed doctor. I need to get my hands on the bas—" Glancing at her, he amended, "On the person responsible."

Kent stepped to the bed. "Can you identify your assailant?"

Emmett shook his head, then winced. "No. I'd decided to do some investigating, but when I went into the hall someone struck me over the head. All I saw was a pale blur."

"*I* saw." Skirt swishing, Maud excitedly rounded the foot of the four-poster. "I was coming up the stairs, to visit Juliet. Mr. Carleton fell and I saw someone running away from the scene of the crime, toward the opposite end of the corridor.'' She paused, eyes dramatically wide. ''It was Ravi, I know it was!''

''Did you see his face?'' Kent asked sharply.

''No, but I'd recognize that light-colored robe anywhere.''

''Dash it all,'' Henry said. ''You can't base a deadly accusation on such flimsy evidence.''

Pouting, she folded her arms. ''I know what I saw.''

His gait oddly uneven, he walked to her side and slipped an arm around her waist. ''Darling,'' he murmured, ''were you wearing your spectacles?''

Her cheeks pinkened. ''Of course not. You know I'd just come from having tea with you in the drawing room. I wanted to tell Juliet the news straightaway.''

''What news?'' Juliet said.

Henry toyed nervously with the curled end of his mustache. ''Later, Your Grace. Now is hardly the time or the place—''

''Oh, fiddle,'' Maud said with an airy wave. ''Now is as good a time as any. Henry plans to ask Father for my hand in marriage.''

Juliet smiled in surprised delight. ''Maud, how wonderful! We'll be neighbors.''

Kent clapped Henry on the back. ''Never thought you'd give up your wandering ways.''

''To become a dreary country gentleman with a throng of squawking children,'' Juliet couldn't resist teasing.

''Er . . . yes.'' Running a finger under his collar, he walked to the door. ''If you'll excuse me, I have a dinner engagement.''

''You're limping,'' Kent observed. ''Have you injured yourself?''

Henry reddened to his ears. Glancing at Maud, he mumbled, ''I, er . . .''

''He had to protect my honor.'' An unholy gleam in her eyes, Maud swept to his side. ''I'll see you out, darling.''

As they left the room, Juliet bit back a giggle. Maud must have been forced to use her method for subduing an ardent suitor; a marriage proposal had been the outcome.

"Praise God my daughter didn't wed such a rake," Emmett said. "Lord Higgleston would be justified in refusing the alliance."

Juliet sat beside him on the bed. "Oh, I don't know, Papa. I suspect Maud will keep Henry on the straight and narrow."

"But I doubt we can trust her powers of observation," Kent said, pacing before them, hands on his hips. "That couldn't have been Ravi she saw running away."

"I wouldn't be so sure, Kent," Emmett said, his face grim. "He was fanatically loyal to your father, which would make him my enemy. I was on my way to find him when I was hit over the head."

"I trust Ravi." Kent sank slowly into a chair. "I've known him all my life. I can't believe he'd hurt anyone."

"*Someone* here must have a hidden side, a motive we haven't considered," Emmett said. "How about Chantal's other daughter?"

"Rose? For Christ's sake, she's my half sister . . . Emily's half sister. And a harmless girl, besides."

"I'm sorry, Kent, but we must consider everyone." Emmett turned to Juliet. "She must be about your age, Princess. What's she like?"

She saw an image of the girl's milk-pure complexion and liquid brown eyes. The girl who'd crept in to leave the diary.

"She's impetuous and emotional . . . almost childish at times. And she hates the Carletons, just as her father did."

Emmett frowned. "Has she been unkind to you?"

"No, she's just loyal to the past. She venerated her father."

"That's no proof," Kent said.

Yet shadows dimmed the light in his eyes. Juliet's heart wrenched. How dreadful it must be for him to suspect the people he loved. Rising from the bed, she went to him and dropped to her knees to lay her cheek against his thigh. He grasped her shoulders, his fingers pressing hard, as if he gained strength from her closeness.

"I'm sorry, Kent. I'm sorry to bring up these suspicions."

"I know, darling." He brushed his lips across her hair. "But I'd give my own life to keep you safe."

Emmett coughed self-consciously. "About Rose. Does she have an alibi for the attempts on your life?"

"No one here does," Juliet said, turning to him. "And she reveres Dreamspinner. She might well be the one who stole it."

"Stole?" Emmett said, astonishment quirking his mustache.

"The necklace disappeared a few days ago."

Bowing his head, Kent raked his fingers through his hair. "Of course, there's another possibility. Chantal hated Dreamspinner. Maybe she wanted to get rid of it."

"I'm inclined to agree with her on that," Emmett said, grimacing. "The necklace means nothing to me anymore. And yet . . ." He stared down at the floor. "I can't believe she's a criminal. At one time I knew Chantal Hutton as well as I know myself. She's a generous and warmhearted woman. Only someone cold-blooded could kill her own daughter."

"Cold-blooded," Kent said slowly, "or mad."

"Nonsense. Chantal is as sane as you or I."

Juliet studied her father's confident face, then tried to picture Chantal thrusting a rock over the parapet and lacing the cream with a lethal dose of morphine. Somehow she couldn't reconcile the images with Chantal's forthright manner. Yet no one here seemed to fit that deadly role.

Emmett pushed to his feet. "I should like to question Ravi. Where can we find him?"

"He often takes tea with Chantal," Kent said. "In her apartment."

Seeing her father's startled frown, Juliet said gently, "You should know, Papa. She and Ravi are . . ."

His eyes widened, then narrowed to reflective interest. "Indeed. Now, there's a curious development."

"Shall we go, then?" she said, scrambling up.

"You're staying here," Kent said.

"No," Emmett said, "we shouldn't leave her alone."

"He's right," Juliet agreed.

Kent drilled her with a furious glare. She refused to flinch. Abruptly he muttered what sounded like a curse and turned, snatching her hand. "Come along, then."

She walked out, flanked by her husband and her father. If Papa felt any pain from the vicious lump on his head, he showed no sign. She glanced from one man to the other; both wore the same look of concentrated ferocity. A kernel of contentment rested within her disquiet, a warm appreciation that they'd closed ranks to protect her. Yet she chafed at the notion that she wasn't free to roam about her own home at will.

Dusk light seeped through the occasional deep-set window. In silence they climbed the winding stairs of the north tower, the stone cool against Juliet's hand. When they reached the landing, Emmett deferred to Kent with a nod.

Before he could knock, the door opened. Ravi stopped, a tea tray balanced on his palm. His muddy brown eyes widened slightly. "Yes, sahib?"

"I should like to speak to you. Chantal and Rose, as well."

"Chantal is resting. I will ask—"

"Don't ask. I'll see the three of you. *Now.*"

He pushed the door wide and walked inside. Juliet and her father followed.

Chantal stood in a doorway, golden candlelight from the bedroom silhouetting her queenly figure. Her blond hair cascaded loose over a low-cut dressing gown; her face bore the softness of a woman just loved. Her dishabille gave Juliet the uncomfortable feeling of having interrupted a tryst. She looked sharply at Ravi, who set down the tray. Could the lovers also have engineered a murder plot?

Chantal frowned at Emmett. "This is most unexpected."

"So I see."

"Pardon the intrusion," Kent said. "I've some questions to ask, and I'd like Rose to be present. Is she here?"

Chantal lifted a tentative hand to her bosom. "I'm not certain. I've been . . . in my own room. Having tea."

For how long? Juliet wondered. Had Chantal switched a lighter gown for that dark henna silk? Or was Maud right? Ravi wore his customary pale robe. . . .

Kent strode to a closed door and rapped hard. After a moment, the panel swung open and Rose poked her head out, her sable hair swinging girlishly free.

"Kent? Why are you here—?" Looking beyond him, she scowled, then marched out. The white lace ends of a fichu dangled to her skirt of dove-gray silk. Juliet tensed. Could she be the one Maud had seen?

"Mama, really!" Rose said. "You promised *he* wasn't coming back, that he'd only be here this afternoon."

Chantal followed her daughter's gaze to Emmett. "Mr. Carleton is a guest of Kent and Juliet. I trust you'll be civil."

"But Mama—"

"Sit down." She made an imperious wave of her hand, the bracelets chiming.

Rose gave a disgruntled sniff, but plopped down on a hassock and folded her arms.

"Thank you," Emmett murmured to Chantal.

She regarded him, her mouth set in a bitter line. Even from halfway across the room, Juliet felt the intensity of that shared stare. How must Chantal feel to look back on a lost lover, a lover who had given her a cherished daughter, then married someone else? Slipping her hand into Kent's, Juliet treasured his solid warmth. Thank heavens she had made the right choice.

Chantal swung away. "Excuse me. I'll only be a moment."

"Wait—" Kent started, but she'd disappeared into her bedroom, leaving the door ajar.

"Let her go," Emmett said gruffly. "It wasn't fair of us to intrude without warning."

Ravi glowered as he glided to the mantelpiece to light the candles in a pair of brass candelabra. Rose glared at the both of them. Releasing Juliet's hand, Kent paced the dhurri rug.

Barely two minutes passed before Chantal emerged. She'd drawn up her cornsilk hair and fastened it with a jeweled comb. A lace shawl covered the magnificent expanse of her bosom, and Juliet caught the aroma of sweet woodruff. A woman's armor, she thought, Chantal wanted to look her best. For Emmett? Or because she sensed a confrontation brewing and strove to conceal her guilt?

Without preamble, Kent said, "A short while ago, someone struck Emmett over the head."

Paling, Chantal braced a hand on the cane back of a chair. "Struck—?" Her widened blue eyes veered to Emmett, as if searching for injury. "Dear heavens. I'm sorry, Emmett."

"The blow knocked him senseless, so he didn't see his assailant." Kent paused. "But Lady Maud saw."

A moment of tense silence spun out. Rose clenched her fichu. Emmett shifted impatiently. Ravi stepped to Chantal's side. The tableau reminded Juliet of sitting on the edge of her seat at a stage play, waiting breathlessly for the next line.

"So tell us," Rose demanded. "Who did she see?"

"First I'd like to know where each of you have been for the past hour and a half."

"Since she returned from the cemetery," Ravi said, laying a dusky hand on her shoulder, "Chantal has been with me."

She wheeled on him. "It can't have been as long as that."

An odd frantic entreaty underscored her voice. What was she hiding? Juliet wondered. Was Chantal afraid to ally herself with a man she knew to be a murderer? A thought stunned her. Ravi loved Chantal. Could he be seeking revenge on Emmett for hurting her?

His austere expression softened to gentle regret as Ravi cupped her cheek. *"Jauneman,"* he murmured, "I am indeed certain."

Scowling, Rose jumped up. "Don't, Mama. Don't let that heathen touch you in front of other people."

Ravi narrowed his eyes to slits. "You would do well to mind your manners."

Eyes flashing and bosom heaving, she stepped toward him. "You would chastise me? As if you had the right! Kent, tell him—"

"Please, darling," Chantal said swiftly. "Calm yourself. You'll make yourself ill. Perhaps you should go to your room."

"I won't be sent away like a naughty child." Her slim fingers trembled around the fichu; her breath came in audible gasps. "No one must know, Mama. No one must know about you and that . . . that dark-skinned pagan. You . . . who had the love of a duke. You're desecrating Father's memory. . . ."

Suddenly she swayed. Whiteness outlined her tense lips. Eyes rolling back, lashes closing, she crumpled to the rug.

Alarmed, Juliet raced to her side. Everyone crowded around.

Chantal dropped to her knees beside her daughter. "Dear God!" she wailed, taking the limp hand. "What's happened to my baby?"

"It's only a swoon," said Emmett, standing behind her. "Common in high-strung girls. She'll likely be fine in a moment."

Yet he frowned in concern. Juliet touched the girl's brow. The skin felt clammy, all color gone. The only sign of life was the shallow wheeze of her breathing.

Kent lightly slapped his sister's cheek. She lay still. Deathly still, Juliet thought fearfully.

He looked up. "She needs smelling salts. Chantal?"

She lifted a hand to her throat. "Yes . . . yes, perhaps I have a vial somewhere. I'll see if I can find it." Rising, she vanished into her bedroom.

"The doctor was summoned to examine me," Emmett said. "Perhaps he should take a look at the girl."

"See if he's arrived yet," Kent told Ravi. "Then fetch a tisane from the kitchen."

Ravi inclined his turbaned head and hurried out.

As the door closed, Juliet said, "Should we put her in bed?"

Nodding, Kent slid his arms beneath his sister's pliant form. His strides long, he shouldered open the heavy oak door.

Following, Juliet entered a neat bedroom, three of the walls forming the octagonal shape of the tower. Light spilled from an oil lamp atop a small desk. He gently lay Rose on the frilly blue coverlet. Against the white linen pillow, her brown hair haloed her ashen features. She stirred, and a panting moan escaped her pale lips. Yet her eyes remained shut.

Juliet glanced from Kent to her father, who hovered in the doorway. "She's having trouble breathing. She'll rest more comfortably if I loosen her corset. Why don't you both wait outside?"

Emmett nodded and ducked out.

Kent seized her hand. "I'd rather not leave you alone, Juliet."

She gave him a reassuring smile. "I'll be perfectly fine, darling. You'll be close by."

He scowled at her. Then he glanced at Rose, who lay unmoving, her hand curled in childish fashion beside her pale cheek. His expression relaxed into brotherly concern. After planting a kiss on Juliet's brow, he walked out, leaving the door ajar.

She rolled the girl onto her side and undid the row of buttons down the back of her gown. Then she plucked at the tight lacing until the strings hung free. Immediately Rose seemed to breathe easier. She lay limp, lashes dark against her wan face. She looked so dainty and vulnerable that Juliet felt a twist of compassion.

Rose was an odd girl, modest yet passionate about her place in the castle hierarchy. Though Juliet couldn't condone Rose for lashing out at Ravi, she could see that the girl's sensitivity to slights lay rooted in her bastardy, in her yearning to be recognized as a duke's true daughter.

Resolving to spend more time with Rose, Juliet turned to inspect the small chamber while she waited for Chantal to bring the smelling salts. There were several arched windows and another, closed door. On the desk lay a tidy stack of papers, probably the unfinished play. The walls bore framed sketches in William Deverell's lyrical style. She went to examine the one over the desk. Beneath a gilded canopy, an exotically robed man sat on a throne as several men paid him homage. In spidery script, she read *The Maharaja of Kashmir*.

The ruler who had once owned Dreamspinner, Juliet mused. Rose had hung the sketch in a place of honor, where she could view it while she sat at work. She truly *was* fanatically devoted to the necklace—

Abruptly metal grated on metal. The sound startled Juliet. She spun toward the bed. Empty.

She looked to the door. Closed. Her blood chilled. Rose stood there, her hand on the iron bolt, her back to the thick oak panel.

She was smiling, and a strange slyness shone in her dark eyes. Around the milk-pale skin of her throat glinted green stones in the design of a peacock.

Dreamspinner.

Shadows danced on the crimson hangings and shivered in the corners. Hands in his pockets, Kent paced a restive circle of the sitting room. His gaze strayed to Rose's door, which stood ajar. His sister would recover. And Juliet was safe, he told himself for the tenth time. Yet to have her gone from his sight made him nervous as a cat.

Drat Rose and her untimely outburst! He'd felt so close to ferreting out the murderer. He'd sensed fear like a tangible presence in the air. The killer's fear of being found out. Now the perception had vanished along with the suspects.

He crossed paths with Emmett, who strode back and forth before the darkened windows. "What the hell's taking Chantal so long?" Kent growled.

Lifting his broad shoulders in a distracted shrug, Emmett toyed with his handlebar mustache. "I've been thinking about the past, Kent."

"What about it?"

Emmett frowned at Chantal's open door, then took a step toward Rose's room. "There's something I'd nearly forgotten. Something that might . . ."

"Might what?"

"Might have a bearing on the murderer's identity."

Kent felt his every nerve jolt. "What is it?"

"It involves a vow of secrecy I made to Chantal long ago." Emmett drew a heavy breath. "But for Juliet's safety, I must break that vow. You see, Chantal's mother spent years in a lunatic asylum. She died about the time Emily was born."

Kent stared. "I never knew that."

"Chantal never told anyone but me. She was afraid William would disdain her for her bad blood. She confided in me only because she needed my help in paying for her mother's treatment."

A chill sped through Kent, leaving his mouth dry and his palms damp. "Madness . . ."

"Can be inherited," Emmett finished.

The two men looked at each other. In whom had the bad seed been planted?

Chantal hastened out of the bedroom. Her shawl hung askew and her mouth drooped with worry. "I've found the salts at last. Had to rummage through every drawer of my dressing table."

She swept toward her daughter's bedroom. Kent grasped her arm. "You're not going in there alone," he snapped.

"Why not?" Her blue eyes widened. "What's happened? Oh, dear heaven . . . did Rose . . ."

"Did Rose what?"

She parted her lips. Candlelight wavered across her stark features. Fear shone in her gaze. A mother's fear. A sane fear . . .

With sudden sickening certainty, Kent knew the truth.

At the same instant, realization dawned on Emmett's face. In grim unison they swung toward the bedroom.

The door shut with a quiet click. Immediately came the chilling grate of a bolt sliding home.

Juliet stood transfixed by the insane glow in those brown eyes. Just as Dreamspinner glowed with a deadly life.

Understanding deluged her in sickening dread. Rose was the killer. Rose had plotted her death. . . .

Furious beating sounded on the door. "Juliet!" came Kent's muffled voice. "Juliet, answer me!"

Then her father's hoarse voice: "Princess, talk to me! Are you all right?"

Sensing that she mustn't show fear, she called, "I'm fine."

Annoyance contorted Rose's girlish features. "Go away, both of you! Kent, this has nothing to do with you."

More pounding. "Rose, open this door!"

Sadness drew on her lips. "He never understood," she murmured, shaking her head so that the dark hair swirled around her loosened gown. "Twice now he's let himself be led astray."

Silence came from without. What were the men doing?

Wiping damp palms on her skirt, Juliet tried to think. Could she overpower Rose? Perhaps if she kept the girl talking, Kent could find a way to get the door opened.

"You're the person who struck Papa today," she said. "And you pushed Emily to her death."

Rose's gaze wavered for an instant. "She forced me to it. I caught her stealing out of the library with Dreamspinner." Her lip curled in disgust. "She admitted that she intended to disobey Kent and give the necklace to her dear Papa, to win his favor. I couldn't let her do that."

Give the necklace to Papa. So that was the secret action Emily had intended. Juliet's heart ached for the noble Emily.

Rose must have lured her sister onto the parapet.

Imagining Emily struggling in terror made Juliet's blood run cold. "She was the duchess. The jewels were hers to dispose of as she wished."

With the tenderness of a lover, Rose caressed the necklace. "Dreamspinner belongs to the Deverells. Father deemed it so." Eyes hardening, she took a step forward. "Emmett Carleton came here today to talk you into giving him the necklace."

"That isn't true. He came to end the feud—"

A powerful thudding shook the door. Kent! The solid oak panel held firm. Fear tasting acrid in her mouth, Juliet knew she must rely on her own wits.

"Kent will let you keep the necklace. Unlock the door, Rose. He only wants to help you."

"No, he's fallen under your spell." A curious blackness descended over her face. Reaching into her pocket, she drew forth a dagger. "I'm sorry, Juliet. I wanted to like you, and for a time I did. Then I saw the truth. I can't let a Carleton's blood defile the Deverell line. I can't let you give away Dreamspinner, either."

The blade glinting in the lamplight, she walked closer.

Pity snaked around the icy horror inside Juliet. Rose truly believed in her own righteousness. . . .

The door hinges groaned but held under Kent's repeated strikes. Juliet knew with dreadful surety that she dare not wait.

She took a step backward; her thighs met the hard edge of the desk. Wildly she looked around for a weapon. Her hands closed on a silver inkwell behind her.

"You're making a mistake," she said, forcing calmness into her voice. "You see, Dreamspinner is only a clever forgery. Augusta sold the real stones years ago."

Dagger upraised, Rose stopped. Confusion clouded her big brown eyes. "You're lying."

"Pry one of the stones out of its mounting," Juliet said swiftly. "They're green glass, not emeralds. There's probably paint on the underside to enhance the color."

Blinking uncertainly, Rose looked down at the necklace. Juliet seized the chance and hurled the inkpot.

It struck Rose's arm. Black ink drenched her gray sleeve. Squealing, she dropped the knife. The blade went skittering under the bed.

Juliet dove for the small door. Wrenching it open, she dashed outside. A cool wind blew her hair. The moon shone through a haze of clouds, casting shadows on the narrow walkway, on the toothlike embrasures.

Alarm dried her throat. The parapet where Emily had died . . .

Sobbing in desperation, she pounded over the stone flags. The stairs. She must reach the stairs leading down to the courtyard.

A heavy weight thrust her off balance. Her back slammed against the hard surface of an embrasure. Wiry arms thrust her toward the edge. She caught a dizzying glimpse of the wall sweeping downward to the glimmering river and the rocky bank.

Terror tore a scream from her throat. She sobbed and struggled. Rose pushed with the iron strength of a madwoman. The drop loomed before Juliet. She scrabbled frantically for purchase. The limestone crumbled to dust in her fingers. . . .

Heedless of the pain numbing his shoulder, Kent thrust again and again at the door. With grunts of fury, Emmett applied his own shoulder to the task. The hinges creaked ominously. Yet still the oaken door held despairingly firm.

An idea sprang into Kent's beleaguered brain. "The courtyard," he gasped out. "There's a stairway leading to the parapet . . . another door into the bedroom."

Giving a grim nod, Emmett ran out.

"Oh, dear God," moaned Chantal, wringing her hands. "This is all my fault. I didn't want to let myself believe . . ."

A scream echoed faintly. Juliet.

Please, God. Don't take my love from me again.

The grisly image of her lying in a pool of blood gave

his aching muscles renewed power. In desperation he battered the door. The hinges screeched. With an ear-splitting crash, the panel gave way.

Rushing through the opening, he glanced around the room. Empty. The papapet door stood ajar. He dashed outside. Down the walkway, moonlight gilded a dark-haired woman leaning over an embrasure.

Rose. Maniacal fervency lit her features. Christ! She'd thrust Juliet half off the wall—

He ran. Gravel sprayed from beneath his feet. Tears of fear misted his eyes. His shoulder burned with each jarring step.

Juliet began to slip downward. Over his own sobbing breaths, he heard her gasp. She snatched futilely at the powdery stone.

No . . . no . . . no. Not again. Not again.

He shoved at Rose; she went staggering back. In the same swift motion he seized Juliet under the arms and yanked her to him.

He buried his face in the fragrant tumble of her hair. His heart thudded. Oh, God, he'd almost lost his beloved Juliet . . . and their precious baby.

She gulped in air and clutched limply at his shoulders. "Kent . . . oh, Kent. You're here."

"Yes, darling," he crooned. "You're safe now. I love you."

"Don't!" Rose cried shrilly. "You can't love a Carleton."

He lifted his head. Renewed panic stiffened his muscles. A distance down the parapet, his sister had scrambled onto an embrasure. Moonlight silvered her slim figure and glinted off Dreamspinner.

"Stop her!" Chantal cried, from behind. "Kent, she'll fall!"

Releasing Juliet, he darted toward Rose. At the same instant, Emmett pounded up the stairs and emerged onto the walkway. Closer to the girl, he lunged at her and grasped her skirt.

"You'll never have Dreamspinner!" she screamed. "I'll take it with me into eternity!"

She yanked hard; her gown ripped. Almost calmly,

she stepped off the wall. Moonlight gleamed on her fanatical expression, on the glass stones of the necklace. Arms flailing, she fell from sight.

Kent froze. Darkness spun before his eyes. A kaleidoscope of images flashed inside his head. Rose sitting a horse for the first time. Rose crouched adoringly at their father's knee. Rose standing witness at Emily's wedding . . .

Oh, God. Oh, God. His sister. His little sister.

A soft embrace surrounded him. Juliet. Sagging against her, he let her warmth seep into him. Tears slid down his icy cheeks. Her murmured words of comfort glided over him, over the vast raw wound inside him.

"It wasn't your fault," she said. "You couldn't have known. There's nothing you could have done."

Chantal's weeping shivered through the night air. "My daughter. If only I'd not blinded myself . . ."

Emmett gazed down at Rose's body on the rocks below. Slowly he turned away and gathered Chantal close.

"You gave her a mother's love," he said heavily. "It was the feud, the hatred, that twisted her."

"But it's over now," Juliet whispered. "The feud is ended."

The words penetrated the dark well of Kent's despair. The love in her eyes struck him with a healing ray of hope. Holding her tight, he took a fierce breath.

"Yes," he said. "The hatred is over forever."

Epilogue

The lusty howl of an infant echoed through the nave.

Sunlight jeweled by stained glass shone on the party gathered around the marble christening font. The vicar finished pouring the water and hastily handed the small, squalling bundle to its godmother. Maud Hammond-Gore gathered the baby against the gentle mound of her belly, jiggled her a moment until the sobs lulled, then passed the child to her wide-eyed husband.

Standing at Kent's side, Juliet stood on tiptoe and whispered, "Henry looks terrified, don't you think?"

"It's good practice for him," he murmured close to her ear. "He'll soon discover the joys of fatherhood."

His hand closed around hers, imbuing her with his steady warmth and solid security. In dreamy contentment, she listened to the vicar intone the closing prayers. Then the group filed out of the tiny church and into the June sunshine.

Henry promptly handed the baby to Juliet. "Er . . . I believe this is yours."

Maud squinted proudly at the baby. "She is a beauty, isn't she?"

Juliet smiled down at Emily's adorable face and wide green eyes peeking out from the lace-edged bonnet. Her milky scent blended with the aroma of roses climbing the stone wall of the church. Kent tickled her chin; the infant seized his finger, drew it to her mouth, and began to gum it vigorously.

"Ouch!" he said. "That's no way to treat your father."

"Might we deduce she's hungry?" Maud said, patting her belly. "*We* certainly are."

Juliet laughed. "Emily had a feeding before church. As for you, there'll be plenty of feasting back at the castle."

"Enough deducing, darling," Henry said, casting an indulgent look at his wife. "Shall we go on?"

As they strolled away, her parents came out of the throng of well-wishers. They made a perfect couple, Juliet thought fondly, Emmett the distinguished businessman in his charcoal-gray suit and Dorothea the elegant lady in her fashionable sapphire gown. He'd been right to hide the past from Mama. Untouched by tragedy, she looked serene and lovely.

"You certainly spoke your mind in there," Emmett told the baby. "I suspect you'll take after your mother in that respect."

Emily cooed and waved a tiny fist.

"Don't let his gruff manner fool you," said Kent. "Like me, he prefers your mother exactly as she is."

Juliet's heart skipped a beat. A smile transformed his rugged features into the breathtakingly handsome man she loved so much. Desire shimmered deep inside her, bearing the promise of brilliant joy. . . .

"Come to Grandmama now." Heedless of her pristine collar, Dorothea nestled the baby against her shoulder. Bright-eyed and gurgling, Emily gazed around the courtyard.

"Ah," said Emmett, "Lady Emily's a fine granddaughter. Three months old and so curious about the world."

A secretive smile touched Juliet's lips. "Perhaps it won't be so very long before you'll have a grandson, too."

Kent cocked his head and stared. "You're not . . ."

Nodding, she held her breath. "I am."

His stunned look gentled; he slid an arm around her. "Another baby . . ."

"How delightful," exclaimed Dorothea. She rubbed her cheek against Emily's. "Did you hear that, darling? A sister or brother for you to play with."

"Fine news indeed," Emmett said. "If the child's a boy, perhaps he'll take an interest in business matters."

"Or in my inventions," Kent countered with a grin.

"Why not both?" Emmett suggested. "I've been meaning to discuss financing this newfangled machine of yours. Engines that run on petrol are the wave of the future."

"We can speak of the thresher when I return to London. The queen has been badgering me about an agricultural bill she wishes Parliament to pass."

"Bring the whole family. Victoria has summoned me, as well."

"Oh, Papa," Juliet said, gazing at his beaming face. "Do you mean . . ."

"We wanted to surprise you, darling," Dorothea said proudly. "He's to be knighted at last."

Suddenly a Pekingese puppy ran barking through the crowd, his feathery tail dancing on air. Ducking through the sea of guests, little Hannah Forster chased the dog. No longer did she need the wooden crutch. Her knee-length pink dress revealed legs that were coltishly slim and blessed straight.

Augusta hurried around the corner of the church. She paused only to smile at Emily, then continued after the puppy. "Rajah! Naughty boy, you were supposed to remain with the coachman."

Laughing, everyone drifted to their carriages to return to the castle. As Emmett and Dorothea carried the infant to the landau, Kent held back and murmured, "Our passion has borne fruit again, my Lady Botanist. But you've only just finished rebuilding your greenhouse. Are you happy about having another child so soon?"

"Another babe won't hinder me," Juliet said, touching his smooth-shaven cheek. "I want Emily to have all the sisters and brothers I never had."

His eyes darkened despite the warming sunshine, and he clung tight to her hands. "I know. I can't help remembering my own sister. Perhaps if I'd paid more heed to Rose . . ."

Her heart melted. "Don't torture yourself, darling. Her madness was hereditary, not your fault at all."

He released a heavy sigh. "I suppose Chantal suffered more than I. To lose both her daughters."

"We can be thankful she has Ravi. In her last letter, she seemed almost happy again, touring India with him."

"Mmmm." Lifting her hand, Kent brushed his lips across the back in a caress that made her shiver. "It was kind of Emmett to let Ravi take over the management of his new tea estate."

Dazzlingly glad to see the light return to his eyes, Juliet smiled. His heat radiated to her; his strength aroused both quiet contentment and restless longing. She reached up on tiptoe to kiss his hard mouth. "Kent, I'm so happy you and Papa have put aside your differences."

He smiled, a slow, seductive gentling of his noble face. His hands found her waist and rubbed enticingly. "Perhaps tonight you'd be willing to demonstrate your gratitude."

"By candlelight?" she teased. "Or shall we make love in darkness, for nostalgia's sake?"

His eyes gleamed. "Whatever pleases my duchess. I intend to spend my life pleasing you."

His low-pitched voice made her stomach tighten deliciously.

"And I," she said, kissing him again, "intend to spend my life spinning dreams of our future."